Gilbert Burnet, Richard Baxter, Robert Parsons

The lives of Sir Matthew Hale, Lord Chief Justice of England, Wilmot, Earl of Rochester

Gilbert Burnet, Richard Baxter, Robert Parsons

The lives of Sir Matthew Hale, Lord Chief Justice of England, Wilmot, Earl of Rochester

ISBN/EAN: 9783337104900

Printed in Europe, USA, Canada, Australia, Japan

Cover: Foto ©Raphael Reischuk / pixelio.de

More available books at **www.hansebooks.com**

THE
LIVES

OF

Sir MATTHEW HALE, Knt.

Lord Chief Justice of ENGLAND;

WILMOT, Earl of Rochester;

AND

Queen MARY.

Written by Bishop BURNETT.

To this EDITION are added,

RICHARD BAXTER's Additional NOTES to the Life of Sir MATTHEW HALE.

AND

A SERMON Preached at the Funeral of the Earl of Rochester, by the Rev. Mr. PARSONS.

LONDON:

Printed for T. DAVIES, in Ruffel-Street, Covent-Garden.

M.DCC.LXXIV.

THE

PREFACE.

NO part of *history is more instructive and delighting, than the lives of great and worthy men : the shortness of them invites many readers, and there are such little and yet remarkable passages in them, too inconsiderable to be put in a general history of the age in which they lived, that all people are very desirous to know them. This makes Plutarch's lives to be more generally read than any of all the books which the ancient Greeks or Romans writ.*

But the lives of heroes and princes are commonly filled with the account of the great things done by them, which do rather belong to a general, than a particular history; and do rather amuse the readers fancy with a splendid shew of greatness, than offer him what is really so useful to himself: and indeed the lives of princes are

either

either writ with so much flattery, by those who intended to merit by it at their own hands, or others concerned in them; or with so much spite, by those who being ill used by them have revenged themselves on their memory, that there is not much to be built on them; and though the ill nature of many makes what is satyrically writ to be generally more read and believed, than when the flattery is visible and coarse, yet certainly resentment may make the writer corrupt the truth of history, as much as interest; and since all men have their blind sides, and commit errors, he that will industriously lay these together, leaving out, or but slightly touching, what should be set against them to balance them, may make a very good man appear in very bad colours: so upon the whole matter, there is not that reason to expect either much truth, or great instruction, from what is written concerning heroes or princes; for few have been able to imitate the patterns Suetonius set the world in writing the lives of the Roman emperors, with the same freedom that they had led them: but the lives of private men, though they seldom entertain the reader with such a variety of passages as the other do; yet certainly they offer him things that are more imitable, and do pre-

sent

sent wisdom and virtue to him, not only in a fair idea, which is often look'd on as a piece of the invention or fancy of the writer, but in such plain and familiar instances, as do both direct him better, and persuade him more; and there are not such temptations to bias those who writ them, so that we may generally depend more on the truth of such relations as are given in them.

In the age in which we live, religion and virtue have been proposed and defended with such advantages, with that great force of reason, and those persuasions, that they can hardly be matched in former times; yet after all this, there are but few much wrought on by them, which perhaps flows from this, among other reasons, that there are not so many excellent patterns set out, as might both in a shorter and more effectual manner recommend that to the world, which discourses do but coldly; the wit and stile of the writer being more considered than the argument which they handle, and therefore the proposing virtue and religion in such a model, may perhaps operate more than the perspective of it can do; and for the history of learning, nothing does so preserve and improve it, as the writing the lives of those who have been eminent in it.

There

There is no book the ancients have left us, which might have informed us more than Diogenes Laertius his lives of the philosophers, if he had had the art of writing equal to that great subject which he undertook, for if he had given the world such account of them, as Gassendus has done of Peiresk, how great a stock of knowledge might we have had, which by his unskilfulness is in a great measure lost; since we must now depend only on him, because we have no other, or better author, that has written on that argument.

For many ages there were no lives writ but by monks, through whose writings there runs such an incureable humour of telling incredible and inimitable passages, that little in them can be believed or proposed as a pattern. Sulpitius Severus and Jerom shewed too much credulity in the lives they writ, and raised Martin and Hilarion beyond what can be reasonable believed: after them, Socrates, Theodoret, Sozomen, and Palladius, took a pleasure to tell uncouth stories of the monks of Thebais, and Nitra; and those who came after them, scorned to fall short of them, but raised their saints above those of former ages, so that one would have thought that undecent way of writing could raise no higher;

and

and this humour infected even those who had otherwise a good sense of things, and a just apprehension of mankind, as may appear in Matthew Paris, who though he was a writer of great judgment and fidelity, yet he has corrupted his history with much of that alloy: but when emulation and envy rose among the several orders or houses, then they improved in that art of making romances, instead of writing lives, to that pitch, that the world became generally much scandalized with them. The Franciscans and Dominicans tried who could say the most extravagant things of the founders, or other saints of their orders, and the Benedictines, who thought themselves possest of the belief of the world, as well as of its wealth, endeavoured all that was possible still to keep up the dignity of their order, by out-lying the others all they could; and whereas here or there, a miracle, a vision, or trance, might have occured in the lives of former saints, now every page was full of those wonderful things.

Nor has the humour of writing in such a manner, been quite laid down in this age, though more awakened and better enlightened, as appears in the life of Philip Nerius, and a great many more: and the jesuits at Antwerp, are

now

now taking care to load the world with a vast and voluminous collection of all those lives that has already swelled to eleven volumes in folio, in a small print, and yet being digested according to the calender, they have yet but ended the month of April. The life of monsieur Renty is writ in another manner, where there are so many excellent passages, that he is justly to be reckoned amongst the greatest patterns that France has afforded in this age.

But while some have nourished infidelity, and a scorn of all sacred things, by writing of those good men in such a strain, as makes not only what is so related to be disbelieved, but creates a distrust of the authentical writings of our most holy faith; others have fallen into another extream, in writing lives too jejunely, swelling them up with trifling accounts of the childhood and education, and the domestick and private affairs of those persons of whom they writ, in which the world is little concerned; by these they become so flat, that few care to read them; for certainly those transactions are only fit to be delivered to posterity, that may carry with them some useful piece of knowledge to after-times.

I have

I have now an argument before me, which will afford indeed only a short history, but will contain in it as great a character as perhaps can be given of any in this age; since there are few instances of more knowledge and greater virtues meeting is one person. I am upon one account (besides many more) unfit to undertake it, because I was not at all known to him, so I can say nothing from my own observation; but upon second thoughts I do not know whether this may not qualify me to write more impartially, though perhaps more defectively, for the knowledge of extraordinary persons does most commonly biass those who were much wrought on by the tenderness of their friendship for them, to raise their stile a little too high when they write concerning them: I confess I knew him as much as the looking often upon him could amount to. The last year of his being in London, he came always on Sundays (when he could go abroad) to the chapel of the Rolls, where I then preached: in my life I never saw so much gravity, tempered with that sweetness, and set off with so much vivacity, as appeared in his looks and behaviour, which disposed me to a veneration for him, which I never had for any, with whom I was not acquainted: I was seeking an opportunity

of

of being admitted to his converſation; but I underſtood that between a great want of health, and a multiplicity of buſineſs, which his employment brought upon him, he was maſter of ſo little of his time, that I ſtood in doubt whether I might preſume to rob him of any of it, and ſo he left the town before I could reſolve on deſiring to be known to him.

My ignorance of the law of England, made me alſo unfit to write of a man, a great part of whoſe character, as to his learning, is to be taken from his ſkill in the Common Law, and his performance in that. But I ſhall leave that to thoſe of the ſame robe; ſince if I engaged much in it, I muſt needs commit many errors, writing of a ſubject that is foreign to me.

The occaſion of my undertaking this, was given me firſt by the earneſt deſires of ſome that have great power over me, who having been much obliged by him, and holding his memory in high eſtimation, thought I might do it ſome right by writing his life; I was then engaged in the hiſtory of the reformation, ſo I promiſed that as ſoon as that was over, I ſhould make the beſt uſe I could of ſuch informations and memorials as ſhould be brought me.

This

*This I have now performed in the best man-
ner I could, and have brought into method all
the parcels of his life, or the branches of his
character, which I could either gather from the
informations that were brought me, or from
those that were familiarly acquainted with him,
or from his writings. I have not applied any
of the false colours with which art, or some
forced eloquence, might furnish me in writing
concerning him ; but have endeavoured to set
him out in the same simplicity in which he lived.
I have said little of his domestick concerns, since
though in these he was a great example, yet it
signifies nothing to the world, to know any particular exercises, that might be given to his
patience ; and therefore I shall draw a veil
over all these, and shall avoid saying any thing
of him, but what may offord the reader some profitable instruction. I am under no temptations of
saying any thing, but what I am perfuaded is
exactly true, for where there is so much excellent
truth to be told, it were an inexcusable fault
to corrupt that, or prejudice the reader against
it, by the mixture of falshoods with it.*

*In short, as he was a great example while he
lived, so I wish the setting him thus out to posterity,*

rity, in his own true and native colours, may have its due influence on all persons, but more particularly on those of that profession, whom it more immediately concerns, whether on the bench or at the bar.

THE

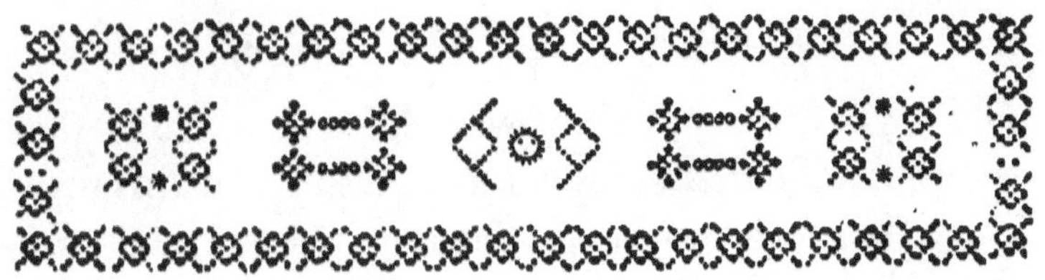

THE
LIFE AND DEATH

OF

Sir MATTHEW HALE, Knt.

LATE

Lord Chief Juſtice of England.

MATTHEW HALE, was born at
Alderly in Gloceſterſhire, Nov. 1, 1609.
His grandfather was Robert Hale, an
eminent clothier in Wotton-under-edge, in that
county, where he and his anceſtors had lived for
many deſcents ; and they had given ſeveral parcels
of land for the uſe of the poor, which were enjoyed
by them to this day. This Robert acquired an
eſtate of ten thouſand pounds, which he divided
almoſt equally amongſt his five ſons ; beſides the
portions he gave his daughters, from whom a nu-
merous poſterity has ſprung. His ſecond ſon was
Robert Hale, a Barriſter of Lincoln's-Inn ; he
married Joan, the daughter of Matthew Poyntz, of

B

Alderly,

Alderly, Efquire, who was defcended from that noble family of the Poyntz's of Acton : of this marriage there was no other iffue but this one fon. His Grandfather by his mother was his godfather, and gave him his own name at his baptifm. His father was a man of that ftrictnefs of confcience, that he gave over the practice of the law, becaufe he could not underftand the reafon of giving colour in pleadings, which as he thought was to tell a lye, and that, with fome other things commonly practifed, feemed to him contrary to that exactnefs of truth and juftice which became a chriftian, fo that he withdrew himfelf from the Inns of Court to live on his eftate in the country. Of this I was informed by an ancient gentleman, that lived in a friendfhip with his fon for fifty years, and he heard Judge Jones, that was Mr. Hale's contemporary, declare this in the King's-bench. But as the care he had to fave his foul, made him abandon a profeffion in which he might have raifed his family much higher, fo his charity to his poor neighbours made him not only deal his alms largely among them while he lived, but at his death he left (out of his fmall eftate which was but 100 l. a year) 20 l. a year to the poor of Wotton, which his fon confirmed to them, with fome addition, and with this regulation, that it fhould be diftributed among fuch poor houfe-keepers, as did not receive the alms of the parifh ; for to give it to thofe, was only, as he ufed to fay, to fave fo much money to the rich, who by law were bound to relieve the poor of the parifh.

Thus

Thus he was defcended rather from a good, than a noble family, and yet what was wanting in the infignificant titles of high birth, and noble blood, was more than made up in the true worth of his anceftors. But he was foon deprived of the happinefs of his father's care and inftruction, for as he loft his mother before he was three years old, fo his father died before he was five; fo early was he caft on the providence of God. But that unhappinefs was in a great meafure made up to him: for after fome oppofition made by Mr. Thomas Poyntz, his uncle by his mother, he was committed to the care of Anthony Kingfcot, of Kingfcot, Efquire, who was his next kinfman, after his uncles, by his mother.

Great care was taken of his education, and his guardian intended to breed him to be a divine, and being inclined to the way of thofe then called Puritans, put him to fome fchools that were taught by thofe of that party, and in the feventeenth year of his age, fent him to Magdalen-Hall in Oxford, where Obadiah Sedgwick was his tutor. He was an extraordinary proficient at fchool, and for fome time at Oxford. But the Stage-players coming thither, he was fo much corrupted by feeing many plays, that he almoft wholly forfook his ftudies. By this he not only loft much time, but found that his head came to be thereby filled with fuch vain images of things, that they were at beft unprofitable, if not hurtful to him; and being afterwards fenfible of the mifchief of this, he refolved

upon

upon his coming to London, (where he knew the opportunities of fuch fights would be more frequent and inviting) never to fee a play again, to which he conftantly adhered.

The corruption of a young man's mind, in one particular, generally draws on a great many more after it, fo he being now taken off from following his ftudies, and from the gravity of his deportment, that was formerly eminent in him, far beyond his years, fet himfelf to many of the vanities incident to youth, but ftill preferved his purity, and a great probity of mind. He loved fine clothes, and delighted much in company : and being of a ftrong robuft body, he was a great mafter of all thofe exercifes that required much ftrength. He alfo learned to fence, and handle his weapons, in which he became fo expert, that he worfted many of the mafters of thofe arts : but as he was exercifing himfelf in them, an inftance appeared, that fhewed a good judgment, and gave fome hopes of better things. One of his mafters told him, he could teach him no more, for he was now better at his own trade than himfelf was. This Mr. Hale look'd on as flattery ; fo to make the mafter difcover himfelf, he promifed him the houfe he lived in, for he was his tenant, if he could hit him a blow on the head : and bad him do his beft, for he would be as good as his word. So after a little engagement, his mafter being really fuperiour to him, hit him on the head, and he performed his promife ; for he gave him the houfe freely : and

was

was not unwilling at that rate to learn fo early, to diftinguifh flattery from plain and fimple truth.

He was now fo taken up with martial matters, that inftead of going on in his defign of being a fcholar, or a divine, he refolved to be a foldier: and his tutor Sedgwick going into the Low-countries, chaplain to the renowned Lord Vere, he refolved to go along with him, and to trail a pike in the prince of Orange's army; but a happy ftop was put to this refolution, which might have proved fo fatal to himfelf, and have deprived the age of the great example he gave, and the ufeful fervices he afterwards did his country. He was engaged in a fuit of law with Sir William Whitmore, who laid claim to fome part of his eftate, and his guardian being a man of a retired temper, and not made for bufinefs, he was forced to leave the univerfity, after he had been three years in it, and go to London to follicit his own bufinefs. Being recommended to ferjeant Glanvill for his councellor, and he obferving in him a clear apprehenfion of things, and a folid judgment, and a great fitnefs for the ftudy of the law, took pains upon him to perfuade him to forfake his thoughts of being a foldier, and to apply himfelf to the ftudy of the law: and this had fo good an effect on him, that on the 8th of November, 1629, when he was paft the twentieth year of his age, he was admitted into Lincoln's-Inn: and being then deeply fenfible how much time he had loft, and that idle and vain things had over-run and almoft corrupted his mind,

B 3

he

he refolved to redeem the time he had loft, and followed his ftudies with a diligence that could fcarce be believed, if the fignal effects of it did not gain it credit. He ftudied for many years at the rate of fixteen hours a day: he threw afide all fine clothes, and betook himfelf to a plain fa-fhion, which he continued to ufe in many points to his dying day.

But, fince the honour of reclaiming him from the idlenefs of his former courfe of life, is due to the memory of that eminent lawer, ferjeant Glan-vill, and fince my defign in writing is to propofe a pattern of heroic virtue to the world, I fhall men-tion one paffage of the ferjeant which ought never to be forgotten. His father had a fair eftate, which he intented to fettle on his elder brother, but he being a vicious young man, and there appearing no hopes of his recovery, he fettled it on him, that was his fecond fon. Upon his death, his eldeft fon finding that what he had before looked on, as the threatnings of an angry father, was now but too certain, became melancholy, and that by degrees wrought fo great a change on him, that what his father could not prevail in while he lived, was now effected by the feverity of his laft will, fo that it was now too late for him to change in hopes of an eftate that was gone from him. But his brother obferving the reality of the change, refolved within himfelf what to do: fo he called him, with many of his friends together to a feaft, and after other difhes had been ferved up to the

dinner,

dinner, he ordered one that was covered to be set before his brother, and desired him to uncover it; which he doing, the company was surprized to find it full of writings. So he told them, that he was now to do what he was sure his father would have done, if he had lived to see that happy change, which they now all saw in his brother: and therefore he freely restored to him the whole estate. This is so great an instance of a generous and just disposition, that I hope the reader will easily pardon this digression, and that the rather, since that worthy serjeant was so instrumental in the happy change that followed in the course of Mr. Hale's life.

Yet he did not at first break off from keeping too much company with some vain people, till a sad accident drove him from it, for he, with some other young students, being invited to be merry out of town, one of the company called for so much wine, that, notwithstanding all that Mr. Hale could do to prevent it, he went on in his ex-cess till he fell down as dead before them, so that all that were present, were not a little affrighted at it, who did what they could to bring him to himself again. This did particularly affect Mr. Hale, who thereupon went into another room, and shutting the door, fell on his knees, and prayed earnestly to God, both for his friend, that he might be restored to life again; and that him-self might be forgiven for giving such countenance to so much excess: and he vowed to God, that

B 4

he

he would never again keep company in that manner, nor drink a health while he lived. His friend
recovered, and he moſt religiouſly obſerved his
vow, till his dying day. And though he was
afterwards preſt to drink healths, particularly the
king's, which was ſet up by too many as a diſtin-
guiſhing mark of loyalty, and drew many into
great exceſs after his Majeſty's happy reſtoration;
but he would never diſpenſe with his vow, though
he was ſometimes roughly treated for this, which
ſome hot and indiſcreet men called obſtinacy.

This wrought an entire change on him: now
he forſook all vain company, and divided himſelf
between the duties of religion, and the ſtudies of
his profeſſion. In the former he was ſo regular,
that for ſix and thirty years time he never once
failed going to church on the Lord's day; this
obſervation he made when an ague firſt interrupted
that conſtant courſe, and he reflected on it as an
acknowledgment of God's great goodneſs to him,
in ſo long a continuance of his health.

He took a ſtrict account of his time, of which
the reader will beſt judge, by the ſcheme he drew
for a diary, which I ſhall inſert copied from the
original, but I am not certain when he made it; it
is ſet down in the ſame ſimplicity in which he writ
it for his own private uſe.

Morning.

I. To lift up the heart to God in thankfulneſs
for renewing my life.

II. To

II. To renew my covenant with God in Chrift. 1. By renewed acts of faith receiving Chrift, and rejoycing in the height of that relation.   2. Refolution of being one of his people, doing him allegiance.

III. Adoration and prayer.

IV. Setting a watch over my own infirmities and paffions, over the fnares laid in our way. *Perimus licitis.*

Day Employment.

There muft be an employment, two kinds.

I. Our ordinary calling, to ferve God in it.   It is a fervice to Chrift though never fo mean. Colof. 3. Here faithfulnefs, diligence, chearfulnefs. Not to overlay myfelf with more bufinefs than I can bear.

II. Our fpiritual employments: mingle fomewhat of God's immediate fervice in this day.

Refrefhments.

I. Meat and drink, moderation feafoned with fomewhat of God.

II. Recreations.   1. Not our bufinefs. 2. Suitable.   No games, if given to covetoufnefs or paffion.

If alone.

I. Beware of wandering vain luftful thoughts; fly from thyfelf rather than entertain thefe.

II. Let thy folitary thoughts be profitable, view the evidences of thy falvation, the ftate of thy foul,

the

the coming of Chrift, thy own mortality, it will make thee humble and watchful.

Company.

Do good to them. Ufe God's name reverently. Beware of leaving an ill impreffion of ill example. Receive good from them, if more knowing.

Evening.

Caft up the accompts of the day. If ought amifs, beg pardon. Gather refolution of more vigilance. If well, blefs the mercy and grace of God that hath fupported thee.

Thefe notes have an imperfection in the wording of them, which fhews they were only intended for his privacies. No wonder, a man who fet fuch rules to himfelf, became quickly very eminent and remarkable.

Noy, the attorney-general, being then one of the greateft men of the profeffion, took early notice of him, and called often for him, and directed him in his ftudy, and grew to have fuch friendfhip for him, that he came to be called *Young Noy.* He paffing from the extreme of vanity in his apparel, to that of neglecting himfelf too much, was once taken when there was a prefs for the king's fervice, as a fit perfon for it; for he was a ftrong and well-built man: but fome that knew him coming by, and giving notice who he was, the prefs-men let him go. This made him return to more decency in his clothes, but never to any fuperfluity or vanity in them.   Once

Once as he was buying some cloth for a new suit, the draper, with whom he differed about the price, told him he should have it for nothing, if he would promise him an hundred pounds when he came to be Lord Chief Justice of England; to which he answered, that he could not with a good conscience wear any man's cloth, unless he payed for it; so he satisfied the draper, and carried away the cloth. Yet that same draper lived to see him advanced to that same dignity.

While he was thus improving himself in the study of the law, he not only kept the hours of the hall constantly in term-time, but seldom put himself out of commons in vacation time, and continued then to follow his studies with an unwearied diligence; and not being satisfied with the books wrote about it, or to take things upon trust, was very diligent in searching all records. Then did he make divers collections out of the books he had read, and mixing them with his own observations, digested them into a common-place book; which he did with so much industry and judgment, that an eminent judge of the King's-bench borrowed it of him when he was Lord Chief Baron: He unwillingly lent it, because it had been writ by him before he was called to the bar, and had never been thoroughly revised by him since that time, only what alterations had been made in the law by subsequent statutes, and judgments, were added by him as they had happened: but the judge, having perused it, said, that though

though

though it was compofed by him fo early, he did not think any lawyer in England could do it better, except he himfelf would again fet about it.

He was foon found out by that great and learned antiquary, Mr. Selden, who though much fuperiour to him in years, yet came to have fuch a liking of him, and of Mr. Vaughan, who was afterwards Lord Chief Juftice of the Common-pleas, that as he continued in a clofe friendfhip with them while he lived, fo he left them at his death two of his four executors.

It was this acquaintance that firft fet Mr. Hale on a more enlarged purfuit of learning, which he had before confined to his own profeffion, but becoming as great a mafter in it, as ever any was, very foon, he who could never let any of his time go away unprofitably, found leifure to attain to as great a variety of knowledge, in as comprehenfive a manner as moft men have done in any age.

He fet himfelf much to the ftudy of the Roman law, and though he liked the way of judicature in England by juries much better than that of the civil law, where fo much was trufted to the judge; yet he often faid, that the true grounds and reafons of law were fo well delivered in the Digefts, that a man could never underftand law as a fcience fo well as by feeking it there, and therefore lamented much that it was fo little ftudied in England.

He looked on readinefs in arithmetick as a thing which might be ufeful to him in his own employ-

ment,

ment, and acquired it to such a degree, that he would often on the sudden, and afterwards on the bench, resolve very hard queftions, which had puzled the beft accomptants about town. He refted not here, but ftudied the algebra, both *fpeciofa* and *numerofa*, and went through all the other mathematical fciences, and made a great collection of very excellent inftruments, fparing no coft to have them as exact as art could make them. He was alfo very converfant in philofophical learning, and in all the curious experiments, and rare difcoveries of this age; and had the new books, written on thofe fubjects, fent him from all parts, which he both read and examined fo critically, that if the principles and hypothefes, which he took firft up, did any way prepoffefs him, yet thofe, who have differed moft from him, have acknowledged, that in what he has writ concerning the Torricellian experiment, and of the rarefaction and condenfation of the air, he fhews as great an exactnefs, and as much fubtilty in the reafoning he builds on them, as thefe principles to which he adhered could bear. But indeed, it will feem fcarce credible, that a man fo much employed, and of fo fevere a temper of mind, could find leifure to read, obferve, and write fo much of thefe fubjects as he did. He called them his diverfions, for he often faid when he was weary with the ftudy of the law, or divinity, he ufed to recreate himfelf with philofophy, or the mathematicks; to thefe he added great fkill in phyfick, anatomy, and chyrurgery:

and

and he ufed to fay, " No man could be abfolutely " a mafter in any profeffion, without having fome " fkill in other fciences : " for, befides the fatis- faction he had in the knowledge of thefe things, he made ufe of them often in his employments. In fome examinations he would put fuch queftions to phyficians, or furgeons, that they have profeffed the college of phyficians could not do it more ex- actly ; by which he difcovered great judgment, as well as much knowledge, in thefe things : and in his ficknefs he ufed to argue with his doctors about his diftempers, and the methods they took with them, like one of their own profeffion ; which one of them told me, he underftood as far as fpe- culation without practice could carry him.

To this he added great fearches into ancient hiftory, and particularly into the rougheft and leaft delightful part of it, chronology. He was well ac- quainted with the ancient Greek philofophers, but want of occafion to ufe it, wore out his knowledge of the Greek tongue; and though he never ftudied the Hebrew tongue, yet by his great converfation with Selden, he underftood the moft curious things in the Rabinical learning.

But above all thefe, he feemed to have made the ftudy of divinity the chief of all others, to which he not only directed every thing elfe, but alfo arrived at that pitch in it, that thofe, who have read what he has written on thefe fubjects, will think, they muft have had moft of his time and thoughts. It may feem extravagant, and al-

moft

moſt incredible, that one man, in no great compaſs of years, ſhould have acquired ſuch a variety of knowledge, and that in ſciences that require much leiſure and application. But as his parts were quick, and his apprehenſions lively, his memory great, and his judgment ſtrong; ſo his induſtry was almoſt indefatigable. He roſe always betimes in the morning, was never idle, ſcarce ever held any diſcourſe about news, except with ſome few in whom he confided entirely. He entered into no correſpondence by letters, except about neceſſary buſineſs, or matters of learning, and ſpent very little time in eating or drinking; for as he never went to public feaſts, ſo he gave no entertainments but to the poor; for he followed our Saviour's direction (of feaſting none but theſe) literally: and in eating and drinking he obſerved not only great plainneſs and moderation, but lived ſo philoſophi-cally, that he always ended his meal with an ap-petite: ſo that he loſt little time at it, (that being the only portion which he grudged himſelf) and was diſpoſed to any exerciſe of his mind, to which he thought fit to apply himſelf immediately after he had dined; by theſe means he gained much time, that is otherwiſe unprofitably waſted.

He had alſo an admirable equality in the temper of his mind, which diſpoſed him for what ever ſtudies he thought fit to turn himſelf to; and ſome very uneaſy things, which he lay under for many years, did rather engage him to, than diſtract him from, his ſtudies.

When

When he was called to the bar, and began to make a figure in the world, the late unhappy wars broke out, in which it was no eafy thing for a man to preferve his integrity, and to live fecurely, free from great danger and trouble. He had read the life of Pomponius Atticus, wrote by Nepos, and having obferved, that he had paffed through a time of as much diftraction, as ever was in any age or ftate, from the wars of Marius and Scilla, to the beginnings of Auguftus his reign, without the leaft blemifh on his reputation, and free from any confiderable danger, being held in great efteem by all parties, and courted and favoured by them; he fet him as a pattern to himfelf, and obferving that befides thofe virtues which are neceffary to all men, and at all times, there were two things that chiefly preferved Atticus, the one was his engaging in no faction, and medling in no public bufi-nefs; the other was his conftant favouring and relieving thofe that were loweft, which was afcrib-ed by fuch as prevailed to the generofity of his temper, and procured him much kindnefs from thofe on whom he had exercifed his bounty, when it came to their turn to govern: He refolv-ed to guide himfelf by thofe rules as much as was poffible for him to do.

He not only avoided all public employment, but the very talking of news; and was always both favourable and charitable to thofe who were de-preffed, and was fure never to provoke any in particular, by cenfuring or reflecting on their acti-

ons;

ons; for many that have conversed much with him, have told me, they never heard him once speak ill of any person.

He was employed in his practice by all the king's party. He was affigned council to the earl of Strafford, and archbishop Laud, and afterwards to the blessed king himself, when brought to the infamous pageantry of a mock-trial, and offered to plead for him with all the courage, that so glorious a cause ought to have infpired him with, but was not suffered to appear, because the king refusing, as he had good reason, to submit to the court, it was pretended, none could be admitted to speak for him. He was also council for the duke of Hamilton, the earl of Holland, and the lord Capel: his plea for the former of these I have published in the memoirs of that duke's life. Afterwards also, being council for the lord Craven, he pleaded with that force of argument, that the then attorney-general threatened him for appearing against the government; to whom he answered, " he was " pleading in defence of those laws, which they " declared they would maintain and preserve; " and he was doing his duty to his client, so that " he was not to be daunted with threatenings."

Upon all these occasions he had difcharged himfelf with so much learning, fidelity, and courage, that he came to be generally employed for all that party; nor was he fatisfied to appear for their juft defence in the way of his profeffion, but he also relieved them often in their neceffities; which he

C

did

did in a way that was no lefs prudent than charitable, confidering the dangers of that time : for he did often depofit confiderable fums in the hands of a worthy gentleman of the king's party, who knew their neceffities well, and was to diftribute his charity according to his own difcretion, without either letting them know from whence it came, or giving himfelf any account to whom he had given it.

Cromwell, feeing him poffeffed of fo much practice, and he being one of the eminenteft men of the law, who was not at all afraid of doing his duty in thofe critical times, refolved to take him off from it, and raife him to the bench.

Mr. Hale faw well enough the fnare laid for him, and though he did not much confider the prejudice it would be to himfelf, to exchange the eafy and fafer profits he had by his practice, for a judge's place in the Common-pleas, which he was required to accept of, yet he did deliberate more on the lawfulnefs of taking a commiffion from ufurpers; but having confidered well of this, he came to be of opinion, " that it being abfolutely " neceffary, to have juftice and property kept up " at all times, it was no fin to take a commiffion " from ufurpers, if he made no declaration of his " acknowledging their authority," which he never did. He was much urged to accept of it by fome eminent men of his own profeffion, who were of the king's party, as fir O lando Bridgeman, and fir Geoffery Palmer; and was alfo fatisfied

con-

concerning the lawfulness of it, by the resolution of some famous divines, in particular Dr. Sheldon, and Dr. Henchman, who were afterwards promoted to the fees of Canterbury and London.

To these were added the importunities of all his friends, who thought that in a time of so much danger and oppreffion, it might be no small fecurity to the nation, to have a man of his integrity and abilities on the bench: and the ufurpers themfelves held him in that eftimation, that they were glad to have him give a countenance to their courts, and by promoting one that was known to have different principles from them, affected the reputation of honouring and trufting men of eminent virtues, of what perfuafion foever they might be, in relation to public matters.

But he had greater fcruples concerning the proceeding againft felons, and putting offenders to death by that commiffion, fince he thought the fword of juftice belonging only by right to the lawful prince, it feemed not warrantable to proceed to a capital fentence by an authority derived from ufurpers; yet at firft he made diftinction between common and ordinary felonies, and offences againft the ftate; for the laft he would never meddle in them, for he thought thefe might be often legal and warrantable actions, and that the putting men to death on that account was murder; but for the ordinary felonies, he at firft was of opinion, that it was as neceflary, even in times of ufurpation, to execute juftice in thofe cafes, as in matters

of

of property; but after the king was murdered, he laid by all his collections of the pleas of the crown, and that they might not fall into ill hands, he hid them behind the wainscotting of his ſtudy, for he ſaid, " there was no more occaſion to uſe " them, till the king ſhould be again reſtored to " his right," and ſo upon his Majeſty's reſtoration he took them out, and went on in his deſign to perfect that great work.

Yet, for ſome time after he was made a judge, when he went the circuit, he did ſit on the crown-ſide, and judged criminals : but, having conſidered farther of it, he came to think, that it was at leaſt better not to do it ; and ſo after the ſecond or third circuit, he refuſed to ſit any more on the crown-ſide, and told plainly the reaſon, for in matters of blood, he was always to chooſe the ſafer ſide. And indeed he had ſo carried himſelf in ſome trials, that they were not unwilling he ſhould withdraw from medling farther in them, of which I ſhall give ſome inſtances.

Not long after he was made a judge, which was in the year 1653, when he went the circuit, a trial was brought before him at Lincoln, concerning the murder of one of the townſmen, who had been of the king's party, and was killed by a ſoldier of the garriſon there. He was in the fields with a fowling piece on his ſhoulder, which the ſoldier ſeeing, he came to him and ſaid, it was contrary to an order which the Protector had made, " That none who had been of the
" king's

" king's party fhould carry arms;" and fo he would have forced it from him; but as the other did not regard the order, fo being ftronger than the foldier, he threw him down, and having beat him, he left him. The foldier went into the town, and told one of his fellow-foldiers how he had been ufed, and got him to go with him, and lie in wait for the man that he might be revenged on him. They both watched his coming to town, and one of them went to him to demand his gun, which he refufing, the foldier ftruck at him, and as they were ftruggling, the other came behind, and ran his fword into his body, of which he prefently died. It was in the time of the affizes, fo they were both tried: againft the one there was no evidence of forethought felony, fo he was only found guilty of man-flaughter, and burnt on the hand; but the other was found guilty of murder: and though colonel Whàley, that commanded the garrifon, came into the court and urged, that the man was killed only for difobeying the Protector's orders, and that the foldier was but doing his duty; yet the judge regarded both his reafons and threatenings very little, and therefore he not only gave fentence againft him, but ordered the execution to be fo fuddenly done, that it might not be poffible to procure a reprieve, which he believed would have been obtained, if there had been time enough granted for it.

Another occafion was given him of fhewing both his juftice and courage, when he was in an-

other

other circuit. He underſtood that the Protector had ordered a jury to be returned for a trial in which he was more than ordinarily concerned: upon this information, he examined the ſheriff about it, who knew nothing of it, for he ſaid he referred all ſuch things to the under-ſheriff; and having next aſked the under-ſheriff concerning it, he found the jury had been returned by order from Cromwell; upon which he ſhewed the ſtatute, that all juries ought to be returned by the ſheriff, or his lawful officer; and this not being done according to law, he diſmiſſed the jury, and would not try the cauſe: upon which the Protector was highly diſpleaſed with him, and at his return from the circuit, he told him in anger, he was not fit to be a judge; to which all the anſwer he made was, that it was very true.

Another thing met him in the circuit, upon which he reſolved to have proceeded ſeverely. Some Anabaptiſts had ruſhed into a church, and had diſturbed a congregation, while they were receiving the ſacrament, not without ſome violence; at this he was highly offended, for he ſaid, it was intolerable for men, who pretended ſo highly to liberty of conſcience, to go and diſturb others; eſpecially thoſe who had the encouragement of the law on their ſide: but theſe were ſo ſupported by ſome great magiſtrates and officers, that a ſtop was put to his proceedings; upon which he declared, he would meddle no more with the trials on the crown-ſide.

When

When Penruddock's trial was brought on, there was a special meffenger fent to him, requiring him to affift at it. It was in vacation time, and he was at his country-houfe at Alderly: he plainly refufed to go, and faid, the four terms, and two circuits, were enough, and the little interval that was between, was little enough for his private affairs, and fo he excufed himfelf: he thought it was not neceffary to fpeak more clearly, but if he had been urged to it, he would not have been afraid of doing it.

He was at that time chofen a parliament-man, (for there being then no houfe of lords, judges might have been chofen to fit in the houfe of commons) and he went to it, on defign to obftruct the mad and wicked projects then on foot, by two parties, that had very different principles and ends.

On the one hand, fome that were perhaps more fincere, yet were really brain-fick, defigned they knew not what, being refolved to pull down a ftanding miniftry, the law, and property of England, and all the antient rules of this government, and fet up in its room an indigefted enthufiaftical fcheme, which they called the kingdom of Chrift, or of his faints; many of them being really in ex-pectation, that one day or other Chrift would come down, and fit among them, and at leaft they thought to begin the glorious thoufand years mentioned in the Revelation.

Others at the fame time, taking advantages from the fears and apprehenfions, that all the fober men

of

of the nation were in, leaſt they ſhould fall under
the tyranny of a diſtracted ſort of people, who, to
all their other ill principles, added great cruelty,
which they had copied from thoſe at Munſter in
the former age, intended to improve that opportunity to raiſe their own fortunes and families. A-
midſt theſe, judge Hale ſteered a middle courſe;
for as he would engage for neither ſide, ſo he, with
a great many more worthy men, came to parliament, more out of a deſign to hinder miſchief,
than to do much good; wiſely foreſeeing, that the
inclinations for the royal family were daily growing ſo much, that in time the diſorders, then in
agitation, would ferment to that happy reſolution
in which they determined in May 1660. And
therefore all that could be then done, was to op-
poſe the ill deſigns of both parties, the enthuſiaſts
as well as the uſurpers. Among the other extravagant motions made in this parliament, one was,
to deſtroy all the records in the Tower, and to
ſettle the nation on a new foundation; ſo he took
this province to himſelf, to ſhew the madneſs of
this propoſition, the injuſtice of it, and the miſchiefs
that would follow on it; and did it with ſuch
clearneſs, and ſtrength of reaſon, as not only
ſatisfied all ſober perſons, (for it may be ſuppoſed
that was ſoon done) but ſtopt even the mouths of
the frantic people themſelves.

Thus he continued adminiſtering juſtice till the
Protector died, but then he both refuſed the
mournings that were ſent to him and his ſervants

for

for the funeral, and likewise to accept of the new commiffion that was offered him by Richard, and when the reft of the judges urged it upon him, and employed others to prefs him to accept of it, he rejected all their importunities, and faid, he could act no longer under fuch authority.

He lived a private man till the parliament met that called home the king, to which he was re-turned knight of the fhire from the county of Gloucefter. It appeared at that time how much he was beloved and efteemed in his neighbourhood, for though another, who ftood in competition with him, had fpent near a thoufand pounds to procure voices, (a great fum to be employed that way in thofe days) and he had been at no coft, and was fo far from foliciting it, that he had ftood out long againft thofe who prefs'd him to appear, and he did not promife to appear till three days before the election, yet he was preferred. He was brought thi-ther almoft by violence, by the lord (now earl of) Berkeley, who bore all the charge of the enter-tainments on the day of his election, which was confiderable, and had engaged all his friends and intereft for him : and whereas by the writ, the knight of the fhire muft be *miles gladio cinctus*, and he had no fword, that noble lord girt him with his own fword during the election ; but he was foon weary of it, for the embroidery of the belt did not fuit well with the plainnefs of his cloaths: and indeed the election did not hold long, for as foon as ever he came into the field, he was

chofen

chofen by much the greater number, though the poll continued for three or four days.

In that parliament he bore his fhare in the happy period then put to the confufions that threatened the utter ruin of the nation, which, contrary to the expectations of the moft fanguine, fettled in fo ferene and quiet a manner, that thofe who had formerly built fo much on their fuccefs, calling it an anfwer from heaven to their folemn appeals to the providence of God, were now not a little confounded, to fee all this turned againft themfelves, in an inftance much more extraordinary than any of thofe were, upon which they had built fo much. His great prudence and excellent temper led him to think, that the fooner an act of indemnity were paffed, and the fuller it were of graces and favours, it would fooner fettle the nation, and quiet the minds of the people; and therefore he applied himfelf with a particular care to the framing and carrying it on, in which it was vifible he had no concern of his own, but merely his love of the public that fet him on to it.

Soon after this, when the courts in Weftminfter-hall came to be fettled, he was made lord chief baron; and when the earl of Clarendon (then lord chancellor) delivered him his commiffion, in the fpeech he made according to the cuftom on fuch occafions, he expreffed his efteem of him in a very fingular manner, telling him among other things, " that if the king could have found out " an honefter and fitter man for that employment,

" he

" he would not have advanced him to it; and
" that he had therefore preferred him, becaufe he
" knew none that deferved it fo well." It is ordinary for perfons fo promoted to be knighted, but
he defired to avoid having that honour done him,
and therefore for a confiderable time declined all
opportunities of waiting on the king, which the
lord chancellor obferving, fent for him upon bufinefs one day, when the king was at his houfe, and
told his Majefty there was his modeft chief baron,
upon which he was unexpectedly knighted.

He continued eleven years in that place, managing the court, and all proceedings in it, with
fingular juftice. It was obferved by the whole
nation, how much he raifed the reputation and
practice of it: and thofe who held places and offices in it, can all declare, not only the impartiality of his juftice, for that is but a common virtue,
but his generofity, his vaft diligence, and his great
exactnefs in trials. This gave occafion to the only
complaint that ever was made of him, that he did
not difpatch matters quick enough; but the great
care he ufed, to put fuits to a final end, as it made
him flower in deciding them; fo it had this good
effect, that caufes, tried before him, were feldom,
if ever, tried again.

Nor did his adminiftration of juftice lie only in
that court: he was one of the principal judges
that fat in Clifford's-Inn, about fettling the difference between landlord and tenant, after the
dreadful fire of London. He being the firft that

offered

offered his service to the city, for accommodating all the differences that might have arisen about the rebuilding it, in which he behaved himself to the satisfaction of all persons concerned : so that the sudden and quiet building of the city, which is justly to be reckoned one of the wonders of the age, is in no small measure due to the great care, which he and sir Orland Bridgeman, (then lord chief justice of the Common-pleas, afterwards lord keeper of the great seal of England) used, and to the judgment they shewed in that affair : since without the rules then laid down, there might have otherwise followed such an endless train of vexatious suits, as might have been little less chargeable than the fire itself had been. But, without detracting from the labours of the other judges, it must be acknowledged, that he was the most instrumental in that great work ; for he first, by way of scheme, contrived the rules upon which he and the rest proceeded afterwards, in which his readiness at arithmetic, and his skill in architecture, were of great use to him.

But it will not seem strange that a judge behaved himself as he did, who, at the entry into his employment, set such excellent rules to himself, which will appear in the following paper copied from the original under his own hand.

Things

Things neceffary to be continually had in remembrance.

I. That in the adminiftration of juftice, I am intrufted for God, the king and country; and therefore,

II. That it be done, 1. uprightly; 2. deliberately; 3. refolutely.

III. That I reft not upon my own underftanding or ftrength, but implore and reft upon the direction and ftrength of God.

IV. That in the execution of juftice I carefully lay afide my own paffions, and not give way to them, however provoked.

V. That I be wholly intent upon the bufinefs I am about, remitting all other cares and thoughts, as unfeafonable and interruptions.

VI. That I fuffer not myfelf to be prepoffeffed with any judgment at all, till the whole bufinefs and both parties be heard.

VII. That I never engage myfelf in the beginning of any caufe, but referve myfelf unprejudiced till the whole be heard.

VIII. That in bufinefs capital, though my nature prompt me to pity; yet to confider, that there is alfo a pity due to the country.

IX. That I be not too rigid in matters purely confcientious, where all the harm is diverfity of judgment.

X. That

X. That I be not biassed with compassion to the poor, or favour to the rich, in point of justice.

XI. That popular, or court applause, or distaste, have no influence in any thing I do in point of distribution of justice.

XII. Not to be solicitous what men will say or think, so long as I keep myself exactly according to the rule of justice.

XIII. If in criminals it be a measuring cast, to incline to mercy and acquittal.

XIV. In criminals that consist merely in words, when no more harm ensues, moderation is no injustice.

XV. In criminals of blood, if the fact be evident, severity is justice.

XVI. To abhor all private solicitations, of what kind soever, and by whom soever, in matters depending.

XVII. To charge my servants, 1. not to interpose in any business whatsoever; 2. not to take more than their known fees; 3. not to give any undue precedence to causes; 4. not to recommend council.

XVIII. To be short and sparing at meals, that I may be the fitter for business.

He would never receive private addresses or recommendations from the greatest persons in any matter, in which justice was concerned. One of the first peers of England went once to his chamber

ber

ber and told him, " that having a fuit in law to
" be tried before him, he was then to acquaint
" him with it, that he might the better underftand
" it, when it fhould come to be heard in court."
Upon which the lord chief baron interrupted
him, and faid, " he did not deal fairly to come to
" his chamber about fuch affairs, for he never
" received any information of caufes but in open
" court, where both parties were to be heard
" alike ;" fo he would not fuffer him to go on :
whereupon his grace (for he was a duke) went
away not a little diffatisfied, and complained of it
to the king, as a rudenefs that was not to be en-
dured. But his Majefty bid him content himfelf
that he was no worfe ufed, and faid, " he verily
" believed he would have ufed himfelf no better,
" if he had gone to folicit him in any of his own
" caufes."

Another paffage fell out in one of his circuits,
which was fomewhat cenfured as an affectation of
an unreafonable ftrictnefs, but it flowed from his
exactnefs to the rules he had fet himfelf. A gentleman had fent him a buck for his table, that had
a trial at the affizes ; fo when he heard his name,
he afked, " if he was not the fame perfon that
" had fent him venifon," and finding he was the
fame, he told him, " he could not fuffer the trial
" to go on, till he had paid him for his buck ;"
to which the gentleman anfwered, " that he never
" fold his venifon, and that he had done nothing
" to him, which he did not do to every judge that
" had

" had gone that circuit," which was confirmed by
several gentlemen then present : but all would not
do, for the lord chief baron had learned from Solomon, that a gift perverteth the ways of judgment, and therefore he would not suffer the trial to
go on, till he had paid for the present ; upon which
the gentleman withdrew the record : and at Salis-
bury the dean and chapter having, according to the
custom, presented him with six sugar loaves in his
circuit, he made his servants pay for the sugar before he would try their cause.

It was not so easy for him to throw off the importunities of the poor, for whom his compassion
wrought more powerfully than his regard to
wealth and greatness ; yet when justice was concerned, even that did not turn him out of the
way.   There was one that had been put out of a
place for some ill behaviour, who urged the lord
chief baron to set his hand to a certificate, to
restore him to it, or provide him with another ;
but he told him plainly, his fault was such that he
could not do it ; the other pressed him vehemently,
and fell down on his knees, and begged it of him
with many tears ; but finding that could not pro-
vail, he said he should be utterly ruined if he did
it not ; and he should curse him for it every day.
But that having no effect, he then fell out in all
the reproachful words, that passion and despair
could inspire him with, to which all the answer
the lord chief baron made, was, " that he could
" very well bear all his reproaches, but he could

" not

" not for all that set his hand to his certificate."
He saw he was poor, so he gave him a large charity and sent him away.

But now he was to go on after his pattern,
Pomponius Atticus, still to favour and relieve them
that were lowest; so besides great charities to the
nonconformists, who were then as he thought too
hardly used, he took great care to cover them all
he could, from the severities some designed against
them, and discouraged those who were inclined to
stretch the laws too much against them. He lamented the differences that were raised in this
church very much, and according to the impartiality of his justice, he blamed some things on both
sides, which I shall set down with the same freedom that he spake them. He thought many of
the nonconformists, had merited highly in the
business of the king's restoration, and at least deserved that the terms of conformity should not
have been made stricter, than they were before the
war. There was not then that dreadful prospect
of popery, that has appeared since: but that which
afflicted him most was, that he saw the heats and
contentions which followed upon those different
parties and interests, did take people off from the
indispensable things of religion, and slackened the
zeal of otherways good men for the substance
of it, so much being spent about external and
indifferent things. It also gave advantages to
atheists, to treat the most sacred points of our
holy faith as ridiculous, when they saw the pro-

D

sessors

feffors of it contend, fo fiercely, and with fuch bitternefs, about leffer matters. He was much offended at all thofe books that were written to expofe the contrary fect to the fcorn and contempt of the age in a wanton and petulant ftile; he thought fuch writers wounded the chriftian religion, through the fides of thofe who differed from them: while a fort of lewd people, who having affumed to tbemfelves the title of wits (though but very few of them have a right to it) took up from both hands, what they had faid, to make one another fhew ridiculous, and from thence perfuaded the world to laugh at both, and at all religion for their fakes. And therefore he often wifhed there might be fome law, to make all fcurrility or bitternefs in difputes about religion punifhable. But as he lamented the proceedings too rigouroufly againft the nonconformifts, fo he declared himfelf always of the fide of the church of England, and faid thofe of the feparation were good men, but they had narrow fouls, who would break the peace of the church, about fuch inconfiderable matters, as the points in difference were.

He fcarce ever medled in ftate intrigues, yet upon a propofition that was fet on foot by the lord keeper Bridgeman, for a comprehenfion of the more moderate diffenters, and a limited indulgence towards fuch as could not be brought within the comprehenfion, he difpenfed with his maxim, of avoiding to engage in matters of ftate. There were feveral meetings upon that occafion. The

divine

divine of the church of England that appeared
most considerable for it, was doctor Wilkins, afterwards promoted to the bishoprick of Chester, a
man of as great a mind, as true a judgment, as
eminent virtues, and of as good a soul, as any I
ever knew. He being determined, as well by his
excellent temper, as by his foresight and prudence,
by which he early perceived the great prejudices
that religion received, and the vast dangers the reformation was like to fall under by those divisions,
set about that project with the magnanimity that
was indeed peculiar to himself; for though he was
much censured by many of his own side, and se-
conded by very few, yet he pushed it as far as he
could. After several conferences with two of the
eminentest of the presbyterian divines, heads were
agreed on, some abatements were to be made, and
explanations were to be accepted of. The particulars of that project being thus concerted,
they were brought to the lord chief baron, who
put them in form of a bill, to be presented to the
next sessions of parliament.

But two parties appeared vigorously against this
design, the one was of some zealous clergymen,
who thought it below the dignity of the church to
alter laws, and change settlements for the sake of
some whom they esteemed schismatics : they also
believed, it was better to keep them out of the
church, than bring them into it, since a faction
upon that would arise in the church, which they
thought might be more dangerous than the schism

itself

itself was. Besides they said, if some things were now to be changed in compliance with the humour of a party, as soon as that was done, another party might demand other concessions, and there might be as good reasons invented for these as for those : many such concessions might also shake those of our own communion, and tempt them to forsake us, and go over to the church of Rome, pretending that we changed so often, that they were thereby inclined to be of a church that was constant and true to herself. These were the reasons brought, and chiefly insisted on, against all comprehension; and they wrought upon the greater part of the house of commons, so that they passed a vote against the receiving of any bill for that effect.

There were others that opposed it upon different ends : they designed to shelter the papists from the execution of the law, and saw clearly that nothing could bring in popery so well as a toleration. But to tolerate popery bare-faced, would have startled the nation too much ; so it was necessary to hinder all the propositions for union, since the keeping up the differences was the best colour they could find, for getting the toleration to pass only as a slackening the laws against dissenters, whose numbers and wealth made it adviseable to have some regard to them ; and under this pretence popery might have crept in more covered, and less regarded : so these councils being more acceptable to some concealed papists then in great power, as

has

has fince appeared but too evidently, the whole projećt for comprehenfion was let fall, and thofe who had fet it on foot, came to be looked on with an ill eye, as fecret favourers of the diffenters, underminers of the church, and every thing elfe that jealoufy and diftafte could caft on them.

But upon this occafion the lord chief baron, and Dr. Wilkins, came to contraćt a firm and familiar friendfhip; and the lord chief baron having much bufinefs, and little time to fpare, did, to enjoy the other the more, what he had fcarce ever done before, he went fometimes to dine with him. And though he lived in great friendfhip with fome other eminent clergymen, as Dr. Ward, bifhop of Salifbury; Dr. Barlow, bifhop of Lincoln; Dr. Barrow, late mafter of Trinity college; Dr. Tillotfon, dean of Canterbury; and Dr. Stillingfleet, dean of St. Paul's, (men fo well known and fo much efteemed, that as it was no wonder the lord chief baron valued their converfation highly, fo thofe of them that are yet alive will think it no leffening of the charaćter they are fo defervedly in, that they are reckoned among judge Hale's friends) yet there was an intimacy and freedom in his converfe with bifhop Wilkins, that was fingular to him alone. He had during the late wars lived in a long and intire friendfhip with the apoftolical primate of Ireland bifhop Ufher: their curious fearches into antiquity, and the fympathy of both their tempers, led them to a great agreement almoft in every thing. He held alfo

D 3

great

great converfation with Mr. Baxter, who was his
neighbour at Acton, on whom he looked as a
perfon of great devotion and piety, and of a very
fubtile and quick apprehenfion : their converfation
lay moft in metaphyfical and abftracted ideas and
fchemes.

He looked with great forrow on the impiety and
atheifm of the age, and fo he fet himfelf to oppofe
it, not only by the fhining example of his own
life, but by engaging in a caufe, that indeed could
hardly fall into better hands : and as he could not
find a fubject more worthy of himfelf, fo there
were few in the age that underftood it fo well, and
could manage it more fkilfully. The occafion
that firft led him to write about it was this. He
was a ftrict obferver of the Lord's day, in which,
befides his conftancy in the public worfhip of God,
he ufed to call all his family together, and repeat
to them the heads of the fermons, with fome additions of his own, which he fitted for their capacities and circumftances, and that being done,
he had a cuftom of fhutting himfelf up for two or
three hours, which he either fpent in his fecret
devotions, or on fuch profitable meditations as
did then occur to his thoughts. He writ them
with the fame fimplicity that he formed them in
his mind, without any art, or fo much as a thought
to let them be publifhed: he never corrected them,
but laid them by, when he had finifhed them,
having intended only to fix and preferve his own
reflections in them ; fo that he ufed no fort of care

to polish them, or make the first draught perfecter than when they fell from his pen. These fell into the hands of a worthy person, and he judging, as well he might, that the communicating them to the world, might be a public service, printed two volumes of them in octavo a little before the author's death, containing his

CONTEMPLATIONS,

I. Of our latter end.
II. Of wisdom, and the fear of God.
III. Of the knowledge of Christ crucified.
IV. The victory of faith over the world.
V. Of humility.
VI. Jacob's vow.
VII. Of contentation.
VIII. Of afflictions.
IX. A good method to entertain unstable and troublesome times.
X. Changes and troubles, a poem.
XI. Of the redemption of time.
XII. The great audit.
XIII. Directions touching keeping the Lord's day, in a letter to his children.
XIV. Poems written upon Christmas-day.

In the 2d Volume.

I. An enquiry touching happiness.
II. Of the chief end of man.

                    III.

III. Upon Eclef. xii. 1. Remember thy Creator.

IV. Upon the Pfal. li. 10. Create a clean heart in me ; with a poem.

V. The folly and mifchief of fin.

VI. Of felf-denial.

VII. Motives to watchfulnefs, in reference to the good and evil angels.

VIII. Of Moderation of the affections.

IX. Of worldly hope and expectation.

X. Upon Heb. xiii. 14. We have here no continuing city.

XI. Of contentednefs and patience.

XII. Of moderation of anger.

XIII. A preparative againft affliction.

XIV. Of fubmiffion, prayer, and thankfgiving.

XV. Of prayer and thankfgiving on Pf. cxvi. 12.

XVI. Meditations on the Lord's prayer, with a paraphrafe upon it.

In them there appears a generous and true fpirit of religion, mix'd with a moft ferious and fervent devotion, and perhaps with the more advantage, that the ftile wants fome correction, which fhews they were the genuine productions of an excellent mind, entertaining itfelf in fecret with fuch contemplations. The ftile is clear and mafculine, in a due temper between flatnefs and affectation, in which he expreffes his thoughts both eafily and decently. In writing thefe difcourfes, having run over moft of the fubjects that his own circumftances led him chiefly to confider, he began to be in some pain to chuse new arguments, and therefore resolved to fix on a theme that should hold him longer.

He was soon determined in his choice, by the immoral and irreligious principles and practices, that had so long vexed his righteous soul: and therefore began a great design against atheism ; the first part of which is only printed, of the origination of mankind, designed to prove the creation of the world, and the truth of the Mosaical history.

The second part was of the nature of the soul, and of a future state.

The third part was concerning the attributes of God, both from the abstracted ideas of him, and the light of nature ; the evidence of providence, the notions of morality, and the voice of conscience.

And the fourth part was concerning the truth and authority of the scriptures, with answers to the objections against them. On writing these he spent seven years. He wrote them with so much consideration, that one who perused the original under his own hand, which was the first draught of it, told me, he did not remember any considerable alteration, perhaps not of twenty words in the whole work.

The way of his writing them (only on the evenings of the Lord's day, when he was in town, and not much oftener when he was in the country) made, that they are not so contracted, as it is

very

very likely he would have writ them, if he had been more at leifure to have brought his thoughts into a narrower compafs, and fewer words.

But making fome allowance for the largenefs of the ftile, that volume that is printed, is generally acknowledged to be one of the perfecteft pieces both of learning and reafoning that has been writ on that fubject; and he who read a great part of the other volumes told me, they were all of a piece with the firft.

When he had finifhed this work, he fent it by an unknown hand to bifhop Wilkins, to defire his judgment of it; but he that brought it, would give no other account of the author, but that he was not a clergyman. The bifhop and his worthy friend Dr. Tillotfon, read a great deal of it with much pleafure, but could not imagine who could be the author, and how a man that was mafter of fo much reafon, and fo great a variety of know-ledge, fhould be fo unknown to them, that they could not find him out, by thofe characters which are fo little common. At laft Dr. Tillotfon guef-fed it muft be the lord chief baron, to which the other prefently agreed, wondering he had been fo long in finding it out. So they went immediately to him, and the bifhop thanking him for the en-tertainment he had received from his works, he blufhed extremely, not without fome difpleafure, apprehending that the perfon he had trufted had difcovered him. But the bifhop foon cleared that, and told him, " he had difcovered himfelf, for the

" learning

" learning of that book was fo various, that
" none but he could be the author of it."   And
that bifhop having a freedom in delivering his opinion of things and perfons, which perhaps few
ever managed both with fo much plainnefs and
prudence, told him, " there was nothing could
" be better faid on thefe arguments, if he could
" bring it into a lefs compafs, but if he had not
" leifure for that, he thought it much better to have
" it come out, though a little too large, than that
" the world fhould be deprived of the good which
" it muft needs do."   But our judge had never
the opportunity of revifing it, fo a little before
his death he fent the firft part of it to the prefs.

In the beginning of it, he gives an effay of his
excellent way of methodizing things, in which he
was fo great a mafter, that whatever he undertook, he would prefently caft into fo perfect a
fcheme, that he could never afterwards correct it.
He runs out copioufly upon the argument of the
impoffibility of an eternal fucceffion of time, to
fhew that time and eternity are inconfiftent one
with another ; and that therefore all duration that
was paft, and defined by time, could not be from
eternity ; and he fhews the difference between
fucceffive eternity already paft, and one to come:
fo that though the latter is poffible, the former is
not fo ; for all the parts of the former have actually
been, and therefore being defined by time, cannot
be eternal ; whereas the other are ftill future to all
eternity, fo that this reafoning cannot be turned
                                                    to

to prove the poffibility of eternal fucceffions, that have been, as well as eternal fucceffions that fhall be. This he follows with a ftrength I never met with in any that managed it before him.

He brings next all thofe moral arguments, to prove that the world had a beginning; agreeing to the account Mofes gives of it, as that no hiftory rifes higher, than near the time of the deluge; and that the firft foundation of kingdoms, the invention of arts, the beginnings of all religions, the gradual plantation of the world, and increafe of mankind, and the confent of nations do agree with it. In managing thefe, as he fhews profound fkill both in hiftorical and philofophical learning, fo he gives a noble difcovery of his great candour and probity, that he would not impofe on the reader with a falfe fhew of reafoning by arguments that he knew had flaws in them; and, therefore, upon every one of thefe he adds fuch allays, as in a great meafure leffened and took off their force, with as much exactnefs of judgment, and ftrictnefs of cenfure, as if he had been fet to plead for the other fide: and indeed fums up the whole evidence for religion, as impartially as ever he did in a trial for life or death to the jury, which, how equally and judicioufly he always did, the whole nation well knows.

After that, he examines the ancient opinions of the philofophers, and enlarges with a great variety of curious reflections in anfwering that only argument, that has any appearance of ftrength for

the

the cafual production of man, from the origination
of infects out of putrified matter, as is commonly
fuppofed ; and he concluded the book, fhewing
how rational and philofophical the account which
Mofes gives of it is. There is in it all a fagacity
and quicknefs of thought, mixed with great and
curious learning, that I confefs I never met together in any other book on that fubject. Among
other conjectures, one he gives concerning the deluge is, " that he did not think the face of the
" earth and the waters were altogether the fame
" before the univerfal deluge, and after ; but pof-
" fibly the face of the earth was more even than
" now it is ; the feas poffibly more dilated and
" extended, and not fo deep as now." And a little
after, " poffibly the feas have undermined much
" of the appearing continent of earth." This I
the rather take notice of, becaufe it hath been
fince his death made out in a moft ingenious and
moft elegantly written book by Mr. Burnet, of
Chrift's college in Cambridge, who has given
fuch an effay towards the proving the poffibility
of an univerfal deluge, and from thence has collected with great fagacity what paradife was before it, as has not been offered by any philofopher
before him.

While the judge was thus employing his time,
the lord chief juftice Keyling dying, he was on
the 18th of May 1671, promoted to be lord chief
juftice of England. He had made the pleas of the
crown one of his chief ftudies, and by much
fearch.

fearch, and long obfervation, had compofed that great work concerning them, formerly mentioned. He that holds the high office of jufticiary in that court, being the chief truftee, and affertor of the liberties of his country, all people applauded this choice, and thought their liberties could not be better depofited than in the hands of one, that as he underftood them well, fo he had all the juftice and courage that fo facred a truft required. One thing was much obferved and commended in him, that when there was a great inequality in the ability and learning of the councellors that were to plead one againft another, he thought it became him, as the judge, to fupply that; fo he would enforce what the weaker council managed but indifferently, and not fuffer the more learned to carry the bufinefs by the advantage they had over the others in their quicknefs and fkill in law, and readinefs in pleading, till all things were cleared in which the merits and ftrength of the ill-defended caufe lay. He was not fatisfied barely to give his judgment in caufes, but did, efpecially in all intricate ones, give fuch an account of the reafons that prevailed with him, that the council did not only acquiefce in his authority, but were fo convinced by his reafons, that I have heard many profefs that he brought them often to change their opinions; fo that his giving of judgment was really a learned lecture upon that point of law: and which was yet more, the parties themfelves, though intereft does too commonly corrupt the judgment,

were

were generally satisfied with the juftice of his decifions, even when they were made againft them.
His impartial juftice, and great diligence, drew
the chief practice after him, into whatfoever court
he came: fince, though the courts of the Common pleas, the Exchequer and the King's-bench,
are appointed for the trial of caufes of different
natures, yet it is eafy to bring moft caufes into
any of them, as the council or attornies pleafe;
fo as he had drawn the bufinefs much after him,
both into the Common-pleas, and the Exchequer,
it now followed him into the king's-bench, and
many caufes that were depending in the Exchequer
and not determined, were let fall there, and
brought again before him in the court to which
he was now removed. And here did he fpend the
reft of his publick life and employment: but
about four years and a half after this advancement, he, who had hitherto enjoyed a firm and
vigorous health, to which his great temperance,
and the equality of his mind, did not a little conduce, was on a fudden brought very low by an
inflammation in his midriff, which in two days
time broke the conftitution of his health to fuch a
degree that he never recovered it; he became fo
afthmatical, that with great difficulty he could
fetch his breath; that determined in a dropfy, of
which he afterwards died. He underftood phyfick
fo well, that, confidering his age, he concluded
his diftemper muft carry him off in a little time;
and therefore he refolved to have fome of the laft
months

months of his life referved to himfelf, that, being freed of all worldly cares, he might be preparing for his change. He was alfo fo much difabled in his body, that he could hardly, though fupported by his fervants, walk through Weftminfter-hall, or endure the toil of bufinefs. He had been a long time wearied with the diftractions that his employment had brought on him, and his profeffion was become ungrateful to him ; he loved to apply himfelf wholly to better purpofes, as will appear by a paper that he wrote on this fubject, which I fhall here infert :

" Firft, if I confider the bufinefs of my pro-
" feffion, whether as an advocate or as a judge, it
" is true I do acknowledge by the inftitution of
" Almighty God, and the difpenfation of his pro-
" vidence, I am bound to induftry and fidelity in
" it : and as it is an act of obedience unto his
" will, it carries with it fome things of religious
" duty, and I may and do take comfort in it, and
" expect a reward of my obedience to him, and
" the good that I do to mankind therein, from the
" bounty and beneficence and promife of Almighty
" God : and it is true alfo that without fuch em-
" ployments civil focieties cannot be fupported,
" and great good redounds to mankind from them,
" and in thefe refpects the confcience of my own
" induftry, fidelity and integrity in them, is a
" great comfort and fatisfaction to me. But yet
" this I muft fay concerning thefe employments,
" confidered fimply in themfelyes, that they are

" very

" very full of cares, and anxieties and perturba-
" tions.

" Secondly, That though they are beneficial to
" others, yet they are of the leaft benefit to the
" perfon employed in them.

" Thirdly, That they do neceffarily involve the
" party, whofe office it is, in great dangers, dif-
" ficulties, and calumnies.

" Fourthly, That they only ferve for the meri-
" dian of this life, which is fhort and uncertain.

" Fifthly, That tho' it be my duty faithfully to
" ferve in them, while I am called to them, and
" till I am duly called from them, yet they are great
" confumers of that little time we have here, which,
" as it feems to me, might be better fpent in a
" pious contemplative life, and a due provifion for
" eternity. I do not know a better temporal em-
" ployment than Martha had, in teftifying her
" love and duty to our Saviour, by making pro-
" vifion for him ; yet our Lord tells her, that
" though fhe was troubled about many things,
" there was only one thing neceffary, and Mary
" had chofen the better part."

By this the reader will fee that he continued
in his ftation upon no other confideration, but
that being fet in it by the providence of God, he
judged he could not abandon that poft which
was affigned him, without preferring his own private inclination to the choice God had made for
him ; but now that fame providence having by
this great diftemper difengaged him from the obligation

gation of holding a place, which he was no longer
able to difcharge, he refolved to refign it. 'This
was no fooner furmifed abroad, than it drew upon
him the importunities of all his friends, and the
clamour of the whole town to divert him from it,
but all was to no purpofe; there was but one argument that could move him, which was, that
he was obliged to continue in the employment
God had put him in for the good of the public;
but to this he had fuch an anfwer, that even thofe
who were moft concerned in his withdrawing,
could not but fee, that the reafons inducing him
to it, were but too ftrong; fo he made application
to his majefty for his writ of eafe, which the king
was very unwilling to grant him, and offered to
let him hold his place ftill, he doing what bufinefs
he could in his chamber; but he faid, " he could
" not with a good confcience continue in it,
" fince he was no longer able to difcharge the
" duty belonging to it."

But yet fuch was the general fatisfaction which
all the kingdom received by his excellent adminiftration of juftice, that the king, though he could
not well deny his requeft, yet he deferred the
granting of it as long as was poffible: nor could
the lord chancellor be prevailed with to move the
king to haften his difcharge, though the chief
juftice often preffed him to it.

At laft having wearied himfelf, and all his
friends, with his importunate defires, and growing
fenfibly weaker in body, he did upon the twenty-

fift

firſt day of February, 28. Car. An. Dom. 167⅚, go before a maſter of chancery, with a little parchment deed, drawn by himſelf, and written all with his own hand, and there ſealed and delivered it, and acknowledged it to be enrolled, and afterwards he brought the original deed to the lord chancellor, and did formally ſurrender his office in theſe words

" Omnibus Chriſti fidelibus ad quos præſens
" ſcriptura pervenerit, Matheus Hale, miles ca-
" pitalis juſticiarius domini regis ad placita-coram
" ipſo rege tenenda aſſignatus ſalutem in domino
" ſempiternam, noveritis me præfatum Matheum
" Hale, militem jam ſenem factum & variis cor-
" poris mei ſenilis morbis & infirmitatibus dire
" laborantem & adhuc detentum. Hâc chartâ
" mea reſignare & ſurſum reddere ſereniſſimo do-
" mino noſtro Carolo ſecundo, Dei gratia Angliæ
" Scotiæ Franciæ & Hiberniæ, regi, fidei defen-
" ſori, &c. Predictum officium capitalis juſticiarii
" ad placita coram ipſo rege tenenda, humillime
" petens quod hoc ſcriptum irrotaletur de recordo.
" In cujus rei teſtimonium huic chartæ meæ
" reſignationis ſigillum meum oppoſui, dat viceſi-
" mo primo die Februarii anno regni dict. dom.
" regis nunc viceſimo octavo."

He made this inſtrument, as he told the lord chancellor, for two ends; the one was to ſhew the world his own free concurrence to his removal:

another

another was to obviate an objection heretofore
made, that a chief juftice being placed by writ,
was not removeable at pleafure, as judges by patent were ; which opinion, as he faid, was once
held by his predeceffor the lord chief juftice Keyling, and though he himfelf was always of another opinion, yet he thought it reafonable to
prevent fuch a fcruple.

He had the day before furrendered to the king
in perfon, who parted from him with great grace,
wifhing him moft heartily the return of his health,
and affuring him, " that he would ftill look upon
" him as one of his judges, and have recourfe
" to his advice when his health would permit,
" and in the mean time would continue his pen-
" fion during his life."

The good man thought this bounty too great,
and an ill precedent for the king, and therefore
writ a letter to the lord treafurer, earneftly defiring
that his penfion might be only during pleafure ;
but the king would grant it for life, and make it
payable quarterly.

And yet for a whole month together, he would
not fuffer his fervant to fue out his patent for his
penfion; and when the firft payment was received,
he ordered a great part of it to charitable ufes, and
faid, he intended moft of it fhould be fo employed
as long as it was paid him.

At laft he happened to die upon the quarter day,
which was Chriftmas day ; and though this might
have given fome occafion to a difpute whether the

penfion

penſion for that quarter were recoverable, yet the king was pleaſed to decide that matter againſt himſelf, and ordered the penſion to be paid to his executors.

As ſoon as he was diſcharged from his great place, he returned home with as much chearful-neſs as his want of health would admit of, being now eaſed of a burthen he had been of late groaning under, and ſo made more capable of enjoying that which he had much wiſhed for, according to his elegant tranſlation of, or rather paraphraſe upon, thoſe excellent lines in Seneca's Thyeſtes. Act. 2.

> *Stet quicunque volet potens,*
> *Aulæ culmine lubrico :*
> *Me dulcis ſaturet quies.*
> *Obſcuro poſitus loco.*
> *Leni perfruar otio :*
> *Nullis nota quiritibus,*
> *Ætas per tacitum fluat.*
> *Sic cum tranſierint mei,*
> *Nullo cum ſtrepitu dies,*
> *Plebeius moriar ſenex.*
> *Illi mors gravis incubat,*
> *Qui notus nimis omnibus,*
> *Ignotus moritur ſibi.*

" Let him that will aſcend the tottering ſeat
" Of courtly grandeur, and become as great
" As are his mounting wiſhes : as for me,
" Let ſweet repoſe and reſt my portion be ;

" Gi

" Give me fome mean obfcure recefs, a fphere
" Out of the road of bufinefs, or the fear
" Of falling lower; where I fweetly may
" Myfelf and dear retirement ftill enjoy.
" Let not my life or name be known unto
" The grandees of the time, toft to and fro
" By cenfures or applaufe; but let my age
" Slide gently by, not overthwart the ftage
" Of public action; unheard, unfeen,
" And unconcern'd, as if I ne'er had been.
" And thus, while I fhall pafs my filent days
" In fhady privacy, free from the noife
" And buftles of the mad world, then fhall I
" A good old innocent plebeian die.
" Death is a mere furprife, a very fnare
" To him, that makes it his life's greateft care
" To be a public pagent, known to all,
" But unacquainted with himfelf, doth fall.

Having now attained to that privacy, which he
had no lefs ferioufly than pioufly wifhed for, he
called all his fervants that had belonged to his
office together, and told them, he had now laid
down his place, and fo their employments were
determined; upon that, he advifed them to fee for
themfelves, and gave to fome of them very confiderable prefents, and to every one of them a
token, and fo difmiffed all thofe that were not his
domefticks. He was difcharged the 15th of February 1675-6, and lived till the Chriftmas following, but all the while was in fo ill a ftate of
health,

health, that there was no hopes of his recovery.
He continued ſtill to retire often, both for his devotions and ſtudies, and as long as he could go, went
conſtantly to his cloſet; and when his infirmities
encreaſed on him, ſo that he was not able to go
thither himſelf, he made his ſervants carry him
thither in a chair. At laſt, as the winter came on,
he ſaw with great joy his deliverance approaching,
for beſides his being weary of the world, and
his longings for the bleſſedneſs of another ſtate, his
pains encreaſed ſo on him, that no patience inferior to his could have borne them without a great
uneaſineſs of mind; yet he expreſſed to the laſt
ſuch ſubmiſſion to the will of God, and ſo equal a
temper under them, that it was viſible then what
mighty effects his philoſophy and chriſtianity had
on him, in ſupporting him under ſuch a heavy
load.

He could not lie down in bed above a year before his death, by reaſon of the aſthma, but ſat
rather than lay in it.

He was attented on in his ſickneſs by a pious
and worthy divine, Mr. Evan Griffith, miniſter of
the pariſh; and it was obſerved, that in all the
extremities of his pain, whenever he prayed by
him, he forbore all complaints or groans, but with
his hands and eyes lifted up, was fixed in his devotions. Not long before his death, the miniſter
told him, " There was to be a ſacrament next
" Sunday at church, but he believed he could not
" come and partake with the reſt, therefore he

" would

" would give it him in his own houfe : " But he anfwered, " No; his heavenly father had pre-
" pared a feaft for him, and he would go to his
" father's houfe to partake of it : " So he made himfelf be carried thither in his chair, where he received the facrament on his knees, with great devotion, which, it may be fuppofed, was the greater, becaufe he apprehended it was to be his laft, and fo took it as his viaticum and provifion for his journey. He had fome fecret unaccountable prefages of his death, for he faid, " that, if he
" did not die on fuch a day," (which fell to be the 25th of November) " he believed he fhould
" live a month longer," and he died that very day month. He continued to enjoy the free ufe of his reafon and fenfe to the laft moment, which he had often and earneftly prayed for during his ficknefs. And when his voice was fo funk that he could not be heard, they perceived by the almoft conftant lifting up of his eyes and hands, that he was ftill afpiring towards that bleffed ftate, of which he was now fpeedily to be poffeffed.

He had for many years a particular devotion for Chriftmas-day, and after he had received the facrament, and been in the performance of the publick worfhip of that day, he commonly wrote a copy of verfes on the honour of his Saviour, as a fit expreffion of the joy he felt in his foul, at the return of that glorious anniverfary. There are feventeen of thofe copies printed, which he wrote on feventeen feveral Chriftmas-days, by which the

world

world has a tafte of his poetical genius, in which,
if he had thought it worth his time to have excelled, he might have been eminent as well as in
other things; but he wrote them rather to entertain himfelf, than to merit the laurel.

I fhall here add one which has not been yet
printed, and it is not unlikely it was the laft he
writ; it is a paraphrafe on Simeon's fong; I take
it from his blotted copy not at all finifhed, fo the
reader is to make allowance for any imperfection
he may find in it.

" Bleffed Creator, who before the birth
" Of time, or e'er the pillars of the earth
" Were fix't or form'd, did'ft lay that great defign
" Of man's redemption, and did'ft define
" In thine eternal councils all the fcene
" Of that ftupendious bufinefs, and when
" It fhould appear, and though the very day
" Of its epiphany, concealed lay
" Within thy mind, yet thou wert pleas'd to fhow
" Some glimpfes of it, unto men below,
" In vifions, types, and prophefies, as we
" Things at a diftance in perfpective fee :
" But thou wert pleas'd to let thy fervant know
" That that bleft hour, that feem'd to move fo flow
" Through former ages, fhould at laft attain
" Its time, e'er my few fands, that yet remain,
" Are fpent ; and that thefe aged eyes
" Should fee the day, when Jacob's ftar fhould rife.

" And

" And now thou haſt fulfill'd it, bleſſed Lord,
" Diſmiſs me now, according to thy word;
" And let my aged body now return
" To reſt, and duſt, and drop into an urn;
" For I have liv'd enough, mine eyes have ſeen
" Thy much deſired ſalvation, that hath been
" So long, ſo dearly wiſh'd, the joy, the hope
" Of all the ancient patriarchs, the ſcope
" Of all the propheſies, and myſteries,
" Of all the types unveil'd, the hiſtories
" Of Jewiſh church unriddl'd, and the bright
" And orient ſun ariſen to give light
" To Gentiles, and the joy of Iſrael,
" The worlds redeemer, bleſt Emanuel.
" Let this ſight cloſe mine eyes, 'tis loſs to ſee,
" After this viſion, any ſight but thee.

Thus he uſed to ſing on the former Chriſtmas-days, but now he was to be admitted to bear his part in the new ſongs above; ſo that day which he had ſpent in ſo much ſpiritual joy, proved to be indeed the day of his jubilee and deliverance; for between two and three in the afternoon, he breathed out his righteous and pious ſoul. His end was peace, he had no ſtrugglings, nor ſeemed to be in any pangs in his laſt moments. He was buried on the 4th of January, Mr. Griffith preach-ing the funeral ſermon, his text was Iſa. lvii. 1.
" 'The righteous periſheth, and no man layeth it
" to heart; and merciful men are taken away,
" none conſidering that the righteous is taken
" away

" away from the evil to come." Which how fitly
it was applicable upon this occasion, all that consider the course of his life, will easily conclude.
He was interred in the church-yard of Alderly, a-
mong his anceftors; he did not much approve of
burying in churches, and used to say, " the
" churches were for the living, and the church-
" yards for the dead." His monument was like
himself, decent and plain; the tomb-stone was
black marble, and the sides were black and white
marble, upon which he himself had ordered this
bare and humble infcription to be made,

HIC INHUMATUR CORPUS
MATTHEI HALE, MILITIS;
ROBERTI HALE, ET JOANNÆ,
UXORIS EJUS, FILII UNICI.
NATI IN HAC PAROCHIA DE AL-
DERLY, PRIMO DIE NOVEMBRIS,
ANNO DOM. 1609.
DENATI VERO IBIDEM VICESIMO
QUINTO DIE DECEMBRIS, AN-
NO DOM. 1676.
ÆTATIS SUÆ, LXVII.

Having thus given an account of the moft remarkable things of his life, I am now to present
the reader with fuch a character of him, as the
laying his feveral virtues together will amount to:
in which I know how difficult a tafk I undertake;
for to write defectively of him, were to injure him,

and

and leſſen the memory of one to whom I intend to do all the right that is in my power. On the other hand, there is ſo much here to be commended, and propoſed for the imitation of others, that I am afraid ſome may imagine, I am rather making a picture of him, from an abſtracted idea of great virtues and perfections, than ſetting him out, as he truly was : but there is great encouragement in this, that I write concerning a man ſo freſh in all peoples rememberance, that is ſo lately dead, and was ſo much and ſo well known, that I ſhall have many vouchers, who will be ready to juſtify me in all that I am to relate, and to add a great deal to what I can ſay.

It has appeared in the account of his various learning, how great his capacities were, and how much they were improved by conſtant ſtudy. He roſe always early in the morning, he loved to walk much abroad, not only for his health, but he thought it opened his mind, and enlarged his thoughts to have the creation of God before his eyes. When he ſet himſelf to any ſtudy, he uſed to caſt his deſign into a ſcheme, which he did with a great exactneſs of method ; he took nothing on truſt, but perſued his enquires as far as they could go, and as he was humble enough to confeſs his ignorance, and ſubmit to myſteries which he could not comprehend, ſo he was not eaſily impoſed on, by any ſhews of reaſon, or the bugbears of vulgar opinions. He brought all his knowledge as much to ſcientifical principles, as he poſſibly could,

which

which made him neglect the study of tongues, for the bent of his mind lay another way. Difcourfing once of this to fome, they faid, " they looked " on the common law, as a ftudy that could not " be brought into a fcheme, nor formed into a " rational fcience, by reafon of the indigeftednefs " of it, and the multiplicity of the cafes in it, " which rendered it very hard to be underftood, " or reduced into a method ;" but he faid, " he " was not of their mind," and fo quickly after, he drew with his own hand, a fcheme of the whole order and parts of it, in a large fheet of paper, to the great fatisfaction of thofe to whom he fent it. Upon this hint, fome preffed him to compile a body of the Englifh law. It could hardly ever be done by a man who knew it better, and would with more judgment and induftry have put it into method ; but he faid, " as it was a great " and noble defign, which would be of vaft ad- " vantage to the nation ; fo it was too much for " a private man to undertake : it was not to be " entered upon, but by the command of a prince, " and with the communicated endeavours of fome " of the moft eminent of the profeffion."

He had great vivacity in his fancy, as may appear by his inclination to poetry, and the lively illuftrations, and many tender ftrains in his contemplations ; but he look'd on eloquence and wit, -as-things to be ufed very chaftly, in ferious matters, which fhould come under a feverer enquiry : therefore he was both, when at the bar, and on

the

the bench,- a great enemy to all eloquence or rhetoric in pleading : he said, " If the judge or jury " had a right underſtanding, it ſignified nothing, " but a waſte of time, and loſs of words ; and if " they were weak, and eaſily wrought on, it was " a more decent way of corrupting them, by " bribing their fancies, and byaſing their affecti- " ons ;" and wondered much at that affeⅽtation of the French lawyers in imitating the Roman orators in their pleadings. For the oratory of the Romans, was occaſioned by their popular govern- ment, and the factions of the city, ſo that thoſe who intended to excell in the pleading of cauſes, were trained up in the ſchools of the Rhetors, till they became ready and expert in that luſcious way of diſcourſe. It is true, the compoſures of ſuch a man as Tully was, who mixed an extraordinary quickneſs, an exact judgment, and a juſt decorum with his ſkill in rhetoric, do ſtill entertain the rea- ders of them with great pleaſure : but at the ſame time it muſt be acknowledged, that there is not that chaſtity of ſtile, that cloſeneſs of reaſoning, nor that juſtneſs of figures in his orations, that is in his other writings ; ſo that a great deal was ſaid by him, rather becauſe he knew it would be acceptable to his auditors, than that it was ap- proved of by himſelf ; and all who read them, will acknowledge, they are better pleaſed with them as eſſays of wit and ſtile, than as pleadings, by which ſuch a judge as ours was, would not be much wrought on. And if there are ſuch grounds

to

to cenfure the performances of the greateft mafter
in eloquence, we may eafily infer what naufeous
difcourfes the other orators made, fince in oratory,
as well as in poetry, none can do indifferently. So
our judge wondered to find the French, that live
under a monarchy, fo fond of imitating that which
was an ill effect of the popular government of Rome.
He therefore pleaded himfelf always in few words,
and home to the point: and when he was a judge,
he held thofe that pleaded before him, to be the
main hinge of the bufinefs, and cut them fhort,
when they made excurfions about circumftances of
no moment, by which he faved much time, and
made the chief difficulties be well ftated and
cleared.

There was another cuftom among the Romans,
which he as much admired, as he defpifed their
rhetoric, which was, that the juris-confults were
the men of the higheft quality, who were bred
to be capable of the chief employment in the ftate,
and became the great mafters of their law: thefe
gave their opinions of all cafes that were put to
them freely, judging it below them to take any
prefent for it; and indeed they were the only true
lawyers among them, whofe refolutions were of
that authority, that they made one claffis of thofe
materials out of which Trebonian compiled the
digefts under Juftinian; for the orators or caufidici
that pleaded caufes, knew little of the law, and
only employed their mercenary tongues, to work
on the affections of the people, and fenate or the
pretors;

pretors: even in moſt of Tully's orations there is little of law, and that little which they might ſprinkle in their declamations, they had not from their own knowledge, but the reſolution of ſome juris-conſult: according to that famous ſtory of Servius Sulpitius, who was a celebrated orator, and being to receive the reſolution of one of thoſe that were learned in the law, was ſo ignorant, that he could not underſtand it; upon which the juris-conſult reproached him, and ſaid, " it was " a ſhame for him that was a nobleman, a ſena- " tor, and a pleader of cauſes, to be thus ignorant " of law:" this touched him ſo ſenſibly, that he ſet about the ſtudy of it, and became one of the moſt eminent juris-conſults that ever were at Rome. Our judge thought it might become the greatneſs of a prince, to encourage ſuch ſort of men, and of ſtudies; in which, none in the age he lived in was equal to the great Selden, who was truly in our Engliſh law, what the old Roman juris-conſults were in theirs.

But where a decent eloquence was allowable, judge Hale knew how to have excelled as much as any, either in illuſtrating his reaſonings, by proper and well purſued ſimilies, or by ſuch tender expreſſions, as might work moſt on the affections, ſo that the preſent lord chancellor, has often ſaid of him ſince his death, that he was the greateſt orator he had known; for though his words came not fluently from him, yet when they were out, they were the moſt ſignificant, and expreſſive,

that

that the matter could bear ; of this fort there are many in his contemplations made to quicken his own devotion, which have a life in them becoming him that ufed them, and a foftnefs fit to melt even the harfheft tempers, accommodated to the gravity of the fubject, and apt to excite warm thoughts in the readers, that as they fhew his excellent temper that brought them out, and applied them to himfelf, fo they are of great ufe to all, who would both inform and quicken their minds. Of his illuftrations of things by proper fimilies, I fhall give a large inftance out of his book of the origination of mankind, defigned to expofe the feveral different hypothefes the philofophers fell on, concerning the eternity and original of the univerfe, and to prefer the account given by Mofes, to all their conjectures ; in which, if my tafte does not mifguide me, the reader will find a rare and very agreeable mixture, both of fine wit, and folid learning and judgment.

[" That which may illuftrate my meaning, in this preference of the revealed light of the holy fcriptures, touching this matter, above the effays of a philofophical imagination, may be this. Suppofe that Greece being unacquainted with the curiofity of mechanical engines, though known in fome remote region of the world, and that an excellent artift had fecretly brought and depofited in fome field or foreft, fome excellent watch or clock, which had been fo formed, that the original of its motion were hidden, and involved in

F   fome

some close contrived piece of mechanism, that this watch was so framed, that the motion thereof might have lasted a year, or some such time as might give a reasonable period for their philosophical discanting concerning it, and that in the plain table there had been not only the description and indication of hours, but the configurations and indications of the various phases of the moon, the motion and place of the sun in the ecliptic, and divers other curious indications of celestial motions, and that the scholars of the several schools of Epicurus, of Aristotle, of Plato, and the rest of those philosophical sects, had casually in their walk, found this admirable automaton; what kind of work would there have been made by every sect, in giving an account of this phenomenon? We should have had the Epicurean sect have told the bystanders, according to their preconceived hypothesis, that this was nothing else but an accidental concretion of atoms, that happily falling together had made up the index, the wheels, and the ballance, and that being happily fallen into this posture, they were put into motion. Then the Cartesian falls in with him, as to the main of their supposition, but tells him, that he doth not sufficiently explicate how the engine is put into motion, and therefore to furnish this motion, there is a certain materia subtilis that pervades this engine, and the moveable parts, consisting of certain globular atoms apt for motion, they are thereby, and by the mobility of the globular atoms put into

motion.

motion. A third finding fault with the two former, becaufe thofe motions are fo regular, and do
exprefs the various phenomena of the diftribution
of time, and of the heavenly motions ; therefore
it feems to him, that this engine and motion alfo,
fo analogical to the motions of the heavens, was
wrought by fome admirable conjunction of the
heavenly bodies, which formed this inftrument and
its motions, in fuch an admirable correfpondency
to its own exiftence. A fourth, difliking the fup-
pofitions of the three former, tells the reft, that
he hath a more plain and evident folution of the
phenomenon, namely, the univerfal foul of the
world, or fpirit of nature, that formed fo many
forts of infects with fo many organs, faculties,
and fuch congruity of their whole compofition,
and fuch curious and various motions as we may
obferve in them, hath formed and fet into motion
this admirable automaton, and regulated and ordered it, with all thefe congruities we fee in it.
Then fteps in an Ariftotelian, and being diffatisfied with all the former folutions, tells them,
gentlemen, you are all miftaken, your folutions
are inexplicable and unfatisfactory, you have taken
up certain precarious hypothefes, and being prepoffeffed with thefe creatures of your own fancies,
and in love with them, right or wrong, you form
all your conceptions of things according to thofe
fancied and preconceived imaginations. The fhort
of the bufinefs is, this machina is eternal, and fo
are all the motions of it, and in as much as a

circular

circular motion hath no beginning or end, this motion that you fee both in the wheels and index, and the fucceffive indications of the celeftial motions, is eternal, and without beginning. And this is a ready and expedite way of folving the phenomena, without fo much ado as you have made about it.

And whilft all the mafters were thus contriving the folution of the phenomenon, in the hearing of the artift that made it, and when they had all fpent their philofophizing upon it, the artift that made this engine, and all this while liftened to their admirable fancies, tells them, gentlemen, you have difcovered very much excellency of invention touching this piece of work that is before you, but you are all miferably miftaken: for it was I that made this watch, and brought it hither, and I will fhew you how I made it. Firft, I wrought the fpring, and the fufee, and the wheels, and the ballance, and the cafe, and table; I fitted them one to another, and placed thefe feveral axes that are to direct the motions of the index to difcover the hour of the day, of the figure that difcovers the phafes of the moon, and the other various motions that you fee; and then I put it together, and wound up the fpring, which hath given all thefe motions, that you fee in this curious piece of work, and that you may be fure I tell you true, I will tell you the whole order and progrefs of my making, difpofing, and ordering of this piece of work; the feveral materials of it, the manner of

the

the forming of every individual part of it, and how long I was about it. This plain and evident difcovery renders all thefe excogitated hypothefes of thofe philofophical enthufiafts vain and ridiculous, without any great help of rhetorical flourifhes, or logical confutations. And much of the fame nature is that difparity of the hypothefes of the learned philofophers in relation to the origination of the world and man, after a great deal of duft raifed, and fanciful explications and unintelligible hypothefes. The plain, but divine narrative, by the hand of Mofes, full of fenfe, and congruity, and clearnefs, and reafonablenefs in itfelf, does at the fame moment give us a true and clear difcovery of this great miftery, and renders all the effays of the generality of the heathen philofophers to be vain, inevident, and indeed inexplicable theories, the creatures of phantafy, and imagination, and nothing elfe."]

As for his virtues, they have appeared fo confpicuous in all the feveral tranfactions and turns of his life, that it may feem needlefs to add any more of them, than has been already related; but there are many particular inftances which I knew not how to fit to the feveral years of his life, which will give us a clearer and better view of him.

He was a devout chriftian, a fincere proteftant, and a true fon of the church of England; moderate towards diffenters, and juft even to thofe from whom he differed moft; which appeared fignally in the care he took of preferving the quakers

from

from that mifchief that was like to fall on them, by declaring their marriages void, and fo baftarding their children; but he confidered marriage and fucceffion as a right of nature, from which none ought to be barred, what miftake foever they might be under, in the points of revealed religion.

And therefore in a trial that was before him, when a quaker was fued for fome debts owing by his wife before he married her, and the quaker's council pretended, that it was no marriage that had paft between them, fince it was not folemnized according to the rules of the church of England; he declared, that he was not willing on his own opinion to make their children baftards, and gave directions to the jury to find it fpecial. It was a reflection on the whole party, that one of them to avoid an inconvenience he had fallen in, thought to have preferved himfelf by a defence, that if it had been allowed in law, muft have made their whole iffue baftards, and incapable of fucceffion, and for all their pretended friendfhip to one another, if this judge had not been more their friend, than one of thofe they fo called, their pofterity had been little beholding to them. But he governed himfelf indeed by the law of the gofpel, of doing to others, what he would have others do to him; and therefore becaufe he would have thought it a hardfhip not without cruelty, if amongft papifts all marriages were nulled which had not been made with all the ceremonies in the roman

ritual,

ritual, so he applying this to the case of the sectaries, he thought all marriages made according to the several persuasions of men, ought to have their effects in law.

He used constantly to worship God in his family, performing it always himself, if there was no clergymen present: but as to his private exercises in devotion, he took that extraordinary care to keep what he did secret, that this part of his character must be defective, except it be acknowledged that his humility in covering it, commends him much more than the highest expressions of devotion could have done.

From the first time that the impressions of religion settled deeply in his mind, he used great caution to conceal it: not only in obedience to the rules given by our Saviour, of fasting, praying, and giving alms in secret; but from a particular distrust he had of himself, for he said he was afraid, he should at some time or other, do some enormous thing, which if he were look'd on as a very religious man, might cast a reproach on the profession of it, and give great advantages to impious men to blaspheme the name of God: but a tree is known by its fruits, and he lived not only free of blemishes, or scandal, but shined in all the parts of his conversation: and perhaps the distrust he was in of himself, contributed not a little to the purity of his life, for he being thereby obliged to be more watchful over himself, and to depend more on the aids of the Spirit of God, no wonder

F 4

der

der if that humble temper produced thofe excellent effects in him.

He had a foul enlarged and raifed above that mean appetite of loving money, which is generally the root of all evil. He did not take the profits that he might have had by his practice: for in common cafes, when thofe who came to afk his council gave him a piece, he ufed to give back the half, and fo made ten fhillings his fee, in ordinary matters that did not require much time or ftudy. If he faw a caufe was unjuft, he for a great while would not meddle farther in it, but to give his advice that it was fo; if the parties after that, would go on, they were to feek another councel- lor, for he would affift none in acts of injuftice. If he found the caufe doubtful or weak in point of law, he always advifed his clients to agree their bufinefs: yet afterwards he abated much of the fcrupulofity he had about caufes that appeared at firft view unjuft, upon this occafion. There were two caufes brought to him, which by the igno- rance of the party or their attorney, were fo ill reprefented to him, that they feemed to be very bad, but he enquiring more narrowly into them, found they were really very good and juft: fo after this he flackened much of his former ftrictnefs, of refufing to meddle in caufes upon the ill circum- ftances that appeared in them at firft.

In his pleading he abhorred thofe too common faults of mif-reciting evidences, quoting precedents, or books falfly, or afferting things confidently;

by

by which ignorant juries, or weak judges, are too often wrought on. He pleaded with the fame fincerity that he ufed in the other parts of his life, and ufed to fay, " it was as great a difhonour as " a man was capable of, that for a little money " he was to be hired to fay or do otherwife than " as he thought :" all this he afcribed to the un- meafurable defire of heaping up wealth, which corrupted the fouls of fome that feemed otherwife born and made for great things.

When he was a practitioner, differences were often referred to him, which he fettled, but would accept of no reward for his pains, though offered by both parties together, after the agreement was made ; for he faid, " in thofe cafes he was made " a judge, and a judge ought to take no money." If they told him, he loft much of his time in con- fidering their bufinefs, and fo ought to be acknow- ledged for it ; his anfwer was, (as one that heard it told me,) " can I fpend my time better, than " to make people friends ? muft I have no time " allowed me to do good in ? "

He was naturally a quick man, yet by much practice on himfelf, he fubdued that to fuch a de- gree, that he would never run fuddenly into any conclufion concerning any matter of importance. Feftina lente was his beloved motto, which he ordered to be engraven on the head of his ftaff, and was often heard to fay, " that he had obferved " many witty men run into great errors, becaufe " they did not give themfelves time to think, but

" the

" the heat of imagination making some notions
" appear in good colours to them, they without
" staying till that cooled, were violently led by
" the impulses it made on them ; whereas calm and
" slow men, who pass for dull in the common
" estimation, could search after truth and find it
" out, as with more deliberation, so with greater
" certainty."

He laid aside the tenth penny of all he got for the poor, and took great care to be well informed of proper objects for his charities; and after he was a judge, many of the perquesites of his place, as his dividend of the rule and box money, were sent by him to the jails to discharge poor prisoners, who never knew from whose hands their relief came. It is also a custom for the marshall of the king's-bench, to present the judges of that court with a piece of plate for a new-year's gift, that for chief justice being larger than the rest: this he intended to have refused, but the other judges told him it belonged to his office, and the refusing it would be a prejudice to his successors, so he was persuaded to take it, but he sent word to the marshal, that instead of plate, he should bring him the value of it in money, and when he received it, he immediately sent it to the prisons, for the relief and discharge of the poor there. He usually invited his poor neighbours to dine with him, and made them set at table with himself; and if any of them were sick, so that they could not come, he would send meat warm to them

from

from his table: and he did not only relieve the poor in his own parish, but fent fupplies to the neighbouring parifhes, as there was occafion for it: and he treated them all with the tendernefs and familiarity that became one, who confidered they were of the fame nature with himfelf, and were reduced to no other neceffities but fuch as he himfelf might be brought to: but for common beggars, if any of thefe came to him, as he was in his walks, when he lived in the country, he would afk fuch as were capable of working, why they went about fo idly; if they anfwered, it was becaufe they could find no work, he often fent them to fome field, to gather all the ftones in it, and lay them on a heap, and then would pay them liberally for their pains: this being done, he ufed to fend his carts, and caufed them to be carried to fuch places of the highway as needed mending.

But when he was in town, he dealt his charities very liberally, even among the ftreet beggars, and when fome told him, that he thereby encouraged idlenefs, and that moft of thefe were notorious cheats, he ufed to anfwer, " that he believed moft " of them were fuch, but among them there were " fome that were great objects of charity, and " preffed with grievous neceffities: and that he had " rather give his alms to twenty who might be " perhaps rogues, than that one of the other fort " fhould perifh for want of that fmall relief " which he gave them."

He

He loved building much, which he affected chiefly becaufe it employed many poor people: but one thing was obferved in all his buildings, that the changes he made in his houfes, was always from magnificence to ufefulnefs, for he avoided every thing that looked like pomp or vanity, even in the walls of his houfes: he had good judgment in architecture, and an excellent faculty in contriving well.

He was a gentle landlord to all his tenants, and was ever ready upon any reafonable complaints, to make abatements, for he was merciful as well as righteous. One inftance of this was, of a widow that lived in London, and had a fmall eftate near his houfe in the country; from which her rents were ill returned to her, and at a coft which fhe could not well bear: fo fhe bemoaned herfelf to him, and he according to his readinefs to affift all poor people, told her, he would order his fteward to take up her rents, and the returning them fhould coft her nothing. But after that, when there was a falling of rents in that country, fo that it was neceffary to make abatements to the tenant; yet he would have it lie on himfelf, and made the widow be paid her rent as formerly.

Another remarkable inftance of his juftice and goodnefs was, that when he found ill money had been put into his hands, he would never fuffer it to be vented again; for he thought it was no excufe for him to put falfe money in other peoples hands, becaufe fome had put it in his: a great

heap.

heap of this he had gathered together, for many had fo far abufed his goodnefs, as to mix bafe money among the fees that were given him : it is like he intended to have deftroyed it, but fome thieves who had obferved it, broke into his chamber and ftole it, thinking they had got a prize; which he ufed to tell with fome pleafure, imagining how they found themfelves deceived, when they perceived what fort of booty they had fallen on.

After he was made a judge, he would needs pay more for every purchafe he made than it was worth; if it had been a horfe he was to buy, he would have out-bid the price : and when fome reprefented to him, that he made ill bargains, he faid, " it became judges to pay more for what " they bought, than the true value ; that fo thofe " with whom they dealt, might not think they " had any right to their favour, by having fold " fuch things to them at an eafy rate :" and faid it was fuitable to the reputation, which a judge ought to preferve, to make fuch bargains, that the world might fee they were not too well ufed upon fome fecret account.

In fum, his eftate did fhew how little he had minded the raifing a great fortune, for from a hundred pounds a year, he raifed it not quite to nine hundred, and of this a very confiderable part came in by his fhare of Mr. Selden's eftate; yet this, confidering his great practice while a counfellor, and his conftant, frugal, and modeft

way of living, was but a fmall fortune. In the
fhare that fell to him by Mr. Selden's will, one
memorable thing was done by him, with the other
executors, by which they both fhewed their regard
to their dead friend, and their love of the public.
His library was valued at fome thoufands of pounds,
and was believed to be one of the curioufeft collections in Europe; fo they refolved to keep this
intire, for the honour of Selden's memory, and
gave it to the univerfity of Oxford, where a noble
room was added to the former library for its reception, and all due refpects have been fince fhewed by that great and learned body, to thofe their
worthy benefactors, who not only parted fo
generoufly with this great treafure, but were a
little put to it how to oblige them, without croffing the will of their dead friend. Mr. Selden
had once intended to give his library to that
univerfity, and had left it fo by his will; but having occafion for a manufcript, which belonged to
their library, they afked of him a bond of a thoufand pounds for its reftitution; this he took fo ill
at their hands, that he ftruck out that part of his
will by which he had given them his library, and
with fome paffion declared they fhould never have
it. The executors ftuck at this a little, but having confidered better of it, came to this refolution,
that they were to be the executors of Mr. Selden's
will, and not of his paffion; fo they made good
what he had intended in cold blood, and paft over
what his paffion had fuggefted to him.

The

The parting with fo many excellent books, would have been as uneafy to our judge, as any thing of that nature could be, if a pious regard to his friend's memory had not prevailed over him; for he valued books and manufcripts above al. things in the world.   He himfelf had made a great and rare colle&tion of manufcripts belonging to the law of England; he was forty years in ga-thering it: he himfelf faid it coft him above fifteen hundred pounds, and calls it in his will, a treafure worth having and keeping, and not fit for every man's view; thefe all he left to Lincoln's-Inn, and for the information of thofe who are curious to fearch into fuch things, there fhall be a catalogue of them added at the end of this book.

By all thefe inftances it does appear, how much he was raifed above the world, or the love of it.   But having thus maftered things with-out him, his next ftudy was to overcome his own inclinations.   He was as he faid himfelf na-turally paffionate; I add, as he faid himfelf, for that appeared by no other evidence, fave that fometimes his colour would rife a little; but he fo governed himfelf, that thofe who lived long about him, have told me they never faw him dif-ordered with anger, though he met with fome trials, that the nature of man is as little able to bear, as any whatfoever.   There was one who did him a great injury, which it is not neceffary to mention, who coming afterwards to him for his

advice in the settlement of his estate, he gave it
very frankly to him, but would accept of no fee
for it, and therefore shewed both that he could
forgive as a christian, and that he had the soul of
a gentleman in him, not to take money of one
that had wronged him so heinously.   And when
he was asked by one, how he could use a man so
kindly, that had wronged him so much, his answer was, " he thanked God he had learned to
" forget injuries."   And besides the great temper
he expressed in all his public employments, in his
family he was a gentle master :   he was tender of
all his servants, he never turned any away, except they were so faulty, that there was no hope
of reclaiming them :   when any of them had been
long out of the way, or had neglected any part
of their duty ; he would not see them at their
first coming home, and sometimes not till the next
day, least when his displeasure was quick upon
him, he might have chid them indecently ; and
when he did reprove them, he did it with that
sweetness and gravity, that it appeared he was
more concerned for their having done a fault, than
for the offence given by it to himself : but if they
became immoral or unruly, then he turned them
away, for he said, " he that by his place ought
" to punish disorders in other people, must by no
" means suffer them in his own house." He advanced his servants according to the time they had
been about him, and would never give occasion
to envy among them, by raising the younger
clerks

clerks above thofe who had been longer with him. He treated them all with great affeﬁion, rather as a friend, than a mafter, giving them often good advice and inftruﬁion. He made thofe who had good places under him, give fome of their profits to the other fervants who had nothing but their wages. When he made his will, he left legacies to every one of them; but he exprefſed a more particular kindnefs for one of them Robert Gibbon, of the Middle Temple, Efq; in whom he had that confidence, that he left him one of his executors. I the rather mention him, becaufe of his noble gratitude to his worthy benefaﬁor and mafter, for he has been fo careful to preferve his memory, that as he fet thofe on me, at whofe defire I undertook to write his life; fo he has procured for me a great part of thofe memorials, and informations, out of which I have compofed it.

The judge was of a moft tender and compaſſionate nature. This did eminently appear in his trying and giving fentence upon criminals, in which he was ftriﬁly careful, that not a circumftance fhould be negleﬁed, which might any way clear the faﬁ. He behaved himfelf with that regard to the prifoners, which became both the gravity of a judge, and the piety that was due to men, whofe lives lay at ftake, fo that nothing of jeering or unreafonable feverity ever fell from him. He alfo examined the witneſſes in the fofteft manner, taking care that they fhould be put under no confufion, which might diforder their memory: and

he

he fummed all the evidence fo equally when he charged the jury, that the criminals themfelves never complained of him. When it came to him to give fentence, he did it with that compofednefs and decency, and his fpeeches to the prifoners, directing them to prepare for death, were fo weighty, fo free of all affectation, and fo ferious and devout, that many loved to go to the trials, when he fat judge, to be edified by his fpeeches, and behaviour in them, and ufed to fay, they heard very few fuch fermons.

But though the pronouncing the fentence of death was a piece of his employment, that went moft againft the grain with him ; yet in that, he could never be mollified to any tendernefs which hindered juftice. When he was once preffed to recommend fome (whom he had condemned) to his majefty's mercy and pardon ; he anfwered, he could not think they deferved a pardon, whom he himfelf had adjudged to die : fo that all he would do in that kind, was to give the king a true account of the circumftances of the fact, after which, his majefty was to confider whether he would interpofe his mercy, or let juftice take place.

His mercifulnefs extended even to his beafts, for when the horfes that he had kept long, grew old, he would not fuffer them to be fold, or much wrought, but ordered his men to turn them loofe on his grounds, and put them only to eafy work, fuch as going to market and the like ; he ufed old dogs alfo with the fame care ; his fhepherd having one

that

that was become blind with age, he intended to have killed or loft him, but the judge coming to hear of it, made one of his fervants bring him home and feed him till he died : and he was fcarce ever feen more angry than with one of his fervants for neglecting a bird, that he kept, fo that it died for want of food.

He was a great encourager of all young perfons, that he faw followed their books diligently, to whom he ufed to give directions concerning the method of their ftudy, with a humanity and fweet-nefs, that wrought much on all that came near him ; and in a fmiling pleafant way, he would admonifh them, if he faw any thing amifs in them: particularly if they went too fine in their clothes, he would tell them, it did not become their pro-feffion. He was not pleafed to fee ftudents wear long perriwigs, or attornies go with fwords ; fo that fuch young men as would not be perfuaded to part with thofe vanities, when they went to him laid them afide, and went as plain as they could, to avoid the reproof which they knew they might otherwife expect.

He was very free and communicative in his dif-courfe, which he moft commonly fixed on fome good and ufeful fubject, and loved for an hour or two at night, to be vifited by fome of his friends. He neither faid nor did any thing with affectation, but ufed a fimplicity that was both natural to himfelf, and very eafy to others : and though he never ftudied the modes of civility or court breed-

ing,

ing, yet he knew not what it was to be rude or harſh with any, except he were impertinently addreſſed to in matters of juſtice, then he would raiſe his voice a little, and ſo ſhake off thoſe importunities.

In his furniture, and the ſervice of his table, and way of living, he liked the old plainneſs ſo well, that as he would ſet up none of the new faſhions, ſo he rather affected a coarſeneſs in the uſe of the old ones; which was more the effect of his philoſophy than diſpoſition, for he loved fine things too much at firſt. He was always of an equal temper, rather chearful than merry; many wondered to ſee the evenneſs of his deportment, in ſome very ſad paſſages of his life.

Having loſt one of his ſons, the manner of whoſe death had grievous circumſtances in it; one coming to ſee him and condole, he ſaid to him, " thoſe were the effects of living long, ſuch muſt " look to ſee many ſad and unacceptable things;" and having ſaid that, he went to other diſcourſes, with his ordinary freedom of mind; for though he had a temper ſo tender, that ſad things were apt enough to make deep impreſſion upon him, yet the regard he had to the wiſdom and providence of God, and the juſt eſtimate he made of external things, did to admiration maintain the tranquility of his mind, and he gave no occaſion by idleneſs to melancholly to corrupt his ſpirit, but by the perpetual bent of his thoughts, he knew well how to divert them from being oppreſſed with the exceſſes of ſorrow.

He

He had a generous and noble idea of God in his mind, and this he found did above all other confiderations preferve his quiet: and indeed that was fo well eftablifhed in him, that no accidents, how fudden foever, were obferved to difcompofe him. Of which an eminent man of that profeffion, gave me this inftance: in the year 1666, an opinion did run through the nation, that the end of the world would come that year. This, whether fet on by aftrologers, or advanced by thofe who thought it might have fome relation to the number of the beaft' in the Revelation, or promoted by men of ill defigns, to difturb the public peace, had fpread mightily among the people ; and judge Hale going that year the weftern circuit, it happened, that as he was on the bench at the affizes, a moft terrible ftorm fell out very unexpectedly, accompanied with fuch flafhes of lightning, and claps of thunder, that the like will hardly fall out in an age ; upon which a whifper or rumour run through the croud, that now the world was to end, and the day of judgment to begin ; and at this there followed a general confternation in the whole affembly, and all men forgot the bufinefs they were met about, and betook themfelves to their prayers : this added to the horror raifed by the ftorm looked very difmally ; in fo much that my author, a man of no ordinary refolution, and firmnefs of mind, confeffed it made a great impreffion on himfelf. But he told me, that he did obferve the judge was not a whit affected, and was going on with the bufinefs of the court in his ordinary manner; from which he made this conclufion, that his thoughts were fo well fixed, that he believed if the world had been really to end, it would have given him no confiderable difturbance.

But I fhall now conclude all that I fhall fay concerning him, with what one of the greateft men of the profeffion of the law, fent me as an abftract of the character he had made of him, upon long obfervation, and much converfe with him : it was fent me, that from thence, with the other materials, I might make fuch a reprefentation of him to the world, as he indeed deferved ; but I refolved not to fhred it out in parcels, but to fet it down intirely as it was fent me, hoping that as the reader will be much delighted with it, fo the noble perfon that fent it, will not be offended with me for keeping it intire, and fetting it in the beft light I could. ·It begins abruptly, being defigned to fupply the defects of others, from whom I had earlier and more copious informations.

" He would never be brought to difcourfe of public matters in private converfation, but in queftions of law, when any young lawyer put a cafe to him he was very communicative, efpecially while he was at the bar : but when he came to the bench, he grew more referv'd, and would never fuffer his opinion in any cafe to be known, till he was obliged to declare it judicially : and he concealed his opinion in great cafes fo carefully, that the reft of the judges in the fame court could

never

never perceive it; his reafon was, becaufe every judge ought to give fentence according to his own perfuafion and confcience, and not to be fwayed by any refpect or difference to another man's opinion: and by this means it hath happened fome times, that when all the barons of the exchequer had delivered their opinions, and agreed in their reafons and arguments; yet he coming to fpeak laft, and differing in judgment from them, hath expreffed himfelf with fo much weight and folidity, that the barons have immediately retracted their votes and concurred with him: He hath fet as a judge in all the courts of law, and in two of them as chief; but ftill wherever he fat, all bufinefs of confequence followed him, and no man was content to fit down by the judgment of any other court, till the cafe were brought before him, to fee whether he were of the fame mind: and his opinion being once known, men did readily acquiefce in it; and it was very rarely feen, that any man attempted to bring it about again, and he that did fo, did it upon great difadvantages, and was always looked upon as a very contentious perfon: fo that what Cicero fays of Brutus, did very often happen to him, *etiam quos contra ftatuit æquos placatofque dimifit.*

" Nor did men reverence his judgment and opinion in courts of law only, but his authority was as great in courts of equity, and the fame refpect and fubmiffion was paid to him there too; and this appeared not only in his own court of

equity

equity in the exchequer chamber, but in the chancery too, for thither he was often called to advife and affift the lord chancellor, or lord keeper for the time being; and if the caufe were of difficult examination, or intricated and entangled with variety of fettlements, no man ever fhewed a more clear and difcerning judgment: if it were of great value, and great perfons interefted in it, no man ever fhewed greater courage and integrity in laying afide all refpect of perfons: when he came to deliver his opinion, he always put his difcourfe into fuch a method, that one part gave light to the other, and where the proceedings of chancery might prove inconvenient to the fubject, he never fpared to obferve and reprove them, and from his obfervations and difcourfes, the chancery hath taken occafion to eftablifh many of thofe rules by which it governs itfelf at this day.

" He did look upon equity as a part of the common law, and one of the grounds of it; and therefore as near as he could, he did always reduce it to certain rules and principles, that men might ftudy it as a fcience, and not think the adminiftration of it had any thing arbitrary in it. Thus eminent was this man in every ftation, and into what court foever he was called, he quickly made it appear, that he deferved the chief feat there.

" As great a lawyer as he was, he would never fuffer the ftrictnefs of law to prevail againft confcience; as great a chancellor as he was, he would make ufe of all the niceties and fubtilties in law,

when

when it tended to fupport right and equity.   But
nothing was more admirable in him, than his patience: he did not affect the reputation of quicknefs
and difpatch, by a hafty and captious hearing of
the councel : he would bear with the meaneft, and
gave every man his full fcope, thinking it much
better to loofe time than patience.   In fumming
up of an evidence to a jury, he would always require the bar to interrupt him if he did miftake,
and to put him in mind of it, if he did forget the
leaft circumftance; fome judges have been difturbed
at this as a rudenefs, which he always looked upon
as a fervice and refpect done to him.

" His whole life was nothing elfe but a continual courfe of labour and induftry, and when he
could borrow any time from the public fervice, it
was wholly employed either in philofophical or divine meditations, and even that was a public fervice
too as it hath proved; for they have occafioned his
writing of fuch treatifes, as are become the choiceft
entertainments of wife and good men, and the
world hath reafon to wifh that more of them were
printed.   He that confiders the active part of his
life, and with what unwearied diligence and application of mind, he difpatched all mens bufinefs
which came under his care, will wonder how he
could find any time for contemplation : he that
confiders again the various ftudies he paft through,
and the many collections and obfervations he hath
made, may as juftly wonder how he could find
any time for action : but no man can wonder at

the

the exemplary piety and innocence of such a life so spent as this was, wherein as he was careful to avoid every idle word, so 'tis manifest he never spent an idle day. They who come far short of this great man, will be apt enough to think that this is a panegyric, which indeed is a history, and but a little part of that history which was with great truth to be related of him : men who despair of attaining such perfection, are not willing to believe that any man else did ever arrive at such a height.

" He was the greatest lawyer of the age, and might have had what practice he pleased ; but though he did most conscientiously affect the labours of his profession, yet at the same time he despised the gain of it; and of those profits which he would allow himself to receive, he always set apart a tenth penny for the poor, which he ever dispensed with that secrecy, that they who were relieved, seldom or never knew their benefactor. He took more pains to avoid the honours and preferments of the gown, than others do to compass them. His modesty was beyond all example, for where some men, who never attained to half his knowledge, have been puffed up with a high conceit of themselves, and have affected all occasions of raising their own esteem by depreciating other men, he on the contrary was the most obliging man that ever practised : if a young gentleman happened to be retained to argue a point in law, where he was on the contrary side, he would very often mend

the

the objections when he came to repeat them, and always commend the gentleman if there were any room for it, and one good word of his was of more advantage to a young man, than all the favour of a court could be."

Having thus far perfued his hiftory and character, in the public and exemplary parts of his life, without interrupting the thread of the relation, with what was private and domeftic, I fhall conclude with a fhort account of thefe.

He was twice married, his firft wife was Ann daughter of fir Henry Moore of Faly in Berkfhire, grandchild to fir Francis Moore, ferjeant at law; by her he had ten children, the four firft died young, the other fix lived to be all married; and he outlived them all, except his eldeft daughter, and his youngeft fon, who are yet alive.

His eldeft fon Robert married Frances the daughter of fir Francis Chock, of Avington in Berkfhire, and they both dying in a little time one after another left five children, two fons Matthew and Gabriel, and three daughters, Ann, Mary, and Frances, and by the judge's advice, they both made him their executor, fo he took his grandchildren into his own care, and among them he left his eftate.

His fecond fon Matthew, married Ann the daughter of Mr. Matthew Simmonds, of Hilfley, in Gloucefterfhire, who died foon after, and left one fon behind him named Matthew.

His

His third fon Thomas, married Rebekah the daughter of Chriftian Le Brune, a Dutch merchant, and died without iffue.

His fourth fon Edward, married Mary the daughter of Edmond Goodyere, Efq; of Heythorp, in Oxfordfhire, and ftill lives ; he has two fons, and three daughters.

. His eldeft daughter Mary, was married to Edward Alderly, fon of Edward Alderly, of Innifhannon, in the county of Cork in Ireland, who dying, left her with two fons and three daughters ; fhe is fince married to Edward Stephens, fon to Edward Stephens, Efq; of Cherington in Gloucefterfhire. His youngeft daughter Elizabeth, was married to Edward Webb, Efq; barrifter at law, fhe died, leaving two children, a fon and a daughter.

His fecond wife was Ann, the daughter of Mr. Jofeph Bifhop, of Faly in Berkfhire, by whom he had no children ; he gives her a great character in his will, as a moft dutiful, faithful, and loving wife, and therefore trufted the breeding of his grand-children to her care, and left her one of his executors, to whom he joined fir Robert Jenkinfon, and Mr. Gibbon. .So much may fuffice of thofe defcended from him.

In after times, it is not be doubted, but it will be reckoned no fmall honour to derive from him ; and this has made me more particular in reckoning up his iffue. I fhall next give an account of the iffues of his mind, his books, that are either

printed,

printed, or remain in manuscript; for the last ot these by his will, he has forbid the printing ot any of them after his death, except such as he should give order for in his life : but he seems to have changed his mind afterwards, and to have left it to the discretion of his executors, which of them might be printed : for though he does not express that, yet he ordered by a codicil, " that if " any book of his writing, as well touching the " common law, as other subjects, should be prin- " ted, than what should be given for the consi- " deration of the copy, should be divided into " ten shares, of which he appointed seven to go " among his servants, and three to those who had " copied them out, and were to look after the " impression." The reason, as I have understood it, that made him so unwilling to have any of his works printed after his death, was, that he apprehended in the licensing them, (which was necessary before any book could be lawfully prin- ted, by a law then in force, but since his death determined) some things might have been struck out or altered; which he had observed not without some indignation, had been done to a part of the reports, of one whom he had much esteemed.

This in matters of law, he said, might prove to be of such mischievous consequences, that he thereupon resolved none of his writings should be at the mercy of licensers; and therefore, because he was not sure, that they should be pub- lished without expurgations or interpolations, he

forbade

forbade the printing any of them; in which he afterwards made some alteration, at least he gave occasion by his codicil, to infer that he had altered his mind.

This I have the more fully explained, that his last will may be no way misunderstood, and that his worthy executors, and his hopeful grand-children, may not conclude themselves to be under an indispensible obligation of depriving the public of his excellent writings.

A CATALOGUE of all his Printed Books.

1. THE primitive origination of mankind, considered and examined according to the light of nature. Folio

2. Contemplations moral and divine, part 1. 8vo.

3. Contemplations moral and divine, part 2. 8vo.

4. Difficiles Nugæ, or observations touching the Torricellian experiment, and the various solutions of the same, especially touching the weight and elasticity of the air. 8vo.

5. An essay touching the gravitation, or non-gravitation of fluid bodies, and the reasons thereof. 8vo.

6. Observations touching the principles of natural motions, and especially touching rarefaction, and condensation; together with a reply to certain remarks, touching the gravitation of fluids. 8vo.

7. The life and death of Pomponius Atticus, written by his contemporary and acquaintance

Cor.

Cornelius Nepos, tranflated out of his fragments; together with obfervations, political and moral, thereupon. 8vo.

8. Pleas of the crown, or a methodical fummary of the principal matters relating to that fubject. 8vo.

MANUSCRIPTS not yet publifhed.

1. CONCERNING the fecondary origination of mankind. Fol.

2. Concerning religion, 5 vol. in Fol. viz. 1. De deo, Vox metaphyfica, pars 1 & 2. 2. Pars 3. Vox naturæ, providentiæ, ethicæ, confcientiæ. 3. Liber fextus, feptimus, octavus. 4. Pars 9. Concerning the holy fcriptures, their evidence and authority. 5. Concerning the truth of the holy fcriptures, and the evidences thereof.

3. Of policy in matters of religion. Fol.

4. De anima, to Mr. B. Fol.

5. De anima, tranfactions between him and Mr. B. Fol.

6. Tentamina, de ortu, natura & immortalitate animæ. Fol.

7. Magnetifmus magneticus. Fol.

8. Magnetifmus phyficus. Fol.

9. Magnetifmus divinus.

10. De generatione animalium & vegetabilium. Fol. lat.

11. Of the law of nature. Fol.

12. A letter of advice to his grand-children. 4to.

13. Placita coronæ, 7 vol. Fol.

13. Pra.

14. Preparatory notes concerning the right of the crown. Fol.

15. Incepta de juribus coronæ. Fol. ·

16. De prerogativa regis. Fol.

17. Preparatory notes touching parliamentary proceedings, 2 vol. 4to.

18. Of the jurisdiction of the house of lords, 4to.

19. Of the jurisdiction of the admiralty.

20. Touching ports and customs. Fol.

21. Of the right of the sea and the arms thereof, and customs. Fol.

22. Concerning the advancement of trade. 4to.

23. Of sheriffs account. Fol.

24. Copies of evidences. Fol.

25. Mr. Selden's discourses. 8vo.

26. Excerpta ex schedis Seldenianis.

27. Journal of the 18 and 21 Jacobi regis. 4to.

28. Great common place book of reports or cases in the law, in law French. Fol.

In Bundles.

ON *quod tibi fieri,* &c. Matth. vii. 12. Touching punishments, in relation to the Socinian controversy.

Policies of the church of Rome.

Concerning the laws of England.

Of the amendment of the laws of England.

Touching provision for the poor.

Upon Mr. Hobbs's manuscript.

Concerning the time of the abolition of the Jewish laws.

In

In Quarto.

Quod fit deus.
Of the ſtate and condition of the ſoul and body
after death.

Notes concerning matters of law.

To theſe I ſhall add the Catalogue of the
Manuscripts which he left to the Hon.
Society of Lincoln's-Inn, with that part of
his Will that concerns them.

ITEM, As a teſtimoney of my honour and
reſpect to the ſociety of Lincoln's-Inn,
where I had the greateſt part of my education,
I give and bequeath to that honourable ſociety the ſeveral manuſcript books contained in
a ſchedule annexed to my will: they are a
treaſure worth having and keeping, which I
have been near forty years in gathering, with
very great induſtry and expence. My deſire is,
that they be kept ſafe, and all together, in
remembrance of me; they were fit to be bound
in leather and chained, and kept in archives:
I deſire they may not be lent out, or diſpoſed
of: only if I happen hereafter to have any of
my poſterity of that ſociety, that deſires to
tranſcribe any book, and give very good caution to reſtore it again in a prefixed time,
ſuch as the benchers of that ſociety in coun-

H   cil

cil ſhall approve of; then, and not otherwiſe, only one book at one time may be lent out to them by the ſociety; ſo that there be no more but one book of thoſe books abroad out of the library at one time. They are a treaſure that are not fit for every man's view: nor is every man capable of making uſe of them: only I would have nothing of theſe books printed, but intirely preſerved together, for the uſe of the induſtrious learned members of that ſociety.

A Catalogue of the Books given by him to Lincoln's-Inn, according to the ſchedule annexed to his will.

PLacita de tempore regis Johannis, 1 vol. ſtitcht.

Placita coram rege. E. 1.   2 vol.

Placita coram rege E. 2.   3 vol.

Placita coram rege E. 3. 3 vol.

Placita coram rege R. 2.   1 vol.

Placita coram rege H. 4. H 5.   1 vol.

Placita de banco, E. 1. ab anno 1, ad annum 21.   1 vol.

Tranſcripts of many pleas, coram rege & de banco E. 1.   1 vol.

The pleas in the exchequer, ſtiled communia, from 1 E. 3. to 46 E. 3.   5 vol.

Cloſe rolls of king John, verbatim, of the moſt material things, 1 vol.

The principal matters in the cloſe and patent

rolls,

rolls, of H. 3. tranfcribed verbatim, from 9 H. 3. to 56 H. 3. 5 vol. velum, marked K. L.

The principal matters in the clofe and patent rolls, E. 1. with feveral copies and abftracts of records, 1 vol. marked F.

A long book of abftracts of records, by me.

Clofe and patent rolls, from 1 to 10 E. 3, and other records of the time of H. 3. 1 vol. marked W.

Clofe rolls of 15 E. 3. with other records, 1 vol. marked N.

Clofe rolls from 17 to 38 E. 3.   2 vol.

Clofe and patent rolls from 40 E. 3 to 50 E. 3. 1 vol. marked B.

Clofe rolls of E. 2. with other records, 1 vol. R.

Clofe and patent rolls, and charter rolls in the time of king John for the clergy, 1 vol.

A great volume of records of feveral natures, G.

The leagues of the kings of England, tempore E. 1. E. 2. E. 3.   1 vol.

A book of ancient leagues and military provifions, 1 vol.

The reports of iters of Derby, Nottingham, and Bedford, tranfcribed, 1 vol.

Itinera foreft de Pickering & Lancafter, tranfcript ex originali, 1 vol.

An ancient reading, very large, upon charta de foreftæ, and of the foreft laws.

The tranfcript of the iter forefta de Dean, 1 vol.

Quo warranto and liberties of the county of Gloucefter, with the pleas of the chace of Kingfwood, 1 vol.

H 2

Tran-

Tranfcript of the black book of the admiralty, laws of the army, impofitions and feveral honours, 1 vol.

Records of patents, inquifitions, &c. of the county of Leicefter, 1 vol.

Mufter and military provifions of all forts, extracted from the records, 1 vol.

Gervafius Tilburienfis, or the black book of the exchequer, 1 vol.

The king's title to the pre-emption of tin, a thin vol.

Calender of the records in the tower, a fmall vol.

A mifcellany of divers records, orders, and other things of various natures, marked E.   1 vol.

Another of the like nature in leather cover, 1 vol.

A book of divers records and things relating to the chancery, 1 vol.

Titles of honour and pedigrees, efpecially touching Clifford, 1 vol.

Hiftory of the marches of Wales collected by me, 1 vol.

Certain collections touching titles of honour, 1 vol.

Copies of feveral records touching premunire, 1 vol.

Extract of commiffions tempore H. 7. H. 8. R. and the proceedings in the court military, between Ray and Ramfey, 1 vol.

Petitions in parliament tempore E. 1. E. 2. E. 3. H. 4.   3 vols.

Summons of parliament, from 49 H. 3. to 22 E. 4.   3 vol.

The

The parliament rolls from the beginning of E. 1. to the end of R. 3. in 19 volumes, viz. 1 of E. 1. 1 of E. 2. with the ordinations. 2 of E. 3. 3 of R. 2. 2 of H. 4. 2 of H. 5. 4 of H. 6. 3 of E. 4. 1 of R. 3. all tranfcribed at large.

Mr. Elfing's book touching proceedings in parliament, 1 vol.

Noye's collection touching the king's fupplies, 1 vol. ftitcht.

A book of various collections out of records and regifter of Canterbury, and claims at the coronation of R. 2. 1 vol.

Tranfcript of bifhop Ufher's notes, principally concerning chronology, 3 large vol.

A tranfcript out of dooms-day book of Gloucefterfhire and Herefordfhire, and of fome pipe-rolls, and old accompts of the cuftoms, 1 vol.

Extracts and collections out of records touching titles of honour, 1 vol.

Extracts of pleas, patents and clofe-rolls, tempore H. 3. E. 1. E. 2. E. 3. and fome old antiquities of England, 1 vol.

Collections and memorials of many records and antiquities, 1 vol. Seldeni.

Calender of charters, and records in the tower, touching Gloucefterfhire.

Collection of notes and records of various natures, marked M. 1 vol. Seldeni.

Tranfcript of the iters of London, Kent, Cornwall, 1 vol.

                                          Ex-

Extracts out of the leiger-books of Battell, Eve-
sham, Winton, &c. 1 vol. Seldeni.

Copies of the principal records in the red book,
in the exchequer, 1 vol.

Extracts of records and treaties, relating to sea
affairs, 1 vol.

Records touching customs, ports, partition of
the lands of Gi. de Clare, &c.

Extract of pleas in the time of R. 1. king
John, E. 1. &c. 1 vol.

Cartæ antiquæ in the tower, transcribed, in 2
vol.

Chronological remembrances, extracted out of
the notes of bishop Usher, 1 vol. stitched.

Inquisitiones de legibus Walliæ, 1 vol.

Collections or records touching knighthood.

Titles of honour. Seldeni. 1 vol.

Mathematicks and fortifications, 1 vol.

Processus curiæ militaris, 1 vol.

A book of honour stitched, 1 vol.

Extracts out of the registry of Canterbury.

Copies of several records touching proceedings
in the military court, 1 vol.

Abstracts of summons and rolls of parliament,
out of the book Dunelm, and some records alpha-
betically digested, 1 vol.

Abstracts of divers records in the office of first
fruits, 1 vol. stitched.

Mathematical and astrological calculations, 1 vol.

A book of divinity.

Two

Two large repositories of records, marked A. and B.

[All thofe above are in folio.]

The proceedings of the forefts of Windfor, Dean, and Effex, in 4to. 1 vol.

[Thofe that follow are moft of them in vellum or parchment.]

Two books of old ftatutes, one ending H. 7. the other 2 H. 5. with the fums, 2 vol.

Five laft years of E. 2.   1 vol.

Reports tempore E. 2.   1 vol.

The year book of R. 2. and fome others, 1 vol.

An old chronicle from the creation to E. 3, 1 vol.

A mathematical book, efpecially of optiques, 1 vol.

A Dutch book of geometry and fortification.

Murti Benevenlani geometrica, 1 vol.

Reports tempore E. 1. under titles, 1 vol.

An old regifter and fome pleas, 1 vol.

Bernardi Bratrack peregrinatio, 1 vol.

Iter Cantii and London, and fome reports, tempore E. 2. 1 vol.

Reports tempore E. 1. and E. 2. 1 vol.

Leiger book, Abbatiæ de bello.

Ifidori opera.

Liber altercationis, & chriftianiæ philofophæ, contra paganos.

Hiftoria Petri manducatorii.

Hornii aftronomica,

Hiftoria ecclefiæ Dunelmenfis,

Holandi chymica.

H 4

De

De alchymiæ fcriptoribus.

The black book of the new law, collected by me, and digefted into alphabetical titles, written with my own hand, which is the original copy.

MATTHEW HALE.

The Conclusion.

THUS lived and died fir Matthew Hale, the renowned lord chief juftice of England. He had one of the bleffings of virtue in the higheft meafure of any of the age, that does not always follow it, which was, that he was univerfally much valued and admired by men of all fides and perfuafions. For as none could hate him but for his juftice and virtues, fo the great eftimation he was generally in, made, that few durft undertake to defend fo ungrateful a paradox, as any thing faid to leffen him would have appeared to be. His name is fcarce ever mentioned fince his death, without particular accents of fingular refpect. His opinion in points of law generally paffes as an uncontroulable authority, and is often pleaded in all the courts of juftice: and all that knew him well, do ftill fpeak of him as one of the perfecteft patterns of religion and virtue they ever faw.

The commendations given him by all forts of people are fuch, that I can hardly come under the cenfures of this age, for any thing I have faid con-- cerning him ; yet if this book lives to after times, it will be looked on perhaps as a picture, drawn

more

more according to fancy and invention, than after the life ; if it were not that thofe who knew him well, eftablifhing its credit in the prefent age, will make it pafs down to the next with a clearer authority.

I fhall perfue his praife no further in my own words, but fhall add what the prefent lord chancellor of England faid concerning him, when he delivered the commiffion to the lord chief juftice Rainsford, who fucceeded him in that office, which he began in this manner.

" The vacancy of the feat of the chief juftice
" of this court, and that by a way and means fo
" unufual, as the refignation of him, that lately
" held it, and this too proceeding from fo deplorable
" a caufe, as the infirmities of that body, which
" began to forfake the ableft mind that ever pre-
" fided here, hath filled the kingdom with lamen-
" tations, and given the king many and penfive
" thoughts, how to fupply that vacancy again."
And a little after fpeaking to his fucceffor, he faid,
" The very labours of the place, and that weight
" and fatigue of bufinefs which attends it, are no
" fmall difcouragements ; for what fhoulders may
" not juftly fear the burthen which made him
" ftoop that went before you ? Yet I confefs you
" have a greater difcouragement than the meer
" burthen of your place, and that is the unimitable
" example of your laft predeceffor : *onerofum eft*
" *fuccedere bono principi,* was the faying of him
" in the panegyrick ; and you will find it fo too
" that are to fucceed fuch a chief juftice, of fo
" inde-

" indefatigable an induſtry, ſo invincible a pati-
" ence, ſo exemplary an integrity, and ſo magna-
" nimous a contempt of worldly things, without
" which no man can be truly great; and to all
" this a man that was ſo abſolute a maſter of the
" ſcience of the law, and even of the moſt ab-
" ſtruſe and hidden parts of it, that one may
" truly ſay of his knowledge in the law, what St.
" Auſtin ſaid of St. Hierom's knowledge in divi-
" nity, *quod Hieronimus neſcivit, nullus mortalium*
" *unquam ſcivit.* And therefore the king would
" not ſuffer himſelf to part with ſo great a man,
" till he had placed upon him all the marks of
" bounty and eſteem, which his retired and weak
" condition was capable of."

To this high character, in which the expreſſions,
as they well become the eloquence of him who
pronounced them, ſo they do agree exactly to the
ſubject, without the abatements that are often to
be made for rhetoric; I ſhall add that part of the
lord chief juſtice's anſwer, in which he ſpeaks of
his predeceſſor.

" —— A perſon in whom his eminent virtues,
" and deep learning, have long managed a conteſt
" for the ſuperiority, which is not decided to this
" day, nor will it ever be determined, I ſuppoſe,
" which ſhall get the upper hand. A perſon that
" has ſat in this court theſe many years, of whoſe
" actions there I have been an eye and an ear
" witneſs, that by the greatneſs of his learning
" always charmed his auditors to reverence and

" atten-

“ attention : a perſon, of whom I think I may
“ boldly ſay, that as former times cannot ſhew
“ any ſuperiour to him, ſo I am confident ſuc-
“ ceeding and future time will never ſhew any
“ equal : theſe conſiderations hightened by what I
“ have heard from your lordſhip concerning him,
“ made me anxious and doubtful, and put me to
“ a ſtand, how I ſhould ſucceed ſo able, ſo good,
“ and ſo great a man : it doth very much trouble
“ me, that I who in compariſon of him am but
“ like a candle lighted in the ſun-ſhine, or like a
“ glow-worm at mid-day, ſhould ſucceed ſo great
“ a perſon, that is and will be ſo eminently fa-
“ mous to all poſterity, and I muſt ever wear this
“ motto in my breaſt to comfort me, and in my
“ actions to excuſe me,

“ *Sequitur, quamvis non paſſibus æquis.*”

Thus were panegyricks made upon him while
yet alive, in that ſame court of juſtice which he
had ſo worthily governed. As he was honoured
while he lived, ſo he was much lamented when he
died : and this will ſtill be acknowledged as a juſt
inſcription for his memory, though his modeſty
forbid any ſuch to be put on his tomb-ſtone.

THAT HE WAS ONE OF THE GREATEST
PATTERNS THIS AGE HAS AFFORDED,
WHETHER IN HIS PRIVATE DEPORT-
MENT AS A CHRISTIAN, OR IN HIS
PUBLIC EMPLOYMENTS, EITHER AT
THE BAR OR ON THE BENCH.

ADDI-

ADDITIONAL NOTES

OF THE

LIFE AND DEATH

OF

Sir MATTHEW HALE, Knt.

Written by RICHARD BAXTER,

At the Requeſt of EDWARD STEPHENS, Eſq; Publiſher of his Contemplations, and his familiar Friend.

To the READER.

SINCE the hiſtory of judge Hale's life is publiſhed (written by Dr. Burnet very well) ſome men have thought, that becauſe my familiarity with him was known, and the laſt time of a man's life is ſuppoſed to contain his matureſt judgment, time, ſtudy, and experience correcting former overſights; and this great man who was moſt diligently and thirſtily learning to the laſt, was like to be ſtill wiſer, the notice that I had of him in the latter years of his life ſhould not be omitted.

I was

I was never acquainted with him till 1667, and therefore have nothing to fay of the former part of his life; nor of the latter, as to any public affairs, but only of what our familiar converfe acquainted me : but the vifible effects made me wonder at the induftry and unwearied labours of his former life. Befides the four volumes againft atheifm and infidelity, in folio, which I after mention, when I was defired to borrow a manufcript of his law collections, he fhewed me, as I remember, about two and thirty folios, and told me, he had no other on that fubject, (collections out of the tower records, &c.) and that the amanuenfis work that wrote them, coft him a thoufand pound. He was fo fet on ftudy, that he refolvedly avoided all neceffary diverfions, and fo little valued either grandeur, wealth, or any worldly vanity, that he avoided them to that notable degree, which incompetent judges took to be an excefs. His habit was fo coarfe and plain, that I, who am thought guilty of a culpable neglect therein, have been bold to defire him to lay by fome things which feemed too homely. The houfe which I furrendered to him, and wherein he lived at Acton, was indeed well fituate but very fmall, and fo far below the ordinary dwellings of men of his rank, as that divers farmers thereabout had better ; but it pleafed him. Many cenfured him for chufing his laft wife below his quality : but the good man more regarded his own daily comfort, than men's thoughts and talk. As far as I could difcern, he chofe one very fuitable to his ends; one of his own judgment and temper, prudent and loving and fit to pleafe him; and that would not draw on him the trouble of much acquaintance and relations. His houfekeeping was according to the reft, like his eftate and mind, but not like his place and honour: for he refolved never to grafp at riches, nor take great fees, but would refufe what many others thought too little. I wondered when he told me how fmall his eftate was, after fuch ways of getting as were before him : but as he had little, and defired little, fo he was content with little, and fuited his dwelling, table, and retinue thereto. He greatly fhunned the vifits of many, or great perfons, that came not to him on neceffary bufinefs, becaufe all his hours were precious to him, and therefore he contrived the avoiding of them, and the free enjoyment of his beloved privacy.

I muft with a glad remembrance acknowledge, that while we were fo unfuitable in places and worth, yet fome fuitablenefs of judgment and difpofition made our frequent converfe pleafing to us both. The laft time fave one, that I was at his houfe, he made me lodge there, and in the morning inviting me to more frequent vifits faid, no man fhall be more welcome; and he was no diffembler. To fignify his love, he put my name as a legatee in his will, bequeathing me forty fhillings. Mr. Stephens gave me two manufcripts, as appointed by him for me, declaring his judgment of our church contentions and their cure (after

men-

mentioned). Though they are imperfect as written on the same question at several times, I had a great mind to print them, to try whether the common reverence of the author would cool any of our contentious clergy : but hearing that there was a restraint in his will, I took out part of a copy in which I find these words, " I do expresly " declare, that I will have nothing of my writings " printed after my death, but only such as I shall " in my life-time deliver out to be printed." And not having received this in his life-time, nor to be printed in exprefs terms, I am afraid of croffing the will of the dead, though he ordered them for me.

It shewed his mean estate as to riches, that in his will he is put to diftribute the profits of a book or two when printed, among his friends and fervants. Alas! we that are great loofers by printing, know that it muft be a fmall gain that muft thus accrue to them. Doubtlefs, if the lord chief juftice Hale had gathered money as other lawyers do that had lefs advantage, as he wanted not will, fo he would not have wanted power to have left them far greater legacies. But the fervants of a felf-denying mortified mafter, muft be content to fuffer by his virtues, which yet if they imitate him, will turn to their final gain.

God made him a public good, which is more than to get riches. His great judgment and known integrity, commanded refpect from thofe that knew him; fo that I verily think, that no one

fubject

subject since the days that history hath notified the affairs of England to us, went off the stage with greater and more universal love and honour; (and what honour without love is, I understand not.) I remember when his successor, the lord chief justice Rainsford, falling into some melancholly, came and sent to me for some advice, he did it as he said, because judge Hale desired him so to do; and expressed so great respect to his judgment and writings, as I perceived much prevailed with him. And many have profited by his contemplations, who would never have read them, had they been written by such a one as I. Yet among all his books and discourses, I never knew of these until he was dead.

His resolution for justice was so great, that I am persuaded, that no wealth nor honour would have hired him knowingly to do one unjust act.

And though he left us in sorrow, I cannot but acknowledge it a great mercy to him, to be taken away when he was. Alas! what would the good man have done, if he had been put by plotters, and traitors, and swearers, and forswearers, upon all that his successors have been put to? In likelihood, even all his great wisdom and sincerity, could never have got him through such a wilderness of throns, and briars, and wild beasts, without tearing in pieces his entire reputation, if he had never so well secured his conscience. O! how seasonably did he avoid the tempest and go to Christ.

And

And so have so many excellent persons since
then, and especially within the space of one year,
as may well make England tremble at the prog-
noftick, that the righteous are taken as from the
evil to come. And alas! what an evil is it like to
be? We feel our loss. We fear the common
danger. But what believer can chufe but acknowledge God's mercy to them, in taking them up to
the world of light, love, peace and order, when
confufion is coming upon this world, by darknefs,
malignity, perfidioufnefs and cruelty. Some think
that the laft conflagration fhall turn this earth
into hell. If so who would not firft be taken from
it? And when it is fo like to hell already, who
would not rather be in heaven?

Though fome miftook this man for a meer philofopher or humanift, that knew him not within;
yet his moft ferious defcription of the fufferings of
Chrift, and his copious volumes to prove the truth
of the fcripture, chriftianity, our immortality, and
the Deity, do prove fo much reality in his faith
and devotion, as makes us paft doubt of the reality of his reward and glory.

When he found his belly fwell, his breath and
ftrength much abate, and his face and flefh decay,
he chearfully received the fentence of death: and
though Dr. Gliffon by meer oximel fquilliticum,
feemed a while to eafe him, yet that alfo foon failed
him; and he told me, he was prepared and contented comfortably to receive his change. And
accordingly he left us, and went into his native

I

country

country of Gloucefterfhire to die, as the hiftory
tells you.

Mr. Edward Stephens being moft familiar with
him, told me his purpofe to write his life: and
defired me to draw up the meer narrative of my
fhort familiarity with him; which I did as follow-
eth: by hearing no more of him, caft it by; but
others defiring it, upon the fight of the publifhed
hiftory of his life by Dr. Burnet, I have left it to
the difcretion of fome of them, to do with it
what they will.

And being half dead already in thofe deareft
friends who were half myfelf, am much the more
willing to leave this mole-hill and prifon of earth,
to be with that wife and bleffed fociety, who being
united to their head in glory, do not envy, hate,
or perfecute each other, nor forfake God, nor
fhall ever be forfaken by him.

R. B.

Note, That this narrative was written two years
    before Dr. Burnet's; and it's not to be doubt-
    ed, but that he had better information of
    his manufcripts, and fome other circumftances,
    than I. But of thofe manufcripts directed to
    me, about the foul's immortality, of which I
    have the originals under his hand, and alfo
    of his thoughts of the fubjects mentioned
    by me, from 1671, till he went to die in
    Gloucefterfhire, I had the fulleft notice.

ADDI-

ADDITIONAL NOTES

On the Life and Death of

Sir MATTHEW HALE, Knt.

————

To my Worthy Friend Mr. Stephens, the Publisher of Judge Hale's Contemplations.

Sir,

YOU desired me to give you notice of what I knew in my personal converse, of the great lord chief justice of England, sir Matthew Hale. You have partly made any thing of mine unmeet for the sight of any but yourself and his private friends (to whom it is useless) by your divulging those words of his extraordinary favour to me, which will make it thought, that I am partial in his praises. And indeed that excessive esteem of his, which you have told men of, is a divulging of his imperfection, who did over-value so unworthy a person as I know myself to be.

I will promise you to say nothing but the truth; and judge of it and use it as you please.

 My

My acquaintance with him was not long : and
I look'd on him as an excellent perfon ftudied in
his own way, which I hoped I fhould never have
occafion to make much ufe of;   but I thought not
fo verfed in our matters as ourfelves.   I was confirmed in this conceit by the firft report I had from
him, which was his wifh, that Dr. Reignolds,
Mr. Calamy, and I, would have taken bifhopricks,
when they were offered us by the lord chancellor,
as from the king, in 1660, (as one did). I thought
he underftood not our cafe, or the true ftate of
Englifh prelacy.   Many years after when I lived
at Acton, he being lord chief baron of the exchequer, fuddenly took a houfe in the village.   We
fat next feats together at church for many weeks,
but neither did he ever fpeak to me or I to him.
At laft, my extraordinary friend (to whom I was
more beholding than I muft here exprefs,) ferjeant
Fountain, afked me, why I did not vifit the lord
chief baron ?   I told him, becaufe I had no reafon
for it, being a ftranger to him ; and had fome
againft it, viz. that a judge, whofe reputation was
neceffary to the ends of his office, fhould not be
brought under court fufpicion, or difgrace, by his
familiarity with a perfon, whom the intereft and
diligence of fome prelates had rendered fo odious,
as I knew myfelf to be with fuch, I durft not be
fo injurious to him.   The ferjeant anfwered, it is
not meet for him to come firft to you ; I know
why I fpeak it : let me intreat you to go firft to
him.   In obedience to which requeft I did it; and

fo

ſo we entered into neighbourly familiarity. I lived then in a ſmall houſe, but it had a pleaſant garden and backſide, which the (honeſt) landlord had a deſire to ſell. The judge had a mind to the houſe; but he would not meddle with it, till he got a ſtranger to me, to come and enquire of me whether I was willing to leave it? I told him, I was not only willing but deſirous, not for my own ends, but for my landlord's ſake, who muſt needs ſell it: and ſo he bought it, and lived in that poor houſe, till his mortal ſickneſs ſent him to the place of his interment.

I will truly tell you the matter and the manner of our converſe. We were oft together, and almoſt all our diſcourſe was philoſophical, and eſpecially about the nature of ſpirits and ſuperiour regions; and the nature, operations, and immortality of man's ſoul. And our diſpoſition and courſe of thoughts, were in ſuch things ſo like, that I did not much croſs the bent of his conference. He ſtudied phyſicks, and got all new or old books of philoſophy that he could meet with, as eagerly as if he had been a boy at the univerſity. Mouſnerius, and Honoratus Faber, he deſervedly much eſteemed; but yet took not the latter to be without ſome miſtakes. Mathematicks he ſtudied more than I did, it being a knowledge which he much more eſteemed than I did; who valued all knowledge by the greatneſs of the benefit, and neceſſity of the uſe; and my unſkilfulneſs in them, I acknowledge my great defect, in which he much

I 3

excelled.

excelled. But we were both much addicted to know and read all the pretenders to more than ordinary in phyſicks; the Platoniſts, the Peripateticks, the Epicureans (and eſpecially their Gaſſendus,) Teleius, Campanella, Patricius, Lullius, White, and every ſect that made us any encourging promiſe. We neither of us approved of all in Ariſtotle; but he valued him more than I did. We both greatly diſliked the principles of Carteſius and Gaſſendus (much more of the Bruitiſts, Hobbs and Spinoſa); eſpecially their doctorine de motu, and their obſcuring, or denying nature itſelf, even the principia motus, the virtutes formales, which are the cauſes of operations.

Whenever we were together, he was the ſpring of our diſcourſe (as chuſing the ſubject): and moſt of it ſtill was of the nature of ſpirits, and the immortality, ſtate, and operations of ſeparated ſouls. We both were conſcious of human darkneſs, and how much of our underſtandings, quiet in ſuch matters, muſt be fetcht from our implicit truſt in the goodneſs and promiſes of God, rather than from a clear and ſatisfying conception of the mode of ſeparated ſouls operations; and how great uſe we have herein of our faith in Jeſus Chriſt, as he is the undertaker, mediator, the Lord and lover of ſouls, and the actual poſſeſſor of that glory. But yet we thought, that it greatly concerned us, to ſearch as far as God allowed us, into a matter of ſo great moment; and that even little and obſcure proſpects into the heavenly ſtate,

are

are more excellent than much and applauded knowledge of tranfitory things.

He was much in urging difficulties and objections; but you could not tell by them what was his own judgment: for when he was able to anfwer them himfelf, he would draw out anothers anfwer.

He was but of a flow fpeech, and fometimes fo hefitating, that a ftranger would have thought him a man of low parts, that knew not readily what to fay (though ready at other times). But I never faw Cicero's doctrine de Oratore, more verified in any man, that furnifhing the mind with all forts of knowledge, is the chief thing to make an excellent orator: for when there is abundance and clearnefs of knowledge in the mind, it will furnifh even a flow tongue to fpeak that which by its congruence and verity fhall prevail. Such a one never wants moving matter, nor an anfwer to vain objectors.

The manner of our converfe was as fuitable to my inclination as the matter. For whereas many bred in univerfities, and called fcholars, have not the wit, manners, or patience, to hear thofe that they difcourfe with fpeak to the end, but through lift and impotency cannot hold, but cut off a man's fpeech when they hear any thing that urgeth them, before the latter part make the former intelligible or ftrong (when oft the proof and ufe is referved to the end), liker fcolds than fcholars; as if they commanded filence at the end of each fentence to him that fpeaketh, or elfe would have two talk at once. I do not remember, that ever he and I did interrupt each other in any difcourfe. His wifdom and accuftomed patience caufed him ftill to ftay for the end. And though my difpofition have too much forwardnefs to fpeak, I had not fo little wit or manners, as to interrupt him; whereby we far better underftood each other, than we could have done in chopping and maimed difcourfe.

He was much for coming to philofophical knowledge by the help of experiments: but he thought, that our new philofophers, as fome call the Cartefians, had taken up many fallacies as experiments, and had made as unhappy a ufe of their trials, as many empericks and mountebanks do in medicine: and that Ariftotle was a man of far greater experience, as well as ftudy, than they. He was wont to fay, that lads at the univerfities had found it a way to be thought wifer than others, to join with boafters that cried down the ancients before they underftood them : for he thought that few of thefe contemners of Ariftotle, had ever fo far ftudied him, as to know his doctrine, but fpoke againft they knew not what; even as fome fecular theologues take it to be the way to be thought wife men and orthodox, to cant againft fome party or fect which they have advantage to contemn. It muft coft a man many years ftudy to know what Ariftotle held. But to read over Magirus (and perhaps the Conimbricenfes or Zabarell), and then prate againft Ariftotle, requireth but a little time and labour. He could well bear

it,

it, when one that had thoroughly studied Aristotle, dissented from him in any particular upon reason; but he loathed it in ignorant men, that were carried to it by shameful vanity of mind.

His many hard questions, doubts and objections to me, occasioned me to draw up a small tract of the nature and immortality of man's soul, as proved by natural light alone (by way of questions and answers): in which I had not baulked the hardest objections and difficulties that I could think of (conceiving that atheists and sadduces are so unhappily witty, and satan such a tutor, that they are as like to think of them as I). But the good man, when I sent it to him, was wiser than I, and sent me word in his return, that he would not have me publish it in English (nor without some alterations of the method); because though he thought I had sufficiently answered all the objections, yet ordinary readers would take deeper into their minds such hard objections as they never heard before, than the answer (how full soever) would be able to overcome: whereupon, not having leisure to translate and alter it, I cast it by.

He seemed to reverence and believe the opinion of Dr. Willis, and such others, *de animis brutorum*, as being not spiritual substances. But when I sent him a confutation of them, he seemed to acquiesce, and as far as I could judge, did change his mind; and had higher thoughts of sensitive natures, than they that take them to be some evanid qualities,

proceed-

proceeding from contexture, attemperation, and motion.

Yet he and I did think, that the notion of immateriality, had little fatisfactory to acquaint us with the nature of a fpirit (not telling us any thing what it is, but what it is not). And we thought, that the old Greek and Latin doctors (cited by Fauftus Rhegiculis, whom Mamertus anfwereth), did mean by a body or matter (of which they faid fpirits did confift), the fame thing as we now mean by the fubftance of fpirits, diftinguifhing them from meer accidents. And we thought it a matter of fome moment, and no fmall difficulty, to tell what men mean here by the word [fubftance], if it be but a relative notion, becaufe it doth *fubftare accidentibus & fubfiftere per fe*, relation is not proper fubftance. It is fubftance that doth fo fubfift : it is fomewhat, and not nothing, nor an accident. Therefore if more than relation muft be meant, it will prove hard to diftinguifh fubftance from fubftance by the notion of immateriality. Souls have no fhadows : they are not palpable and grofs ; but they are SUBSTANTIAL LIFE, as VIRTUES. And it is hard to conceive, how a created *vis vel virtus* fhould be the adequate *conceptus* of a fpirit, and not rather an inadequate, fuppofing the *conceptus* of *fubftantia fundamentalis* (as Dr. Gliffon calls it *de vita naturæ*), feeing *omnis virtus eft rei alicui virtus.*

Yet he yielded to me, that *virtus feu vis vitalis,* is not *animæ accidens,* but the *conceptus formalis*
fpiritus,

fpiritus, fuppofing *fubftantia* to be the *conceptus fundamentalis* : and both together exprefs the effence of a fpirit.

Every created being is paffive ; for *recipit in fluxum caufæ primæ*. God tranfcendeth our defining fkill : but where there is receptivity, many ancients thought there were fome pure fort of materiality : and we fay, there is receptive fubftantiality : and who can defcribe the difference (laying afide the formal virtues that difference things) between the higheft material fubftance, and the loweft fubftance, called immaterial.

We were neither of us fatisfied with the notions of penetrability and indivifibility, as fufficient differences. But the *virtutes fpecificæ* plainly difference.

What latter thoughts, a year before he died, he had of thefe things, I know not : but fome fay, that a treatife of this fubject, the foul's immortality, was his laft finifhed work (promifed in the end of his treatife of man's origination) ; and if we have the fight of that, it will fuller tell us his judgment.

One thing I muft notify to you, and to thofe that have his manufcripts, that when I fent him a fcheme, with fome elucidations, he wrote me on that and my treatife of the foul, almoft a quire of paper of animadverfions ; by which you muft not conclude at all of his own judgment : for he profeffed to me, that he wrote them to me, not as his judgment, but (as his way was) as the hardeft

objections

objections which he would have fatisfaction in. And when I had written him a full anfwer to all, and have been oft fince with him, he feemed fatisfied. You will wrong him therefore, if you fhould print that written to me as his judgment.

As to his judgment about religion; our difcourfe was very fparing about controverfies. He thought not fit to begin with me about them, nor I with him: and as it was in me, fo it feemed to be in him, from a conceit, that we were not fit to pretend to add much to one another.

About matters of conformity, I could gladly have known his mind more fully: but I thought it unmeet to put fuch queftions to a judge, who muft not fpeak againft the laws; and he never offered his judgment to me. And I knew, that as I was to reverence him in his own profeffion, fo in matters of my profeffion and concernment, he expected not, that I fhould think as he, beyond the reafons which he gave.

I muft fay, that he was of opinion, that the wealth and honour of the bifhops was convenient, to enable them the better to relieve the poor, and refcue the inferiour clergy from oppreffion, and to keep up the honour of religion in the world. But all this on fuppofition, that it would be in the hands of wife and good men, or elfe it would do as much harm. But when I afked him, whether great wealth and honour would not be moft earneftly defired and fought by the worft of men, while good men would not feek them? And whether

he

he that was the only fervent feeker, was not likelieft to obtain (except under fome rare extraordinary prince)? And fo whether it was not like to entail the office on the worft, and to arm Chrift's enemies againft him to the end of the world (which a provifion that had neither alluring nor much difcouraging temptation, might prevent), he gave me no anfwer. I have heard fome fay, if the pope were a good man, what a deal of good might he do? But have popes therefore bleft the world.

I can truly fay, that he greatly lamented the negligence, and ill lives, and violence of fome of the clergy; and would oft fay, what have they their calling, honour and maintenance for, but to feek the inftructing and faving of men's fouls?

He much lamented, that fo many worthy minifters were filenced, the church weakened, papifts ftrengthened, the caufe of love and piety greatly wronged and hindered by the prefent differences about conformity. And he hath told me his judgment, that the only means to heal us was, a new act of uniformity, which fhould neither leave all at liberty, nor impofe any thing but neceffary.

I had once a full opportunity to try his judgment far in this. It pleafed the lord keeper Bridgman to invite Dr. Manton and myfelf (to whom Dr. Bates at our defire was added), to treat with Dr. Wilkins and Dr. Burton about the terms of our reconciliation and reftoration to our minifterial liberty. After fome days conference, we came to

agree-

agreement in all things, as to the necessary terms. And because Dr. Wilkins and I had special intimacy with judge Hale, we desired him to draw it up in the form of an act, which he willingly did, and we agreed to every word. But it pleased the house of commons, hearing of it, to begin their next session with a vote, that no such bill should be brought in ; and so it died.

Query 1. Whether after this and other such agreement, it be ingenuity, or somewhat else, that hath ever since said, we know not what they would have ? And that at once call out to us, and yet strictly forbid us to tell them what it is we take for sin, and what we desire.

2. Whether it be likely, that such men as bishop Wilkins, and Dr. Burton, and judge Hale, would consent to such terms of our concord, as should be worse than our present condition of division and convulsion is ? And whether the maintainers of our dividing impositions, be all wiser and better men than this judge and that bishop were ?

3. And whether it be any distance of opinion, or difficulty of bringing us to agreement, that keepeth England in its sad divisions, or rather some mens opinion, that our unity itself is not desirable, lest it strengthen us ? The case is plain.

His behaviour in the church was conformable, but prudent. He constantly heard a curate, too low for such an auditor. In common-prayer he behaved himself as others, saying that, to avoid

the

the differencing of the gospels from the epistles, and the bowing at the name of Jesus, from the names, Christ, Saviour, God, &c. He would use some equality in his gestures, and stand up at the reading of all God's word alike.

I had but one fear or suspicion concerning him, which since I am assured was groundless : I was afraid least he had been too little for the practical part of religion, as to the working of the soul towards God, in prayer, meditation, &c. because he seldom spake to me of such subjects, nor of practical books, or sermons; but was still speaking of philosophy, or of spirits, souls, the future state, and the nature of God. But at last I understood, that his averseness to hypocrisy made him purposely conceal the most of such his practical thoughts and works, as the world now findeth by his contemplations and other writings.

He told me once, how God brought him to a fixed honour and observation of the Lord's day ; that when he was young, being in the west, the sickness or death of some relation at London, made some matter of estate to become his concernment; which required his hastening to London from the west : and he was commanded to travel on the Lord's day : but I cannot well remember how many cross accidents befel him in his journey; one horse fell lame, another died, and much more; which struck him with such sense of divine rebuke, as he never forgot.

When

When I went out of the houfe, in which he fucceeded me, I went into a greater, over-againft the church- door. The town having great need of help for their fouls, I preached between the public fermons in my houfe, taking the people with me to the church (to common-prayer and fermon) morning and evening. The judge told me, that he thought my courfe did the church much fervice ; and would carry it fo refpectfully to me at my door, that all the people might perceive his approbation. But Dr. Reeves could not bear it, but complained againft me; and the bifhop of London caufed one Mr. Rofle of Brainford, and Mr. Philips, two juftices of the peace, to fend their warrants to apprehend me. I told the judge of the warrant, but afked him no council, nor he gave me none; but with tears fhewed his forrow : (the only time that ever I faw him weep). So I was fent to the common goal for fix months, by thefe two juftices, by the procurement of the faid Dr. Reeves (his majefty's chaplain, dean of Windfor, dean of Wolverhampton, parfon of Horfeley, parfon of Acton). When I came to move for my releafe upon a habeas corpus (by the council of my great friend ferjeant Fountain), I found, that the character which judge Hale had given of me, ftood me in fome ftead ; and every one of the four judges of the common-pleas, did not only acquit me, but faid more for me than my council, (viz. judge Wild, judge Archer, judge Tyrel, and the lord chief juftice Vaughan) ; and made me

fenfible

fenfible, how great a part of the honour of his majefty's government, and the peace of the kingdom, confifted in the juftice of the judges.

And indeed judge Hale would tell me, that bifhop Ufher was much prejudiced againft lawyers, becaufe the worft caufes find their advocates : but that he and Mr. Selden had convinced him of the reafons of it, to his fatisfaction : and that he did by acquaintance with them, believe that there were as many honeft men among lawyers, proportionably, as among any profeffion of men in England (not excepting bifhops or divines).

And I muft needs fay, that the improvement of reafon, the diverting men from fenfuality and idlenefs, the maintaining of propriety and juftice, and confequently the peace and welfare of the kingdom, is very much to be afcribed to the judges, and lawyers.

But this imprifonment brought me the great lofs of converfe with judge Hale : for the parliament in the next act againft conventicles, put into it diverfe claufes, fuited to my cafe ; by which I was obliged to go dwell in another county, and to forfake both London and my former habitation ; and yet the juftices of another county were partly enabled to perfue me.

Before I went, the judge had put into my hand four volumes (in folio), which he had written, to prove the being and providence of God, the immortality of the foul, and life to come, the truth of chriftianity, and of every book of the fcripture

K

by

by itfelf, befides the common proofs of the whole. Three of the four volumes I had read over, and was fent to the goal before I read the fourth. I turned down a few leaves for fome fmall animadverfions, but had no time to give them him. I could not then perfuade him to review them for the prefs. The only fault I found with them of any moment, was that great copioufnefs, the effect of his fulnefs and patience, which will be called tedioufnefs by impatient readers.

When we were feparated, he (that would receive no letters from any man, about any matters which he was to judge) was defirous of letter-converfe about our philofophical and fpiritual fubjects. I having then begun a Latin methodus theologiæ, fent him one of the fchemes (before mentioned), containing the generals of the philofophical part, with fome notes upon it; which he fo over-valued, that he urged me to proceed in the fame way. I objected againft putting fo much philofophy (though moftly but de homine) in a method of theology: but he rejected my objections, and refolved me to go on.

At laft it pleafed God to vifit him with his mortal ficknefs. Having had the ftone before (which he found thick pond-water better eafe him of, than the gravel fpring-water), in a cold journey, an extraordinary flux of urine took him firft, and then fuch a pain in his fide, as forced him to let much blood, more than once, to fave him from fudden fuffocation or oppreffion. Ever after which

he

he had death in his lapfed countenance, flefh and ftrength, with fhortnefs of breath. Dr. Willis, in his life-time, wrote his cafe without his name, in an obfervation in his pharmaceut, &c. which was fhortly printed after his own death, and before his patient's : but I dare fay it fo crudely, as is no honour to that book.

When he had ftriven a while under his difeafe, he gave up his place, not fo much from the apprehenfion of the nearnefs of his death (for he could have died comfortably in his public work), but from the fenfe of his difability to difcharge his part : but he ceafed not his ftudies, and that upon points which I could have wifhed him to let go (being confident, that he was not far from his end).

I fent him a book which I newly publifhed, for reconciling the controverfies about predeftination, redemption, grace, free-will, but defired him not to beftow too much of his precious time upon it : but (before he left his place) I found him at it fo oft, that I took the boldnefs to tell him, that I thought more practical writings were moft fuitable to his cafe, who was going from this contentious world. He gave me but little anfwer ; but I after found, that he plied practicals and contemplatives in their feafon ; which he never thought meet to give me any account of. Only in general he oft told me, that the reafon and feafon of his writings (againft atheifm, &c. aforefaid) were, both in his circuit and at home, he ufed to fet apart fome time for

                     meditation,

meditation, especially after the evening public worship every Lord's day; and that he could not so profitable keep his thoughts in connection and method, otherwise, as by writing them down; and withal, that if there were any thing in them useful it was the way to keep it for after use: and therefore for the better management, for the accountableness and the after use, he had long accustomed to pen his meditations; which gave us all of that nature that he hath left us.

Notwithstanding his own great furniture of knowledge, and he was accounted by some, somewhat tenacious of his conceptions (for men that know much, cannot easily yield to the expectations of less knowing men), yet I must say, that I remember not that ever I conversed with a man that was readier to receive and learn. He would hear as patiently, and recollect all so distinctly, and then try it so judiciously (not disdaining to learn of an inferiour in some things, who in more had need to learn of him), that he would presently take what some stand wrangling against many years. I never more perceived in any man, how much great knowledge and wisdom facilitate additions, and the reception of any thing not before known. Such a one presently perceiveth that evidence which another is incapable of.

For instance, the last time, save one, that I saw him (in his weakness at Acton), he engaged me to explicate the doctrine of divine government (and decree), as consistent with the sin of man.

And

And when I had diftinctly told him, 1. What God did, as the author of nature, phyfically. 2. What he did, as legiflator, morally. And 3. What he did, as benefactor, and by fpecial grace. 4. And where permiffion came in, and where actual operation. 5. And fo, how certainly God might caufe the effects, and not caufe the volitions, as determinate to evil, [though the volition and effect being called by one name (as theft, murder, adultery, lying, &c.) oft deceive men]: he took up all that I had faid in order, and diftinctly twice over repeated each part in its proper place, and with its reafon : and when he had done, faid, that I had given him fatisfaction.

Before I knew what he did himfelf in contemplations, I took it not well, that he more than once told me, " Mr. Baxter, I am more beholden " to you than you are aware of; and I thank you " for all, but efpecially for your fcheme, and your " catholic theology." For I was forry, that a man (that I thought) fo near death, fhould fpend much of his time on fuch controverfies (though tending to end them). But he continued after, near a year, and had leifure for contemplations which I knew not of.

When I parted with him, I doubted which of us would be firft at heaven : but he is gone before, and I am at the door, and fomewhat the willinger to go, when I think fuch fouls as his are there.

When he was gone to Gloucefterfhire, and his contemplations were publifhed by you, I fent him

K 3

the

the confeſſion of my cenſures of him, how I had feared that he had allowed too great a ſhare of his time and thoughts to ſpeculation, and too little to practicals ; but rejoiced to ſee the conviction of my error : and he returned me a very kind letter, which was the laſt.

Some cenſured him for living under ſuch a curate at Acton, thinking it was in his power to have got Dr. Reeves, the parſon, to provide a better. Of which I can ſay, that I once took the liberty to tell him, that I feared too much tepidity in him, by reaſon of that thing ; not that he needed him-ſelf a better teacher, who knew more, and could over-look ſcandals ; but for the ſake of the poor ignorant people, who greatly needed better help. He anſwered me, that if money would do it, he would willingly have done it ; but the Dr. was a man, not to be dealt with ; which was the hardeſt word that I remember I ever heard him uſe of any. For I never knew any man more free from ſpeaking evil of others behind their backs. When-ever the diſcourſe came up to the faultineſs of any individuals, he would be ſilent : but the ſorts of faulty perſons he would blame with cautelous free-dom, eſpecially idle, proud, ſcandalous, contenti-ous, and factious clergymen. We agreed in no-thing more than that which he oft repeateth in the papers which you gave me, and which he oft ex-preſſed, viz. that true religion conſiſteth in great, plain, neceſſary things, the life of faith and hope, the love of God and man, an humble ſelf-denying mind,

mind, with mortification of worldly affection, car--nal luft, &c. And that the calamity of the church, and withering of religion, hath come from proud and bufy men's additions, that cannot give peace to themfelves and others, by living in love and quietnefs on this chriftian fimplicity of faith and practice, but vex and turmoil the church with thefe needlefs and hurtful fuperfluities ; fome by their decifions of words, or unneceffary controverfies ; and fome by their reftlefs reaching after their own worldly intereft, and corrupting the church, on pretence of raifing and defending it ; fome by their needlefs ceremonies, and fome by their fuper-ftitious and caufelefs fcruples. But he was efpeci-ally angry at them that would fo manage their differences about fuch things, as to fhew, that they had a greater zeal for their own additions, than for the common faving truths and duties which we were all agreed in ; and that did fo manage their feveral little and felfifh caufes, as wounded or injured the common caufe of the chri-ftian and reformed churches. He had a great diftafte of the books called, a friendly debate, &c. and ecclefiaftical polity, as from an evil fpirit, injur-ing fcripture phrafe, and tempting the atheifts to contemn all religion, fo they might but vent their fpleen, and be thought to have the better of their adverfaries ; and would fay, how eafy is it to re-quite fuch men, and all parties to expofe each other to contempt ? (Indeed, how many parifhes in England afford too plenteous matter of reply

K 4

to

to one that took that for his part ; and of tears to ferious obfervers) ?

His main defire was, that as men fhould not be pevifhly quarrelfom againft any lawful circumftances, forms or orders in religion, much lefs think themfelves godly men, becaufe they can fly from other mens circumftances, or fettled lawful orders as fin ; fo efpecially, that no human additions of opinion, order, modes, ceremonies, profeffions, or promifes, fhould ever be managed to the hindering of chriftian love and peace, nor of the preaching of the gofpel, nor the wrong of our common caufe, or the ftrengthening of atheifm, infidelity, prophanenefs or popery ; but that chriftian verity and piety, the love of God and man, and a good life, and our common peace in thefe, might be firft refoved on and fecured, and all our additions might be ufed, but in due fubordination to thefe, and not to any injury of any of them ; nor fects, parties, or narrow interefts be fet up againft the common duty, and the public intereft and peace.

I know you are acquainted, how greatly he valued Mr. Selden, being one of his executors ; his books and picture being ftill near him. I think it meet therefore to remember, that becaufe many Hobbifts do report, that Mr. Selden was at the heart an infidel, and inclined to the opinions of Hobbs, I defired him to tell me the truth herein : and he oft profeffed to me, that Mr. Selden was a refolved ferious chriftian ; and that he was a great adverfary to Hobbs's errors ; and that he had feen

him

him openly oppofe him fo earneftly, as either to depart from him, or drive him out of the room. And as Mr. Selden was one of thofe called Erafti-ans (as his book de Synedriis, and others fhew), yet owned the office properly minifterial. So moft lawyers that ever I was acquainted with, taking the word jurifdiction, to fignify fomething more than the meer doctoral, prieftly power, and power over their own facramental communion in the church which they guide, do ufe to fay, that it is primarily in the magiftrate (as no doubt all power of corporal coercion, by mulcts and penalties is). And as to the accidentals to the proper power of priefthood, or the keys, they truly fay with Dr. Stillingfleet, that God hath fettled no one form.

Indeed, the lord chief juftice thought, that the power of the word and facraments in the minifte-rial office, was of God's inftitution; and that they were the proper judges appointed by Chrift, to whom they themfelves fhould apply facraments, and to whom they fhould deny them. But that the power of chancellors courts, and many modal additions, which are not of the effence of the prieftly office, floweth from the king, and may be fitted to the ftate of the kingdom. Which is true, if it be limited by God's laws, and exercifed on things only allowed them to deal in, and contradict not the orders and powers fettled by Chrift and his apoftles.

On this account he thought well of the form of government in the church of England ; (lament-

ing

ing the mifcarriages of many perfons), and the want of parochial reformation : but he was greatly for uniting in love and peace, upon fo much as is neceffary to falvation, with all good, fober, peaceable men.

And he was much againft the corrupting of the chriftian religion (whofe fimplicity and purity he juftly took to be much of its excellency), by mens bufy additions, by wit, policy, ambition, or any thing elfe which fophifticateth it, and maketh it another thing, and caufeth the lamentable contentions of the world.

What he was as a lawyer, a judge, a chriftian, is fo well known, that I think for me to pretend that my teftimony is of any ufe, were vain. I will only tell you what I have written by his picture, in the front of the great bible which I bought with his legacy, in memory of his love and name, viz. " Sir Matthew Hale, that unwearied ftudent, that prudent man, that folid philofopher, that famous lawyer, that pillar and bafis of juftice (who would not have done an unjuft act for any worldly price or motive), the ornament of his majefty's government, and honour of Eng'and ; the higheft faculty of the foul of Weftminfter-hall, and pattern to all the reverend and honourable judges; that godly, ferious, practical chriftian, the lover of goodnefs and all good men ; a lamenter of the clergy's felfifhnefs, and unfaithfulnefs, and difcord, and of the fad divifions following hereupon ; an earneft defire of their reformation, concord, and

the

the church's peace, and of a reformed act of uniformity, as the beft and neceffary means thereto;
that great contemner of the riches, pomp and
vanity of the world; that pattern of honeft plainnefs and humility, who while he fled from the
honours that perfued him, was yet lord chief juftice
of the king's bench, after his being long lord chief
baron of the exchequer; living and dying, entering on, ufing, and voluntarily furrendering his
place of judicature, with the moft univerfal love,
and honour, and praife, that ever did Englifh
fubject in this age, or any that juft hiftory doth
acquaint us with, &c. &c. &c. This man fo wife,
fo good, fo great, bequeathing me in his teftament
the legacy of forty fhillings, meerly as a teftimony
of his refpect and love, I thought this book, the
teftament of Chrift, the meeteft purchafe by that
price, to remain in memorial of the faithful
love, which he bare and long expreffed to his inferiour and unworthy, but honouring friend, who
thought to have been with Chrift before him, and
waiteth for the day of his perfect conjunction with
the fpirits of the juft made perfect."

RICHARD BAXTER.

SOME
PASSAGES
OF THE
LIFE AND DEATH

Of the Right Honourable

JOHN Earl of Rocheſter,

Who died July 26, 1680.

Written by his own direction on his death bed,

By GILBERT BURNET, D. D.

Late Lord Biſhop of SARUM.

THE
PREFACE.

THE celebrating the praiſes of the dead, is an argument ſo worn out by long and frequent uſe, and now become ſo nauſeous, by the flattery that uſually attends it, that it is no wonder if funeral orations, or panegyricks, are more conſidered for the elegancy of ſtyle, and fineneſs of wit, than for the authority they carry with them as to the truth of matters of faĉt. And yet I am not hereby deterred from meddling with this kind of argument, nor from handling it with all the plainneſs I can ; delivering only what I myſelf heard and ſaw, without any borrowed ornament. I do eaſily foreſee how many will be engaged for the ſupport of their impious maxims and immoral practices, to diſparage what I am to write. Others will cenſure it, becauſe it comes from one of my profeſſion ; too many ſuppoſing us to be induced to frame ſuch diſcourſes for carrying on what they are pleaſed to call our trade. Some will think I dreſs it up too artificially, and others, that I preſent it too plain and naked.

But being reſolved to govern myſelf by the exaĉt rules of truth, I ſhall be leſs concerned in the cenſures I may fall under. It may ſeem liable to great exception, that I ſhould diſcloſe ſo many things, that were diſcovered to me, if not under the ſeal of confeſſion, yet under the confidence of friendſhip. But this noble lord himſelf not only releaſed me from all obligation of this kind, when I waited on him in his laſt ſickneſs, a few days before he died ; but gave it me in charge not to ſpare him in any thing which I thought might be of uſe to the living ; and was not ill pleaſed to be laid open, as well in the worſt, as in the

beſt

best and *last* part of his life, being so sincere in his repentance, that he was not unwilling to take shame to himself, by suffering his faults to be exposed for the benefit of others.

I write with one great disadvantage, that I cannot reach his chief design without mentioning some of his faults: but I have touched them as tenderly as occasion would bear; and I am sure with much more softness than he desired, or would have consented unto, had I told him how I intended to manage this part. I have related nothing with personal reflections on any others concerned with him, wishing rather that they themselves reflecting on the sense he had of his former disorders, may be thereby led to forsake their own, than that they should be any ways reproached by what I write: and therefore, though he used very few reserves with me, as to his course of life, yet since others had a share in most parts of it, I shall relate nothing but what more immediately concerned himself; and I shall say no more of his faults, than is necessary to illustrate his repentance.

The occasion that led me into so particular a knowledge of him, was an intimation given me by a gentleman of his acquaintance, of his desire to see me. This was some time in October, 1679, when he was slowly recovering out of a great disease. He had understood that I often attended on one well known to him, that died the summer before; he was also then entertaining himself in that state of his health, with the first part of the history of the reformation, then newly come out, with which he seemed not ill pleased: and we had accidentally met in two or three places some time before. These were the motives that led him to call for my company. After I had waited on him once or twice he grew into that freedom with me, as to open to me all his thoughts, both of religion and morality: and to give me a full view of his past life; and seemed not uneasy at my frequent visits. So till he went

from

from London, which was in the beginning of April, I waited on him often. As soon as I heard how ill he was, and how much he was touched with a sense of his former life, I writ to him, and received from him an answer, that, without my knowledge, was printed since his death, from a copy which one of his servants conveyed to the press. In it there is so undeserved a value put on me, that it had been very indecent for me to have published it : yet that must be attributed to his civility and way of breeding : and indeed he was particularly known to so few of the clergy, that the good opinion he had of me, is to be imputed only to his unacquaintance with others.

My end in writing is so to discharge the last commands this lord left on me, as that it may be effectual to awaken those who run on to all the excesses of riot ; and that in the midst of those heats which their lusts and passions raise in them, they may be a little wrought on by so great an instance of one who had run round the whole circle of luxury; *and, as Solomon says of himself,* Whatsoever his eyes desired, he kept it not from them ; and withheld his heart from no joy. *But when he looked back on all that on which he had wasted his time and strength, he esteemed it* vanity and vexation of spirit : *though he had both as much natural wit, and as much acquired by learning, and both as much improved with thinking and study, as perhaps any libertine of the age ; yet when he reflected on all his former courses, even before his mind was illuminated with better thoughts, he counted them madness and folly. But when the powers of religion came to operate on him, then he added a detestation to the contempt he formerly had of them, suitable to what became a sincere penitent, and expressed himself in so clear and so calm a manner, so sensible of his failings towards his Maker and his Redeemer, that as it wrought not a little on those that were about him ; so, I hope, the making it public may have a more general*

A

influence,

influence, chiefly on those on whom his former conversation might have had ill effects.

I have endeavoured to give his character as fully as I could take it : for I who saw him only in one light, in a sedate and quiet temper, when he was under a great decay of strength and loss of spirits, cannot give his picture with that life and advantage that others may, who knew him when his parts were more bright and lively : yet the composure he was then in, may perhaps be supposed to balance any abatement of his usual vigour, which the declination of his health brought him under. I have written this discourse with as much care, and have considered it as narrowly as I could. I am sure I have said nothing but truth ; I have done it slowly, and often used my second thoughts in it, not being so much concerned in the censures which might fall on myself, as cautious that nothing should pass that might obstruct my only design of writing, which is the doing what I can towards the reforming a loose and lewd age. And if such a signal instance concurring with all the evidence that we have for our most holy faith, has no effect on those who are running the same course, it is much to be feared they are given up to a reprobate sense.

SOME

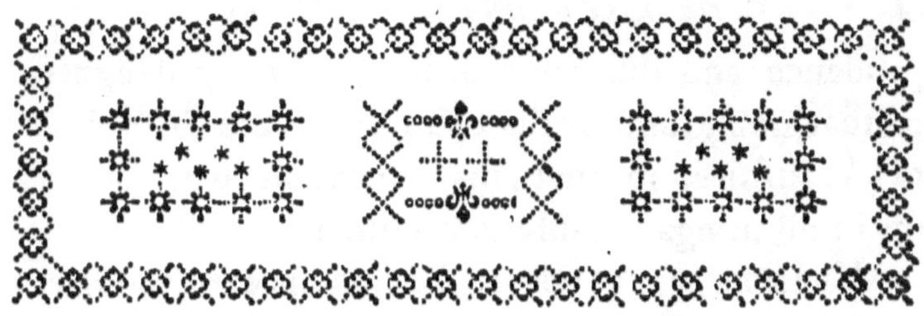

SOME

PASSAGES

Of the LIFE and DEATH of

JOHN Earl of ROCHESTER.

JOHN WILMOT, earl of Rochefter, was born in April, Anno Dom. 1648. His Father was Henry earl of Rochefter, but beft known by the title of the lord Wilmot, who bore fo great a part in all the late wars, that mention is often made of him in the hiftory; and had the chief fhare in the honour of the prefervation of his majefty that now reigns, after Worcefter fight, and the conveying him from place to place, till he happily efcaped into France: but dying before the king's return, he left his fon little other inheritance but the honour and title derived to him, with the pre-tenfions fuch eminent fervices gave him to the king's favour: thefe were carefully managed by the great

A 2

prudence

prudence and difcretion of his mother, a daughter of that noble and antient family of the St. John's of Wiltfhire, fo that his education was carried on in all things fuitably to his quality.

When he was at fchool, he was an extraordinary proficient at his book; and thofe fhining parts which have fince appeared with fo much luftre, began then to fhew themfelves: he acquired the Latin to fuch perfection, that to his dying day he retained a great relifh of the finenefs and beauty of that tongue, and was exactly verfed in the incomparable authors that writ about Auguftus's time, whom he read often with that peculiar delight which the greateft wits have ever found in thofe ftudies.

When he went to the univerfity, the general joy which over ran the whole nation upon his majefty's reftauration, but was not regulated with that fobriety and temperance, that became a ferious gratitude to God for fo great a bleffing, produced fome of its ill effects on him: he began to love thefe diforders too much: his tutor was that eminent and pious divine Dr. Blandford, afterwards promoted to the fees of Oxford and Worcefter; and under his infpection he was committed to the more immediate care of Mr. Phineas Berry, a fellow of Wadham College, a very learned and good-natured man; whom he afterwards ever ufed with much refpect, and rewarded him as became a great man. But the humour of that time wrought fo much on him, that he broke off the courfe of his ftudies, to which no means could ever effectually

recall

recall him ; till when he was in Italy his governour Dr. Balfour, a learned and worthy man, now a celebrated phyſician in Scotland, his native country, drew him to read ſuch books as were moſt likely to bring him back to love learning and ſtudy : and he often acknowledged to me, in particular three days before his death, how much he was obliged to love and honour this his governour, to whom he thought he owed more than to all the world, next after his parents, for his great fidelity and care of him while he was under his truſt.   But no part of it affected him more ſenſibly, than that he engaged him by many tricks (ſo he expreſſed it) to delight in books and reading ; ſo that ever after he took occaſion in the intervals of thoſe woeful extravagancies that conſumed moſt of his time, to read much; and though the time was generally but indifferently employed, for the choice of the ſubjects of his ſtudies was not always good, yet the habitual love of knowledge, together with theſe fits of ſtudy, had much awakened his underſtanding, and prepared him for better things, when his mind ſhould be ſo far changed as to reliſh them.

He came from his travels in the eighteenth year of his age, and appeared at court with as great advantages as moſt ever had.   He was a graceful and well-ſhaped perſon, tall, and well made, if not a little too ſlender : he was exactly well bred, and what by a modeſt behaviour natural to him, what by a civility became almoſt as natural, his converſation was eaſy and obliging.   He had a ſtrange

A 3

vivacity

vivacity of thought, and vigour of expreffion: his wit had a fubtilty and fublimity both, that it was fcarce imitable. His ftyle was clear and ftrong; when he ufed figures, they were very lively, and yet far enough out of the common road: he had made himfelf mafter of the antient and modern wit, and of the modern French and Italian, as well as the Englifh. He loved to talk and write of fpeculative matters, and did it with fo fine a thread, that even thofe who hated the fubjects that his fancy ran upon, yet could not but be charmed with his way of treating of them. Boileau among the French, and Cowley among the Englifh wits, were thofe he admired moft. Sometimes other men's thoughts mixed with his compofures; but that flowed rather from the impreffions they made on him when he read them, by which they came to return upon him as his own thoughts, than that he fervilely copied from any; for few men had a bolder flight of fancy, more fteadily governed by judgment than he had. No wonder a young man fo made, and fo improved, was very acceptable in a court.

Soon after his coming thither, he laid hold on the firft occafion that offered to fhew his readinefs to hazard his life in the defence and fervice of his country. In Winter 1665, he went with the earl of Sandwich to fea, when he was fent to lye for a Dutch Eaft-India fleet; and was in the Revenge, commanded by Sir Thomas Tiddiman, when the attack was mas made on the port of Bergen in Norway, the Dutch fhips having got into that port.

It

It was as defperate an attempt as ever was made; during the whole action, the earl of Rochefter fhewed as brave and as refolute a courage as was poffible: a perfon of honour told me he heard the lord Clifford, who was in the fame fhip, often magify his courage at that time very highly. Nor did the rigours of the feafon, the hardnefs of the voyage, and the extreme danger he had been in, deter him from running the like on the very next occafion; for the fummer following he went to fea again, without communicating his defign to his neareft relations. He went aboard the fhip commanded by Sir Edward Spragge, the day before the great fea fight of that year: almoft all the volunteers that were in the fame fhip were killed. Mr. Middleton (brother to Sir Hugh Middleton) was fhot in his arms: during the action, Sir Edward Spragge, not being fatisfied with the behaviour of one of the captains, could not eafily find a perfon that would chearfully venture through fo much danger, to carry his commands to that captain. This lord offered himfelf to the fervice; and went in a little boat, through all the fhot, and delivered his meffage, and returned back to Sir Edward, which was much commended by all that faw it. He thought it neceffary to begin his life with thefe demonftrations of his courage, in an element and way of fighting, which is acknowledged to be the greateft trial of clear and undaunted valour.

He had fo entirely laid down the intemperance that was growing on him before his travels, that at his return he hated nothing more. But falling

 into

into company that loved thefe exceffes, he was, though not without difficulty, and by many fteps, brought back to it again. And the natural heat of his fancy, being inflamed by wine, made him fo extravagantly pleafant, that many to be more diverted by that humour, ftudied to engage him deeper and deeper in intemperance ; which at length did fo entirely fubdue him, that, as he told me, for five years together he was continually drunk ; not all the while under the vifible effects of it, but his blood was fo inflamed, that he was not in all that time cool enough to be perfectly mafter of himfelf. This led him to fay and do many wild and unaccountable things : by this, he faid, he had broke the firm conftitution of his health, that feemed fo ftrong, that nothing was too hard for it ; and he had fuffered fo much in his reputation, that he almoft defpaired to recover it. There were two principles in his natural temper, that being heightened by that heat, carried him to great exceffes : a violent love of pleafure, and a difpofition to extravagant mirth. The one involved him in great fenfuality ; the other led him to many odd adventures and frolics, in which he was oft in hazard of his life. The one being the fame irregular appetite in his mind, that the other was in his body, which made him think nothing diverting that was not extravagant. And though in cold blood he was a generous and good natured man, yet he would go far in his heats, after any thing that might turn to a jeft, or matter of diverfion. He faid to me, he

never

never improved his intereſt at court, to do a premeditate miſchief to other perſons. Yet he laid out his wit very freely in libels and ſatires, in which he had a peculiar talent of mixing his wit with his malice, and fitting both with ſuch apt words, that men were tempted to be pleaſed with them : from thence his compoſures came to be eaſily known, for few had ſuch a way of tempering theſe together as he had : ſo that when any thing extraordinary that way came out, as a child is fathered ſometimes by its reſemblance, ſo was it laid at his door as its parent and author.

Theſe exerciſes in the courſe of his life were not always equally pleaſant to him ; he had often ſad intervals, and ſevere reflections on them : and though then he had not theſe awakened in him from any deep principle of religion, yet the horror that nature raiſed in him, eſpecially in ſome ſickneſſes, made him too eaſy to receive ſome ill principles, which others endeavoured to poſſeſs him with ; ſo that he was too ſoon brought to ſet himſelf to ſecure and fortify his mind againſt that, by diſpoſſeſſing it all he could of the belief or apprehenſions of religion. The licentiouſneſs of his temper, with the briſkneſs of his wit, diſpoſed him to love the converſation of thoſe who divided their time between lewd actions and irregular mirth. And ſo he came to bend his wit, and direct his ſtudies and endeavours to ſupport and ſtrengthen theſe ill principles both in himſelf and others.

A_n

An accident fell out after this, which confirmed him more in thefe courfes ; when he went to fea in the year 1665, there happened to be in the fame fhip with him Mr. Montague, and another gentleman of quality ; thefe two, the former efpecially, feemed perfuaded that they fhould never return into England. Mr. Montague, faid, he was fure of it ; the other was not fo pofitive. The earl of Rochefter, and the laft of thefe entered into a formal engagement, not without ceremonies of religion, that if either of them died, he fhould appear and give the other notice of the future ftate, if there was any. But Mr. Montague would not enter into the bond. When the day came that they thought to have taken the Dutch fleet in the port of Bergen, Mr. Montague, though he had fuch a ftrong prefage in his mind of his approaching death, yet he generoufly ftaid all the while in the place, of greateft danger : the other gentleman fignalized his courage in a moft undaunted manner, till the end of the action ; when he fell on a fudden into fuch a trembling that he could fcarce ftand ; and Mr. Montague going to him to hold him up, as they were in each others arms, a cannon ball killed him outright, and carried away Mr. Montague's belly, fo that he died within an hour after. The earl of Rochefter told me that that thefe prefages they had in their minds made fome impreffion on him, that there were feparated beings ; and that the foul either by a natural fagacity, or fome fecret notice communicated

cated

cated to it, had a fort of divination: but that gentleman's never appearing was a great fnare to him during the reft of his life. Though when he told me this he could not but acknowledge, it was an unreafonable thing for him to think, that beings in another ftate were not under fuch laws and limits, that they could not command their own motions, but as the Supreme Power fhould order them ; and that one who had fo corrupted the natural principles of truth, as he had, had no reafon to expect that fuch an extraordinary thing fhould be done for his conviction.

He told me of another odd prefage that one had of his approaching death in the lady Warre, his mother-in-law's houfe : the chaplain had dreamt that fuch a day he fhould die, but being by all the family put out of the belief of it, he had almoft forgot it ; till the evening before at fupper, there being thirteen at table, according to a fond conceit that one of thefe muft foon die, one of the young ladies pointed to him, that he was to die. He remembering his dream fell into fome diforder, and the lady Warre reproving him for his fuperftition, he faid, he was confident he was to die before morning, but he being in perfect health, it was not much minded. It was Saturday night, and he was to preach next day. He went to his chamber and fat up late, as appeared by the burning of his candle, and he had been preparing his notes for his fermon, but was found dead in his bed the next morning : thefe things he faid made him inclined to believe, the

foul

foul was a fubftance diftinct from matter ; and this often returned into his thoughts. But that which perfected his perfuafion about it, was, that in the ficknefs which brought him fo near death before I firft knew him, when his fpirits were fo low and fpent that he could not move nor ftir, and he did not think to live an hour ; he faid his reafon and judgment were fo clear and ftrong, that from thence he was fully perfuaded that death was not the fpending or diffolution of the foul, but only the feparation of it from matter. He had in that ficknefs great remorfes for his paft life, but he afterwards told me, they were rather general and dark horrors, than any convictions of finning againft God. He was forry he had lived fo as to wafte his ftrength fo foon, or that he had brought fuch an ill name upon himfelf, and had an agony in his mind about it, which he knew not well how to exprefs : but at fuch times, though he complied with his friends in fuffering divines to be fent for, he faid, he had no great mind to it ; and that it was but a piece of his breeding, to defire them to pray by him, in which he joined little himfelf.

As to the Supreme Being, he had always fome impreffion of one ; and profeffed often to me, that he had never known an entire atheift, who fully believed there was no God. Yet when he explained his notion of this being, it amounted to no more than a vaft power, that had none of the attributes of goodnefs or juftice, we afcribe to the deity ; thefe were his thoughts about religion, as himfelf

told

told me. For morality, he freely owned to me, that though he talked of it, as a fine thing, yet this was only becaufe he thought it a decent way of fpeaking; and that as they went always in cloaths, though in their frolicks they would have chofen fometimes to have gone naked, if they had not feared the people; fo fome of them found it ne-ceffary for human life to talk of morality, yet he confeffed they cared not for it, further than the reputation of it was neceffary for their credit and affairs; of which he gave me many inftances, as their profeffing and fwearing friendfhip, where they hated mortally; their oaths and imprecations on their addreffes to women, which they intended ne-ver to make good; the pleafure they took in de-faming innocent perfons, and fpreading falfe reports of fome perhaps in revenge, becaufe they could not engage them to comply with their ill defigns; the delight they had in making people quarrel; their unjuft ufage of their creditors, and putting them off by any deceitful promife they could invent, that might deliver them from prefent importunity. So that in deteftation of thefe courfes he would often break forth into fuch hard expreffions concerning himfelf, as would be indecent for another to repeat.

· Such had been his principles and practices in a courfe of many years, which had almoft quite ex-tinguifhed the natural propenfities in him to juftice and virtue. He would often go into the country, and be for fome months wholly employed in ftudy, or the fallies of his wit, which he came to direct

chiefly

chiefly to fatire. And this he often defended to me; by faying there was fome people that could not be kept in order, or admonifhed but in this way. I replied, that it might be granted that a grave way of fatire was fometimes no improfitable way of reproof; yet they who ufed it only out of fpite, and mixed lies with truth, fparing nothing that might adorn their poems, or gratify their revenge, could not excufe that way of reproach, by which the innocent often fuffer; fince the moft malicious things if wittily expreffed, might ftick to and blemifh the beft men in the world, and the malice of a libel could hardly confift with the charity of an admonition. To this, he anfwered, a man could not write with life, unlefs he were heated by revenge: for to make a fatire without refentments, upon the cold notions of philofophy, was as if a man would in cold blood cut mens throats who had never offended him: and he faid, the lies in thefe libels came often in as ornaments that could not be fpared without fpoiling the beauty of the poem.

For his other ftudies, they were divided between the comical and witty writings of the antients and moderns, the Roman authors and books of phyfic; which the ill ftate of health he was fallen into, made more neceffary to himfelf, and which qualified him for an odd adventure, which I fhall but juft mention. Being under an unlucky accident, which obliged him to keep out of the way, he difguifed himfelf, fo that his neareft friends could not have known him, and fet up in Tower-ftreet for

an

an Italian mountebank, where he practifed phyfic for
fome weeks not without fuccefs. In his latter
years he read books of hiftory more. He took
pleafure to difguife himfelf as a porter, or as a beggar ; fometimes to follow fome mean amours,
which for the variety of them, he affected. At
other times, merely for diverfion, he would go a-
bout in odd fhapes, in which he acted his part fo
naturally, that even thofe who were in the fecret,
and faw him in thefe fhapes, could perceive nothing by which he might be difcovered.

I have now made the defcription of his former
life and principles, as fully as I thought neceffary
to anfwer my end in writing ; and yet with thofe
referves that I hope I have given no juft caufe of
offence to any. I have faid nothing but what I
had from his own mouth, and have avoided the
mentioning of the more particular paffages of his
life, of which he told me not a few : but fince
others were concerned in them, whofe good only I
defign, I will fay nothing that may either provoke
or blemifh them. It is their reformation, and not
their difgrace, I defire : this tender confideration of
others has made me fupprefs many remarkable
and ufeful things he told me ; but finding that
though I fhould name none, yet I muft at leaft relate fuch circumftances, as would give too great
occafion for the reader to conjecture concerning
the perfons intended right or wrong, either of which
were inconvenient enough, I have chofen to pafs
them quite over. But I hope thofe that know how

much

much they were engaged with him in his ill courfes, will be fomewhat touched with this tendernefs I exprefs towards them, and be thereby the rather induced to reflect on their ways, and to confider without prejudice or paffion what fenfe this noble lord had of their cafe, when he came at laft ferioufly to reflect upon his own.

I now turn to thofe parts of this narrative, wherein I myfelf bore fome fhare, and which I am to deliver upon the obfervations I made, after a long and free converfation with him for fome months. I was not long in his company, when he told me, he fhould treat me with more freedom than he had ever ufed to men of my profeffion. He would conceal none of his principles from me, but lay his thoughts open without any difguife ; nor would he do it to maintain debate, or fhew his wit, but plainly tell me what ftuck with him ; and protefted to me, that he was not fo engaged to his old maxims, as to refolve not to change, but that if he could be convinced, he would chufe rather to be of another mind : he faid, he would impartially weigh what I fhould lay before him, and tell me freely when it did convince, and when it did not. He expreffed this difpofition of mind to me in a manner fo frank, that I could not but believe him, and be much taken with his way of difcourfe : fo we entered into almoft all the parts of natural and revealed religion, and of morality. He feemed pleafed, and in a great meafure fatisfied, with what I faid upon many of thefe heads ; and

though

though our freeft converfation was when we were alone, yet upon feveral occafions, other perfons were witneffes to it.   I underftood from many hands that my company was not diftafteful to him, and that the fubjects about which we talked moft were not unacceptable : and he expreffed himfelf often not ill pleafed with many things I faid to him, and particularly when I vifited him in his laft ficknefs ; fo that I hope it may not be altogether unprofitable to publifh the fubftance of thofe matters about which we argued fo freely, with our reafoning upon them : and perhaps what had fome effects on him, may be not altogether ineffectual upon others. I followed him with fuch arguments as I faw were moft likely to prevail with him : and my not urging other reafons proceeded not from any diftruft I had of their force, but from the neceffity of ufing thofe that were moft proper for him.   He was then in a low ftate of health, and feemed to be flowly recovering of a great difeafe.   He was in the milk diet, and apt to fall into hectical fits ; any accident weakened him ; fo that he thought he could not live long ; and when he went from London, he faid, he believed he fhould never come to town more.   Yet during his being in town he was fo well, that he went often abroad, and had great vivacity of fpirit.   So that he was under no fuch decay, as either darkened or weakened his underftanding ; nor was he any way troubled with the fpleen, or vapours, or under the power of me-lancholly.   What he was then compared to what he had been formerly, I could not fo well judge,

who had feen him but twice before. Others have
told me they perceived no difference in his parts.
This I mention more particularly, that it may not
be thought that melancholly, or the want of fpirits,
made him more inclined to receive any impreffions :
for indeed I never difcovered any fuch thing in him.

Having thus opened the way to the heads of our
difcourfe, I fhall next mention them. The three
chief things we talked about, were morality, natural religion, and revealed religion, chriftianity in
particular. For morality, he confeffed, he faw the
neceffity of it, both for the government of the
world, and for the prefervation of health, life and
friendfhip ; and was very much afhamed of his former practices, rather becaufe he had made himfelf
a beaft, and had brought pain and ficknefs on his
body, and had fuffered much in his reputation,
than from any deep fenfe of a Supreme Being, or
another ftate : but fo far this went with him, that
he refolved firmly to change the courfe of his life ;
which he thought he fhould effect by the ftudy of
philofophy, and had not a few no lefs folid than
pleafant notions concerning the folly and madnefs
of vice : but he confeffed he had no remorfe for
his paft actions, as offences againft God, but only
as injuries to himfelf and to mankind.

Upon this fubject I fhewed him the defects of
philofophy, for reforming the world : that it was
a matter of fpeculation, which but few either had
the leifure, or the capacity to enquire into. But
the principle that muft reform mankind, muft be
obvious

obvious to every mans underftanding. That philofophy in matters of morality, beyond the great
lines of our duty, had no very certain fixed rule;
but in the leffer offices and inftances of our duty,
went much by the fancies of men and cuftoms of
nations; and confequently could not have authority
enough to bear down the propenfities of nature,
appetite or paffion: for which I inftanced in thefe
two points; the one was, about that maxim of
the ftoics, to extirpate all fort of paffion and concern for any thing. That, take it by one hand,
feemed defireable, becaufe if it could be accompli-
fhed, it would make all the accidents of life eafy;
but I think it cannot, becaufe nature, after all our
ftriving againft it, will ftill return to itfelf: yet on
the other hand it diffolved the bonds of nature and
friendfhip, and flackened induftry, which will move
but dully, without an inward heat: and if it delivered a man from any troubles, it deprived him
of the chief pleafures of life, which arife from
friendfhip. The other was concerning the reftraint
of pleafure, how far that was to go. Upon this
he told me the two maxims of his morality then
were, that he fhould do nothing to the hurt of any
other, or that might prejudice his own health;
and he thought that all pleafure, when it did not
interfere with thefe, was to be indulged as the
gratification of our natural appetites. It feemed
unreafonable to imagine thefe were put into a man
only to be reftrained, or curbed to fuch a narrow-

B 2

nefs;

nefs : this he applied to the free ufe of wine and women.

To this I anfwered, that if appetites being natural, was an argument for the indulging them, then the revengeful might as well alledge it for murder, and the covetous for ftealing ; whofe appetites are no lefs keen on thofe objects; and yet it is acknowledged that thefe appetites ought to be curb'd. If the difference is urged from the injury that another perfon receives, the injury is as great if a man's wife is defiled, or his daughter corrupted: and it is impoffible for a man to let his appetites loofe to vagrant lufts, and not to tranfgrefs in thefe particulars : fo there was no curing the diforders that muft arife from thence, but by regulating thefe appetites ; and why fhould we not as well think that God intended our brutifh and fenfual appetites fhould be governed by our reafon, as that the fiercenefs of beafts fhould be managed and tamed by the wifdom, and for the ufe of man? So that it is no real abfurdity to grant, that appetites were put into men, on purpofe to exercife their reafon in the reftraint and government of them, which to be able to do, minifters a higher and more lafting pleafure to a man, than to give them their full fcope and range. And if other rules of philofophy be obferved, fuch as the avoiding thofe objects that ftir paffion, nothing raifes higher paffions than ungoverned luft, nothing darkens the underftanding and depreffes a man's mind more, nor is any thing managed with more frequent returns

of

of other immoralities, such as oaths and imprecations, which are only intended to compass what
is desired : the expence that is necessary to maintain these irregularities, makes a man false in his
other dealings.   All this he freely confessed was
true : upon which I urged, that if it was reasonable for a man to regulate his appetite in things
which he knew were hurtful to him ; was it not
as reasonable for God to prescribe a regulation of
those appetites, whose unrestrained course did produce such mischievous effects ?   That it could not
be denied, but doing to others what we would
have others do unto us, was a just rule. Those
men then that knew how extreme sensible they
themselves would be of the dishonour of their families in the case of their wives or daughters, must
needs condemn themseves for doing that which
they could not bear from another : and if the peace
of mankind, and the intire satisfaction of our
whole life, ought to be one of the chief measures
of our actions, then let all the world judge,
whether a man that confines his appetite, and
lives contented at home, is not much happier than
those that let their desires run after forbidden objects.   The thing being granted to be better in
itself, then the question falls between the restraint
of appetite in some instances, and the freedom of
a man's thoughts, the soundness of his health, his
application to affairs, with the easiness of his whole
life.   Whether the one is not to be done before
the other ?   As to the difficulty of such a restraint,

B 3

though

though it is not eafy to be done, when a man
allows himfelf many liberties, in which it is not
poffible to ftop ; yet thofe who avoid the occafions
that may kindle thefe impure flames, and keep
themfelves well imployed, find the victory and dominion over them no fuch impoffible, or hard matter, as may feem at firft view. So that though the
philofophy and morality of this point were plain,
yet there is not ftrength enough in that principle
to fubdue nature, and appetite. Upon this I urged,
that morality could not be a ftrong thing, unlefs a
man were determined by a law within himfelf; for if
he only meafured himfelf by decency, or the laws
of the land, this would teach him only to ufe fuch
cautions in his ill practices, that they fhould not
break out too vifibly ; but would never carry him
to an inward and univerfal probity. That virtue
was of fo complicated a nature, that unlefs a man
came intirely within its difcipline, he could not
adhere fteadfaftly to any one precept ; for vices are
often made neceffary fupports to one another.
That this cannot be done, either fteadily, or with
any fatisfaction, unlefs the mind does inwardly
comply with, and delight in the dictates of virtue ;
and that could not be effected, except a man's
nature were internally regenerated, and changed
by a higher principle : till that came about, corrupt nature would be ftrong, and philofophy but
feeble; efpecially when it ftruggled with fuch appetites or paffions as were much kindled, or deeply
rooted in the conftitution of ones body. This,

he

he faid, founded to him like enthufiafm, or cant-
ing: he had no notion of it, and fo could not underftand it. He comprehended the dictates of reafon
and philofophy, in which as the mind became
much converfant, there would foon follow, as he
believed, a greater eafinefs in obeying its precepts.
I told him on the other hand, that all his fpecu-
lations of philofophy would not ferve him in any
ftead to the reforming of his nature and life, till
he applied himfelf to God for inward affiftances.
It was certain, that the impreffions made in his
reafon governed him, as they were lively prefented
to him; but thefe are fo apt to flip out of our memory, and we fo apt to turn our thoughts from them,
and at fome times the contrary impreffions are fo
ftrong, that let a man fet up a reafoning in his
mind againft them, he finds that celebrated faying
of the poet,

Vido meliora proboque, deteriora fequor,

    " I fee what is better and approve it, but fol-
        low what is worfe,"

to be all that philofophy will amount to. Whereas thofe who upon fuch occafions apply themfelves to God, by earneft prayer, feel a difengagement from fuch impreffions, and themfelves endued
with a power to refift them; fo that thofe bonds
which formerly held them fall off.

    This he faid muft be the effect of a heat in na-
ture: it was only the ftrong diverfion of the
thoughts, that gave the feeming victory, and he

B 4

did

did not doubt but if one could turn to a problem
in Euclid, or to write a copy of verfes, it would
have the fame effect. To this I anfwered, that if
fuch methods did only divert the thoughts, there
might be fome force in what he faid : but if they
not only drove out fuch inclinations, but begat
impreffions contrary to them, and brought men
into a new difpofition and habit of mind ; then
he muft confefs there was fomewhat more than
a diverfion in thefe changes, which were brought
on our minds by true devotion. I added that reafon and experience were the things that determined our perfuafions : that experience without reafon
may be thought the delufion of our fancy, fo reafon without experience had not fo convincing an
operation ; but thefe two meeting together, muft
needs give a man all the fatisfaction he can defire.
He could not fay, it was unreafonable to believe
that the Supreme Being might make fome thoughts
ftir in our minds with more or lefs force, as it
pleafed : efpecially the force of thefe motions,
being, for moft part, according to the impreffion
that was made on our brains : which that power
that directed the whole frame of nature,
could make grow deeper as it pleafed : it was
alfo reafonable to fuppofe God a being of fuch
goodnefs that he would give his affiftance to fuch
as defired it : for though he might upon fome
greater occafions in an extraordinary manner turn
fome peoples minds, yet fince he had endued
man with a faculty of reafon, it is fit than men
fhould

fhould employ that as far as they could, and beg
his affiftance ; which certainly they can do.   All
this feemed reafonable, and at laft probable.   Now
good men who felt upon their frequent applications
to God in prayer, a freedom from thofe ill impreffions, that formerly fubdued them, and inward
love to virtue and true goodnefs, an eafinefs and
delight in all the parts of holinefs, which was fed
and cherifhed in them by a ferioufnefs in prayer,
and did languifh as that went off, had as real a
perception of an inward ftrength in their minds,
that did rife and fall with true devotion, as they perceived the ftrength of their bodies increafed or abated,
according as they had or wanted good nourifh-
ment.

After many difcourfes upon this fubject, he ftill
continued to think all was the effect of fancy : He
faid, that he underftood nothing of it, but acknowledged that he thought they were happy whofe fancies were under the power of fuch impreffions ;
fince they had fomewhat on which their thoughts
refted and centered ; but when I faw him in his
laft ficknefs, he then told me, he had another fenfe
of what we had talked concerning prayer and inward affiftances. This fubject led us to difcourfe
of God, and of the notion of religion in general.
He believed there was a Supreme Being : he could
not think the world was made by chance, and the
regular courfe of nature feemed to demonftrate the
eternal power of its author. This, he faid, he
could never fhake off ; but when he came to ex-

plain

plain his notion of the deity, he said, he looked on
it as a vast power that wrought every thing by the
necessity of its nature : and thought that God had
none of those affections of love or hatred, which
bred perturbation in us, and by consequence he
could not see that there was to be either reward or
punishment.   He thought our conceptions of God
were so low, that we had better not think much of
him : and to love God seemed to him a presumptuous
thing, and the heat of fanciful men.   Therefore
he believed there should be no other religious worship, but a general celebration of that being, in
some short hymn : all the other parts of worship he
esteemed the inventions of priests, to make the
world believe they had a secret of incensing and ap-
peasing God as they pleased.   In a word, he was
neither persuaded that there was a special providence
about human affairs ;   nor that prayers were of
much use, since that was to look on God as a weak
being, that would be overcome with importunities.
And for the state after death, though he thought
the soul did not dissolve at death, yet he doubted
much of rewards or punishments ;   the one he
thought too high for us to attain by our slight services; and the other was too extreme to be inflicted
for sin.   This was the substance of his speculations
about God and religion.

I told him his notions of God was so low, that
the Supreme Being seemed to be nothing but nature.
For if that being had no freedom or choice of its
own actions, nor operated by wisdom or goodness,
all those reasons which led him to acknowledge a

God,

God, were contrary to this conceit; for, if the order
of the univerfe perfuaded him to think there was a
God, he muft at the fame time conceive him to be
both wife and good, as well as powerful, fince
thefe all appeared equally in the creation; though his
wifdom and goodnefs had ways of exerting themfelves, that were far beyond our notions or meafures. If God was wife and good, he would naturally love, and be pleafed with thofe that refemble him in thefe perfections, and diflike thofe
that were oppofite to him. Every rational being
naturally loves itfelf, and is delighted in others like
itfelf, and is averfe from what is not fo. Truth is
a rational nature's acting in conformity to itfelf in
all things, and goodnefs is an inclination to promote the happinefs of other beings : fo truth and
goodnefs were the effential perfections of every
reafonable being, and certainly moft eminently in
the Deity : nor does his mercy or love raife paffion
or perturbation in him; for we feel that to be a
weaknefs in ourfelves, which indeed only flows from
our want of power or fkill to do what we wifh or
defire : it is alfo reafonable to believe God would
affift the endeavours of the good, with fome helps
fuitable to their nature. And that it could not be
imagined, that thofe who imitated him, fhould not
be fpecially favoured by him ; and therefore fince
this did not appear in this ftate, it was moft reafonable to think it fhould be in another, where the
rewards fhall be an admiffion to a more perfect ftate
of conformity to God, with the felicity that follows it, and the punifhments fhould be a total

exclufion

exclufion from him, with all the horror and darknefs that muft follow that.   Thefe feemed to be the
natural refults of fuch feveral courfes of life, as well
as the effects of divine juftice, rewarding or punifh-
ing.   For fince he believed the foul had a diftinct
fubfiftance, feparated from the body, upon its diffolution, there was no reafon to think it paffed into
a ftate of utter oblivion, of what it had been in
formerly : but that as the reflections on the good
or evil it had done, muft raife joy or horror in it ;
fo thofe good or ill difpofitions accompanying the
departed fouls, they muft either rife up to a higher perfection, or fink to a more depraved and miferable ftate.   In this life variety of affairs and
objects do much cool and divert our minds ; and
are on the one hand often great temptations to the
good, and give the bad fome eafe in their trouble ;
but in a ftate wherein the foul fhall be feparated
from fenfible things, and employed in a more
quick and fublime way of operation, this muft very
much exalt the joys and improvements of the good,
and as much heighten the horror and rage of the
wicked, fo that it feemed a vain thing to pretend to
believe a Supreme Being, that is wife and good, as
well as great, and not to think a difcrimination will
be made between the good and the bad, which, it
is manifeft, is not fully done in this life.

As for the government of the world, if we believe the fupreme power made it, there is no reafon
to think he does not govern it ; for all that we can
fancy againft it, is the diftraction which that infinite

variety

variety of second causes, and the care of their concernments, must give to the first, if it infpects them all. But as among men, thofe of weaker capacities are wholly taken up with fome one thing, whereas thofe of more inlarged powers, can without diftraction, have many things within their care; as the eye can at one view receive a great variety of objects in that narrow compafs without confufion, fo if we conceive the divine underftanding to be as far above ours, as his power of creating and framing the whole univerfe, is above our limited activity; we will no more think the government of the world a diftraction to him ; and if we have once overcome this prejudice, we fhall be ready to acknow-- ledge a providence directing all affairs, a care well becoming the Great Creator.

As for worfhiping him, if we imagine our wor- fhip is a thing that adds to his happinefs, or gives him fuch a fond pleafure as weak people have to hear themfelves commended ; or that our repeated addreffes do overcome him through our mere impor- tunity, we have certainly very unworthy thoughts of him. The true ends of worfhip come within another confideration, which is this, a man is ne- ver entirely reformed till a new principle governs his thoughts ; nothing makes that principle fo ftrong, as deep and frequent meditations of God ; whofe nature though it be far above our compre- henfion, yet his goodnefs and wifdom are fuch perfections as fall within our imagination : and he that thinks often of God, and confiders him as governing

verning the world, and as ever obferving all his actions, will feel a very fenfible effect of fuch meditations, as they grow more lively and frequent with him ; fo the end of religious worfhip, either public or private, is to make the apprehenfions of God have a deeper root and a ftronger influence on us. The frequent returns of thefe are neceffary, left if we allow too long intervals between them, thefe impreffions may grow feebler, and other fuggeftions may come in their room ; and the returns of prayer are not to be confidered as favours extorted by mere importunity, but as rewards conferred on men fo well difpofed and prepared for them, according to the promifes that God has made for anfwering our prayers ; thereby to engage and nourifh a devout temper in us, which is the chief root of all true holinefs and virtue.

It is true, we cannot have fuitable notions of the divine effence ; as indeed we have no juft idea of any effence whatfoever, fince we commonly confider all things, either by their outward figure, or by their effects, and from thence make inferences what their nature muft be : fo though we cannot frame any perfect image in our minds of the divinity, yet we may from the difcoveries God has made of himfelf, form fuch conceptions of him, as may poffefs our minds with great reverence for him, and beget in us fuch a love of thofe perfections as to engage us to imitate them. For when we fay we love God, the meaning is, we love that being that is holy, juft, good, wife, and infinitely perfect : and

loving

loving thefe attributes in that objec, will certainly carry us to defire them in ourfelves. For whatever we love in another, we naturally, according to the degree of our love, endeavour to refemble it. In fum, the loving and worfhipping God, though they are juft and reafonable returns and expreffions of the fenfe we have of his goodnefs to us ; yet they are exacted of us not only as a tribute to God, but as a mean to beget in us a conformity to his nature, which is the chief end of pure and undefiled religion.

If fome men have at feveral times found out inventions to corrupt this, and cheat the world ; It is nothing but what occurs in every fort of employment, to which men betake themfelves ; mountebanks corrupt phyfic, petty-foggers have entangled the matters of property, and all profeffions have been vitiated by the knaveries of a number of their calling.

With all thefe difcourfes he was not equally fatisfied : he feemed convinced that the impreffions of God being much in mens minds, would be a powerful means to reform the world ; and did not feem determined againft providence. But for the next ftate, he thought it more likely that the foul began anew, and that her fenfe of what fhe had done in this body, lying in the figures that are made in the brain, as foon as fhe diflodged, all thefe perifhed, and that the foul went into fome other ftate to begin a new courfe. But I faid on this head, that this was at beft a conjecture, raifed

in

in him by his fancy; for he could give no reason
to prove it true : nor was all the remembrance our
souls had of past things seated in some material
figures lodged in the brain : though it could not
be denied but a great deal of it lay in the brain.
That we have many abstracted notions and ideas
of immaterial things which depend not on bodily
figures : some sins, such as falshood, and ill nature,
were seated in the mind, as lust and appetite were
in the body ; and as the whole body was the re-
cepticle of the soul, and the eyes and ears were
the organs of seeing and hearing, so was the brain
the seat of memory : yet t he power and faculty of memory, as well as of seeing and hearing,
lay in the mind ; and so it was no unconceiveable
thing that either the soul by its own strength, or
by the means of some subtiler organs, which
might be fitted for it in another state, should still
remember as well as think. But indeed we know
so little of the nature of our souls, that it is a
vain thing for us to raise an hypothesis out of the
conjectures we have about it, or to reject one,
because of some difficulties that occur to us ; since
it is as hard to understand how we remember
things now, as how we shall do it in another state :
only we are sure we do it now, and so we shall
be then, when we do it.

When I pressed him with the secret joys that a
good man felt, particularly as he drew near death,
and the horrors of ill men especially at that time ;
he was willing to ascribe it to the impressions they

had

had from their education : but he often confessed,
that whether the business of religion was true or
not, he thought those who had the persuasions of
it, and lived so that they had quiet in their con-
sciences, and believed God governed the world,
and acquiesced in his providence, and had the hope
of an endless blessedness in aother state, the happi-
est men in the world ; and said, he would give
all that he was master of, to be under those persuasions, and to have the supports and joys that
must needs flow from them. I told him the main
root of all corruptions in mens principles was
their ill life ; which, as it darkened their minds,
and disabled them from discerning better things ;
so it made it necessary for them to seek out such
opinions as might give them ease from those cla-
mours, that would otherwise have been raised within
them. He did not deny, but that after the doing of
some things he felt great and severe challenges within himself ; but he said, he felt not these after
some others which I would perhaps call far greater
sins, than those that affected him more sensibly.
This I said, might flow from the disorders he had
cast himself into, which had corrupted his judgment, and vitiated his taste of things ; and by his
long continuance in, and frequent repeating of
some-immoralities, he had made them so familiar
to him, that they were become as it were natural ;
and then it was no wonder if he had not so exact a sense of what was good or evil ; as a feverish
man cannot judge of tastes.

C

He

He did acknowledge, the whole syftem of religion, if believed, was a greater foundation of quiet
than any other thing whatfoever ; for all the quiet
he had in his mind, was, that he could not think
fo good a being as the Deity would make him
miferable.   I afked, if when by the ill courfe of
his life he had brought fo many difeafes on his
body, he could blame God for it ; or expect that
he fhould deliver him from them by a miracle.
He confeffed there was no reafon for that.   I then
urged, that if fin fhould caft the mind, by a natural
effect, into endlefs horrors and agonies, which
being feated in a being not fubject to death, muft
laft for ever, unlefs fome miraculous power inter-
pofed, could he accufe God for that which was the
effect of his own choice and ill life ?

He faid, they were happy that believed ; for it
was not in every man's power.

And upon this we difcourfed long about revealed
religion.   He faid, he did not underftand the bufinefs of infpiration ; he believed the penmen of the
fcriptures had heats and honefty, and fo writ ; but
could not comprehend how God fhould reveal his
fecrets to mankind.   Why was not man made a
creature more difpofed for religion, and better
illuminated ?   He could not apprehend how there
fhould be any corruption in the nature of man, or
a lapfe derived from Adam.   God's communicating his mind to one man, was the putting it in
his power to cheat the World : for prophefies and
miracles, the world had been always full of ftrange
                                            ftories ;

stories; for the boldness and cunning of contrivers meeting with the simplicity and credulity of the people, things were easily received; and being once received, passed down without contradiction. The incoherences of stile in the scriptures, the odd transitions, the seeming contradictions, chiefly about the order of time, the cruelties enjoined the Israelities in destroying the Canaanites, circumcision, and many other rites of the Jewish worship; seemed to him unsuitable to the divine nature : and the first three chapters of Genesis he thought could not be true, unless they were parables. This was the substance of what he excepted to revealed religion in general, and to the old testament in particular.

I answered to all this, that believing a thing upon the testimony of another, in other matters where there was no reason to suspect the testimony, chiefly where it was confirmed by other circumstances, was not only a reasonable thing, but it was the hinge on which all the government and justice in the world depended : since all the courts of justice proceed upon the evidence given by witnesses; for the use of writings, is but a thing more lately brought into the world. So then if the credibility of the thing, the innocence and disinterestedness of the witnesses, the number of them, and the publickest confirmations that could possibly be given, do concur to persuade us of any matter of fact, it is a vain thing to say, because it is possible for so many men to agree in a lye, that there-

fore

fore thefe have done it. In all other things a man gives his affent when the credibility is ftrong on the one fide, and there appears nothing on the other fide to balance it. So fuch numbers agree-ing in their teftimony to thefe miracles; for in-ftance, of our Saviour's calling Lazarus out of the grave the fourth day after he was buried, and his own rifing again after he was certainly dead; if there had been never fo many impoftures in the world, no man can with any reafonable colour pretend this was one. We find both by the Jewifh and Roman writers that lived in that time, that our Saviour was crucified, and that all his difciples and followers believed certainly that he arofe again. They believed this upon the teftimony of the apoftles, and many hundreds who faw it, and died confirming it. They went about to perfuade the world of it with great zeal, though the knew they were to get nothing by it, but reproach and fufferings : and by many wonders which they wrought they confirmed their teftimony. Now to avoid all this, by faying it is poffible this might be a contrivance, and to give no prefumption to make it fo much as probable, that it was fo, is in plain Englifh to fay, "we are refolved, let the evi-" dence be what it will, we will not believe it."

He faid, if a man fays he cannot believe, what help is there ? for he was not mafter of his own belief, and believing was at higheft but a probable opinion. To this I anfwered, that if a man will let a wanton conceit poffefs his fancy againft thefe

things,

things, and never confider the evidence for religion on the other hand, but reject it upon a flight view of it, he ought not to fay he cannot, but he wil not believe : and while a man lives an ill courfe of life, he is not fitly qualified to examine the matter aright. Let him grow calm and virtuous, and upon due application examine things fairly, and then let him pronounce according to his con- fcience, if to take it at its loweft, the reafons on the one hand are not much ftronger than they are on the other. For I found he was fo poffeffed with the general conceit, that a mixture of knaves and fools had made all extraordinary things be eafily believed, that it carried him away to determine the matter, without fo much as looking on the hiftorical evidence for the truth of chriftianity, which he had not enquired into, but had bent all his wit and ftudy to the fupport of the other fide. As for that, that believing is at beft but an opini- on ; if the evidence be but probable, it is fo ; but if it be fuch that it cannot be queftioned, it grows as certain as knowledge : for we are no lefs certain that there is a great town called Conftantinople, the feat of the Ottoman empire, than that there is another called London. We as little doubt that queen Elizabeth once reigned, as that king Charles now reigns in England. So that beliving may be as certain, and as little fubject to doubting, as feeing or knowing.

There are two forts of believing divine matters; the one is wrought in us by our comparing all the

C 3

evidences

evidences of matter of fact, for the confirmation
of revealed religion, with the prophecies in the
fcripture; where things were punctually predicted,
fome ages before their completion; not in dark and
doubtful words uttered like oracles, which might
bend to any event; but in plain term·, as the fore-
telling that Cyrus by name fhould fend the Jews back
from the captivity, after the fixed period of feventy
years: the hiftory of the Syrian and Egyptian kings,
fo punctually foretold by Daniel, and the prediction
of the deftruction of Jerufalem, with many circum-
flances relating to it, made by our Saviour; join-
ing thefe to the excellent rule and defign of the
fcripture in matters of morality, it is at leaft as
reafonable to believe this as any thing elfe in the
world. Yet fuch a believing as this, is only a
general perfuafion in the mind, which has not that
effect, till a man applying himfelf to the directions
fet down in the fcriptures (which upon fuch evidence cannot be denied to be as reafonable, as for
a man to follow the prefcriptions of a learned phy-
fician, and when the rules are both good and eafy,
to fubmit to them for the recovery of his health)
and by following thefe, finds a power entering
within him, that frees him from the flavery of his
appetites and paffions, that exalts his mind above
the accidents of life, and fpreads an inward purity
in his heart, from which a ferene and calm joy a-
rifes within him: and good men, by the efficacy
thefe methods have upon them, and from the re-·
turns of their prayers, and other endeavours, grow

affured

assured that these things are true, and answerable to the promises they find registered in scripture. All this, he said, might be fancy; but to this I answered, that as it were unreasonable to tell a man that is abroad, and knows he is awake, that perhaps he is in a dream, and in his bed, and only thinks he is abroad, or that as some go about in their sleep, so he may be asleep still; so good and religious men know, though others might be abused by their fancies, that they are under no such deception; and find they are neither hot nor enthusiastical, but under the power of calm and clear principles. All this he said he did not understand, and that it was to assert or beg the thing in question, which he could not comprehend.

As for the possibility of revelation, it was a vain thing to deny it; for as God gives us the sense of seeing material objects by our eyes, and opened in some a capacity of apprehending high and sublime things, of which other men seemed utterly incapable; so it was a weak assertion that God cannot awaken a power in some mens minds, to apprehend and know some things, in such a manner that others are not capable of it. This is not half so incredible to us as sight is to a blind man, who yet may be convinced there is a strange power of seeing that governs men, of which he finds himself deprived. As for the capacity put into such mens hands to deceive the world, we are at the same time to consider, that besides the probity of their tempers, it cannot be thought but God can so forci-

C 4.

bly

bly blind up a man in some things that it should not be in his power to deliver them, otherwise than as he gives him in commission: besides, the confirmation of miracles are a divine credential to warrant such persons in what they deliver to the world, which cannot be imagined can be joined to a lye, since this were to put the omnipotence of God to attest that which no honest man would do. For the business of the fall of man, and other things, of which we cannot perhaps give ourselves a perfect account; we who cannot fathom the secrets of the council of God, do very unreasonably to take on us to reject an excellent system of good and holy rules, because we cannot satisfy ourselves about some difficulties in them. Common experience tells us, there is a great disorder in our natures, which is not easily rectified; all philosophers were sensible of it, and every man that designs to govern himself by reason, feels the struggle between it and nature; so that it is plain, there is a lapse of the high powers of the soul.

But why, said he, could not this be rectified by some plain rules given; but men must come and shew a trick to persuade the world they speak to them in the name of God? I answered, that religion being a design to recover and save mankind, was to be so opened, as to awaken and work upon all sorts of people; and generally men of a simplicity of mind, were those that were the fittest objects for God to shew his favour to; therefore it was necessary that messengers sent from heaven
should

should appear with such alarming evidence as might awaken the world, and prepare them by some aftonishing signs, to listen to the doctrine they were to deliver. Philosophy, that was only a matter of fine speculation, had few votaries; and as there was no authority in it to bind the world to believe its dictates, so they were only received by some of nobler and refined natures, who could apply themfelves to and delight in such notions. But true religion was to be built on a foundation, that should carry more weight on it, and to have such convictions, as might not only reach those who were already difposed to receive them, but roufe up such as without great and fenfible excitation would have otherwife flept on in their ill courfes.

Upon this, and fome fuch occafions, I told him, I faw the ill ufe he made of his wit, by which he flurred the graveft things with a flight dafh of his fancy; and the pleafure he found in fuch wanton expreffions, as calling the doing of miracles the fhewing of a trick, did really keep him from examining them with that care which fuch things required.

For the old teftament, we are fo remote from that time, we have fo little knowledge of the language in which it was writ, have fo imperfect an account of the hiftory of thofe ages, know nothing of their cuftoms, forms of fpeech, and the feveral periods they might have, by which they reckon their time, that it is rather a wonder we fhould underftand fo much of it, than that many paffages in it should

should be so dark to us. The chief use of it as to us christians, is, that from writings which the Jews acknowledged to be divinely inspired, it is manifest the Messiah was promised before the destruction of their temple ; which being done long ago, and these prophecies agreeing to our Saviour, and to no other, here is a great confirmation given to the gospel. But though many things in these books could not be understood by us who live above 3000 years after the chief of them were written, it is no such extraordinary matter.

For that of the destruction of the Canaanites by the Israelites, it is to be considered, that if God had sent a plague among them all, that could not have been found fault with. If then God had a right to take away their lives without injustice or cruelty, he had a right to appoint others to do it, as well to execute it by a more immediate way ; and the taking away people by the sword is a much gentler way of dying, than to be smitten with a plague or a famine. And for the children that were innocent of their fathers faults, God could in another state make that up to them. So all the difficulty is, why were the Israelites commanded to execute a thing of such barbarity ? But this will not seem so hard, if we consider that this was to be no precedent for future times ; since they did not do it but upon special warrant and commission from heaven, evidenced to all the world by such mighty miracles as did plainly shew, that they were particularly designed by God to be the executioners of

his

his juſtice ; and God by imploying them in ſo ſevere a ſervice, intended to poſſeſs them with great horror of idolatry, which was puniſhed in ſo extreme a manner.

For the rites of their religion, we can ill judge of them, except we perfectly underſtood the idolatries round about them, to which we find they were much inclined ; ſo they were to be bent by other rites to an extreme averſion from them : and yet by the pomp of many of their ceremonies and ſacrifices, great indulgences were given to a people naturally fond of a viſible ſplendor in religious worſhip.   In all which, if we cannot deſcend to ſuch ſatisfactory anſwers in every particular, as a curious man would deſire, it is no wonder.   The long interval of time, and other accidents, have worn out thoſe things which were neceſſary to give us a clearerer light into the meaning of them.   And for the ſtory of the creation, how far ſome things in it may be parabolical, and how far hiſtorical, has been diſputed ;•there is nothing in it that may not be hiſtorically true.   For if it be acknowledged that ſpirits can form voices in the air, for which we have as good authority as for any thing in hiſtory, then it is no wonder that Eve, being ſo lately created, might be deceived, and think a ſerpent ſpake to her, when the evil ſpirit framed the voice.

But in all theſe things I told him he was in the wrong way, when he examined the buſineſs of religion by ſome dark parts of ſcripture ; therefore I deſired him to conſider the whole contexture of

the

the chriftian religion, the rules it gives, and the methods it prefcribes. Nothing can conduce more to the peace, order, and happinefs of the world, than to be governed by its rules. Nothing is more for the intereft of every man in particular : the rules of fobriety, temperance, and moderation, were the beft prefervers of life, and which was perhaps more of health, humility, contempt of the vanities of the world, and the being well employ-ed, raifes a man's mind to a freedom from the follies and temptations that haunted the greateft part. Nothing was fo generous and great, as to fupply the neceffities of the poor, and to forgive injuries, nothing raifed and maintained a man's reputation fo much, as to be exactly juft and merciful, kind, charitable, and compaffionate, nothing opened the powers of a man's foul fo much as a calm temper, a ferene mind, free of paffion and diforder, nothing made focieties, families, and neighbourhoods fo happy as when thefe rules, which the gofpel prefcribes, took place, of doing as we would have others do to us, and loving our neighbours as ourfelves.

The chriftian worfhip was alfo plain and fimple, fuitable to fo pure a doctrine. The ceremonies of it were few and fignificant, as the admiffion to it by a wafhing with water, and the memorial of our Saviour's death in bread and wine ; the motives in it to perfuade to this purity were ftrong : that God fees us, and will judge us for all our actions : that we fhall be for ever happy or miferable,

able, as we pafs our lives here : the example of
our Savour's life, and the great expreffions of his
love in dying for us, are mighty engagements to
obey and imitate him.   The plain way of expreffion ufed by our Saviour and his apoftles, fhews
there was no artifice, where there was fo much
fimplicity ufed : there were no fecrets kept only
among the priefts, but every thing was open to all
Chriftians . the rewards of holinefs are not entirely put over to another ftate, but good men
are fpecially bleft with peace in their confciencies,
great joy in the confidence they have of the love
of God, and of feeing him for ever, and often a
fignal courfe of bleffings' follows them in their
whole lives; but if at other times calamities fell
on them, thefe were fo much mitigated by the patience they were taught, and the inward affiftances
with which they were furnifhed, that even thofe
croffes were converted to bleffings.

I defired he would lay all thefe things together, and fee what he could except to them,
to make him think this was a contrivance.   Intereft appears in all human contrivances ; our Saviour plainly had none ; he avoided applaufe,
withdrew himfelf from the offers of a crown ; he
fubmitted to poverty and reproach, and much contradiction in his life, and to a moft ignominious
and painful death.   His apoftles had none neither ;
they did not pretend either to power or wealth ;
but delivered a doctrine that muft needs condemn
them, if they ever made fuch ufe of it; they declared
their

their commiſſion fully without reſerves till other times ; they recorded their own weakneſs ; ſome of them wrought with their own hands, and when they received the charities of their converts, it was not ſo much to ſupply their own neceſſities, as to diſtribute to others : they knew they were to ſuffer much for giving their teſtimonies to what they had ſeen and heard ; in which ſo many, in a thing ſo viſible, as Chriſt's reſurrection and aſcenſion, and the effuſion of the Holy Ghoſt which he had promiſed, could not be deceived ; and they gave ſuch public confirmations of it, by the wonders they themſelves wrought, that great multitudes were converted to a doctrine, which, beſides the oppoſition it gave to luſt and paſſion, was borne down and perſecuted for three hundred years, and yet its force was ſuch, that it not only weathered out all thoſe ſtorms, but even grew and ſpread vaſtly under them. Pliny, about threeſcore years after, found their numbers great, and their lives innocent : and even Lucian, amidſt all his raillery, give a high teſtimony to their charity and contempt of life, and the other virtues of the Chriſtians, which is likewiſe more than once done by malice itſelf, Julian the apoſtate.

If a man will lay all this in one balance, and compare with it the few exceptions brought to it, he will ſoon find how ſtrong the one, and how ſlight the other are. Therefore it was an improper way, to begin at ſome cavils about ſome paſſages in the new teſtament, or the old, and from

thence

thence to prepoſſeſs one's mind againſt the whole.
The right method had been firſt to conſider the
whole matter, and from ſo general a view to deſcend to more particular enquiries : whereas they
ſuffered their minds to be foreſtalled with prejudices ;
ſo that they never examined the matter impartially.

To the greateſt part of this he ſeemed to aſſent,
only he excepted to the belief of myſteries in the
chriſtian religion ; which he thought no man could
do, ſince it is not in a man's power to believe that
which he cannot comprehend, and of which he
can have no notion. The believing myſteries, he
ſaid, made way for all the jugglings of prieſts, for
they getting the people under them in that point,
ſet out to them what they pleaſed ; and giving it
a hard name, and calling it a myſtery, the people
were tamed, and eaſily believed it. The reſtrain-
ing a man from the uſe of women, except one in
the way of marriage, and denying the remedy of
divorce, he thought unreaſonable impoſitions on
the freedom of mankind : and the buſineſs of the
clergy, and their maintenance, with the belief of
ſome authority and power, conveyed in their orders,
looked, as he thought, like a piece of contrivance ;
and why, ſaid he, muſt a man tell me, I cannot
be ſaved, unleſs I believe things againſt my reaſon, and then that I muſt pay him for telling me
of them ? Theſe were all the exceptions which
at any time I heard from him to chriſtianity ; to
which I made theſe anſwers.

For

For myfteries, it is plain there is in every thing, somewhat that is unaccountable. How animals or men are formed in their mothers bellies, how feeds grow in the earth, how the foul dwells in the body, and acts and moves it ; how we retain the figures of fo many words or things in our memories, and how we draw them out fo eafily and orderly in our thoughts or difcourfes ? how fight and hearing were fo quick and diftinct, how we move, and how bodies were compounded and united ? thefe things, if we follow them into all the difficulties that we may raife about them, will appear every whit as unaccountable as any myftery of religion ; and a blind or deaf man would judge fight or hearing as incredible as any myftery may be judged by us; for our reafon is not equal to them. In the fame rank, different degrees of age or capacity raife fome far above others, fo. that children cannot fathom the learning, nor weak perfons the councils of more illuminated minds ; therefore it was no wonder if we could not underftand the Divine Effence. We cannot imagine how two fuch different natures as a foul and body fhould fo unite together, and be mutually affected with one anothers concerns ? and how the foul has one principle of reafon, by which it acts intellectually, and another of life, by which it joins to the body and acts vitally ? two principles fo widely differing both in their nature and operation, and yet united in one and the fame perfon. There might be as many hard arguments brought againft the

poffibility

poſſibility of theſe things, which yet every one knows to be true, from ſpeculative notions, as againſt the myſteries mentioned in the ſcriptures. As that of the Trinity, that in one eſſence there are three different principles of operation, which, for want of terms fit to expreſs them by, we call perſons, and are called in ſcripture the Father, Son, and Holy Ghoſt ; and that the ſecond of theſe did unite himſelf in a moſt intimate manner with the human nature of Jeſus Chriſt ; and that the ſuffer-ings he underwent, were accepted of God as a ſacrifice for our ſins ; who thereupon conferred on him a power of granting eternal life to all that ſubmit to the terms on which he offers it ; and that the matter of which our bodies once conſiſted, which may as juſtly be called the bodies we laid down at our deaths, as theſe can be ſaid to be the bodies which we formerly lived in, being refined and made more ſpiritual, ſhall be reunited to our ſouls, and become a fit inſtrument for them in a more perfect eſtate ; and that God inwardly bends and moves our wills, by ſuch impreſſions as he can make on our bodies and minds.

Theſe, which are the chief myſteries of our religion, are neither ſo unreaſonable, that any other objection lies againſt them, but this, that they agree not with our common notions, nor ſo unaccountable, that ſomewhat like them cannot be aſſigned in other things, which are be-lieved really to be, though the manner of them cannot be apprehended : ſo this ought not to be

D

any

any juft objection to the fubmiffion of our reafon
to what we cannot fo well conceive, provided our
belief of it be well grounded. There have been
too many niceties brought indeed rather to darken
than explain thefe : they have been defended by
weak arguments, and illuftrated by fimilies not
always fo very apt and pertinent ; and new fubtilties have been added, which have rather per-
plexed than cleared them. All this cannot be
denied ; the oppofition of hereticks anticntly,
occafioned too much curiofity among the fathers,
which the fcoolmen have wonderfully advanced of
late times. But if myfteries were received, rather
in the fimplicity in which they are delivered in the
fcriptures, than according to the difcantings of
fanciful men upon them, they would not appear
much more incredible, than fome of the common
objects of fenfe and perception. And it is a needlefs fear, that if fome myfteries are acknowledged,
which are plainly mentioned in the new teftament,
it will then be in the power of the priefts to add
more at their pleafure. For it is an abfurd inference from our being bound to affent to fome
truths about the Divine Effence, of which the manner is not underftood, to argue that therefore in
an object prefented daily to our fenfes, fuch as
bread and wine, we fhould be bound to believe
againft their teftimony, that it is not what our
fenfes perceived it to be, but the whole flefh and
blood of Chrift, an entire body being in every
crumb and drop of it. It is not indeed in a man's

power

power to believe thus againſt his ſenſe and reaſon, where the objeƈt is proportioned to them, and fitly applied, and the organs are under no indiſpoſition or diſorder. It is certain that no myſtery is to be admitted, but upon very clear and expreſs authori‑ ties from ſcripture, which could not reaſonably be underſtood in any other ſenſe. And though a man cannot form an explicit notion of a my‑ ſtery, for then it would be no longer a myſtery, yet in general he may believe a thing to be, though he cannot give himſelf a particular account of the way of it ; or rather, though he cannot anſwer ſome objeƈtions which lie againſt it. We know we believe many ſuch in human matters, which are more within our reach ; and it is very unrea‑ ſonable to ſay we may not do it in divine things, which are much more above our apprehenſions.

For the ſevere reſtraint of the uſe of women, it is hard to deny that priviledge to Jeſus Chriſt as a law-giver, to lay ſuch reſtraints, as all inferior legiſlators do ; who when they find the liberties their ſubjeƈts take prove hurtful to them, ſet ſuch limits, and make ſuch regulations, as they judge neceſſary and expedient. It cannot be ſaid, but the reſtraint of appetite is neceſſary in ſome inſtances ; and if it is neceſſary in theſe, perhaps other reſtraints are no leſs neceſſary to fortify and ſecure them. For if it be acknowledged, that men have a property in their wives and daughters, ſo that to defile the one, or corrupt the other, is an unjuſt and injurious thing ; it is certain, that ex-

cept a man carefully governs his appetites, he will
break through thefe reftraints; and therefore our
Saviour knowing that nothing could effectually
deliver the world from the mifchief of unreftrained
appetite, as fuch a confinement, might very reafonably injoin it.   And in all fuch cafes we are to
balance the inconveniences on both hands, and
where we find they are heavieft, we are to acknowledge the equity of the law.   On the one hand there
is no prejudice, but the reftraint of appetite; on
the other are the mifchiefs of being given up to
pleafure, of running inordinately into it, of breaking the quiet of our own family at home, and of
others abroad; the engaging into much paffion, the
doing many falfe and impious things to compafs
what is defired, the wafte of men's eftates, time,
and health.   Now let any man judge, whether the
prejudices on this fide, are not greater than that
fingle one on the other fide, of being denied fome
pleafure? For polygamy, it is but reafonable fince
women are equally concerned in the laws of marriage, that they fhould be confidered as well as
men; but in a ftate of polygamy they are under
great mifery and jealoufy, and are indeed bar-
baroufly ufed.   Man being alfo of a fociable nature, friendfhip and converfe were among the
primitive intendments of marriage, in which, as far
as the man may excel the wife in greatnefs of mind,
and height of knowledge, the wife fomeway makes
that up with her affection and tender care; fo that
from both happily mixed, there arifes a harmony,

which

which is to virtuous minds one of the greatest
joys of life ; but all this is gone in a state of polygamy, which occasions perpetual jarrings and jea-
lousies.   And the variety does but engage men to
a freer range of pleasure, which is not to be put in
the balance with the far greater mischiefs that must
follow the other course.   So that it is plain, our
Saviour considered the nature of man, what it
could bear, and what was fit for it, when he so
restrained us in these our liberties.   And for divorce, a power to break that bond would too much
encourage married persons in the little quarrellings
that may arise between them, if it were in their
power to depart one from another.   For when they
know that cannot be, and that they must live and
die together, it does naturally incline them to lay
down their resentments, and to endeavour to live
together as well as they can.   So the law of the
gospel being a law of love, designed to engage
christians to mutual love, it was fit that all such
provisions should be made, as might advance and
maintain it, and all such liberties be taken away as
are apt to enkindle and foment strife.   This might
fall in some instances to be uneasy and hard enough;
but laws consider what falls out most commonly,
and cannot provide for all particular cases.   The
best laws are in some instances very great grie-
vances : but the advantages being balanced with the
inconveniences, measures are to be taken accordingly.   Upon this whole matter, I said, that
pleasure stood in opposition to other considerations

of

of great weight, and fo the decifion was eafy : and fince our Saviour offers us fo great rewards, it is but reafonable he have a priviledge of loading thefe promifes with fuch conditions, as are not in themfelves grateful to our natural inclinations ; for all that propofe high rewards, have thereby a right to exact difficult performances.

To this, he faid, we are fure the terms are difficult, but are not fo fure of the rewards. Upon this I told him, that we have the fame affurance of the rewards, that we have of the other parts of chriftian religion. We have the promifes of God made to us by Chrift, confirmed by many miracles: we have the earnefts of thefe, in the quiet and peace which follows a good confcience, and in the refurrection of him from the dead who hath promifed to raife us up. So that the reward is fufficiently affured to us ; and there is no reafon it fhould be given to us, before the conditions are performed on which the promifes are made. It is but reafonable we fhould truft God, and do our duty, in hopes of that eternal life, which God who cannot lie hath promifed. The difficulties are not fo great, as thofe which fometimes the commoneft concerns of life bring upon us : the learning fome trades or fciences, the governing our health and affairs, bring us often under as great ftraights : fo that it ought to be no juft prejudice, that there are fome things in religion that are uneafy, fince this is rather the effect of our corrupt natures, which are farther depraved by vicious habits, and can hardly turn to

any

any new courfe of life, without fome pain, than of the dictates of chriftianity, which are in them-felves juft and reafonable, and will be eafy to us when renewed, and in a good meafure reftored to our primitive integrity.

As for the exceptions he had to the maintenance of the clergy, and the authority to which they pretended if they ftretched their defigns too far, the gofpel did plainly reprove them for it; fo that it was very fuitable to that church, which was fo grofly faulty this way, to take the fcriptures out of the hands of the people, fince they do fo manifeftly difclaim all fuch practices.   The priefts of the true chriftian religion have no fecrets among them, which the world muft not know; but are only an order of men dedicated to God, to attend on facred things, who ought to be holy in a more peculiar manner, fince they are to handle the things of God. It was neceffary that fuch perfons fhould have a due efteem paid them, and a fit maintenance ap-pointed for them, that fo they might be preferved from the contempt that follows poverty, and the diftractions which the providing againft it might otherwife involve them in : and as in the order of the world, it was neceffary for the fupport of ma-giftracy and government, and for preferving its efteem, that fome ftate be ufed (though it is a happinefs when great men have philofophical minds to defpife the pageantry of it;) fo the plentiful fupply of the clergy, if well ufed and ap-plied by them, will certainly turn to the advantage '

D 4

of

of religion. And if some men either through ambition or covetousnefs used indirect means, or fervile compliances to afpire to fuch dignities, and
being poffeffed of them, applied their wealth either
to luxury or vain pomp, or made great fortunes
out of it for their families; thefe were perfonal
failings, in which the doctrine of Chrift was not
concerned.

He upon that told me plainly, there was nothing
that gave him, and many others, a more fecret encouragement in their ill ways, than that thofe who
pretended to believe, lived fo that they could not
be thought to be in earneft when they faid it : for
he was fure religion was either a mere contrivance,
or the moft important thing that could be ; fo that
if he once believed, he would fet himfelf in great
earneft to live fuitably to it. The afpirings that
he had obferved at court of fome of the clergy,
with the fervile ways they took to attain to preferment, and the animofities among thofe of feveral
parties about trifles, made him often think they
fufpected the things were not true, which in their
fermons and difcourfes they fo earneftly recommended. Of this he had gathered many inftances ;
I knew fome of them were miftakes and calumnies ;
yet I could not deny but fomething of them might
be too true : and I publifh this the more freely, to
put all that pretend to religion, chiefly thofe that
are dedicated to holy functions, in mind of the
great obligations that lies on them to live fuitable
to their profeffion ; fince otherwife a great deal of
the

the irreligion and atheifm that is among us, may too juftly be charged on them : for wicked men are delighted out of meafure when they difcover ill things in them, and conclude from thence, not only that they are hypocrites, but that religion itfelf is a cheat.

But I faid to him upon this head, that though no good man could continue in the practice of any known fin, yet fuch might, by the violence or furprife of a temptation, to which they are liable as much as others, be of a fudden overcome to do an ill thing, to their great grief all their life after; and then it was a very unjuft inference, upon fome few failings, to conclude that fuch men do not believe themfelves. But how bad foever many are, it cannot be denied but there are alfo many, both of the clergy and laity, who give great and real demonftrations of the power religion has over them, in their contempt of the world, the ftricknefs of their lives, their readinefs to forgive injuries, to relieve the poor, and to do good on all occafions ; and yet even thefe may have their failings, either in fuch things in which their conftitutions are weak, or their temptations ftrong and fudden ; and in all fuch cafes we are to judge of men, rather by the courfe of their lives, than by the errors that they through infirmity or furprife may have flipt into.

Thefe were the chief heads we difcourfed on ; and as far as I can remember, I have faithfully repeated the fubftance of our arguments. I have not concealed the ftrongeft things he faid to me; but

though

though I have not enlarged on all the excurfions
of his wit in fetting them off, yet I have given them
their full ftrength, as he expreffed them, and as
far as I could recollect, have ufed his own words;
fo that I am afraid fome may cenfure me for fetting down thefe things fo largely, which impious
men may make an ill ufe of, and gather together
to encourage and defend themfelves in their vices:
but if they will compare them with the anfwers
made to them, and the fenfe that fo great and refined a wit had of them afterwards, I hope they
may, through the bleffing of God, be not altogether
ineffectual.

The iffue of all our difcourfe was this; he told
me, he faw vice and impiety were as contrary to
human fociety, as wild beafts let loofe would be;
and therefore he firmly refolved to change the whole
method of his life, to become ftrictly juft and true,
to be chafte and temperate, to forbear fwearing
and irreligious difcourfe, to worfhip and pray to
his Maker; and that though he was not arrived at
a full perfuafion of chriftianity, he would never
employ his wit more to run it down, or to corrupt
others.

Of which I have fince a further affurance, from
a perfon of quality, who converfed much with him
the laft year of his life; to whom he would often
fay, that he was happy if he did believe, and that
he would never endeavour to draw him from it.

To all this I anfwered, that a virtuous life would
be very uneafy to him, unlefs vicious inclinations

were

were removed, it would otherwife be a perpetual conftraint. Nor could it be effected without an inward principle to change him ; and that was only to be had by applying himfelf to God for it in frequent and earneft prayer : and I was fure, if his mind was once cleared of thefe diforders, and cured of thofe diftempers, which vice brought on it, fo great an underftanding would foon fee through all thofe flights of wit, that do feed atheifm and irreligion which have a falfe glittering in them, that dazzles fome weak-fighted minds, who have not capacity enough to penetrate further than the furfaces of things ; and fo they ftick in thefe toyls, which the ftrength of his mind would foon break through, if it were once freed from thofe things that depreffed and darkened it.

At this pafs he was when he went from London, about the beginning of April : he had not been long in the country, when he thought he was fo well, that being to go to his eftate in Somerfetfhire, he rode thither poft. This heat and violent motion did fo inflame an ulcer that was in his bladder, that it raifed a very great pain in thofe parts ; yet he with much difficulty came back by coach to the lodge at Woodftock-park. He was then wounded both in body and mind ; he underftood phyfic and his own conftitution and diftemper fo well, that he concluded he could hardly recover ; for the ulcer broke, and vaft quantities of purulent matter paffed with his urine. But now the hand of God touched him, and as he told me, it was not only a general

dark

dark melancholy over his mind, such as he had formerly felt, but a most penetrating cutting sorrow. So that though in his body he suffered extreme pain for some weeks, yet the agonies of his mind sometimes swallowed up the sense of what he felt in his body. He told me, and gave it me in charge to tell it to one for whom he was much concerned, that though there were nothing to come after this life, yet all the pleasures he had ever known in sin, were not worth that torture he had felt in his mind. He considered he had not only neglected and dishonoured, but had openly defied his Maker, and had drawn many others into the like impieties; so that he looked on himself as one that was in great danger of being damned. He then set himself wholly to turn to God unfeignedly, and to do all that was possible in that little remainder of his life which was before him, to redeem those great portions of it that he had formerly so ill employed. The minister that attended constantly on him, was that good and worthy man Mr. Parsons, his mother's chaplain, who hath since his death preached, according to the directions he received from him, his funeral sermon; in which there are so many remarkable passages, that I shall refer my reader to them, and will repeat none of them here, that I may not thereby lessen his desire to edify himself by that excellent discourse, which hath given so great and so general a satisfaction to all good and judicious readers. I shall speak cursorily of every thing, but that which

I

I had immediately from himfelf. He was vifited every week of his ficknefs by his diocefan, that truly primitive prelate, the lord bifhop of Oxford ; who though he lived fix miles from him, yet look-ed on this as fo important a piece of his paftoral care, that he went often to him, and treated him with that decent plainnefs and freedom which is fo natural to him ; and took care alfo that he might not on terms more eafy than fafe, be at peace with himfelf. Dr. Marfhall, the learned and worthy rector of Lincoln College in Oxford, being the minifter of the parifh, was alfo frequently with him ; and by thefe helps he was fo directed and fupported, that he might not on the one hand fatisfy himfelf with too fuperficial a repentance, nor on the other hand be out of meafure oppreffed with a forrow without hope. As foon as I heard he was ill, but yet in fuch a condition that I might write to him, I wrote a letter to the beft purpofe I could. He ordered one that was then with him, to affure me it was very welcome to him ; but not fatisfied with that, he fent me an anfwer, which, as the countefs of Rochefter his mother told me, he dictated every word, and then figned it. I was once unwilling to have publifhed it, becaufe of a compliment in it to myfelf, far above my merit, and not very well fuiting with his condition.

But the fenfe he expreffes in it of the change then wrought on him, hath upon fecond thoughts prevailed with me to publifh it, leaving out what concerns myfelf.

WOODSTOCK-

WOODSTOCK-PARK, OXFORDSHIRE.

" My moſt honoured Dr. Burnett,

" **M**Y ſpirits and body decay ſo equally to-
" gether, that I ſhall write you a letter
" as week as I am in perſon. I begin to value
" churchmen above all men in the world, &c. If
" God be yet pleaſed to ſpare me longer in this world,
" I hope in your converſation to be exalted to that
" degree of piety, that the world may ſee how
" much I abhor what I ſo long loved, and how
" much I glory in repentance and in God's ſervice.
" Beſtow your prayers upon me, that God would
" ſpare me (if it be his good will) to ſhew a true
" repentance and amendment of life for the time to
" come : or elſe, if the Lord pleaſeth to put an
" end to my worldly being now, that he would
" mercifully accept of my death-bed repentance,
" and perform that promiſe that he hath been
" pleaſed to make, that at what time ſoever a ſin-
" ner doth repent, he would receive him. Put up
" theſe prayers, moſt dear doctor, to Almighty
" God, for

" YOUR MOST OBEDIENT,

" LANGUISHING SERVANT,

June 25, 1680.

ROCHESTER."

He

He told me when I faw him, that he hoped I would come to him upon that general infinuation of the defire he had of my company; and he was loth to write more plainly, not knowing whether I could eafily fpare fo much time. I told him, that on the other hand, I looked on it as a prefumption to come fo far, when he was in fuch excellent hands; and though perhaps the freedom formerly between us, might have excufed it with thofe to whom it was known, yet it might have the appearance of fo much vanity, to fuch as were ftrangers to it; fo that till I received his letter, I did not think it convenient to come to him; and then not hearing that there was any danger of a fudden change, I delayed going to him till the twentieth of July. At my coming to his houfe an accident fell out not worth mentioning, but that fome have made a ftory of it. His fervant, being a Frenchman, carried up my name wrong, fo that he miftook it for another, who had fent to him, that he would undertake his cure, and he being refolved not to meddle with him, did not care to fee him: this miftake lafted fome hours, with which I was the better contented, becaufe he was not then in fuch a condition, that my being about him could have been of any ufe to him; for that night was like to have been his laft. He had a convulfion fit, and raved; but opiates being given him, after fome hours reft, his raving left him fo entirely, that it never again returned to him.

I

I cannot eafily exprefs the tranfport he was in, when he awoke and faw me by him ; he broke out in the tendereft expreffions concerning my kindnefs in coming fo far to fee fuch a one, ufing terms of great abhorrence concerning himfelf, which I forbear to relate. He told me, as his ftrength ferved him at feveral fnatches, for he was then fo low, that he could not hold up difcourfe long at once, what fenfe he had of his paft life ; what fad apprehenfion for having fo offended his Maker, and difhonoured his Redeemer ; what horrors he had gone through, and how much his mind was turned to call on God, and on his crucified Saviour, fo that he hoped he fhould obtain mercy, for he believed he had fincerely repented, and had now a calm in his mind after that ftorm that he had been in for fome weeks. He had ftrong apprehenfions and perfuafions of his admittance to heaven, of which he fpake once, not without fome extraordinary emotion. It was indeed the only time that he fpake with any great warmth to me ; for his fpirits were then low, and fo far fpent, that though thofe about him told me he had expreffed formerly great fervour in his devotions ; yet nature was fo much funk, that thefe were in a great meafure fallen off. But he made me pray often with him ; and fpoke of his converfion to God, as a thing now grown up in him to a fettled and calm ferenity. He was very anxious to know my opinion of a death-bed repentance. I told him, that before I gave any refolution in that, it would

be

be convenient that I fhould be acquainted more
particularly with the circumftances and progrefs of
his repentance.

Upon this he satisfied me in many particulars.
He faid, he was now perfuaded both of the truth of
chriftianity, and of the power of inward grace, of
which he gave me this ftrange account. He faid,
Mr. Parfons, in order to his conviction, read to him
the fifty-third chapter of the prophecy of Ifaiah, and
compared that with the hiftory of our Saviour's
paffion, that he might there fee a prophecy concerning it, written many ages before it was done ;
which the Jews that blafphemed Jefus Chrift ftill
kept in their hands, as a book divinely infpired.
He faid to me, that as he heard it read, he felt an
inward force upon him, which did fo enlighten his
mind, and convince him, that he could refift it
no longer ; for the words had an authority which
did fhoot like rays or beams in his mind, fo that
he was not only convinced by the reafonings he had
about it, which fatisfied his underftanding, but by
a power which did fo effectually conftrain him,
that he did ever after as firmly believe in his Saviour, as if he had feen him in the clouds. He
had made it to be read fo often to him, that he had
got it by heart, and went through a great part of
it in difcourfe with me, with a fort of heavenly
pleafure, giving me his reflections on it. Some
few I remember, *Who hath believed our report ?*
(verfe 1.) Here, he faid, was foretold the oppofition the gofpel was to meet with from fuch

E   wretches

wretches as he was.   *He hath no form nor comeliness,
and when we shall see him, there is no beauty that we
should desire him,* (verse 2.)   On this, he said, the
meanness of his appearance and person has made
vain and foolish people disparage him, because he
came not in such a fool's coat as they delight in.
What he said on the other parts I do not well remember; and indeed, I was so affected with what he
said then to me, that the general transport I was
under during the whole discourse, made me less
capable to remember these particulars, as I wish I
had done.

He told me, that he had thereupon received the
sacrament with great satisfaction, and that was
encreased by the pleasure he had in his lady's receiving it with him; who had been for some years
misled into the communion of the church of Rome,
and he himself had been not a little instrumental in
procuring it, as he freely acknowledged: so that
it was one of the joyfullest things that befell him in
his sickness, that he had seen that mischief removed, in which he had so great a hand : and during
his whole sickness, he expressed so much tenderness and true kindness to his lady, that as it easily
defaced the remembrance of every thing wherein he
had been in fault formerly, so it drew from her
the most passionate care and concern for him that
was possible, which indeed deserves a higher character than is decent to give of a person yet alive :
but I shall confine my discourse to the dead.

He

He told me, he had overcome all his resentments to all the world, so that he bore ill-will to no
person, nor hated any upon personal accounts.
He had given a true state of his debts, and had
ordered to pay them all, as far as his estate that
was not settled could go ; and was confident, that
if all that was owing to him were paid to his executors, his creditors would be all satisfied.   He
said, he found his mind now possessed with another
sense of things, than ever he had formerly.   He
did not repine under all his pain, and in one of
the sharpest fits he was under while I was with
him, he said, he did willingly submit ; and looking up to heaven, said, " God's holy will be done,
" I bless him for all he does to me."   He pro-
fessed, he was contented either to die or live, as
should please God ; and though it was a foolish
thing for a man to pretend to chuse whether he
would die or live, yet he wished rather to die.
He knew he could never be so well that life
should be comfortable to him.   He was confident
he should be happy if he died, but he feared if he
lived he might relapse ; and then said he to me,
in what a condition shall I be, if I relapse after all
this ? but, he said, he trusted in the grace and
goodness of God, and was resolved to avoid all
those temptations, that course of life and company,
that was likely to ensnare him : and he desired to
live on no other account, but that he might by
the change of his manners some way take off the
high scandal his former behaviour had given.

                                All

All thefe things at feveral times I had from him, befides fome meffages which very well became a dying penitent to fome of his former friends, and a charge to publifh any thing concerning him, that might be a mean to reclaim others. Praying God, that as his life had done much hurt, fo his death might do fome good.

Having underftood all thefe things from him, and being preffed to give him my opinion plainly about his eternal ftate ; I told him, that though the promifes of the gofpel did all depend upon a real change of heart and life, as the indifpenfible condition upon which they were made ; and that it was fcarce poffible to know certainly whether our hearts are changed, unlefs it appeared in our lives ; and the repentance of moft dying men, being like the howlings of condemned prifoners for pardon, which flowed from no fenfe of their crimes, but from the horror of approaching death ; there was little reafon to encourage any to hope much from fuch forrowing ; yet certainly, if the mind of a finner, even on a death-bed, be truly renewed and turned to God, fo great is his mercy, that he will receive him, even in that extremity. He faid, he was fure his mind was entirely turned, and though horror had given him his firft awaking, yet that was now grown up into a fettled faith and converfion.

There is but one prejudice lies againft all this, to defeat the good ends of divine providence by it upon others, as well as on himfelf ; and that is,

that

that it was a part of his difeafe, and that the lownefs of his fpirits made fuch an alteration in him, that he was not what he had formerly been; and this fome have carried fo far as to fay, that he died mad; thefe reports are raifed by thofe who are unwilling that the laft thoughts or words of a perfon, every way fo extraordinary, fhould have any effect either on themfelves or others; and it is to be feared, that fome have fo far feared their confciences, and exceeded the common meafures of fin and infidelity, that neither this teftimony, nor one coming from the dead, would fignify much towards their conviction.   That this lord was either mad or ftupid, is a thing fo notorioufly untrue, that it is the greateft impudence for any that were about him, to report it, and a very unreafonable credulity in others to believe it.   All the while I was with him, after he had flept out the diforders of the fit he was in the firft night, he was not only without ravings, but had a clearnefs in his thoughts, in his memory, in his reflections on things and perfons, far beyond what I ever faw in a perfon fo low in his ftrength.   He was not able to hold out long in difcourfe, for his fpirits failed; but once for a half hour, and often for a quarter of an hour after he awaked, he had a vivacity in his difcourfe that was extraordinary, and in all things like himfelf.   He called often for his children, his fon, the now earl of Rochefter, and his three daughters, and fpake to them with a fenfe and feeling that cannot be expreffed in writing.

E 3

He

He called me once to look on them all, and said,
" see how good God has been to me, in giving me
" so many blessings, and I have carried myself to
" him like an ungracious and unthankful dog. "
He once talked a great deal to me of public affairs,
and of many persons and things with the same
clearness of thought and expression, that he had
ever done before : so that by no sign but his weakness of body, and giving over discourse so soon,
could I perceive a difference between what his
parts formerly were, and what they were then.

And that wherein the presence of his mind
appeared most, was in the total change of an ill
habit grown so much upon him, that he could
hardly govern himself when he was any ways
heated three minutes without falling into it, I
mean swearing. He had acknowledged to me the
former winter, that he abhorred it, as a base and
indecent thing, and had set himself much to break
it off ; but he confessed, that he was so over-
powered by that ill custom, that he could not
speak with any warmth, without repeated oaths,
which upon any sort of provocation, came almost
naturally from him ; but in his last remorses this
did so sensibly affect him, that by a resolute and
constant watchfulness, the habit of it was perfectly
mastered ; so that upon the returns of pain, which
were very severe and frequent upon him the last
day I was with him, or upon such displeasures as
people sick or in pain are apt to take of a sudden
at those about them ; on all these occasions he
never swore an oath all the while I was there.

Once

Once he was offended with the delay of one he thought made not haste enough with somewhat he called for, and said in a little heat, " that " damned fellow : " soon after, I told him, I was glad to find his style so reformed, and that he had so entirely overcome that ill habit of swearing; only that word of calling any damned, which had returned upon him, was not decent.   His answer was, " Oh that language of friends which was so " familiar to me, hangs yet about me : sure none has " deserved more to be damned than I have done. " And after he had humbly asked God pardon for it, he desired me to call the person to him, that he might ask him forgiveness; but I told him that was needless, for he had said it of one that did not hear it, and so could not be offended by it.

In this disposition of mind did he continue all the while I was with him, four days together ; he was then brought so low, that all hopes of recovery were gone.   Much purulent matter came from him with his urine, which he passed always with some pain, but one day with inexpressible torment; yet he bore it decently, without breaking out into repinings, or impatient complaints. He imagined he had a stone in his passage, but it being searched, none was found.   The whole substance of his body was drained by the ulcer, and nothing was left but skin and bone, and by lying much on his back, the parts there began to mortify : but he had been formerly so low, that he seemed as much past all hopes of life as now;

E 4

which

which made him one morning, after a full and sweet night's rest procured by laudanum, given him without his knowledge, to fancy it was an effort of nature, and to begin to entertain some hopes of recovery : for he said, he felt himself perfectly well, and that he had nothing ailing him, but an extreme weaknefs, which might go off in time ; and then he entertained me with the scheme he had laid down for the rest of his life, how retired, how strict, and how studious he intended to be ; but this was soon over, for he quickly felt, that it was only the effect of a good sleep, and that he was still in a very desperate state.

I thought to have left him on Friday, but not without some paffion he defired me to stay that day ; there appeared no symptom of present death ; and a worthy physician then with him, told me, that though he was so low, that an accident might carry him away on a sudden ; yet without that, he thought he might live yet some weeks. So on Saturday, at four of the clock in the morning, I left him, being the 24th of July. But I durst not take leave of him ; for he had exprefled so great an unwillingnefs to part with me the day before, that if I had not prefently yielded to one day's stay, it was like have given him some trouble, therefore I thought it better to leave him without any formality. Some hours after he afked for me, and when it was told him, I was gone, he feemed to be troubled, and faid, " has my friend left me, then I " fhall die fhortly." After that, he fpake but once

or twice till he died: he lay much filent; once
they heard him praying very devoutly.   And.
on Monday about two of the clock in the morning
he died, without any convulfion, or fo much as
a groan.

The CONCLUSION.

THUS he lived, and thus he died in the
three and thirtieth year of his age.   Náture had fitted him for great things, and his
knowledge and obfervation qualified him to have
been one of the moft extraordinary men, not only
of his nation, but of the age he lived in; and I do
verily believe, that if God had thought fit to have
continued him longer in the world, he had been
the wonder and delight of all that knew him: but
the infinite wife God knew better what was fit for
him, and what the age deferved.   For men who
have fo caft off all fenfe of God and religion, deferve
not fo fignal a blefling, as the example and conviction which the reft of his life might have given
them.   And I am apt to think that the Divine
Goodnefs took pity on him, and feeing the fincerity of his repentance, would try and venture him
no more in circumftances of temptation, perhaps
too hard for human frailty.   Now he is at reft,
and I am very confident enjoys the fruits of his
late, but fincere repentance.   But fuch as live,
and ftill go on in their fins and impieties, and will

not

not be awakened neither by this nor the other alarms that are about their ears, are, it feems, given up by God to a judicial hardnefs and impenitency.

Here is a public inftance of one who lived of their fide, but could not die of it : and though none of all our libertines underftood better than he, the fecret myfteries of fin, had more ftudied every thing that could fupport a man in it, and had more refifted all external means of conviction than he had done ; yet when the hand of God inwardly touched him, he could no longer kick againft thofe pricks, but humbled himfelf under that mighty hand, and as he ufed often to fay in his prayers, he who had fo often denied him, found then no other fhelter but his mercies and compaffions.

I have written this account with all the tendernefs and caution I could ufe, and in whatfoever I may have failed, I have been ftrict in the truth of what I have related, remembering that of Job, " will ye lie for God ? " Religion has ftrength and evidence enough in itfelf, and needs no fupport from lies, and made ftories.   I do not pretend to have given the formal words that he faid, though I have done that where I could remember them. But I have written this with the fame fincerity, that I would have done, had I known I had been to die immediately after I had finifhed it.   I did not take notes of our difcourfes laft winter after we parted ; fo I may have perhaps in the fetting out of my anfwers to him, have enlarged on fe

veral

veral things both more fully and more regularly, than I could fay them in fuch free difcourfes as we had. I am not fo fure of all I fet down as faid by me, as I am of all faid by him to me; but yet the fubftance of the greateft part, even of that, is the fame.

It remains, that I humbly and earneftly befeech all that fhall take this book in their hands, that they will confider it entirely, and not reft fome parts to an ill intention. God the fearcher of hearts, knows with what fidelity I have writ it: but if any will drink up only the poifon that may be in it, without taking alfo the antidote here given to thofe ill principles; or confidering the fenfe that this great perfon had of them, when he reflected ferioufly on them; and will rather confirm themfelves in their ill ways, by the fcruples and objections which I fet down, than be edified by the other parts of it; as I will look on it as a great infelicity, that I fhould have faid any thing that may ftrengthen them in their impieties, fo the fincerity of my intentions will, I doubt not, ex- cufe me at his hands, to whom I offer up this fmall fervice.

I have now performed in the beft manner I could, what was left on me by this noble lord, and have done with the part of an hiftorian. I fhall, in the next place fay fomewhat as a divine. So ex- traordinary a text does almoft force a fermon, though it is plain enough itfelf, and fpeaks with fo loud a voice, that thofe who are not awakened

by

by it, will perhaps confider nothing that I can fay. If our libertines will become fo far fober as to examine their former courfe of life, with that difengagement and impartiality, which they muft acknowledge a wife man ought to ufe in things of greateft confequence, and balance the account of what they have got by their debaucheries, with the mifchiefs they have brought on themfelves and others by them, they will foon fee what a bad bargain they have made. Some diverfion, mirth, and pleafure is all they can promife themfelves; but to obtain this, how many evils are they to fuffer? How have many wafted their ftrength, brought many difeafes on their bodies, and precipitated their age in the purfuit of thofe things? And as they bring old age early on themfelves, fo it becomes a miferable ftate of life to the greateft part of them; gouts, ftranguries, and other infirmities, being fevere reckonings for their paft follies; not to mention the more loathfome difeafes, with their no lefs loathfome and troublefome cures, which they muft often go through, who deliver themfelves up to forbidden pleafures. Many are disfigured befide with the marks of their intemperance and lewdnefs, and which is yet fadder, an infection is derived oftentimes on their innocent but unhappy iffue, who being defcended from fo vitiated an original, fuffer for their exceffes. Their fortunes are profufely wafted, both by their neglect of their affairs, they being fo buried in vice, that they cannot employ either their time or fpirits,

fo

so much exhausted by intemperance, to consider them; and by that prodigal expence which their lusts put them upon. They suffer no less in their credit, the chief mean to recover an entangled estate; for that irregular expence forces them to so many mean shifts, makes them so often false to all their promises and resolutions, that they must needs feel how much they have lost that, which a gentleman, and men of ingenuous tempers, do sometimes prefer even to life itself, their honour and reputation. Nor do they suffer less in the nobler powers of their minds, which, by a long course of such dissolute practices, come to sink and degenerate so far, that not a few whose first blossoms gave the most promising hopes, have so withered, as to become incapable of great and generous undertakings, and to be disabled to every thing, but to wallow like swine in the filth of sensuality, their spirits being dissipated, and their minds so benummed, as to be wholly unfit for business, and even indisposed to think.

That this dear price should be paid for a little wild mirth, or gross and corporal pleasure, is a thing of such unparalelled folly, that if there were not too many such instances before us, it might seem incredible. To all this we must add the horrors that their ill actions raise in them, and the hard shifts they are put to to stave off these, either by being perpetually drunk or mad, or by an habitual disuse of thinking and reflecting on their actions, and (if these arts will not perfectly quiet

them)

them) by taking sanctuary in such atheistical principles, as may at least mitigate the sourness of their
thoughts, though they cannot absolutely settle their
minds.

If the state of mankind and human societies are
considered, what mischiefs can be equal to those
which follow these courses. Such persons are a
plague where ever they come, they can neither be
trusted nor beloved, having cast off both truth and
goodness, which procure confidence and attract
love; they corrupt some by their ill practices,
and do irreparable injuries to the rest, they run
great hazards, and put themselves to much trouble, and all this to do what is in their power to
make damnation as sure to themselves as possibly
they can. What influence this has on the whole
nation is but too visible; how the bonds of nature,
wedlock, and all other relations are quite broken:
virtue is thought an antick piece of formality,
and religion the effect of cowardice or knavery;
these are the men that would reform the world, by
bringing it under a new system of intellectual and
moral principles; but bate them a few bold and
lewd jests, what have they ever done, or designed
to do, to make them to be remembered, except it
be with detestation? They are the scorn of the present age, and their names must rot in the next.
Here they have before them an instance of one,
who was deeply corrupted with the contagion which
he first derived from others, but unhappily heightened it much himself. He was a master indeed

and

and not a bare trifler with wit, as some of those are who repeat, and that but scurvily, what they may have heard from him or some others, and with impudence and laughter will face the world down, as if they were to teach it wisdom; who, God knows, cannot follow one thought a step further than as they have conned it; and take from them their borrowed wit and mimical humour, and they will presently appear, what they indeed are, the least and lowest of men.

If they will, or if they can, think a little, I wish they would consider, that by their own principles they cannot be sure that religion is only a contrivance; all they pretend to is only to weaken some arguments that are brought for it; but they have not brow enough to say, they can prove that their own principles are true, so that at most they bring their cause no higher, than that it is possible religion may not be true. But still it is possible it may be true, and they have no shame left that will deny that it is also probable it may be true; and if so, then what mad men are they who run so great a hazard for nothing? By their own confession, it may be there is a God, a judgment, and a life to come, and if so, then he that believes these things, and lives according to them, as he enjoys a long course of health and quiet of mind, an innocent relish of many true pleasures, and the serenities which virtue raises in him, with the good-will and friendship which it procures him from others; so when he dies, if these things prove

mistakes,

mistakes, he does not out-live his error, nor shall it afterwards raise trouble or disquiet in him, if he then ceases to be; but if these things be true, he shall be infinitely happy in that state, where his present small services shall be so excessively re-warded. The libertines, on the other side, as they know they must die, so the thoughts of death must be always melancholly to them; they can have no pleasant view of that which yet they know can-not be very far from them: the least painful idea they can have of it is, that it is an extinction and ceasing to be, but they are not sure even of that; some secret whispers within make them, whether they will or not, tremble at the apprehensions of another state; neither their tinsel wit, nor super-ficial learning, nor their impotent assaults upon the weak side, as they think, of religion, nor the boldest notions of impiety, will hold them up then. Of all which, I now present so lively an instance, as perhaps history can scarce parallel.

Here were parts so exalted by nature, and im-proved by study, and yet so corrupted and debased by irreligion and vice, that he who was made to be one of the glories of his age, was become a proverb, and if his repentance had not interposed, would have been one of the greatest reproaches of it. He knew well the small strength of that weak cause, and at first despised, but afterwards ab-horred it. He felt the mischiefs, and saw the mad-ness of it; and therefore though he lived to the scandal of many, he died as much to the edification

of

of all thofe who faw him, and becaufe they were but a fmall number, he defired that he might even when dead, yet fpeak. He was willing nothing fhould be concealed that might caft reproach on himfelf and on fin, and offer up glory to God and religion. So that though he lived a hainous finner, yet he died a moft exemplary penitent.

It would be a vain and ridiculous inference for any, from hence to draw arguments about the abftrufe fecrets of predeftination, and to conclude, that if they are of the number of the elect, they may live as they will, and that Divine Grace will at fome time or other violently conftrain them, and irrefiftably work upon them. But as St. Paul was called to that eminent fervice for which he was appointed, in fo ftupendious a manner as is no warrant for others to expect fuch a vocation; fo, if upon fome fignal occafions fuch converfions fall out, which, how far they are fhort of miracles, I fhall not determine, it is not only a vain, but a pernicious imagination, for any to go on in their ill ways upon a fond conceit and expectation that the like will befal them : for whatfoever God's extraordinary dealings with fome may be, we are fure his common way of working is, by offering thefe things to our rational faculties, which, by the affiftances of his grace, if we improve them all we can, fhall be certainly effectual for our reformation ; and if we neglect or abufe thefe, we put ourfelves beyond the common methods of God's mercy, and have no reafon to expect that wonders

F

fhould

fhould be wrought for our conviction; which, though they fometimes happen, that they may give an effectual alarm for the awaking of others, yet it would deftroy the whole defign of religion, if men fhould depend upon, or look for fuch an extraordinary and forcible operation of God's grace.

And I hope, that thofe, who have had fome fharp reflections on their paft life, fo as to be refolved to forfake their ill courfes, will not take the leaft encouragement to themfelves in that defperate and unreafonable refolution of putting off their repentance till they can fin no longer, from the hopes I have expreffed of this lord's obtaining mercy at the laft, and from thence prefume, that they alfo fhall be received when they turn to God on their death-beds: for what mercy foever God may fhew to fuch as really were never inwardly touched before that time; yet there is no reafon to think, that thofe who have dealt fo difingenuoufly with God and their own fouls, as defignedly to put off their turning to him upon fuch confiderations, fhould then be accepted with him. They may die fuddenly, or by a difeafe that may fo diforder their underftandings, that they fhall not be in any capacity of reflecting on their paft lives. The inward converfion of our minds is not fo in our power, that it can be effected without divine grace affifting; and there is no reafon for thofe who have neglected thefe affiftances all their lives, to expect them in fo extraordinary a manner at their death. Nor can one, efpecially in a ficknefs that is

quick

quick and critical, be able to do thofe things that
are often indifpenfably neceffary to make his repentance complete; and even in a longer difeafe,
in which there are larger opportunities for thefe
things. Yet there is great reafon to doubt of a
repentance, begun and kept up merely by terror,
and not from any ingenuous principle. In which,
though 1 will not take on me to limit the mercies
of God, which are boundlefs, yet this muft be
confeffed, that to delay repentance with fuch a
defign, is to put the greateft concernment we have,
upon the moft dangerous and defperate iffue that is
poffible.

But they that will ftill go on in their fins, and be
fo partial to them, as to ufe all endeavours to
ftrengthen themfelves in their evil courfe, even by
thefe very things which the providence of God fets
before them for the cafting down of thefe ftrong
holds of fin : what is to be faid to fuch ? it is to be
feared, that if they obftinately perfift, they will by
degrees come within that curfe, *He that is unjuft, let
him be unjuft ftill : and he that is filthy, let him be
filthy ftill. But if our gofpel is hid, it is hid to them
that are loft, in whom the god of this world hath blinded
the minds of them which believe not, left the light of the
glorious gofpel of Chrift, who is the image of God, fhould
fhine unto them.*

A SERMON

PREACHED AT THE

FUNERAL

Of the Right Honourable

JOHN Earl of Rocheſter,

Who died at Woodſtock-Park, the 26th of July, 1680, and was buried at Spilſbury, in Oxfordſhire, the 9th day of Auguſt.

By ROBERT PARSONS, M. A. Chaplain to the Right Honourable Anne, Counteſs of Rocheſter.

ADVERTISEMENT.

ALL the lewd and profane poems and libels
of the late lord Rochefter, having been (contrary
to his dying requeft, and in defiance of religion,
government, and common decency) publifhed to
the world; and (for the eafier and furer propaga-
tion of vice) printed in penny-books, and cried
about the ftreets of this honourable city, without
any offence or diflike taken at them : it is humbly
hoped that this fhort difcourfe, which gives a true
account of the death and repentance of that noble
lord, may likewife (for the fake of his name)
find a favourable reception among fuch perfons;
though the influence of it cannot be fuppofed to
reach as far as the poifon of the other books is
fpread; which by the ftrength of their own virulent corruption, are capable of doing more mifchief
than all the plays, and fairs, and ftews, in and
about this town can do together.

I say unto you, that likewise joy shall be in heaven over one sinner that repenteth, more than over ninety and nine just persons that need no repentance.

IF ever there were a subject that might deserve and exhaust all the treasures of religious eloquence in the description of so great a man, and so great a sinner as now lies before us ; together with the wonders of the Divine Goodness, in making him as great a penitent ; I think the present occasion affords one as remarkable as any place or age can produce.

Indeed, so great and full a matter it is, that it is too big to come out of my mouth, and perhaps not all of it fit or needful so to do. The greatness of his parts are well enough known, and of his sins too well in the world ; and neither my capacity, nor experience, nor my profession, will allow me to be so proper a judge either of the one or the other. Only as God has been pleased to make me a long while a sad spectator, and a secret mourner for his sins, so as he at last graciously heard the prayers of his nearest relations and true friends, for his conversion and repentance : and it is the good tidings of that especially which God has done for his soul, that I am now to publish and tell abroad to the world, not only by the obligations of mine office, in which I had the honour to be a weak minifter to it, but by his own exprefs and dying commands.

Now although, to defcribe this worthily, would require a wit equal to that with which he lived, and a devotion too equal to that with which he died, and to match either would be a very hard tafk ; yet befides that, I am not fufficient for thefe things, (for who is ?) and that my thoughts have been rather privately bufied to fecure a real repentance to himfelf whilft living, than to publifh it abroad to others in an artificial drefs after he is dead : I fay, befides all this, I think I fhall have lefs need to call in the aids of fecular eloquence. The proper habit of repentance is not fine linen, or any delicate array, fuch as are ufed in the court, or kings houfes, but fack-cloth and afhes : and the way which God Almighty takes to convey it, is not by the words of man's wifdom, but by the plainnefs of his written word, affifted by the inward power and demonftration of the Spirit : and the effects it works, and by which it difcovers itfelf, are not any raptures of wit and fancy ; but the moft humble proftrations both of foul and fpirit, and the captivating all human imaginations-to the obedience of a defpifed religion and a crucified Saviour.

And it is in this array I intend to bring out this penitent to you ; an array which I am fure he more valued, and defired to appear in, both to God and the world, than in all the triumphs of wit and gallantry ; and therefore, (waving all thefe rhetorical
flourifhes,

flourishes, as beneath the folemnity of the occafion, and the majefty of that great and weighty truth I am now to deliver) I fhall content myfelf with the office of a plain hiftorian, to relate faithfully and impartially what I faw and heard, efpecially during his penitential forrows; which, if all that hear me this day had been fpectators of, there would then been no need of a fermon to convince men; but every man would have been as much a preacher to him-felf of this truth, as I am, except thefe forrows: and yet even thefe forrows fhould be turned into joys too, if we would only do what we pray for, that the will of God may be done in earth as it is in heaven; for fo our bleffed Lord affures us; "I fay "unto you, that likewife joy fhall be in heaven over "one finner that repenteth, &c." From which I fhall confider,

I. The finner particularly that is before us.

II. The repentance of this finner, together with the means, the time, and all probable fincerity of it.

III. The joy that is in heaven, and fhould be on earth, for the repentance of this finner.

IV. I fhall apply myfelf to all that hear me; that they would join in this joy, in praife and thankf-giving to God, for the converfion of this finner; and if there be any that have been like him in their fins, that they would alfo fpeedily imitate him in their repentance.

And

And 1. Let us confider the perfon before us, as he certainly was a great finner.   But becaufe man was upright before he was a finner, and to mea-fure the greatnefs of his fall, it will be neceffary to take a view of that heighth from which he fell; give me leave to go back a little, to look into the rock from which he was hewn, the quality, family, education, and perfonal accomplifhments of this great man.   In doing of which, I think no man will charge me with any defign of cuftomary flat-tery, or formality; fince I intend only thereby to fhew the greatnefs and unhappinefs of his folly, in the perverting fo many excellent abilities and ad-vantages for virtue and piety in the fervice of fin, and fo becoming a more univerfal, infinuating, and prevailing example of it.

As for his family, on both fides, from which he was defcended, they were fome of the moft famous in their generations.   His grandfather was that ex-cellent and truly great man, Charles lord Wilmot, vifcount Athlone in Ireland.   Henry his father, who inherited the fame title and greatnefs, was by his late majefty, king Charles I. created baron of Adderbury, in Oxfordfhire, and by his prefent majefty, earl of Rochefter.   He was a man of fignal loyalty and integrity indeed; and of fuch courage and conduct in military affairs, as became a great general.   His mother was the relict of fir Francis Henry Lee, of Ditchly, in the county of Oxford, baronet, grandmother to the prefent right honour-able earl of Litchfield, and the daughter of that

generous

generous and honourable gentleman fir John St. Johns, of Lyddiard, in the county of Wilts, baronet, whofe family was fo remarkable for loyalty, that feveral of his fons willingly offered themfelves in the day of battle, and died for it ; and whilft the memory of the Englifh or Irifh rebellion lafts, that family cannot want a due veneration in the minds of any perfon, that loves either God or the king.

As for his education, it was in Wadham College, Oxford, under the care of that wife and excellent governor Dr. Blandford, the late bifhop of Worcefter ; there it was that he laid a good foundation of learning and ftudy, though he afterwards built upon that foundation hay and ftubble. There he firft fucked from the breaft of his mother the univerfity, thofe perfections of wit, and eloquence, and poetry, which afterwards, by his own corrupt ftomach, where turned into poifon to himfelf and others ; which certainly can be no more a blemifh to thofe illuftrious feminaries of piety and good learning, than a difobedient child is to a wife and virtuous father, or the fall of man to the excellency of Paradife.

A wit he had fo rare and fruitful in its invention, and withal fo choice and delicate in its judgment, that there is nothing wanting in his compofures to give a full anfwer to that queftion, What and where wit is ? except the purity and choice of fubject. For had fuch excellent feeds but fallen upon good ground, and inftead of pitching upon a beaft, or a luft, been raifed up on high, to celebrate the

myfteries

myſteries of the divine love, in pſalms, and hymns, and ſpiritual ſongs ; I perſuade myſelf we might by this time have received from his pen, as excellent an idea of divine poetry, under the goſpel, uſeful to the teaching of virtue, eſpecially in this generation, as his profane verſes have been to deſtroy it. And 1 am confident, had God ſpared him a longer life, this would have been the whole buſineſs of it, as I know it was the vow and purpoſe of his ſickneſs.

His natural talent was excellent, but he had hugely improved it by learning and induſtry, being thoroughly acquainted with all claſſick authors, both Greek and Latin ; a thing very rare, if not peculiar to him among thoſe of his quality, which yet he uſed not, as other poets have done, to tranſlate or ſteal from them ; but rather to better and improve them by his own natural fancy.   And whoever reads his compoſures, will find all things in them ſo peculiarly great, new and excellent, that he will eaſily pronounce, that though he has lent to many others, yet he has borrowed of none ; ·and that he has been as far from a ſordid imitation of thoſe before him, as he will be from being reached by thoſe that follow him.

His other perſonal accompliſhments in all the perfections of a gentleman, for the court or country, whereof he was known of all men to be a very great maſter, is no part of my buſineſs to. deſcribe or underſtand ; and whatever they were in themſelves, I am ſure they were but miſerable comfor

ters

ters to him, fince they only miniftered to his fins, and made his example the more fatal and dangerous; for fo we may own, (nay, I am obliged by him not to hide, but to fhew the rocks which others may avoid) that he was once one of the greateft of finners.

And truly none but one fo great in parts could be fo. His fins were like his parts, from which they fprang, all of them high and extraordinary. He feemed to affect fomething fingular and paradoxical in his impieties, as well as in his writings, above the reach and thought of other men ; taking as much pains to draw others in, and to pervert the right ways of virtue, as the apoftles and primitive faints did to fave their own fouls, and them that heard them. For this was the heightening and amazing circumftance of his fins, that he was fo diligent and induftrious to recommend and propagate them ; not like thofe of old that hated the light, but thofe the prophet mentions, Ifaiah iii. 9. " Who " declare their fins as Sodom, and hide it not ; that " take it upon their fhoulders, and bind it to them " as a crown ; " framing arguments for fin, making profelytes to it, and writing panegyricks upon vice.

Nay, fo confirmed was he in fin, that he oftentimes almoft died a martyr for it. God was pleafed fometimes to punifh him with the effects of his folly, yet till now (he confeffed) they had no power to melt him into true repentance ; or if at any time he had fome lucid intervals from his folly

and

and madnefs, yet (alas) how fhort and tranfitory were they ? All that goodnefs was but as a morning cloud, and as the early dew which vanifhes away ; he ftill returned to the fame excefs of riot, and that with fo much the more greedinefs, the longer he had fafted from it.

And yet even this defperate finner, that one would think had made a covenant with death, and was at an agreement with hell, and juft upon the brink of them both ; God, to magnify the riches of his grace and mercy, was pleafed to fnatch as a brand out of the fire.   As St. Paul, though " before " a blafphemer, a perfecutor, an injurious, yet ob- " tained mercy, that in him Chrift Jefus might " fhew forth all long-fuffering, for a pattern to " them that fhould hereafter believe on him to " everlafting life. " 1 Tim. i. 13, 16.   So God ftruck him to the ground as it were by a light from heaven, and a voice of thunder round about him : infomuch that now the fcales fall from his eyes, as they did from St. Paul's ; his ftony heart was opened, and ftreams of tears gufhed out, the bitter but wholefome tears of true repentance.

And, that this may appear to be fo, I think it neceffary to account for thefe two things.

I. For the means of it ; that it was not barely the effect of ficknefs, or the fear of death ; but the hand of God alfo working in them and by them manifeftly.

II. For the fincerity of it ; which though none but God that fees the heart, can tell certainly,

yet

yet man even alfo may and ought to believe it; not only in the judgment of charity, but of moral juftice, from all evident figns of it, which were poffible to be given by one in his condition.

And 1ft. For the means or method of his repentance. That which prepared the way for it was a fharp and painful ficknefs, with which God was pleafed to vifit him; the way which the Almighty often takes to reduce the wandering finner to the knowledge of God and himfelf. "I will be unto "Ephraim as a lion, and as a young lion unto "the houfe of Judah; I, even I, will tear and go "away, and none fhall relieve him; I will go and "return to my place, till they acknowledge their "offence, and feek my face; and in their affliction "they will feek me early." Hof. v. 14, 15.

And though to forfake our fins then, when we can no longer enjoy them, feems to be rather the effect of impotency and neceffity, than of choice, and fo not fo acceptable or praife-worthy; yet we find, God Almighty often ufes the one to bring about the other; and improves a forced abftinence from fin, into a fettled loathing and a true deteftation of it.

It is true, there are fuch ftubborn natures, that like clay, are rather hardened by the fire of afflictions; ungracious children, that fly in the face of their heavenly father in the very inftant when he is correcting them; or it may be like thofe children who promife wonders then, but prefently after forget all. Such as thefe we have defcribed,

Pfal.

Pfal. lxxviii. 34, 35, 36, 37. " When he flew
" them, then they fought him, and they returned
" and enquired early after God ; then they remem-
" bered that God was their rock, and that the
" high God was their Redeemer ; neverthelefs they
" did but flatter him with their mouth, and lyed
" unto him with their tongues, for their heart was
" not right with him, neither continued they fted-
" faft in his covenant. " And it is probable
this has been the cafe formerly of this perfon.
But there was an evident difference betwixt the
effects of this ficknefs upon him, and many others
before : he had other fentiments of things now,
(he told me) and acted upon quite different principles ; he was not vexed with it as it was painful,
or hindered him from his fins, which he would
have rolled under his tongue all the while, and
longed again to be at ; but he fubmitted patiently
to it, accepting it as the hand of God, and was
thankful, blefling and praifing God not only in,
but for his extremities. There was now no cur-
fing, no railings or reproaches to his fervants, or
thofe about him, which in other ficknefles were
their ufual entertainment, but he treated them
with all the meeknefs and patience in the world,
begging pardon frequently of the meannefs of them
but for a hafty word, which the extremity of his
ficknefs, and the fharpnefs of his pain, might eafily
force from him. His prayers were not fo much for
eafe, or health, or a continuance in life, as for
grace, and faith, and perfect refignation to the will

of

of God. So that I think we may not only chari-
tably but juftly conclude, that his ficknefs was not
the chief ingredient, but through the grace of God,
an effectual means of a true, though late repentance,
as will beft be judged by the marks I am now to
give you of the fincerity of it ; for which I am in
the next place to account.

II. And it was the power of Divine Grace, and
of that only, that broke through all thofe obfta-
cles that ufually attend a man in his circumftances;
that God (who is a God of infinite compaffion and
forbearance) allowed him leifure and opportunity
for repentance ; that he awakened him from his
fpiritual flumber by a pungent ficknefs ; that he
gave him fuch a prefence of mind, as both to provide prudently for his worldly affairs, and yet not to
be diftracted or diverted by them from the thoughts
of a better world ; that lengthened out his day of
grace, and accompanied the ordinary means of falvation, and weak miniftry of his word, with the
convincing and over-ruling power of his Spirit to
his confcience ; which word of God came to him
quick and powerful, fharper than a two edged
fword, piercing even to the dividing afunder of
his foul and fpirit ; and at laft, the Spirit of God
witneffed to his fpirit, that now he was become
one of the children of God.

Now, if the thief upon the crofs (an inftance
too much abufed) was therefore accepted, becaufe
accompanied with all the effects of a fincere convert, which his condition was capable of ; as

G   confeffion

confeſſion of Chriſt's in the midſt of the blaſ-
phemies of phariſees, and his own lewd com-
panion, and deſertion of even Chriſt's diſciples;
if his repentance be therefore judged real, becauſe
he ſeems to be more concerned in the remembrance
of Chriſt's future kingdom than his own death;
if St. Paul was approved by the ſame more abun-
dant labours, which he commended in the Co-
rinthians, " yea, what zeal? what fear? what
" vehement deſire? " 2 Cor. vii. 11. I think I
ſhall make it appear, that the repentace of this perſon was accompanied with the like hopeful ſymp-
toms : and I am ſo ſenſible of that awful preſence
both of God and man before whom I ſpeak, who
are eaſily able to diſcover my failings, that I ſhall
not deliver any thing, but what I know to be a
ſtrict and religious truth.

Upon my firſt viſit to him, (May 26, juſt at
his return from his journey out of the Weſt) he
moſt gladly received me, ſhewed me extraordinary
reſpects upon the ſcore of mine office, thanked
God, who had in mercy and good providence ſent
me to him, who ſo much needed my prayers and
counſels ; and acknowledging how unworthily
heretofore he had treated that order of men, re-
proaching them that they were proud, and prophe-
cied only for rewards ; but now he had learned
how to value them ; that he eſteemed them the
ſervants of the moſt High God, who were to ſhew
to him the way to everlaſting life.

At

At the fame time I found him labouring under ftrange trouble and conflicts of mind ; his fpirit wounded, and his confcience full of terrors.   Upon his journey, he told me, he had been arguing with greater vigour againft God and religion than ever he had done in his life time before, and that he was refolved to run them down with all the arguments and fpite in the world ; but, like the great convert St. Paul, he found it hard to kick againft the pricks.   For God, at that time, had fo ftruck his heart by his immediate hand, that prefently he argued as ftrongly for God and virtue, as before he had done againft it.   That God ftrangely opened his heart, creating in his mind moft awful and tremendous thoughts and ideas of the Divine Majefty, with a delightful contemplation of the Divine nature and attributes, and of the lovelinefs of religion and virtue.   I never (faid he) was advanced thus far towards happinefs in my life before, though upon the commiffion of fome fins extraordinary, I have had fome checks and warnings confiderable from within, but ftill ftruggled with them, and fo wore them off again.   The moft obfervable that I remember, was this : one day at an atheiftical meeting, at a perfon of quality's, I undertook to manage the caufe, and was the principal difputant againft God and piety, and for my performances received the applaufe of the whole company ; upon which my mind was terribly ftruck, and I immediately replied thus to myfelf.   Good God ! that a man that walks upright,

G 2

that

that fees the wonderful works of God, and has the
ufe of his fenfes and reafon, fhould ufe them to the
defying of his Creator! But though this was a
good beginning towards my converfion, to find my
confcience touched for my fins, yet it went off
again; nay, all my life long, I had a fecret value
and reverence for an honeft man, and loved morality in others. But I had formed an odd fcheme
of religion to myfelf, which would folve all that
God or confcience might force upon me; yet I was
not ever well reconciled to the bufinefs of chriftianity, nor had that reverence for the gofpel of Chrift
as I ought to have. Which eftate of mind continued till the fifty-third chapter of Ifaiah was read
to him, (wherein there is a lively defcription of the
fufferings of our Saviour, and the benefits thereof)
and fome other portions of fcripture; by the
power and efficacy of which word, affifted by his
Holy Spirit, God fo wrought upon his heart, that
he declared, that the myfteries of the paffion appeared as clear and plain to him, as ever any thing
did that was reprefented in a glafs; fo that that
joy and admiration, which poffeffed his foul upon
the reading of God's word to him, was remarkable
to all about him; and he had fo much delight in
his teftimonies, that in my abfence, he begged his
mother and lady to read the fame to him frequently,
and was unfatisfied (notwithftanding his great pains
and weaknefs) till he had learned the fifty-third
chapter of Ifaiah without book.

At

At the fame time, difcourfing of his manner of life from his youth up, and which all men knew was too much devoted to the fervice of fin, and that the lufts of the flefh, of the eye, and the pride of life, had captivated him : he was very large and particular in his acknowledgments about it, more ready to accufe himfelf than I or any one elfe can be ; publickly crying out, O bleffed God, can fuch an horrid creature as I am be accepted by thee, who has denied thy being, and contemned thy power ? Afking often, can there be mercy and pardon for me ? will God own fuch a wretch as I ? and in the middle of his ficknefs faid, fhall the unfpeakable joys of heaven be conferred on me ? O mighty Saviour ! never, but through thine infinite love and fatisfaction ! O never, but by the purchafe of thy blood ! adding, that with all abhorrency he did reflect upon his former life ; that fincerely and from his heart he did repent of all that folly and madnefs which he had committed.

Indeed, he had a true and lively fenfe of God's great mercy to him, in ftriking his hard heart, and laying his confcience open, which hitherto was deaf to all God's calls and methods : faying, if that God, who died for great as well as leffer finners did not fpeedily apply his infinite merits to his poor foul, his wound was fuch as no man could conceive or bear, crying out, that he was the vileft wretch and dog that the fun fhined upon, or the earth bore ; that he now faw his error, in not living up to that reafon which God endued him with, and

G 3

which

which he unworthily villified and contemned; wished
he had been a starving leper crawling in a ditch,
that he had been a link-boy or a beggar, or for his
whole life confined to a dungeon, rather than thus
to have finned againſt God.

How remarkable was his faith, in a hearty
embracing and devout confeſſion of all the arti-
ticles of our chriſtian religion, and all the divine
myſteries of the goſpel? ſaying, that that abſurd
and fooliſh philoſophy, which the world ſo much
admired, propagated by the late Mr. Hobbs, and
others, had undone him, and many more of the
beſt parts in the nation? who, without God's great
mercy to them, may never, I believe, attain to ſuch
a repentance.

I muſt not omit to mention his faithful adhe-
rence to, and caſting himſelf entirely upon the
mercies of Jeſus Chriſt, and the free grace of
God, declared to repenting ſinners through him;
with a thankful remembrance of his life, death,
and reſurrection; begging God to ſtrengthen his
faith, and often crying out, Lord, I believe, help
thou mine unbelief.

His mighty love and eſteem of the holy ſcriptures, his reſolutions to read them frequently, and
meditate upon them, if God ſhould ſpare him,
having already taſted the good word; for having
ſpoken to his heart, he acknowledged all the ſeeming abſurdities and contradictions thereof, fancied
by men of corrupt and reprobate judgments, were
vaniſhed,

vanished, and the excellency and beauty appeared, being come to receive the truth in the love of it.

His extraordinary fervent devotions, in his frequent prayers of his own, moſt excellent and correct; amongſt the reſt, for the king, in ſuch a manner as became a dutiful ſubject, and a truly grateful ſervant; for the church and nation, for ſome particular relations, and then for all men; his calling frequently upon me at all hours to pray with him, or read the ſcriptures to him; and toward the end of his ſickneſs, would heartily deſire God to pardon his infirmities, if he ſhould not be ſo wakeful and intent through the whole duty as he wiſhed to be, and that though the fleſh was weak, yet the ſpirit was willing, and hoped God would accept that.

His continual invocation of God's Grace and Holy Spirit to ſuſtain him, to keep him from all evil thoughts, from all temptations and diabolical ſuggeſtions, and every thing which might be prejudicial to that religious temper of mind, which God had now ſo happily endued him withal; crying out, one night eſpecially, how terrible the tempter did aſſault him, by caſting upon him lewd and wicked imaginations; but I thank God (ſaid he) I abhor them all, by the power of his grace, which I am ſure is ſufficient for me; I have overcome them; it is the malice of the devil, becauſe I am reſcued from him; and the goodneſs of God, that frees me from all my ſpiritual enemies.

G 4

His

His great joy at his lady's converſion from Popery to the church of England, (being, as he termed it, a faction ſupported only by fraud and cruelty) which was by her done with deliberation and mature judgment ; the dark miſts of which, have for ſome months before been breaking away, but now cleared, by her receiving the bleſſed ſacrament with her dying huſband, at the receiving of which, no man could expreſs more joy and devotion that he did ; and having handled the word of life, and ſeen the ſalvation of God, in the preparation of his mind, he was now ready to depart in peace.

His hearty concern for the pious education of his children, wiſhing that his ſon might never be a wit, that is (as he himſelf explained it) one of thoſe wretched creatures, who pride themſelves in abuſing God and religion, denying his being, or his providence ; but that he might become an honeſt and religious man, which could only be the ſupport and bleſſing of his family, complaining what a vicious and naughty world they were brought into, and that no fortunes or honours were comparable to the love and favour of God to them, in whoſe name he bleſſed them, prayed for them, and committed them to his protection.

His ſtrict charge to thoſe perſons, in whoſe cuſtody his papers were, to burn all his profane and lewd writings, as being only fit to promote vice and immorality, by which he had ſo highly offended God, and ſhamed and blaſphemed that holy religion into which he had been baptized; and

all

all his obfcene and filthy pictures, which were fo
notorioufly fcandalous.

His readinefs to make reftitution to the utmoft
of his power to all perfons whom he had injured ;
and for thofe whom he could not make a compen-
fation to, he prayed for God's and their pardons.
His remarkable juftice in taking all poffible care
for the payment of his debts, which before, he confeffed, he had not fo fairly and effectually done.

His readinefs to forgive all injuries done againft
him, fome more particularly mentioned, which
were great and provoking ; nay, annexing thereto
all the affurance of a future friendfhip, and hoping
he fhould be as freely forgiven at the hand of God.

How tender and concerned was he for his fervants about him in his extremities, (manifefted by
the beneficence of his will to them) pitying their
troubles in watching with him, and attending him,
treating him with candor and kindnefs, as if they
had been his intimates!

How hearty were his endeavours to be ferviceable to thofe about him, exhorting them to the
fear and love of God, and to make a good ufe of
his forbearance and long-fuffering to finners, which
fhould lead them to repentance. And here I muft
not pafs-by his pious and moft paffionate exclama-
tion to a gentleman of fome character, who came
to vifit him upon his death-bed ; " O remember
" that you contemn God no more, he is an aveng-
" ing God, and will vifit you for your fins ; he will in
" mercy, I hope, touch your confcience fooner or
" later,

" later, as he has done mine.   You and I have been
" friends and finners together a great while, there-
" fore I am the more free with you.   We have
" been all miftaken in our conceits and opinions,
" our perfuafions have been falfe and groundlefs ;
" therefore God grant you repentance. "   And
feeing him the next day again, he faid to him,
" perhaps you were difobliged by my plainnefs to
" you yefterday ; I fpake the words of truth and
" fobernefs to you, (and ftriking his hand upon
" his breaft) faid, I hope God will touch your
" heart. "

Likewife his commands to me, to preach abroad,
and to let all men know (if they knew it not already)
how feverely God had difciplined him for his fins
by his afflicting hand ; that his fufferings were moft
juft, though he had laid ten thoufand times more
upon him ; how he had laid one ftripe upon another becaufe of his grievous provocations, till he
had brought him home to himfelf ; that in his former vifitations he had not that blefled effect he was
now fenfible of.   He had formerly fome loofe
thoughts and flight refolutions of reforming, and
defigned to be better, becaufe even the prefent con-
fequences of fin were ftill peftering him, and were
fo troublefome and inconvenient to him ; but that
now he had other fentiments of things, and acted
upon other principles.

His willingnefs to die, if it pleafed God, refign-
ing himfelf always to the divine difpofal ; but if
God fhould fpare him yet a longer time here, he
hoped

hoped to bring glory to the name of God in the whole courfe of his life, and particularly by his endeavours to convince others, and to aflure them of the danger of their condition, if they continued impenitent, and how gracioufly God had dealt with him.

His great fenfe of his obligations to thofe excellent men, the right reverend my lord bifhop of Oxford, and Dr. Marfhall, for their charitable and frequent vifits to him, and prayers with him; and Dr. Burnett, who came on purpofe from London to fee him, who were all very ferviceable to his repentance.

His extraordinary duty and reverence to his mother, with all the grateful refpects to her imaginable, and kindnefs to his good lady, beyond expreffion, (which may well enhance fuch a lofs to them) and to his children, obliging them with all the endearments that a good hufband or a tender father could beftow.

To conclude thefe remarks, I fhall only read to you his dying remonftrance, fufficiently attefted and figned by his own hand, as his trueft fenfe, (which I hope may be ufeful for that good end he defigned it) in manner and form following.

" **F**OR the benefit of all thofe whom I may
" have drawn into fin by my example and
" encouragement, I leave to the world this my
" laft declaration, which I deliver in the prefence
" of

" of the great God, who knows the secrets of all
" hearts, and before whom I am now appearing
" to be judged.

" That from the bottom of my soul I detest
" and abhor the whole course of my former wick-
" ed life; that I think I can never sufficiently
" admire the goodness of God, who has given me
" a true sense of my pernicious opinions and vile
" practices, by which, I have hitherto lived with-
" out hope, and without God in the world; have
" been an open enemy to Jesus Christ, doing the
" utmost despite to the Holy Spirit of Grace.   And
" that the greatest testimony of my charity to such,
" is to warn them in the name of God, and as they
" regard the welfare of their immortal souls, no
" more to deny his being, or his providence, or
" despise his goodness ; no more to make a mock
" of sin, or contemn the pure and excellent re-
" ligion of my ever blessed redeemer, through
" whose merits alone, I, one of the greatest sin-
" ners, do yet hope for mercy and forgiveness.
" Amen."

Declared and signed in the presence of

ANNE ROCHESTER.

                          · June 19, 1680.
ROBERT PARSONS.

              J. ROCHESTER.

                                And

And now I cannot but mention with joy and admiration that fteady temper of mind which he enjoyed through the whole courfe of his ficknefs and repentance; which muft proceed, not from a hurry and perturbation of mind or body, arifing from the fear of death, or dread of hell only, but from an ingenuous love to God, and an uniform regard to virtue, (fuitable to that folemn declaration of his, I would not commit the leaft fin to gain a kingdom) with all poffible fymptoms of a lafting perfeverance in it, if God fhould have reftored him. To which may be added, his comfortable perfuafions of God's accepting him to his mercy, faying, three or four days before his death, I fhall die, but oh, what unfpeakable glories do I fee! what joys, beyond thought or expreffion, am I fenfible of! I am affured of God's mercy to me through Jefus Chrift. Oh how I long to die, and be with my Saviour!

The time of his ficknefs and repentance was juft nine weeks; in all which time he was fo much mafter of his reafon, and had fo clear an underftanding, (faving thirty hours, about the middle of it, in which he was delirious) that he had never dictated or fpoke more compofed in his life: and therefore, if any fhall continue to fay, his piety was the effect of madnefs or vapours; let me tell them, 'tis highly difingenuous, and that the affertion is as filly as it is wicked. And moreover that the force of what I have delivered may be not evaded by wicked men, who are refolved to

harden

harden their hearts, maugre all convictions, by
faying. this was done in a corner; I appeal, for
the truth thereof, to all forts of perfons who in
confiderable numbers vifited and attended him, and
more particularly to thofe eminent phyficians who
were near him, and converfant with him in the
whole courfe of his tedious ficknefs ; and who,
if any, are competent judges of a phrenfy or
delirium.

There are many more excellent things in my
abfence which have occafionally dropt from his
mouth, that will not come within the narrow compafs of a fermon; thefe, I hope, will fufficiently
prove what I produce them for. And if any fhall
be ftill unfatisfied here in this hard-hearted generation, it matters not, let them at their coft be
unbelievers ftill, fo long as this excellent penitent
enjoyes the comfort of his repentance. And now
from all thefe admirable figns we have great reafon to believe comfortably, that his repentance
was real, and his end happy ; and accordingly imitate the neighbours and coufens of Elizabeth,
(Luke i. 58.) who, when they heard how the
Lord had fhewed great mercy upon her, came and
rejoiced with her.

Thus his dear mother fhould rejoice, that the
fon of her love and of her fears, as well as of her
bowels, is now born again into a better world ;
adopted by his Heavenly Father, and gone before
her to take poffeffion of an eternal inheritance.

II. His truly loving confort fhould rejoice, that God has been fo gracious to them both, as at the fame time to give him a fight of his errors in point of practice, and herfelf (not altogether without his means and endeavours) a fight of hers in point of faith. And truly, confidering the great prejudices and dangers of the Roman religion, I think I may aver that there is joy in heaven, and fhould be on earth, for her converfion as well as his.

III. His noble and moft hopeful iffue fhould rejoice, as their years are capable; not that a dear and loving father has left them, but that fince he muft leave them, he has left them the example of a penitent, and not of a finner; the bleffing of a faint, in recommending them to an all-fufficient Father, and not entailing on them the fatal curfe that attends the pofterity of the wicked and impenitent.

IV. All good men fhould rejoice, to fee the triumphs of the crofs in thefe latter days, and the words of divine wifdom and power. And bad men certainly, whenever they confider it, are moft of all concerned to joy and rejoyce in it, as a condemned malefactor is, to hear that a fellow criminal has got his pardon, and that he may do fo too, if he fpeedily fue for it.

And this joy of all will ftill be the greater, if we compare it with the joy there is in heaven, in the cafe of juft perfons, that need no repentance, viz. that need not fuch a folemn extraordinary repentance, or the whole change of heart and mind,

as

as great finners do : and of this my text pronoun-
ces, that there is, " greater joy in heaven over
" one fuch finner that truly repenteth, than there
" is over ninety and nine juft perfons that need
" not fuch repentance." One reafon of which we
may conceive to be this ; that fuch a penitent's
former failings, are ordinarily the occafion of a
greater and more active piety afterwards ; as our
convert earneftly wifhed, that God would be pleafed to fpare him but one year more, that in that he
might honour his name proportionably to the difhonour done to God in his whole life paft. And
we fee St. Paul laboured more abundantly than all
the apoftles in the planting of the church, becaufe
he had raged furioufly before in the deftruction of
it ; and our Saviour himfelf tells us, that " to
" whom much is forgiven, they will love much;
" but to whom little is forgiven, they will love
" little.

'Tis certainly the more fafe, indeed the only fafe
way to be conftantly virtuous, and he that is wife
indeed, i. e. wife unto falvation, will endeavour to
be one of thofe that need no repentance ; I mean
that intire and whole work of beginning anew,
but will draw out the fame thread through his
whole life, and let not the fun go down upon any
of his fins : but then the other repentance is more
remarkable, and, where it is real, the more effectual, to produce a fervent and a fruitful piety ;
befides, the greater glory to God in the influence
of the example. Which may probably be a farther

reafon

reafon of the exceffive joy of the angels at the converfion of fuch a finner; becaufe they, who are
better acquainted with human nature than we,
knowing it apt, like the Pharifees, to demand a
fign from heaven, for the reformation of corrupted
cuftoms, difcern likewife, that fuch defperate fpiritual recoveries, will feem fo many openings of the
heavens in the defcent of the Holy Dove, vifible to
the ftanders by; and accordingly will have the
greater influence upon them. And 'tis this, in the
laft place, that I am to recommend to all that hear
me this day.

And having thus difcharged the office of an hiftorian, in a faithful reprefentation of the repentance and converfion of this great finner; give me
leave now to befpeak you as an ambaffador of Chrift,
and in his name, earneftly perfuade you to be reconciled to him, and to follow this illuftrious perfon,
not in his fins any more, but in his forrows for
them, and his forfaking them. If there be any in
this place, or elfewhere, who have been drawn
into a complacency or practice of any kind of fin
from his example, let thofe efpecially be perfuaded
to break off their fins by repentance, by the fame
example; that as he has been for the fall, fo he
may now be for the rifing again of many in Ifrael.
God knows there are too many that are wife
enough to difcern and follow the examples of evil,
but to do good from thofe examples they have no
power; like thofe abfurd flatterers we read of, who
could imitate Plato in his crookednefs, Ariftotle in

H

his

his ſtammering, and Alexander the great in the bending of his neck, and the ſhrillneſs of his voice, but either could not, or would not, imitate them in any of their perfeƈtions. Such as theſe I would beſeech, in their cooler ſeaſons, to aſk themſelves that queſtion, " what fruit had you in thoſe things " whereof you are now aſhamed, for the end of theſe " things is death ?" And if any encourage themſelves in their wickedneſs from this example, reſolving however to enjoy the good things that are preſent, to fill themſelves with coſtly wines, and to let no part of pleaſure paſs by them untaſted, ſuppoſing with the goſpel rich man, that when one comes to them from the dead, when ſickneſs or old age approaches, that then they will repent; let ſuch as theſe conſider the dreadful hazard they run by ſuch pernicious counſels. It may be (and it is but juſt with God it ſhould be) that whilſt they are making proviſions for the fleſh to fulfil the luſts thereof, and are ſaying to their ſouls, ſoul thou haſt much goods laid up for many years, therefore take thine eaſe, eat, drink and be merry; perhaps juſt then at the ſame time the hand of God may be writing upon the walls of their habitations, that fatal ſentence, " thou fool, this night ſhall " thy ſoul be required of thee, and then whoſe " ſhall all thoſe things be, which thou haſt pro" miſed ?" And what ſad refleƈtions muſt ſuch a one need make upon his own folly, when he ſees all that mirth and eaſe, which he has promiſed himſelf for ſo many years, muſt be at an end in

a very

a very few hours? And not only fo, but that mirth turned into howlings, and that eafe into a bed of flames; when the foul muft be torn away on a fudden from the things it loved, and go where it will hate to live, and yet cannot die. And were it not better for us to embrace cordially the things which belong to our everlafting peace, before they are hid from our eyes? Were it not better for us all to be wife betimes by preventing fuch a danger, than to open our eyes, as the unhappy rich man did, when we are in a place of torment?

Be perfuaded then with humble, penitent, and obedient hearts to meet the bleffed Jefus, who is now on the way, and comes to us in the perfon and in the bowels of a Saviour, wooing us to accept thofe eafy conditions of pardon and peace offered in his holy gofpel, rather than to ftay till he become our adverfary and our judge too, when he will deliver us over to the tormentors, till we have paid the ut-moft farthing, i. e. to all eternity: when thofe who have made a mock at fin all their lives, and laughed at the pretended cheats of religion and its priefts, fhall find themfelves at laft the greateft fools, and the moft fadly cheated in the world: for God will then laugh at their calamity, and mock when their fear cometh, when it cometh as defolation, and their deftruction as a whirlwind. And fince they would not fuffer his mercy to re-joyce over his juftice, nor caufe any joy in heaven, as the text mentions, in their converfion; his juf-tice will certainly rejoyce over his mercy, and caufe

joy

joy in heaven (as it did at the fall of Babylon) which would not be cured, Rev. xix. 1. in their confusion.   And oh that there was such an heart in them, that they would consider this betimes ! that in the midst of their carnal jollities they would but vouchsafe one regard what may happen hereafter, and what will certainly be the end of these things. For however the fruits of sin may seem pleasant to the eye, and to be desired to make one seem wise and witty to the world, yet alas, they are but empty and unsatisfactory at present, and leave a mortal sting behind them, and bitterness in the latter end; like the book St. John eat, (Rev. x. 10.) " which in his mouth was sweet as honey, but as " soon as he had eat it, his belly was bitter." And that God should please at last to bring men back in their old age from their sinful courses, by a way of weeping, to pluck them as fire-brands out of everlasting burnings; yet if men consider how rare and difficult a thing it is to be born again when one is old, how many pangs and violences to nature there must needs be, to put off the habits and inclinations to old sins, as difficult (saith the prophet) as for the leopard to change his spots, or the Æthiopian his skin : and then when that is done, what scars and weaknesses even a cure must leave behind. I say, he that duly considers this, will think it better to secure his salvation, and all his present true comforts, by preserving his inno-cency, or alleviating his work by a daily repen-tance for lesser failings, than to venture upon one

single

fingle chance of a death-bed repentance ; which is no more to be depended upon, for the performance, or acceptance, than it can encourage any man not to labour, becaufe Elias was fed by ravens, or the Ifraelites with manna from heaven.

If then there be any (though alas that need not be afked) that have made the greatnefs of their wit, or birth, or fortune, inftruments of iniquity to iniquity ; let them now convert them to that original noble ufe for which God intended them, viz. to be inftruments of righteoufnefs unto holinefs.

To thefe efpecially that are thus great, not only God, but this great perfon alfo, by my mouth, being dead yet fpeaketh ; for as St. Paul feemed more efpecially concerned for his brethren and kinfmen according to the flefh, and even the rich man in hell, though fufficiently diftracted by his own fufferings, yet feems hugely defirous that one might be fent from the dead to his brethren, that he might teftify unto them, leaft they alfo come into that place of torment : fo this illuftrious con-vert, after God had opened his eyes to fee his follies, was more efpecially defirous of the falvation of thofe that were his brethren, though not in the flefh, yet in the greatnefs of their quality, and of their fins ; paffionately wifhing, that all fuch were not only almoft, but altogether fuch as he now was, faving his bodily afflictions ; and of great force, methinks, fhould the admonitions of a dying friend be.

Now

Now thefe efpecially I would befeech, as the minifter of Chrift, and fuch as, though we are reviled we blefs, though we are defamed we intreat, to fuffer the word of exhortation, that they would not terminate their eyes upon the outward pomp and pageantry that attends them, as the vulgar Jews did upon their rites and ceremonies; but (as the wifer Ifraelites, who efteemed thofe glittering formalities as the types and images of heavenly things) be quickened by them to the ambition of original honours, and future glory. How much were it to be wifhed, that fuch perfons efpecially would be followers of God and goodnefs, fince whether they will or no, other men will be followers of them.

It is true, the temptations of great perfons are more, and greater than thofe of inferiors; but then their abilities and underftandings are ordinarily greater too; and if they lye more open to the affaults of the devil, they have generally greater fagacity to forefee the danger, and more powerful affiftance to go through it. Nor is piety inconfiftent with greatnefs, any more than it is with policy, but is the beft foundation and fecurity both to the one and the other. The breeding of Mofes at court, without doubt contributed much even to his religious performances, at leaft fo far, as to make them more ufeful and exemplary to others: but then he was fincerely virtuous all the while, as well whilft reputed the fon of Pharaoh's daughter, as when Jethro's fon-in-law.

We

We find chriftians in Cæfar's houfhold as foon as any where elfe in Rome ; and when chriftianity had once gained Conftantine, it fpread itfelf farther over the empire in a few years, than before it had done in fome centuries. Since then fo much good or mifchief depends upon illuftrious examples, will it not better become men to draw the multitude after them to heaven by their piety, than by infectious guilts be at the head of a miferable company of the damned.

'Tis this piety, a timely and exemplary piety, that will perpetuate to men of birth and fortunes, their honours, and their eftates too, as well by deriving on them the bleffing of God, who is the true fountain of honour, as by creating an awe and reverence for them from all orders of men, even to many generations ; a reverence which will be frefh and lafting, when all the trophies of wit and gaiety are laid in the duft. 'Tis this piety that will be the guide of their youth, and the comfort of their age ; for length of days are in her right hand, and in her left hand riches and honour. 'Tis this, and this only, that can make all outward bleffings comfortable, and indeed bleffings to us, by making them the fteps and means of attaining the never fading honours and incomprehenfible glories of that kingdom which is above ; where there fhall be no more fin, nor ficknefs, nor pain, nor tears, nor death, but we fhall reft from all our labours, and our works fhall follow us.

Unto

Unto which God of his infinite mercy bring us,
for the merits and mediation of Jesus Christ
our Saviour; to whom with the Father and
Holy Spirit, let us ascribe all praise and adoration, now and for ever.   Amen.

F I N I S.

AN

ESSAY

ON THE

MEMORY

OF THE LATE

QUEEN MARY.

By GILBERT BURNETT, D. D.

Late Lord Bishop of Sarum.

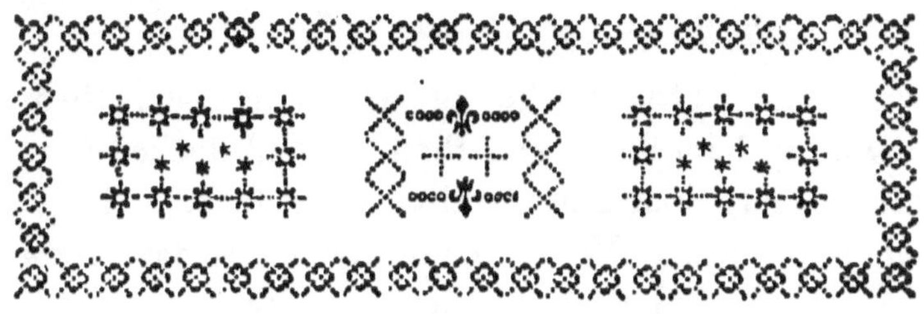

AN
ESSAY
ON THE
MEMORY
OF THE LATE
QUEEN MARY.

"ALL flesh is grass, and all the goodliness "therefore, is as the flower of the field." Some of these flowers have more life and lustre than others ; they are more beautiful, as well as more lasting : yet in the course of things, the grass withereth, and the flower fadeth ; and that sometimes so quick, and by such an unlooked for turn, that in the morning it groweth up and flourisheth, and in the evening it is cut down and

A 2

withered.

withered. One ftroke of a fcythe cuts them down by handfuls; and then the beft decked fpot of ground, does quickly change its face, and lofe all its beauty. We who but the other day faw a great queen, (I fay the other day, for fuch an idea muft live fo long and fo frefh in our minds, that for a great many years we will ftill fay the other day) we who faw her, like the mafter-piece of nature, wrought up by all the polifhings of art and improvement, look with fo frefh a bloom, and fuch promifing appearances, who carried that air of life and joy about her, that animated all who faw her, and who reckoned their own lives both the fafer and happier, becaufe hers was fo firm, muft now lament that all this is taken from us with one fudden and amazing ftroke. The beft part of us, our hearts and hopes, are ftruck down with her; who was the beft, God knows, the much beft part of us all. We look up to heaven with deep, though filent regret, as if we envied her bleffednefs: we look down to the earth, like men that are finking thither: we look to the grave, where what was mortal is lodged till it becomes immortal, with a fort of indignation, that it fhould receive and confume thofe facred remains for which we feel a fort of fuperftition, which though our reafon may check, yet it cannot quite filence or extinguifh.

Nature, even on very extraordinary occafions, is apt to give itfelf fome vent, and to procure to itfelf fome mitigation of its pain. And when it is

too

too full for well chofen expreffions, or regular difcourfes, the broken and inarticulate language of
fighs and tears, gives fome relief: a calm fucceeds
thofe ftorms; they give at leaft a breathing, and
fofter intervals.   Here we feel fuch an oppreffion,
and diftraction of thought, that they choak us
inwardly, and break out only in amazement, and
in a wildnefs of look and behaviour.   We feel fo
great a lofs at prefent, that we need not heighten
it by the gloomy profpect of the fatal confequen-
ces that may follow it: and yet we cannot help
feeing that, which is but too vifible.   We dare
not pretend to enter into the fecret of God's councils, which are wrapt up from the eyes of mortals:
yet they have fuch characters upon them, that from
thence we are induced to make fome conjectures
about them; though after all, thefe are but conjectures, and are often ill grounded.   But whether
we look up to God, or to the outward face of
things, and to thofe appearances that are but too
obvious, we foon find caufe enough to drive back
our thoughts to that dark and native horror that
does now haunt and poffefs them.   Some may perhaps make vain complaints againft God, and try
to eafe their own grief, by accufing his providence:
our hearts may carry us to fay, why was fo much
worth laid in one mind, and fo nobly lodged? Why
was it juft fhewed the world, with advantage
enough to let all men fee what might have been
expected from it ? Why were fo many great ideas
and vaft defigns formed by her ? Why was fhe
furnifhed

furnifhed with fuch fkill and foftnefs in the ma‑
nagement of them ?   and the fad why comes laft,
why was all this fnatched from us fo early and
fo fuddenly ?

It is true, all God's ways are a great depth ;
and we may never prefume to afk of him a reafon
of any of his dealings, which are paft finding out:
but here the fteps of his providence are fo account‑
able, that we ought not to be long in the dark
about them.   So much worth was full ripe for
heaven, and was much too good for earth, efpe‑
cially for fo corrupt a part of it as we are.   If
thofe great bleffings which heaven held forth to
us in her, had attained the ends for which they
were defigned, we might then have hoped that her
crown would have been longer delayed ; and that
our happinefs might have been the more lafting.
The cutting part of our forrow is this, that we
have too good reafon to believe that we have pro‑
cured this to ourfelves.

Unlefs, according to the growing impiety that
fpreads itfelf amongft us, we will conclude that
God has forfaken the earth, and that all things
roll, either under the fullennefs of fate, or the
giddinefs of chance ; if we believe that providence
watches over and governs all that happens here
below, we muft then acknowledge, that fo great
a change as this has made, could not have come
upon us, but by a juft and wife direction.   There‑
fore inftead of thofe irregular thoughts and expref‑
fions by which fo great a commotion of mind may
difcharge

difcharge itfelf, and inftead of thofe wild and de-jecting apprehenfions, which it may be apt to throw upon us, we ought to reduce ourfelves to more order, and to confider more fedately, what we may juftly fear, and how we may wifely pro-vide againft it.

If we will examine what may have brought fo fevere a ftroke upon us, and what may draw after it yet heavier ones, (but can any be heavier!) then if there is yet room for hopes, if our wound is not incurable, and if the breach that is made upon us is not wide as the fea, fo that nothing can hinder our being overflown by it, then, I fay, the fearching into this, is all the referve that is left us, all that can balance fo ineftimable a lofs, or ra-ther all that can fave us from being fwallowed up utterly by it.

Even in a fhipwrack every one is forced, after all his aftonifhment at their common fate, to try by what fhift he himfelf may efcape: for tho' the firft diforders of melancholy may make one wifh rather to perifh in fo terrible a calamity, than to furvive it, yet after all, nature returns to itfelf, and feels felf-prefervation to be too deeply wrought in its compofition, to be eafily fhaken off. While then fuch a load oppreffes us, and when fuch fears compafs us round, all that remains to make the one lighter, and to diffipate the other, is for us to lay our hands on our mouths, becaufe God has done it : but then to lay them on our heart, and to afk

our-

ourfelves what have we done ? And what fhall we do to be faved ?

How juft foever any affliction may feem to be, yet it muft have its bounds. Our religion gives a temper : it does not impofe upon us the dry fullennefs of ftoics ; their moft admired fayings, that fate is inexorable ; that it is in vain to be troubled at that we cannot help : and the famed anfwer of him, who upon the news of his fon's death, faid coldly, I knew I begat him mortal, have an air in them that feems above the prefent ftate of human nature. It looks too favage and contrary to thofe tender affections that are planted in us, and that are in fome fort neceffary for carrying on the common concerns of life. But the extreams on the other hand, are much more boifterous and untractable : while the rages of paffion govern, neither the calmnefs of reafon, nor the authority of religion will be harkened to. Heathenifm was fruitful in the inventions of fury, hecatombs of living creatures were thought poor oblations : human facrifices were offered liberally on thofe occafions, nor was the greateft wafte of treafure, with all the profufion of funeral piles and magnificent buildings, thought a fuitable addreffing of their dead to the invifible ftate, to which they went, unlefs innumerable ghofts were fent after them as a welcome convoy to follow them thither. When the civilizing of the world, and the decencies firft of humanity, then of philofophy, and chiefly when revealed religion came to foften and enlighten

men,

men, thofe outragious folemnities fell off ; tho'
the coftly part was by many kept up with too
much oftentation.   The corrupters of religion
found that the tendernefs of affection, with that
generous difintereffednefs which it gave, offered to
them a harveft that might be fruitful ; and they
were not defective in the art of cultivating it.

Opinions were invented, and practices were
contrived, that drew great wealth into their hands;
and begat a confideration for them, which, if it
had not been over-done by the managers, and that
in a manner too coarfe and too ravenous not to be
found out at laft, was bringing the whole world
under their authority.   Their title feemed fure ;
and it was to have its chief operation, when both
thofe who died, and thofe who lived, were the leaft
able to examine their pretenfions : the fears of the
one, and the forrows of the other, made them very
pliant to their conduct, and implicit under it.

We have a better light, and are governed by
truer meafures : we know there is a wife providence, and a future ftate ; and in thofe two never-
failing fources of quiet and fubmiffion, we give
our forrows juft abatements.   But fince all the
fteps of providence, though juft and wife in themfelves, have not the fame face to us, fome of them
being as bright as others are dark ; we ought not
to look on providence as rigid fate ; but as the
fteady conduct of a mind that is infinitely wife :
we ought therefore to go as far as reafonably we
can, in judging what is the language of that pro-
B   vidence

vidence to us, and what the defigns of it upon us may be.

The livelieft as well as the ufefulleft exercifes of our thoughts, is to fum all that was excellent and imitable in the perfon whofe lofs we lament ; to lay it altogether ; to obferve how amiable it was, what an influence it had, and in what effects it appeared. . This if it refts in the bare commendation of one, that may be fafely praifed, when flattery or intereft cannot be thought to have any fhare in the incenfe, that is then given, it is at leaft a juftice to the memory of a perfon that deferved it, and an homage to virtue itfelf. It will probably go deeper, and have its beft effect upon us : it will engage us to love thofe virtues in ourfelves, which we admire in others, and will reproach us, if we commend that in another, which we take no care to imitate ourfelves. Probably this will not evaporate quite into difcourfe, or wear off with time : fomewhat will ftick, and have a due effect upon us. Some of thofe virtues may fo far infinuate themfelves into us, that we may grow to love and practice them. A noble pattern cannot be much looked at without begetting fome difpofition to copy after it, and to imitate it. A great luftre, though it may fometimes dazzle, yet it enlightens, as well as it ftrikes.

Thofe who are perhaps tied too clofely by fome fatal engagements to practices that they cannot refolve on forfaking, yet have that fecret veneration for true virtue, efpecially for the fublime of it,

and

and faw fo much of that in our bleffed queen, that they may be defirous to fee fuch a juft reprefentation of thofe various branches of her character, as may entertain their admiration at prefent, and be perhaps of fome more ufe to them in other periods of their lives. They may defire to be made wifer, if not better by it. They may hope that what effect foever it may have on the prefent age, it will have fome on thofe that are to come : it will be a lively part of our hiftory, and fet a noble pattern to fucceeding princes. And all perfons, how bad foever they may be themfelves, have too fenfible a fhare in government, not to wifh that their princes were truly and heroically good.

A picture of her, that may have fome life in it, is that which all feemed to defire. Where there were fo many peculiar features, and yet fo much of majefty fpread over them all, it feems as hardly poffible not to hit a great deal of the refemblance, as to hit it all, and to draw truly, and to the life. Every one will at firft view, fay, it is fhe; but this abatement muft be expected, that it has not quite taken her. It has not her air, though it may have her features. The colours may feem to fink, when we remember how the original itfelf looked.

Extraordinary degrees of virtue in fovereign princes happen fo feldom, that it is no wonder if they give the world a furprife that is as great as it is agreeable. When we look through paft ages, and through all the different climates and corners of the world, we find little that is truly eminent, without some great diminution accompanying it.

We accuftom ourfelves by ftudy and obfervation not to be flattered with the hopes of feeing ideas of perfection on the throne. It feems a prefumption to fancy, that our own times fhould have a priviledge that former ages could not boaft. We find that even David, and Solomon much more, had blemifhes almoft equal to their virtues. Few of their fucceffors arrived at their degree of perfection; though they might have all their allay. Hezekiah and Jofiah are the leaft exceptional : yet fome leffer flips occur even in their hiftory. Conftantine and Theodofius were two of the greateft bleffings of the chriftian church ; yet we dare not propofe them as patterns in every thing. Clovis and Charles the great make a mighty figure in hiftory; becaufe, the world is difpofed to remember what was good in them, and to forget the reft. A full picture of thefe would have one fide fo bright, with another fo fpotted, that the whole would look but odly. If the good and bad that was in moft princes, whofe names found the beft, were fet againft one another, as critically as Suetonius has reprefented the Roman emperors, the world would perhaps retract much of the admiration that it has paid them ; and might be for fome time in fufpence, which fide of the character was fuperior, and did preponderate the other.

Female government has had its peculiar blemifhes, with fewer patterns to compenfate for the
faultinefs

faultinefs of others. The fiercenefs of Semiramis's charaƈter does leſſen her greatnefs, and the luxuries of Cleopatra does more than balance her beauties. The cruelties of Irene were fuch, that even her zeal for images could not cover them, in the thickeſt miſt of fuperſtition. Mathildis and the Joans of Naples, are too black to be well thought of, for all the flatteries of popes : and pope Gregory's raptures upon Brunichild have leſſened him, rather than changed her charaƈter. It is true, Pulcheria has a fairer grace, yet fome fufpicions have a little eclipfed her; and her reign was but of a few days continuance, till ſhe chofe a hufband, who was made emperor by the right of marrying her. Amalazuntha has a nobler charaƈter, it is indeed given her by Caſſiodore, that had been her chief miniſter; but he was.the wifeſt and beſt of men in the age : her fate was difmal, and others have caſt black imputations on her; but if that wife fenator is to be believed, ſhe was one of the beſt and greateſt, though the moſt unfortunate of women. Female government has feldom looked fo great, as it did in Ifabel of Caſtile. But if ſhe was a good queen, ſhe was but an indifferent wife ; and all the honour ſhe did her fex, was thrown down in her daughter, who was likewife a fovereign ; whofe violent affeƈtions to her hufband, was as troublefome while he lived, as extravagant after his death ; ſhe keeping the dead body ſtill in view, and making it travel about with her in her journies, which ſhe made only in the night ; neglecting

B 3

glecting

glecting government, and finking into a feeblenefs, that made her become at laft utterly incapable of even the fhadow of it, which was all that had remained in her for many years.

If Jane of Navarre had had a larger fphere, fhe was indeed a perfect pattern : nothing was ever fuggefted to leffen her, but that which was her true glory, her receiving the reformation ; fhe both received it, and brought her fubjects to it. She not only reformed her court, but her whole principality, to fuch a degree, that the golden age feemed to have returned under her ; or rather, chriftianity appeared again with the purity and luftre of its firft beginnings. Nor is there one fingle abatement to be made here, only her principality was narrow ; her dominion was fo little extended, that though fhe had the rank and dignity of a queen, yet it looked liker a fhadow, than the reality of fovereignty; or rather it was fovereignty in minature, though the colours were very bright, it was of the fmalleft form.

Two Marys in this ifland fhewed a greatnefs of genius that has feldom appeared to the world. But the fuperftition and cruelty of the one, and the conduct and misfortunes of the other, did fo leffen them, that the fex had been much funk by their means, if it had not been at the fame time as powerfully fupported by the happieft and moft renowned of all fovereign queens ; I know I need not name her.

The

The great figure fhe made both at home and abroad, her wife conduct and able miniftry were fuch, that the nations flourifhing in trade, and extending itfelf in colonies, the encreafe of our wealth, and the ftrength of our fleets, owe their beginnings to her aufpicious reign. The great tranfactions then abroad in the werld, took their turn from the direction and the fupport that fhe gave them. But that which is above all, and for which we owe her memory the profoundeft acknowledgments, it was by her means that the true religion received its eftablifhment among us. She delivered us from a foreign yoke, fhe freed us from idolatry and fuperftition, and fettled us upon a conftitution that has been ever fince the trueft honour, as well as the greateft fupport of the reformation. So much we owe to the afhes of that great queen, that her memory is ftill frefh and facred among us : her times are efteemed the ftandard of our happinefs, and her name ftill carries a delightful found to every Englifh ear. If there were any defects or diforders in that time, we ought to think mildly of them, and to cenfure them gently. In her we muft own, that female government feemed to have fhined with the faireft glory : we are fure that hiftory can fhew nothing like it.

But the lateft is commonly the frefheft in our thoughts ; and what luftre foever authority in that fex may have caft about it in the laft age, it has come under a cloud in the prefent. A queen has lived in our own times, whofe great defcent gave

B 4

her

her a juſt title to the higheſt gratitude, and whoſe mind ſeemed born with a ſublimity made for empire, that for ſome time, like the northern ſtar, attract-ed the eyes of all the world to her.   But ſhe aban-doned her throne and ſubjects, and choſe rather to wander ingloriouſly, than to maintain her poſt, and exert her ſuperiority of genius in governing well at home, and giving law to thoſe about her.   This had made the diſpoſition to Salick laws become more univerſal.   We have ſeen that which has not only taken off the cloud, which ſhe had caſt on her ſex, but has raiſed it far beyond the precedents or patterns of former times.   In her, that name, which all generations ſhall call bleſſed, has reco-vered the amiable ſound, that it ought ever to have.   We heard it, not without ſome harſhneſs, when we remembered ſome who had carried it: nothing can add to the glorious beginning of that name ; yet our Mary has reſtored it to its firſt ſweetneſs.

We ſeek in vain for a pattern to reſemble her: Her grandmother of Navarre, is the likeſt thing we find to her.   But we do not leſſen that queen's glory, when we ſay that this deſcendant of hers had an auguſter appearance and a more exalted throne. She had a higher ſphere, and ſo we may conclude ſhe was the ſuperior intelligence.   She was all that the other queen had been, even whilſt ſhe was in her princely ſtate.   The world has reaſon to be-lieve, that every thing would have been the ſame in the other, if ſhe had been advanced to an im-

perial

perial crown. But what may be well believed of her, was seen in this branch, that sprang from her root: her worth grew with her advancement. She was not only better known in it, but there was a constant progress in her virtues, even beyond that of her fortune.

Yet after all, this cannot so properly be called a female government; though sovereignty was in her, it was also in another; her administration supplied the others absence. Monarchy here seemed to have lost its very essence; it being a government by one. But as the administration was only in one at a time, so they were more one, than either espousals or a joint tenure of the throne could make them; there was an union of their thoughts, as well as of their persons; and a concurring in the same designs, as well as in the same interests. Both seemed to have one soul; they looked like the different faculties of the same mind. Each of them having peculiar talents, they divided between them the different parts of government, as if they had been several provinces: while he went abroad with the sword in his hand, she staid at home with the scepter in hers: he went as the arbiter of Europe, to force a just, as well as a general peace; she staid to maintain peace and to do justice at home. He was to conquer enemies, and she was to gain friends. He as the guardian of Christendom, was to diffuse himself to all, while she contracted her care chiefly to the concerns of religion and virtue. While he had more business, and

she

fhe more leifure, fhe prepared and fuggefted what he executed. In all this, there was fo clofe, but fo entire an union, that it was not poffible to know how much was proper to any one; or if ever they differed in a thought from one another: but the living are not now to be fpoke of; our thoughts muft run wholly where our forrows carry us.

While we feek for refemblance in her, in facred hiftory we find her fo like Jofiah, that their being of the fame dignity, may excufe the parallel, though the fex is different. He came, after a long and deep corruption; a reign that had fo entirely viti-ated the nation, that neither the judgments of God that fell on Manaffes, nor his own fincere, though late repentance, was able to correct the diforders of his former years. So foon is a nation run into fo depraved a ftate, that its recovery becomes almoft defperate. Jofiah was under much difadvantage in his firft education: his being a king fo young, expofed him to all the flatteries by which thofe about him might hope to infinuate themfelves into his favour; but his happy temper was above it. While he was but growing out of childhood, in the eighth year of his reign, and the fixteenth year of his age, he began to feek after God: he continued four years in this pious courfe of life, before he fet about the reforming of the people, that his own good example might have fuch influence, and give him fuch credit in it, as might balance the flow-nefs of beginning it. When he fet about it, it was the work of fix years to purge the land from
idolatry;

idolatry; and of other six to set forward the repairing the temple. All was not finished before the eighteenth year of his reign, so hard it is to recover a degenerated nation. As they were searching the temple, the book of the law (by which most do understand the original itself) was found, the dreadful threatnings in it struck Josiah with a just horror. He sent to Huldah, a famed prophetess, to see what comfort she could give him; she answered, that the decree was fixed and irreversible; but he should die in peace, and not see those fatal days. This was some mitigation to his grief. He tried all he could to reform his people, but without success; they were weary of him and of his virtue, and were longing for an opportunity to return again to their idolatry. So inveterate was the corruption, that all the exactness of Josiah's care, as well as the strictness of the example that he set his own sons, could not keep them from the spreading contagion, it was so catching. This was the last essay of mercy upon that people, in the best of all their kings. He was fatally engaged in an unequal war, and was killed in the day of battle. His death, upon his own single account, would have given the Jews but too just a cause of a bitter mourning for him; but the miseries that did immediately follow his death, made it to be so long remembered, that in a book writ about a hundred years after, it is said, that they continued their mourning for him to that day. It was no wonder that it was remembered by them

with

with fo folemn and lafting a forrow. A fucceffion of calamities came fo thick after it, that there was fcarce a lucid interval between them; captivity came after captivity; and what by war, what by famine, and what by defertion, in the courfe of four and twenty years after his death, their nation became an aftonifhment, a curfe, and a bye word, to all nations. Jerufalem was laid in heaps, their temple was rafed down to the ground, and Zion became a ploughed field. And if the fecond and final deftruction of that city and nation had not been fo fignal, and fo particularly related by one who was an eye witnefs of it, that it wore out the remembrance of all that had happened in former times, this would have paft for one of the blackeft and the moft amazing fcenes in hiftory.

That pathetical lamentation which Jeremy writ upon it, has ftrains in it fo tender and fo moving, that no man who has not hardened himfelf againft the compaffions of human nature, can read them without a fenfible emotion, though they relate to tranfactions that happened many ages ago; fuch a lively poem as that is, makes them ever look frefh, and feem prefent.

I will make no reflections on any part of this hiftorical deduction. It leads one fo naturally to application, that there is no need of offering any. Here one may go rather too faft, than too flow, and ftretch the matter further than it will bear.

The whole of it, without any ftraining, lets us fee, that in the worft ftate under which a nation

can

can fall, a good prince gives a full ſtop to thoſe judgments that are reſerved for them ; even when they ſeemed to be juſt breaking out upon them ; and that the removal of ſuch princes, is like the letting looſe that hand of juſtice which was reſtrained by their interceſſions. But ſince there is an uniformity in the methods of providence, " and that " which has been, is that which ſhall be, " then ſuch an amazing miſery as accompanied the utter ruin of the Jewiſh nation, ought to make deep impreſſions on all others, and to give theſe words of the prophet a formidable found ; " the righteous " periſh, and the merciful perſons are taken away " from the evil to come ; " which will come the quicker, as well as the more certainly, for their being taken away : and that will be yet the nearer, if while ſuch an appearance of things is in view, no man confiders it, nor lays it to heart.

Here I return to my ſubjeƈt, from which all that has been now ſaid, is not ſo much a digreſſion as it may appear to be to vulgar readers : a ſubjeƈt it is, where the common cenſures of diſcourſes of this kind are not to be much apprehended. On other occaſions of this nature, a few virtues muſt be raiſed, to make the moſt of them that may be ; and ſome few accidents muſt be ſet out with due advantages. For the ſake of theſe, a great deal muſt be forgiven, and the reſt is to be ſhaded or ſhewed as at a diſtance and in perſpeƈtive. Mankind is ſo little diſpoſed to believe much good of others, becauſe moſt men know ſo much ill by themſelves,

felves, and are very unwilling to be made better, that in order to the begetting a full belief of that which is propofed to the imitation of others, the words by which it is expreffed muft be feverely weighed and well chofen. When things of this kind are related with an exactnefs that feems too much ftudied, the wit that is ill placed leffens the effect that might have followed, if the recital had been more natural ; for what is moft genuine will be always the beft received ; nor muft too much be faid, how true or juft foever.

The prefent age may be eafily brought to believe any thing that can be faid upon this fubject, be-caufe the atteftations of it came fo thick from all hands. Yet fuch a character as is now to be offered the world, and to be conveyed down to pofterity, muft be fo managed, that it may not feem too exceffive ; that duty or affection may not be thought to have raifed it too high. The living witneffes, to whom we may now appeal, will foon go off the ftage ; the filent groans as well as the louder cries that are now founding in all our ftreets and in every corner, will foon be drowned and hufhed in filence : and then that which will be now cenfured, as a narrow and fcanty commendation, far below the fubject, and unworthy of it, will ap-pear to fucceeding ages to be a ftrain above human nature; it will pafs for the picture of an ima-ginary perfection, that feems rather to fet forth what our nature ought to rife to, than what has really happened.

This

This precaution is neceſſary, when perſons have lived in the ſhade, known only to a few and in a narrow neighbourhood. But a man may take a freer range when he undertakes to deſcribe one that was always in view, that was under a conſtant obſervation; and where a high elevation did put even that, which humility might endeavour to recover, in a true light. The bright as well as the dark ſides of ſuch perſons muſt be found out. Management may ſerve a turn, and go on for a time with ſecreſy and ſucceſs; but the continued and uninterrupted thread of life, led with ſo uniform an exactneſs, that cenſure itſelf could never find matter to fix on, even ſo long as to keep a doubtful thought in ſuſpence, is that which one may venture on, without the danger of over-doing it, he muſt rather deſpair to do it juſtice.

Where the matter riſes with ſo copious a fruitfulneſs, a nice choice muſt be made; much muſt be omitted, a great deal muſt be only mentioned, rather glanced at than enlarged on. The world is now ſo far beforehand in every thing that can be ſaid, that we muſt own fame has here changed her character, and has given ſuch true and full repreſentations, that there is little left to be done; but put things that are generally known, and univerſally talked of, in a little order, and to tell them as natively as ſhe did them.

Here ariſes an unexampled piece of a character, which may be well begun with; for I am afraid it both began and will end with her. In moſt per-

ſons,

fons, even thofe of the trueft merit, a ftudied management will fometimes appear with a little too
much varnifh, like a nocturnal piece, that has a
light caft through even the moft fhaded parts : fome
difpofition to fet ones felf out, and fome fatisfaction
in being commended, will at fome time or other
fhew itfelf more or lefs.   Here we may appeal to
great multitudes, to all who had the honour to ap-
proach her, and particularly to thofe who were
admitted to the greateft nearnefs, and the moft
conftant attendance, if at any one time, any thing
of this fort did ever difcover itfelf.   When due
acknowledgments were made, or decent things
were faid upon occafions that did well deferve them,
(God knows how frequent thefe were !) thefe
feemed fcarce to be heard ; they were fo little defired that they were prefently paft over, without
fo much as an anfwer that might feem to entertain
the difcourfe, even when it checked it.   She went
off from it to other fubjects, as one that could not
bear it.

So entire a deadnefs to the defire of glory, which
even the philofophers acknowledged was the laft thing
that a wife man put off, feemed to be fomewhat a-
bove human nature, and nearly refembling that ftate
of abfolute perfection, to which fhe has now attained.
The defire of true glory is thought to be the nobleft
principle that can be in fovereigns ; which fets
them on, with the moft conftant zeal, to procure
the good of mankind.   Many have thought that a
zealous purfuit of the one, could not be duly

animated

animated and maintained without the other. It was a part of the felicity of our times, that we have seen the moſt active zeal for the public, and a conſtant delight in doing good, joined with ſuch unaffected humility, ſo regardleſs of applauſe or praiſe, that the moſt critical obſervors could never ſee reaſon to think, that the ſecret flatteries of vanity or ſelf-love did work inwardly, or had any power over her.

An open and native ſincerity, which appeared in genuine characters, in a free and unreſtrained manner, did eaſily perſuade thoſe who ſaw it, that all was of a piece. A conſtant uniform behaviour, when that which is within does not agree with the appearances, ſeems to be a ſtrain above our pitch. Nor could any perſon find any other reaſon to ſuppoſe that it was otherwiſe in this inſtance, but from the ſecret ſenſe that every man has of ſome latent corruption, and the ſtolen inſinuations of pride that he feels within himſelf, which may make him conclude, that the whole race of mankind is ſo tainted, that nothing can be entirely freed from thoſe infirmities which do ſo naturally beſet us. But ſuch perſons ought to make another reflection, that daily obſervation ſhews to be true; that no man lives under ſo exact a guard, and ſuch a conſtant preſence of mind, but that all thoſe hidden diſpoſitions which lurk within him, will ſhoot out ſometimes, and ſhew themſelves on great occaſions, or ſudden accidents. Nature will break through all rules, when it is much excited, or taken at unawares. Therefore it is much more reaſonable,

C

as well as it is more charitable, to think that there are no fecret inclinations, which lie fo quiet that they do never difcover themfelves in a courfe of many years, and of unlooked for accidents, than to imagine that they are fo covered and managed, as to be chained up in perpetual reftraint. There is an air in what is genuine that is foon feen, (I had almoft faid felt.) It looks noble, without ftrains or art ; it pleafes as well as perfuades, with a force that is irrefiftible ; and how filent foever it may be, it looks like the univerfal character : it is a language which nature makes all men underftand, how few foever they are that feek it : this was fo peculiar to her, and fo fingular in her, that it deferved well to be begun with.

In moft of thofe perfons who have been the eminenteft for their piety and virtue, their thoughts have rifen too high for human nature : their notions have become too fierce, and their tempers too fullen and untractable ; they have confidered only what was good and defirable in itfelf, without regarding what the world could bear. They have not foftened themfelves enough into that agreeablenefs of temper, that might give fuch an amiable profpect of virtue, as fhould encourage the world to love and imitate it. Their meditations have foured them too much ; and, by an obftinate perfuing their own ideas, without accommodating themfelves enough to the frailties of others, they have given advantage to thofe who have ftudied to load them with prejudices : their

defigns

defigns have mifcarried, and they themfelves have become morofe and melancholy; defparing of doing any thing, becaufe they could not hope to do every thing. Cato's error has run through the beft fort of men that have ever lived : of projecting a common-wealth like Plato's, when the Romans were run to a dreg. Children muft be gained even by flattering their weakneffes, and by the foftnefs of kindnefs and good humour. The grown ftate of man is often but an advanced childhood : a dotage rather than a ripenefs. It muft be confeffed, that few of thofe who in all other refpects feem to have been born for the good of mankind, have been able to give their notions that turn, to fet them off with that air, and to recommend them with that addrefs, which we of late admired fo much. A charming behaviour, a genuine fweetnefs, and the fprightli-nefs, as well as the freedom of good humour, had foftened all thofe frightful apprehenfions that the world is too willing to entertain of the feverities of virtue, and of the ftrictnefs of true religion. Leffer matters were not much ftood on : an eafy compliance in fome of thefe, how little foever they were liked, on their own account, was intended to give her advantages, in order to the compaffing of greater things. While a frefh and graceful air, more turned to ferioufnefs, but always ferene, that dwelt on her looks, difcovered both the perfect calm that was within, and fhewed the force as well as the amiablenefs of thofe principles which

C 2

were

were the fprings of fo chearful a temper, and fo lively a deportment.

The freedom of chearfulnefs is not always under an exact command : it will make efcapes from rules, and be apt to go too far, and to forget all meafures and bounds : it is feldom kept under a perpetual guard. The opennefs of her behaviour was fubject to univerfal obfervation ; but it was under that regularity of conduct, that thofe who knew her beft and faw her ofteneft, could never difcover her thoughts or her intentions further, than as fhe herfelf had a mind to let them be known. No half word, or change of look, no forgetfulnefs, or run of difcourfe, did ever draw any thing from her, further, or fooner, than as fhe defigned it. This was managed in fo peculiar a way, that no diftruft was fhewed in it, nor diftafte given by it. It appeared to be no other, than that due refervednefs which became her elevation ; and fuited thofe affairs that were to pafs through her hands. When fhe faw caufe for it, fhe had the trueft methods to oblige others to ufe all due freedom with herfelf ; while yet fhe kept them at a fit diftance from her own thoughts.

She would never take any affiftance from thofe arts, that are become fo common to great pofts, that fome perhaps fancy them neceflary : fhe did not cover her purpofes by doubtful expreffions, or fuch general words, as taken ftrictly do fignify little, but in common ufe are underftood to import a great deal more. As fhe would not deceive others,

fo

fo fhe avoided the faying of that which might give them an occafion to deceive themfelves : and when fhe did not intend to promife, fhe took care to explain her meaning fo critically, that it might be underftood that no conftruction of a promife was to be made from general words of favour. In a courfe of feveral years, and of many turns, when great occafion was given for more artificial - methods, and when, according to the maxims of the world, great ufe might have been made of them ; yet fhe maintained her fincerity fo intirely, to the honour of truth, be it faid, as well as to hers, that fhe never once needed explanations to juftify either her words or actions. Integrity preferved her, as well as fhe preferved it.

Such eminent, I am forry to fay, fuch unufual . perfections, had they appeared in one of the meaneft capacity, and of the loweft degree of improvement, yet muft have challenged great veneration. Common obfervation makes it but too apparent, that thofe of the higheft form, that have an exaltation in them, which makes them like another rank of mortals, that have a true flight of thought, a great compafs of knowledge, a ftability and equablenefs of temper, with a deep and correct judgment, who have cultivated the advantages of nature, by fearching and laborious acquifitions ; fuch perfons, I fay, do fwell too much upon the preference that is due to them ; and foil thofe fhining diftinctions that were born with them, by mixtures that need not now be enlarged on. A fubject compofed of fo much perfection, ought not to be digreffed from, to fet out the diforders that appear but too frequently in the fublimeft pieces of mankind. Thefe are fo unacceptable, while virtue has fo benign an afpect, that eminent degrees of it, though joined with a lower proportion of that which feems to have more luftre, is much more valuable, than all that can be called great in human nature, is without it.

But if both thefe fhould happen to meet together, and that in as high a degree as our mortal ftate is capable of, then we muft acknowledge, that this is all that we can expect from our nature, under its prefent depreffion. So few inftances of fuch a mixture have appeared to us, that we muft confefs, it is much more than we ought to look for. The hiftory of princes that have lived at a great diftance from us, is feldom believed to be fo exact, efpecially in the commendatory part, that we rely much upon it. Xenophon has made Cyrus appear to be a prince, fo much perfecter than the world is difpofed to believe, that the picture he gives of him paffes rather for a piece of invention, than of hiftory. When the world fhall have lived beyond the fame of tradition and report, a minute hiftory of his life, if exactly writ, may probably have the fame fate: it will look too great to be credible.

What is good, as well as what is great in human nature, were here fo equally mixed, and both fhined fo bright in her, that though one of thefe is always the better part, yet it is hard to tell, in whether of the two she was the more eminent.

I will say little either of her rank, or of her person: the dignity of the one, and the majesty of the other, were born with her. Her sphere was great, and she was furnished with advantages proportioned to it. She maintained her authority with so becoming a grace; and inspired so particular a respect, that in this regard only, she was absolute and despotical, and could not be resisted. The port of royalty, and the humility of christianity did so happily concur in her, that how different soever their characters may seem to be, they gave a mutual lustre to each other.

She maintained that respect that belonged to her sex, without any of those diminutions, that though generally speaking, they do not much misbecome it, yet do seem a little to lessen it. She would never affect to be above it in common and meaner things: she had a courage that was resolute and firm, mixed with a mildness that was soft and gentle; she had in her all the graces of her own sex, and all the greatness of ours. If she did not affect to be a Zenobia or a Boadicia, it was not because she wanted their courage, but because she understood the decencies of her sex better than they did. The character of a Jean of Navarre, or of our celebrated Elizabeth, was much more valuable in her esteem, than that of a Semiramis, or of a Thomiris. A desire of power, or an eagerness of empire, were things so far below her,

C 4

though

though they generally pafs for heroical qualities, that perhaps the world never yet faw fo great a capacity for government, joined with fo little appetite to it; fo unwillingly affumed, fo modeftly managed, and fo chearfully laid down.

The clearnefs of her apprehenfion, the prefence of her mind, the exactnefs of her memory, the folidity of her judgment, the correctnefs of her expreffions, had fuch particular diftinctions in them, that great enlargements might be made on every one of thefe, if a cloud of witnefies did not make them lefs neceffary. None took things fooner, or retained them longer : none judged truer, or fpoke more exactly. She writ clear and fhort, with a true beauty and force of ftile. She difcovered a fuperiority of genius, even in the moft trifling matters, which were confidered by her only as amufements, and fo gave no occafion for deep reflections. A happinefs of imagination, and a livelinefs of expreffion, appeared upon the commoneft fubjects; on the fudden, and in greateft variety of accidents, fhe was quick but not hafty : and even without the advantages that her condition gave her, fhe had an exaltation of mind, that fubdued as well as charmed all that came near her.

A quicknefs of thought is often fuperficial ; it catches eafily, and fparkles with fome luftre ; but it lafts not long, nor does it go deep : a bright vivacity was here joined with fearching diligence. Her age and her rank had denied her opportunities for much ftudy ; yet fhe had gone far that way,

and

and had read the beſt book in the three languages, that were almoſt equally familiar to her. ·She gave the moſt of her hours to the ſtudy of the ſcriptures, and of books relating to them. It were eaſy to give amazing inſtances of her underſtanding in matters of divinity. She had ſo well conſidered our diſputes with the church of Rome, that ſhe was capable of managing debates in them, with equal degrees of addreſs and judgment: nor was ſhe unacquainted with thoſe unhappy queſtions that have diſtracted us: and had ſuch juſt, as well as large notions about them, that they would have ſoon laid our animoſities, and have compoſed our differences, if there had been temper enough, on all ſides, to have hearkened to them.

She had a generous and a ſublime idea of the chriſtian religion, and a particular affection to the church of England: but an affection that was neither blind nor partial. She ſaw what finiſhings we ſtill wanted; and had dedicated her thoughts and endeavours to the conſidering of the beſt means that might both compleat and eſtabliſh us. She intended to do all that was poſſible, in order to the raiſing a higher ſpirit of true devotion among us, to engage thoſe of our profeſſion to a greater application to their functions; and to diſpoſe us all to a better underſtanding among ourſelves; that we might with united endeavours ſet ourſelves to beat down impiety and immorality. She read and medi-tated much on theſe ſubjects; and judged of them with ſo juſt an exactneſs, that it appeared the

ſtrength

ftrength of her mind went far beyond the compafs of her knowledge. She took that care to be well informed of thefe matters, that when fhe met with hints, either in books or fermons, that related to other fubjects with which fhe was not acquainted, fhe loft none of them : if they feemed to be of importance, fhe called for explanations of them, from thofe whom fhe fuffered to entertain her upon fuch fubjects. She propofed them often with a preface, confeffing her own ignorance ; and when fhe had ftated fome difficulties to them very clearly, fhe would conclude with words that carried in them an air of modefty, that fhined then moft particularly, when fhe feemed to defire an increafe of knowledge. She would fay, " fhe did not " know if there was any difficulty in fuch things " or not ; or, if fhe apprehended or expreffed it " right ; or, if it was only her ignorance." When any new thing was laid before her, fhe feemed glad to have an occafion to own, that fhe knew nothing of that before ; but then fhe would have it to be fully explained to her, till fhe found fhe did thoroughly apprehend it. All thefe intimations were fo carefully laid up by her, that fhe feemed fcarce capable of forgetting them. After feveral years of interval, fhe returned in difcourfe to fome fubjects, that had been formerly opened to her, with a frefh-nefs of apprehenfion about them, as if the firft difcourfe had never been interrupted. She knew none of the learned languages, yet when fome paffages of fcripture were explained to her, by the

genius

genius and phrafes of the original languages, fhe retained them very carefully, even though fhe underftood not the foundation of them. She loved fincerity in every thing, to fuch a degree, that fhe defired to underftand the weak fide as well as the ftrong one of all parties and doctrines. She loved a diftinct knowledge of every thing; and fhe had accuftomed thofe whom fhe admitted to talk to her on fuch fubjects, to hide neither the weaknefs of the one fide, nor the ftrength of the other from her. When fhe delivered her own judgment, which fhe generally avoided to do, unlefs there was fome neceffity for it, fhe did it with that modefty, as well as exactnefs, that it fhewed the force as well as the purity of her mind.

Next to the beft fubjects, fhe beftowed moft of her time on books of hiftory, chiefly of the latter ages, particularly thofe of her own kingdoms, as being the moft proper to give her ufeful inftruction. Lively books, where wit and reafon gave the mind a true entertainment, had much of her time. She was a good judge as well as a great lover of poetry : fhe loved it beft when it dwelt on the beft fubjects. So tender fhe was of poetry, though much more of virtue, that fhe had a particular concern in the defilement, or rather the proftitution of the mufes among us. She made fome fteps to the underftanding philofophy and mathematicks, but fhe ftopped foon ; only fhe went far in natural hiftory and perfpective, as fhe was very exact in geography. She thought fublime
things

things were too high flights for the fex; which fhe oft·talked of with a liberty that was very lively: but fhe might well be familiar with it, after fhe had given fo effectual a demonftration of the improvements it was capable of. Upon the whole matter, fhe ftudied and read more than could be imagined by any, who had not known how many of her hours were fpent in her clofet. She would have made a much greater progrefs, if the frequent returns of ill humours on her eyes, had not forced her to fpare them. Her very diverfions gave indications of a mind that was truly great: fhe had no relifh for thofe lazy ones, that are the too common confumers of moft peoples time, and that make as great waftes on their minds, as they do on their fortunes. If fhe ufed them fometimes, fhe made it vifible, it was only in compliance with forms; becaufe fhe was unwilling to offend others with too harfh a feverity: fhe gave her minutes of leifure with the greateft willingnefs to architecture and gardenage. She had a riches of invention, with a happinefs of contrivance, that had airs in it that were freer and nobler than what was more ftiff, though it might be more regular: fhe knew that this drew an expence after it; fhe had no other inclinations befides this, to any diverfions that were expenceful; and fince this employed many hands, fhe was pleafed to fay, "that fhe "hoped it would be forgiven her." Yet fhe was uneafy when fhe felt the weight of the charge that lay upon it.

When

When her eyes were endangered by reading too much, she found out the amusement of work; and in all those hours that were not given to better employments, she wrought with her own hands, and that sometimes with so constant a diligence, as if she had been to earn her bread by it. It was a new thing, and looked like a sight, to see a queen work so many hours a day. " She looked on " idleness as the great corrupter of human nature; " and believed that if the mind had no employ- " ment given it, it would create some of the worst " sort to itself: and she thought that any thing " that might amuse and divert, without leaving " a dreg and ill impression behind it, ought to fill " up those vacant hours, that were not claimed by " devotion or business. " Her example soon wrought on, not only those that belonged to her, but the whole town to follow it : so that it was become as much the fashion to work, as it had been formerly to be idle. In this, which seemed a nothing, and was turned by some to be the subject of raillery, a greater step was made than perhaps every one was aware of, to the bettering of the age. While she diverted herself thus with work, she took care to give an entertainment to her own mind, as well as to those who were admitted to the honour of working with her : one was appointed to read to the rest ; the choice was suited to the time of the day, and to the employment : some book or poem that was lively, as well as instructing. Few of her sex, not to say of her rank, gave ever less time to dreffing, or feemed lefs curious about it. Thofe parts of it which required more patience, were not given up intirely to it. She read often, all the while herfelf, and generally aloud ; that thofe who ferved about her, might be the better for it : when fhe was indifpofed, another was called to do it : all was intermixed with fuch pleafant reflections of her own, that the glofs was often better liked than the text.   An agreeable vivacity fpread that innocent chearfulnefs among all about her, that whereas in moft courts, the hours of ftrict attendance are the heavieft parts of the day, they were in hers the moft delightful of all others.

Her chearfulnefs may be well termed innocent, for none was ever hurt by it : no natural defects, or real faults, true or falfe, were ever the fubjects of her mirth : nor could fhe bear it in others, if their wit happened to glance that way.   She thought it a cruel and barbarous thing, to be merry on other peoples coft ; or, to make the misfortunes or follies of others, the matter of their diverfion. She fcarce ever expreffed a more intire fatisfaction in any fermon that fhe had heard, than in our late primate's againft evil fpeaking.   When fhe thought fome were guilty of it, fhe would afk them, if they had read that fermon.   This was underftood to be a reprimand, though in the fofteft manner. She had indeed one of the bleffings of virtue, that does not always accompany it : for fhe was as free from cenfures, as fhe was from deferving them. When reflections were made on this, before her,

she

she said, " she afcribed that wholly to the good-
" nefs of God to her : for she did not doubt but
" that many fell under hard chara&ters, that de-
" ferved them as little. She gave it this further
" turn, that God knew her weaknefs, and that
" she was not able to bear fome imputations; and
" therefore he did not try her beyond her ftrength."
In one refpe&, she intended never to provoke cenfure : she was confcientioufly tender of wounding
others; and faid, " she hoped God would ftill
" blefs her in her own good name, as long as she
" was careful not to hurt others; " but as she
was exa& in not wronging any other while she diverted herfelf, fo upon indifferent fubje&s she had
a fpring of chearfulnefs in her, that was never to
be exhaufted : it never run to repetition, or forced
mirth.

A mind that was fo exalted by nature, and was
fo improved by induftry, who was as much above
all about her by her merit, as she was by her
condition, and that owed thofe peculiar advantages
under God, chiefly to herfelf, for very little was
added to her by others, had certainly a right to in-
dulgent cenfures, even though she had given occafion to them. Much ought to have been forgiven
to one that had deferved fo well; but this is perhaps the firft inftance that the world has yet feen,
of one that had fo much in her that deferved to be
valued and admired, without one fingle defe& or
allay, that needed allowances to be made for it.

I have

I have dwelt hitherto upon the more general
parts of her character; I go next to confider what
was more fpecial. Thofe that deferve to be moft
enlarged on, are the difpofitions of her mind, both
with relation to the impreffions of religion, and the
compaffions of human nature. What fhe was inwardly with relation to God, was only known to
him whom fhe now fees face to face. Thofe with
whom fhe talked with more than ordinary freedom
upon thofe matters, faw on many occafions what
an awful fenfe fhe had of God, and of all things
in which his glory was concerned; they faw with
how exact a tendernefs fhe weighed every thing
by which the purity of her own confcience was to
be preferved, unblemifhed as well as unfpotted.

In thofe great fteps of her later years, that carried
a face which at firft appearance feemed liable to
cenfure, and that were the fingle inftances of her
whole life, that might be thought capable of hard
conftructions; fhe weighed the reafons fhe went
on with a caution and exactnefs that well became
the importance of them; the biafs lying ftill againft
that, which to vulgar minds might feem to be
her intereft. She was convinced that the public
good of mankind, the prefervation of that religion,
which fhe was affured was the only true one, and
thofe real extremities to which matters were driven,
ought to fuperfede all other confiderations. She
had generous notions of the liberty of human nature,
and of the true ends of government; fhe thought
it was defigned to make mankind fafe and happy,

and

and not to raise the power of those, into whose hands it was committed, upon the ruins of property and liberty. Nor could she think that religion was to be delivered up to the humours of misguided princes, whose persuasion made them as cruel in imposing on their subjects the dictates of others, as they themselves were implicit in submitting to them: yet after all, her inclinations lay so strong to a duty, that nature had put her under, that she made a sacrifice of herself in accepting that high elevation, that perhaps was harder to her to bear, than if she had been to be made a sacrifice in the severest sense. She saw that not only her own reputation might suffer by it, but that religion too might be concerned in those reproaches that she was to look for. This was much more to her than all that crowns with their gaudy lustre could offer instead of it; but the saving of whole nations seemed to require it; and that being the only visible mean left to preserve the protestant religion, not only here, but every where else, she was thereby determined to it.

She was no enthusiast; and yet she could not avoid thinking, that her being preserved during her childhood in that flexibility of age and understanding, without so much as one single attempt made upon her, was to be ascribed to a special providence watching over her: to that she added, her being early delivered from the danger of all temptations, and the advantages she had afterwards to employ much privacy in so large a course

of

of ſtudy, which had not been poſſible for her to have compaſſed, if ſhe had lived in the conſtant diſſipation of a public court. Theſe concurring had convinced her, that God had conducted her by an immediate hand, and that ſhe was raiſed up to preſerve that religion which was then every where in its laſt agonies ; yet when theſe and many other conſiderations, which ſhe had carefully attended to, determined her, nature ſtill felt itſelf loaded : ſhe bore it with the outward appearances of ſatisfaction, becauſe ſhe thought it became her not to diſcourage others, or to give them an occaſion to believe that her uneaſineſs was of another nature than truly it was ; but in that whole matter ſhe put a conſtraint upon herſelf (upon her temper I mean, for no conſideration whatſoever could have enduced her to have forced her conſcience,) that was more ſenſible and violent to her, than any thing that could have been wiſhed her by the moſt enraged and virulent of all her enemies.

Oh, could any be enemies to ſuch virtue ! and to ſo pure and ſo angelical a mind ! Could ſhe that was the glory of her ſex, the darling of human nature, and the wonder of all that knew her, become the ſubject of hatred or obloquy !

A nobler ſubject calls me from this tranſport ; to look over the other parts of her character, upon this head of religion. Modeſty and humility covered a great deal from common obſervation, indeed all that was poſſible for her to conceal ; but no clouds can quite darken the day ; it caſts a light

even

even when it does not shine out. Her punctual exactness, not only to public offices, but to her secret retirements, was so regular a thing, that it was never put off in the greatest croud of business or little journeys ; then, though the hour was anticipated, the duty was never neglected : she took care to be so early on those occasions, that she might never either quite forget, or very much shorten that, upon which she reckoned that the blessing of the whole day turned. She observed the Lord's day so religiously, that besides her hours of retirement, she was constantly thrice a day in the public worship of God ; and for a great part of the year four times a day while she lived beyond sea. She was constant to her monthly communions, and retired herself more than ordinary for some days before them. In them, as well as in all the other parts of the worship of God, an unexampled seriousness appeared always in her, without one glance let out for observation ; and such care was taken to hide the more solemn elevations of her mind to God, that these things struck all those who saw them, but had never seen any thing like them before. This did spread a spirit of devotion among all that were about her, who could not see so much in her, without feeling somewhat to arise in themselves ; though few could chain themselves down to such a fixed and steady application as they saw in her. Nothing in that was theatrical, nothing given to shew ; every thing was sincere, as well as solemn, and genuine as well as majestical.

Her

Her attention to fermons was fo entire, that as her eye never wandered from a good preacher, fo fhe fhewed no wearinefs of an indifferent one : when fhe was afked, how fhe could be fo attentive to fome fermons that were far from being perfect, fhe anfwered, " That fhe thought it did not become " her, by any part of her behaviour, to difcourage, " or feem to diflike one that was doing his beft." The hardeft cenfure that fhe paft on the worft, was to fay nothing to their advantage ; for fhe never denied her commendations to any thing that deferved them. She was not content to be devout herfelf ; fhe infufed that temper into all that came near her ; chiefly into thofe whom fhe took into her more immediate care, whom fhe ftudied to form with the tendernefs and watchfulnefs of a mother. She charmed them with her inftructions, as fhe overcame them with her kindnefs ; never was miftrefs both feared and loved fo entirely as fhe was. She fcattered books of inftruction to all that were round about her, and gave frequent orders that good books fhould be laid in the places of attendance, that fuch as waited, might not be condemned to idlenefs ; but might entertain themfelves ufefully, while they were in their turns of fervice.

She had a true regard to piety wherever fhe faw it, in what form or party foever. Her judgment tied her to our communion, but her charity was extended to all. The liberty that fome have taken to unchurch great bodies of chriftians, for fome defects and irregularities, were ftrains that fhe could

never

never affent to; nor indeed could fhe well bear them. She longed to fee us in a clofer conjunction with all proteftants abroad, and hoped we might ftrengthen ourfelves at home, by uniting to us as many as could be brought within our body. Few things ever grieved her more, than that thofe hopes feemed to languifh, and that the profpect of fo defired an union vanifhed out of fight.

The raifing the reputation and authority of the clergy, as the chief inftrument for advancing religion, was that to which fhe intended to apply her utmoft diligence. She knew that the only true way to compafs this, was to engage them to be exemplary in their lives, and eminent in their labours; to watch over their flocks, and to edify them by good preaching and diligent catechifing. She was refolved to have the whole nation underftand, that by thefe ways, and by thefe only, divines were to be recommended to favour and preferment. She made it vifible, that the fteps were to be made by merit, and not by friendfhip and importunity. Solicitations and afpirings were practices that affected her deeply; becaufe fhe faw the ufe that was made of them by malicious obfervers; who concluded from thence, that we run to our profeffion as to a trade, for the fake of the gains and honours that we might find in it, and not to fave fouls, or to edify the church. Every inftance of this kind gave her a fenfible wound, becaufe it hardened bad men in the contempt of religion. She therefore charged thofe, whom fhe trufted moft in

D 3

fuch

fuch matters, to look out for the beft men, and the beft preachers, that they might be made known to her. She was under a real anxiety when church-preferments, efpecially the more eminent ones, were to be difpofed of. She reckoned that that was one of the main parts of her care; for which a particular account was to be given to that God, from whom her authority was derived, and to whom fhe had devoted it. When fhe apprehended that friendfhip might give a biafs to thofe whom fhe allowed to fpeak to her on thofe heads; fhe told them of it, with the authority that became her, and that they well deferved. She could deny the moft earneft folicitations, with a true firmnefs, when fhe thought the perfon did not deferve them; for that was fuperior with her to all other confiderations. But when fhe denied things, fhe did it with fo much foftnefs, and upon fo good reafon, that fuch as might be mortified by the repulfe, were yet forced to confefs that fhe was in the right; even when, for the fake of a friend, they wifhed fhe had for once been in the wrong.

It grieved her to hear how low and depauperated a great many of the churches of England were become: which were funk into fuch extreme poverty, that it was fcarce poffible, even by the help of a plurality, to find a fubfiftence in them. She had formed a great and noble defign, to bring them all to a juft ftate of plenty, and to afford a due encouragement; but pluralities and non-refidence, when not enforced by real neceffity, were otherwife fo odious

to

to her, that she resolved to throw such perpetual disgraces upon them, as should oblige all persons to let go the hold that they had got of the cures of souls, over whom they did not watch, and among whom they did not labour.

In a full discourse on this very subject, the day before the fatal illness overtook her; she said, " she had no great hope of mending matters; yet " she was resolved to go on, and never to suffer " herself to be discouraged, or to lose heart: she " would still try what could be done, and persue " her design, how slow or insensible soever the " progress might be." She had taken pains to form a true plan of the primitive constitutions; and had resolved to bring ours, as near it as could be; that so it might become more firm and useful, for attaining the great ends of religion. Neither the spirit of a party, nor of bigotry, lay at the bottom of all this. She did not project any part of it as an art of government, or an instrument of power and dominion.

Her scheme was thus laid; she thought that the christian religion was revealed from heaven, to make mankind happy here, as well as hereafter: and that as mankind and society could not subsist without any religion at all, so also the corruption of christianity had made many nations the worse rather than the better, for that shadow of it that was received among them. She thought that a pious, learned, and laborious clergy, was the chief mean of bringing the world under the power

of

of the chriſtian religion ; and that the treating their perſons with reſpect, was neceſſary to procure them credit in the diſcharge of their function. She intended to carry on all this together, and not any one part of it ſeparate from the reſt. If at any time ſhe knew any thing in thoſe who ſerved at the altar, that expoſed them to juſt cenſures, ſhe covered it all that could be from common obſervation ; but took care that the perſons concerned ſhould be both roundly ſpoke to, and proceeded againſt when ſofter methods did not ſucceed, or that it ſeemed neceſſary that their puniſhment ought to be made as public as their crimes were. She would never ſuffer any to go away with a conceit, that a zeal for the ſervice of the crown, could atone for other faults ; or compound for the great duties of their function. This ſeemed to be the ſetting the intereſts of religion after their own ; but ſhe was reſolved to give them always the preference.

No intimation was ever let fall to her in any diſcourſe, that offered a probable mean of making us better, which was loſt by her. She would call upon ſome to turn that motion over and over again, till ſhe had formed her own thoughts concerning it. The laſt thing that ſhe had ſettled with our late bleſſed primate, was a ſcheme of ſuch rules, as our preſent circumſtances could bear, publiſhed ſince by his majeſty ; which was an earneſt of many others that were to follow in due time. It was indeed an amazing, as well as a delightful

thing,

thing, to fee how well fhe underftood fuch matters, and how much fhe was fet on promoting them.

She judged aright, that the true end of power,
and the beft exercife of it, was to do good, and to
make the world the better for it. She often faid,
that fhe found nothing in it to make it fupportable,
not to fay pleafant, befides that : and fhe wondered
that the true pleafure which accompanied it, did
not engage princes to perfue it more effectually.
Without this fhe thought, that a private life, with
moderate circumftances, was the happier as well
as the fafer ftate. When reflections were once
made before her, of the fharpnefs of fome hiftorians, who had left heavy imputations on the memory of fome princes; fhe anfwered, " that if
" thofe princes were truly fuch, as the hiftorians
" reprefented them, they had well deferved that
" treatment; and others who tread their fteps,
" might look for the fame : for the truth would
" be told at laft, and that with the more acrimony
" of ftile, for being fo long reftrained. It was a
" gentle fuffering to be expofed to the world in
" their true colours, much below what others had
" fuffered at their hands : fhe thought that all fo-
" vereigns ought to read fuch hiftories as Pro-
" copius; for how much foever he may have
" aggravated matters, and how unbecomingly
" foever he may have writ, yet by fuch books they
" might fee, what would be probably faid of them-
" felves, when all terrors and reftraints fhould fall
" off with their lives." She encouraged thofe
whom

whom she admitted to frequent acceſs, to lay before her all the occaſions of doing good that might occur to their thoughts; and was always well pleaſed when new opportunities were offered to her, in which ſhe might exerciſe that which was the moſt valued of all her prerogatives. So deſirous ſhe was to know both how to correct what might be amiſs, and to promote every good deſign, that ſhe not only allowed of great freedom, in bringing propoſitions of that kind to her, but ſhe charged the conſciences of ſome, with a command to keep no-thing of that nature from her, which they thought ſhe ought to know. Nor were ſuch motions ever unacceptable to her; even when other circum-ſtances made it impoſſible for her to put them in execution.

The reforming the manners of her people was one of her chief cares. If a greater progreſs was not made in this, according to the pious wiſhes of ſome, who had good intentions, and much zeal, the true account of that ſlowneſs was this; ſhe had often heard that the hypocriſy of the former times had brought on the atheiſm and impiety of the pre-ſent, and had fortified libertines in their prejudices; therefore ſhe reſolved to guard againſt every thing that might ſeem to revive that. She obſerved that Joſiah was for the ſpace of four years engaged in a religious courſe of life, before he ſet himſelf to the reforming of his people; that by the example he ſet them, he might gain ſo much credit in carrying on that deſign, as might excuſe, as well as compen-

ſate

fate the flowneſs of beginning it. She judged that all people ought to be well poſſeſſed of their intentions in that matter: and ſhe feared, left in the diſ-jointed ſtate, in which our affairs have lain ſo long, the going on with that deſign might have the face of ſerving ſome other end under that appearance, for that will be popular, even when things are in a very corrupt ſtate. Therefore tho' this was no ſooner moved to her, than ſhe ſet it a going, yet finding few inſtruments to concur in it, and ſeeing a violent oppoſition to thoſe that did, ſhe thought that her putting her whole ſtrength to it might be reſerved with great advantage to another time, in which our affairs ſhould have a calmer face, and be brought to a more ſedate ſtate. She did hearken carefully after every thing that ſeemed to give ſome hope, that the next generation ſhould be better than the preſent, with a particular attention. She heard of a ſpirit of devotion and piety, that was ſpreading itſelf among the youth of this great city, with a true ſatisfaction; ſhe enquired often and much about it, and was glad to hear it went on and prevailed. "She lamented that "whereas the devotions of the church of Rome were "all ſhew, and made up of pomp and pageantry; "that we were too bare and naked; and practiſed "not enough to entertain a ſerious temper, or a "warm and an affectionate heart: we might have "light enough to direct, but we wanted flame to "raiſe an exalted devotion."

I have now given some instances of the temper of her mind, in that which concerned God and religion; I go in the next place to consider her with relation to human nature.

Princes are raised so far above the rest of mankind, that they do generally lose sight of those miseries to which the greater part is subject. It would disturb that ease, in which they pass away their hours too much, to hear dismal recitals of the calamities of their people. How much soever they may be lifted up with the glorious title of the parents of their country, yet for the most part they know little of the pressures their people lie under, and they feel them less. Our blessed queen was become the delight of all that knew her, by the obliging tenderness with which she treated all those who came near her: she made the afflictions of the unfortunate easier to them, by the share that she bore of them, and the necessities of the miserable the more supportable, by the relief that she gave them. She was tender of those who deserved her favour; and compassionate towards those who wanted her pity. It was easy for her to reward, for all sorts of bounty flowed readily from her. But it was much harder for her to punish, except when the nature of the crime made mercy become a cruelty, and then she was inflexible, not only to importunity, but to the tenderness of her own compassionate heart.

She was indeed happily framed by nature, which wrought so soon that it prevented education. She

was

was good and gentle, before she was capable of knowing that she ought to be so. · This grew up with her in the whole progress of childhood: she might need instruction, but she wanted no persuasion; and I have been often told that she never once, in the whole course of her education, gave any occasion to reprove her: so naturally did she go into every thing that was good, often before she knew it, and always after she once understood it.

She was but growing out of childhood, when she went among strangers; but she went under the guard of so exact a conduct, and so much discretion; she expressed such a gentleness, access to her was so easy, and her deportment was so obliging; her life was such an example, and her charity was so free, that perhaps no age ever had such an instance. Never was there such an universal love and esteem (one is tempted to seek for other words, if language did afford them) paid to any, as she had from persons of all ranks and conditions in the United Provinces. It was like transport and rapture: the veneration was so profound, that how just soever it might be, it seemed rather excessive. Neither her foreign birth, nor regal extraction, neither the diversity of interests of opinions, nor her want of power and treasure, (equal to her bounty) diminished the respects that were offered her, even from a people, whose constitution gives them naturally a jealousy of too great a merit in those who are at the head of their government.

I am afraid to enlarge too much on the juſtice that was done her in theſe parts; or on that univerſal mourning, with which her departure from them was followed: that ſeemed ſcarce capable of an addition, till now that there has appeared ſo black a gloom of deſponding ſorrow ſpread among them all; deſpair and death ſeeming to dwell on every face, when the dreadful news flew over to them. I am afraid, I ſay, to dwell too much on this, leaſt it may ſeem to reproach thoſe who owed her much more.

In her character, ordinary things, how ſingular ſoever ſhe might be in them, muſt be thrown into the heap. She was a gentle miſtreſs, a kind friend, (if this word is too low for her ſtate, it is not too low for her humility,) and above all ſhe was ſo tender and ſo reſpectful a wife, that ſhe ſeemed to go beyond the perfecteſt ideas that wit or invention has been able to riſe to. The loweſt condition of life, or the greateſt inequality of fortune, has not afforded ſo perfect a pattern. Tenderneſs and complacency ſeemed to ſtrive which of them ſhould be the more eminent. She had no higher ſatisfaction in the proſpect of greatneſs, that was deſcending on her, than that it gave her an occaſion of making him a preſent worthy of himſelf. Nor had crowns or thrones any charm in them, that was ſo pleaſant to her, as that they raiſed him to a greatneſs, which he ſo well deſerved, and could ſo well maintain. She was all zeal and rapture, when any thing was to be done, that could either

expreſs

exprefs affection, or fhew refpect to him. She obeyed with more pleafure, than the moft ambitious could have when they command. This fubject is too hard to be well fet out, and fo it muft be left in general and larger expreffions.

Thofe who ferved her, can never give over when they are relating the inftances of her gentlenefs to them all. She was fo foft when fhe gave her orders, and fo careful of not putting too much upon them; fo tender of them in their ficknefs and afflictions, fo liberal on many different occafions, that as the inftances are innumerable, fo they have peculiarities in them which fhew that every thing in her was of a piece with the reft. She fhewed a fenfibility at the death of thofe whom fhe particularly valued; that perfons of fo exalted a condition, do generally think may mifbecome them. The many tears that fhe fhed upon the death of our good primate, who got the ftart of her, a very few days, fhewed how well fhe underftood his worth, and how much fhe valued it.

So careful fhe was of all that belonged to her, that when fhe faw what her laft ficknefs was like to grow to, fhe made thofe, who had not yet gone through it, withdraw. She would fuffer none to ftay about her, when their attendance might endanger their own health; and yet fhe was fo tender of them, when they fell under that fo juftly dreadful illnefs, that fhe would not fuffer them to be removed, though they happened to be lodged very near herfelf.

Her

Her bounty and her compassions had great matter given them to work upon. And how wide
foever her fphere may have been, fhe went in this
rather beyond her ftrength, than kept within it.
Thofe generous confeffors and exiles whom the
perfecution of France fent over hither, as well as
to the United Provinces, felt the tendernefs as well
as the bounty of the welcome that fhe gave them.
The confufions of Ireland drove over multitudes of
all ranks, who fled hither for fhelter, and were foon
reduced to great ftraights, from a ftate of as great
plenty: moft of thefe were, by her means, both
fupported during their ftay, and enabled to return
home after that ftorm was over: the largenefs of
the fupplies that were given, and the tender manner of giving them, made their exile both the
fhorter and the more tolerable: the miferable among
ourfelves, particularly thofe who fuffered by the
accidents of war, found in her a relief that was
eafily come at, and was copioufly furnifhed. She
would never limit any from laying proper objects
for her charity in her way; nor confine that care
to the minifters of the Almonry: fhe encouraged
all that were about her, or that had free accefs to
her, to acquaint her with the neceffities under
which perfons of true merit might languifh; and
fhe was never uneafy at applications of that kind,
nor was her hand ever fcanty, when the perfon
was deferving, or the extremity was pinching.
She was regular and exact in this; fhe found that
even a royal treafure, though difpenfed by a hand

that

that was yet more royal, could not anfwer all demands. Therefore fhe took care to have a juft account, both of the worth and of the neceffities of thofe who pretended ; and fhe fhewed in this as great an exactnefs, and as attentive a regard, as much memory, and as much diligence, as if fhe had had no cares of a higher nature upon her. It feemed fhe kept tables of journals ; for fhe had a method in it, with which no body was ever acquainted, as far as I could learn. It was very reafonable to believe, that fhe took notes and fet rules to herfelf in this matter.

But fhe was fo exact to the rule of the gofpel, of managing it with deep fecrefy, that none knew what, or to whom, fhe gave, but thofe whom fhe was forced to employ in it. When it was to fall on perfons who had accefs to her, her own hand was the conveyance ; what went through other hands, was charged on them with an injunction of fecrefy ; and fhe herfelf was fo far from fpeaking of fuch things, that when fome perfons were offered to her charity, who had been already named by others, and were relieved by herfelf, fhe would not let thofe who fpoke to her, upon the fame of their being in want, underftand any thing of the notice that had been already taken of it; but either fhe let the thing pafs in filence, or if the neceffity was reprefented as heavier than fhe had underftood it to be, a new fupply was given, without fo much as a hint of what had gone before.

But

But how good foever fhe was in herfelf, fhe carried a heavy load upon her mind : the deep fenfe
that fhe had of the guilt and judgments that
feemed to be hanging over us, as no doubt it gave
her many afflicting thoughts in the prefence of
God, fo it broke often out in many fad ftrains to
thofe to whom fhe gave her thoughts a freer vent.
The impieties and blafphemies, the open contempt
of religion, and the fcorn of virtue, that fhe heard
of from fo many hands, and in fo many different
corners of the nation, gave her a fecret horror, and
offered fo black a profpect, that it filled her with
melancholy reflections, and engaged her into much
fecret mourning.   This touched her the more
fenfibly when fhe at any time heard that fome, who
pretended to much zeal for the crown and the prefent eftablifhment, feemed from thence to think
they had fome right to be indulged in their licencioufnefs, and other irregularities.   She often faid,
" can a bleffing be expected from fuch hands, or
" on any thing that muft pafs through them ? "
She longed to fee a fet of men of integrity and probity, of generous tempers and public fpirits, in whofe
hands the concerns of the crown and nation might
be lodged, with reafonable hopes of fuccefs, and of a
bleffing from above, upon their fervices. She had a juft
efteem of all perfons as fhe found them truly virtuous
and religious ; nor could any other confiderations
have a great effect upon her, when thefe were wanting.   She made a great difference between thofe
that were convinced of the principles of religion,

how

how fatally foever they might be fhut up from having their due effect on them, and thofe who had
quite thrown them off; where thefe were quite
extinguifhed, no hope was left, nor foundation to
build upon : but where they remained, how feeble
or unactive foever, there was a feed ftill within them,
that at fome time or other, and upon fome happy
occafion, might fhoot and grow. Next to open
impiety, the coldnefs, the want of heat and life in
thofe who pretended to religion, the deadnefs and
dif--union of the whole body of proteftants, and the
weaknefs, the humours and affectations, of fome
who feemed to have good intentions, did very fen--
fibly affect her. She faid often, with feeling and
cutting regret, " can fuch dry bones live ? " When
fhe heard what crying fins abounded in our fleets
and armies, fhe gave fuch directions as feemed
practicable, to thofe who fhe thought might in
fome meafure correct them ; and fhe made fome, in
very eminent ftations, underftand, that nothing
could both pleafe, and even oblige her more, than
that care fhould be taken to ftop thofe growing diforders, and to reduce matters to the gravity and
fobriety of former times. The laft great project
that her thoughts were working on, with relation
to a noble and royal provifion for maimed and de-
cayed feamen, was particularly defigned to be fo
conftituted, as to put them in a probable way of
ending their days in the fear of God. Every new
hint that way, was entertained by her with a lively
joy : fhe had fome difcourfe on that head the very day

E 2

before

before fhe was taken ill. It gave her a fenfible concern, to hear that Ireland was fcarce got out of its
miferies, when it was returning to the levities, and
even to the abominations of former times : fhe
fpake of thofe things like one that was trembling
and finking under the weight of them. She took
particular methods to be well informed of the ftate
of our plantations, and of thofe colonies that we
have among infidels : but it was no fmall grief to
her to hear that they were but too generally a reproach to the religion by which they were named,
(I do not fay which they profeffed, for many of
them feem fcarce to profefs it.) She gave a willing
ear to a propofition that was made for erecting
fchools, and the founding of a college among them.
She confidered the whole fcheme of it, and the en-
dowment which was defired for it. It was a noble
one, and was to rife out of fome branches of the
revenue, which made it liable to objections : but
fhe took care to confider the whole thing fo well, that
fhe herfelf anfwered all objections, and efpoufed
the matter with fo affectionate a concern, that fhe
prepared it for the king to fettle it at his coming
over. She knew how heartily he concurred in all
defigns of that nature, though other more preffing
cares denied him the opportunities of confidering
them fo much : fhe digefted and prepared them for
him ; and as fhe knew how large a fhare of zeal
his majefty had for good things, fhe took care alfo
to give him the largeft fhare of the honour of them.
Nor indeed could any thing inflame her more, than

the

the profpect of fetting religion forward, efpecially where there were hopes of working upon infidels; though after all, the infidels at home feemed to be more incurable and defperate than thofe abroad.

Her concern and her character was not limited to that which might feem to be her own immediate province, and was more efpecially put under her care; the foreign churches had alfo a liberal fhare of it. She was not infenfible of the kindnefs of the Dutch; fhe remembered it always with a grateful tendernefs, and was heartily touched with all their concerns. The refugees of France were confidered by her, as thofe whom God had fent to fit fafe under her fhadow, and eafy through her favour. Thofe fcattered remnants of our elder fifter, that had been hunted out of their vallies, were again brought together by their majefties means. It was the king's powerful interceffion that reftored them to their feats, as well as to their edicts. And it was the queen's charity that formed them into bodies, and put them in the method of enjoying thofe advantages, and of tranfmitting them down to the fucceeding ages. She took care alfo of preferving the little that was left of the Bohemian churches : fhe had formed nurferies of religion in fome of the parts of Germany which were exhaufted by war, and difabled to carry on the education of their youth; and to tranfmit to the next age, the faith which they themfelves profeffed.

E 3

Such

Such was the temper of our blessed queen; these were the earnests of what we expected from her; they had been a full return of the most promising expectations in any other; but in her they were only earnests of what we looked for. It was but the dawning of her day; the mists and clouds rose so thick upon it, the disorders of war did so obstruct many great designs, that her light was much intercepted, it could not shine through : she understood well the decencies of things ; they were beauful in their seasons; and they would not have had so fair an appearance, if they had come before the proper time, and the other circumstances that might fit them.   She seemed to have many years before her ; her youth was that which added this particular happiness to all the other blessings that we had in her, that we thought we were secure in a long continuance of it.   We flattered ourselves with the hopes of a reign that should have been lasting. The hopes of that made us neither to doubt nor fear any thing else.   What generous or abstracted thoughts soever we may have in speculation, self-love lies so near us, that after all we are chiefly concerned for our own times.   We think we may more easily deliver over the concerns of the next age to those who are to live in it.   It seems to be the voice of nature that Hezekiah said, " good is " the word of the Lord, that peace and truth shall " be in my days. "   Therefore when the prospect of a fixed happiness goes farther than the reasonable prospect of our own continuance here, we

think

think we ourselves are very safe. It is also a delightful thought to one, that confiders how much all things are out of joint, and into what diforder they have fallen, to hope that fo dexterous a hand was like to have fo long a courfe of life before her, for putting every thing again into proper methods, and in regular channels; and that might have lived till the nation had put on another face, till we had recovered our antient virtue, as well as our much blafted fame; till religion had been not only fecured, but raifed to fuch a degree, as to have fhined out from us through the whole earth, with a benign influence on all the foreign churches, as well as with a dreadful one towards the Roman-church, (I mean not the dreadfulnefs of cruelty; that is her own character, which we ftill leave entire to her, I mean the dazzling her with the brightnefs of virtue and religion among us) and till public liberty had been fettled upon a true bafis. I mean the authority of a well balanced and well conducted government; that fhould have maintained property, and have afferted the generous principles of the freedom of human nature; that fhould have difpenfed juftice, and rewarded virtue, with a gentle but fteady hand, and have repreffed the luxuriant pretenfions of thofe who underftand public liberty fo little, as not to be able to diftinguifh it from licencioufnefs; which ftrikes firft at religion and virtue, and then muft foon fall with its own burden, under the mifery of ufurpations at home, or become an eafy prey to foreign conquerors. A corrupted ftate

E 4

of

of mankind is well prepared to be a fcene of flavery. Liberty cannot be maintained but by virtue, temperance, moderate defires, and contented minds ; and fince thofe are not to be attained to but by religion, this is an uncontefted truth, that liberty and religion live and die together.

All this, and a deal more, both with relation to ourfelves, and to all that are round about us, was that which we thought we had a right to expect from the continuance of fuch a reign : we thought that God had formed her by fo many peculiar characters, and conducted her by fo many happy providences, that from all thefe we had fome right to conclude, that it would be lafting. The appearances were of our fide ; for though fhe tempered the chearfulnefs of youth with the gravity of age, and the ferioufnefs even of old age, yet youth ftill fmiled in her countenance with fo frefh an air, that we thought nature had not gone half its way, and had yet a long career to run. So firm a health, fo regular a courfe of life, and fo calm a temper, that exactnefs of method, and punctualnefs of hours, feemed to add a further fecurity to our hopes : nor did they ftop under the reign or age of a queen Elizabeth.

We felt fo happy an influence from her example, as well as by her government, that even under the terror that her ficknefs gave us, we flattered ourfelves with the hopes that God was only trying us, to give us a jufter value of fo ineftimable a blefling, that fo it might be reftored to us with the more advantage, and an higher endearment. We could

not

not let ourfelves think, that fo terrible a ftroke was fo near us. We, who but a few days before, had been fancying, what our childrens children were to fee in her, were then driven to apprehend that our fun was to fet before it had attained to its noon. Then under the darknefs of that thick cloud, every one began to recollect what he had feen and obferved in her : and though fome knew more than others, yet every one knew enough to ftrike him with amazement and forrow. Then her whole adminiftration, as well as the privater parts of her life, was remembered : every one had fomething to fay, and all added to the common ftock, and increafed the general lamentation.

It is true, a veil ought here to be drawn over that which is facred. The fecrets of government are fo; and muft not break out, till the proper time comes of recording them, and of delivering them down to pofterity ; and then we know what a figure her hiftory muft make. But in this way, and under the due referves of fpeaking of prefent things, fomewhat may be ventured on, without breaking in too far. Her punctualnefs to hours, her patience in audiences, her gentlenefs in commanding, her refervednefs in fpeaking, her caution in promifing, her foftnefs in finding fault, her readinefs in rewarding, her diligence in ordering, her hearkening to all that was fug-gefted, and the copious accounts that fhe gave to him whom both God, and her own choice, had made her oracle, were every one of them furprifing; but all together they feem to look rather like the idea

of

of what ought to be, than that which could in reason be expected from any one person. It might have been supposed that her whole time must have gone to this. If many other things had been omitted, it was that which must have been well allowed of; but that there might be a fulness of leisure for every thing, the day was early begun; she had many hours to spare, and nothing was done in haste; no hurry nor impatience appeared. Her devotions, both private and public, were not so much as shortened; and she found time enough for keeping up the chearfulness of a court, and for admitting all persons to her. She was not so wholly possessed by the greatest cares, that she forgot the smallest. Those who are exact in little things, generally trifle in great ones; and those who mind great things, think they have a right to neglect smaller ones: they think they should rather be lessened if they were too exact in them. But it was a new thing to see one, who never forgot things, which she herself esteemed but trifles, and which she managed with so becoming a grace, that even in these she perserved her own character, yet to carry on the great concerns of government with so firm a conduct, and such an air of majesty.

If any thing was ever found in her, that might seem to fall too low, it was that her humility and modesty did really depress her too much in her own eyes; and that she might too soon be made to think, that the reasons which were offered to her by others, were better than her own. But even this was

only

only in fuch matters, in which the want of practice might make that modeft diftruft feem more
reafonable : and when fhe did fee nothing in that
which was before her, in which confcience had
any fhare, for whenfoever that appeared, fhe was
firm and unmoveable.

Her adminiftration had a peculiar happinefs attending on it : we had reafon to believe that it
went the better with us upon her account. There
was fomewhat in herfelf that difarmed many of
her enemies ; fuch of them as came near her, were
foon conquered by her ; while the dexterity and
fecrefy of her conduct, defeated the defigns of
thofe who were reftlefs and implacable. We
feemed once to be much expofed ; unprofperous
accidents at fea gave our enemies the appearance
of a triumph : they lay along our coafts, and were
for fome time the mafters of our feas. But a fecret
guard feemed then to environ us : all the harm
that they did us, in one inftance of barbarity,
that fhewed what our general treatment might
probably have been, if we had became a prey to
them, did us little hurt : it feemed rather fuffered
by heaven, to unite us againft them. The
nation loft no courage by it ; their zeal was
the more inflamed. This was her firft effay of
government : but then fhe, who upon ordinary
occafions was not out of countenance to own a
fear that did not mifbecome her, did now, when a
vifible danger threatned her, fhew a firmnefs of
mind, and a compofednefs of behaviour, that made

the

the men of the cleareſt courage aſhamed of themſelves.   She covered the inward apprehenſions that
ſhe had, with ſuch an equality of behaviour, that
ſhe ſeemed afraid of nothing, when ſhe had reaſon
to fear the worſt that could happen. She was reſolved, if things ſhould have gone to extremities, to
have ventured herſelf with her people, and either to
have preſerved them, or to have periſhed with them.

This was ſuch a beginning of the exerciſe of
royal power, as might for ever have given her a
diſguſt of it.   She ſeemed all the while to poſſeſs
her ſoul in patience ; and to live in a conſtant re-
ſignation of herſelf to the will of God, without
any anxiety concerning events.   The happy news
of a great victory, and of a greater preſervation of
his majeſty's ſacred perſon, from the ſureſt inſtruments of death, which ſeemed to be ſent with that
direction, that it might ſhew the immediate watch-
fulneſs of providence about him, did ſoon change
the ſcene, and put another face on our affairs.
She only ſeemed the leaſt changed ; ſhe looked
more chearful, but with the ſame tranquility : the
appearances of it had never left her.   Nor was it
a ſmall addition to her joy, that another perſon,
for whom ſhe ſtill retained profound regards, was
alſo preſerved.   She was a true Sabine in the caſe ;
and though ſhe was no part of the cauſe of the
war, yet ſhe would willingly have ſacrificed her
own life, to have preſerved either of thoſe that
ſeemed to be then in danger.   She ſpoke of that
matter, two days after the news came, with ſo ten-

der

der a fenfe of the goodnefs of God to her in it, that it drew tears from her: and then fhe freely confeffed, " that her heart had trembled, not fo " much from the apprehenfion of the danger, that " fhe herfelf was in, as from the fcene that was " then in action at the Boyne: God had heard her " prayers, and fhe bleffed him for it, with as fen- " fible a joy, as for any thing that had ever hap- " pened to her."

The next feafon of her adminiftration concluded the reduction of Ireland. The expectations of fuccefs there, were once fo much funk, that it feemed that that ifland was to be yet, for another year, a field of blood, and a heap of afhes. She laid the blame of this in a great meafure on the licencioufnefs and other diforders that fhe heard had rather increafed, than abated among them. A fudden turn came from a bold but neceffary refolu- tion, that was executed as gallantly as it was generoufly undertaken. In the face of a great army, a handful of men paffed a deep river, forced a town, and made the enemy to retire in hafte. All pofterity will reckon this among the moft fignal performances of war: an inftance that fhewed how far courage could go; and what brave men, well led on, could do. A great victory followed a few days after: the fuccefs of the action was at fo long and fo doubtful a ftand, that there was juft reafon to believe, that pure hands lifted up to heaven, might have great influence, and might have given the turn; from that time fuccefs was lefs doubtful. All was concluded with the happy reduction of the

whole

whole ifland. The reflections that fhe made on this, looked the fame way that all her thoughts did. " Our forces elfewhere, both at fea and " land, were thought to be confiderable, and fo " promifing, that we were in great hopes of " fomewhat that might be decifive; only Ireland " was apprehended to be too weakly furnifhed " for a concluding campaign; yet fo different " are the methods of providence from human ex- " pectations, that nothing memorable happened " any where, but only in Ireland, where little or " nothing was expected."

She was again at the helm when we were threat-ned with a defcent, and an invafion; which was conducted with that fecrefy, that we were in dan-ger of being furprifed by it, when our preparations at fea were not finifhed, and our force at land was not confiderable. The ftruggle was like to have been formidable; and there was a particular vio-lence to be done to herfelf, by reafon of him who was to have conducted it. Then we felt new proofs of the watchfulnefs of heaven. What comes immediately from caufes that fall not under human counfels, nor can be redreffed by fkill or force, may well be afcribed to the fpecialities of provi-dence : and the rather, if nature feems to go out of its courfe, and feafons change their ordinary face. A long uninterrupted continuance of boif-terous weather, that came from the point that was moft contrary to their defigns, made the project impracticable. A fucceffion of turns of weather

fol-

followed after that, happily to us, and as fatally to them. While the fame wind that ftopped their fleets, joined ours. It went not out of that direction, till it ended in one of the moft glorious actions that ever England had ; and then thofe who were brought together to invade us, were forced to be the melancholy fpectators of the deftruction of the beft part of that fleet, on which all their hope was built. In that, without detracting either from the gallantry of our men, or the conduct of our admiral, it muft be acknowledged that providence had the largeft fhare : and if we may prefume to enter into thofe fecrets, and to judge of the hidden caufes of them, we may well conclude, that her piety and her prayers contributed not a little to it.

She bore fuccefs with the fame decency that appeared when the fky feemed to be more clouded. So firm a fituation of mind as fhe had, feemed to be above the power of accidents of any fort whatfoever. Clouds returned again in another year of her adminiftration ; though not with a face that was quite fo black. She thought God was angry with us ; and it was not hard to find out a reafon to juftify the fevereft of his providences.

It feemed much more accountable, that our affairs fhould have met with fome unhappy interruptions, than that fo many bleffings fhould have attended upon us. She had a tender fenfe of any thing that looked like a mifcarriage, under her conduct, and was afraid left fome miftake of hers

might

might have occafioned it. When difficulties grew too hard to be extricated, and that fhe felt an uneafinefs in them, fhe made God her refuge ; and though fhe had neither the principles nor the temper of an enthufiaft, yet fhe often owned that fhe felt a full calm upon her thoughts, after fhe had given them a free vent before God in prayer.

When fad accidents came from the immediate hand of heaven, particularly on the occafion of a great lofs at fea ; fhe faid, " though there was no " occafion for complaint or anger upon thefe, yet " there was a jufter caufe of grief, fince God's " hand was to be feen fo particularly in them." Sometimes fhe feared there might be fome fecret fins that might lie at the root and blaft all ; but fhe went foon off from that, and faid, " where fo " much was vifible, there was no need of divina- " tion concerning that which might be hidden."

When the fky grew clearer, and in her more profperous days, fhe was never lifted up. A great refolution was taken, which has fince changed the fcene very vifibly : it has not only afferted a dominion over thofe feas which we claim as our own, but has for the prefent affumed a more extended empire ; while we are mafters both of the ocean and the Mediterranean ; and have our enemies coafts, as well as the feas, open to us. She had too tender a heart to take any real fatisfaction in the deftruction of their towns, or the ruin of their poor and innocent inhabitants. She fpoke of this with true indignation, at thofe who had begun

fuch

fuch practices, even in full peace ; or after protections had been given.   She was forry that the ftate of war made it neceffary to reftrain another prince from fuch barbarities, by making himfelf feel the effects of them ; and therefore fhe faid, " fhe " hoped, that fuch practices fhould become fo odi- " ous, in all that fhould begin them, and by their " doing fo force others to retaliate, that for the " future they fhould be for ever laid afide."

When her affairs had another face, fhe grew not fecure, nor went fhe off from her dependance upon God.   In all the pleafures of life, fhe maintained a true indifference for the continuance of them ; and fhe feemed to think of parting with them, in fo eafy a manner, that it plainly appeared how little they had got into her heart : fhe had no occafion for thefe thoughts, from any other principle, but a mere difguft of life, and the afpiring to a better. She apprehended fhe felt once or twice fuch indifpofitions upon her, that fhe concluded nature was working towards fome great ficknefs ; fo fhe fet herfelf to take full and broad views of death, that from thence fhe might judge, how fhe fhould be able to encounter it.   But fhe felt fo quiet an indifference upon that profpect, leaning rather toward the defire of a diffolution, that fhe faid, " though fhe did not pray for death, yet fhe " could neither wifh nor pray againft it.   She left " that before God, and referred herfelf intirely to " the difpofal of providence.   If fhe did not wifh " for death, yet fhe did not fear it."

F

As

As this was her temper, when she viewed it at some distance, so she maintained the same calm, when in the closest struggle with it. Here darkness and horror fall upon me; for who can look thro' that scene so unconcerned as she went through it? I know if I would write according to the rules of art, I should draw a veil here, and leave the reader to imagine that, which no pen can properly express. Every thing must seem flat here, upon a subject that gives a flame too high, to be either managed or described. But it is nature and not art that governs me. I will therefore go through what remains, though without the force or flight that it seems to command: I will do it, though but faintly, with a feebleness suitable to the temper of my own mind, without any anxious study to manage so poor a thing, as the credit of writing in proportion to the sublimity of the subject. Let the matter itself speak; that will have a force that will supply all defects.

She only was calm, when all was in a storm about her: the dismal sighs of all that came near her, could not discompose her. She was rising so fast above mortality, that even he who was more to her than all the world besides, and to all whose thoughts she had been upon every other occasion intirely resigned, could not now inspire her with any desires of returning back to life. Her mind seemed to be dis-entangling itself from her body, and so she rose above that tenderness, that went deeper in her than all other earthly things whatfoever.

foever. It feemed all that was mortal was falling off, when that could give her no uneafinefs.

She received the intimations of approaching death with a firmnefs that did neither bend nor foften under that which has made the ftrongeft minds to tremble. Then, when even the moft artificial grow fincere, it appeared how eftablifhed a calm and how fublime a piety poffeffed her. A ready willingnefs to be diffolved, and an entire refignation to the will of God, did not forfake her one minute, nor had any thing been left to be difpatched in her laft hours. Her mind was in no hurry, but foft as the ftill voice that feemed to be calling her foul away to the regions above. So that fhe made her laft fteps with a ftability and ferioufnefs, that how little ordinary foever they may be, were indeed the natural conclufions of fuch a life as fhe had led.

But how quiet foever fhe was, the news of her danger ftruck the whole nation, as well as the town, with fo aftonifhing a terror, as if thunders and earthquakes had been fhaking both heaven and earth. Blacknefs then dwelt on every face; a filent confufion of look, burfting out often into tears and fighs, was fo univerfal, and looked with fo folemn an air, that how much foever fhe deferved the affections of the nation, yet we never thought that fhe poffeffed them fo entirely, as appeared in thofe days of forrow. It was a feafon of great joy: we were celebrating that Bleffed Nativity that gave us all life and the hopes of a bleffed

immortality,

immortality. But it was a fad interruption to that facred feſtivity when we were alarmed with thofe frightful apprehenſions. We were once revived with the hopes of a leſs formidable ſickneſs. This ſpread a joy that was as high and univerſal as our grief had been. We were eafily enough brought to flatter ourſelves with the belief of that which was fo much wiſhed for. But this went foon off; it was an ill-grounded joy, the clouds returned fo much the blacker, by reafon of that miftaken in-terval. Then all that prayed upon any account whatfoever, redoubled their fervour, and cried out, " fpare thy people, and give not thy heritage to re-" proach." We prayed for ourſelves more than for her, when we cried to God for her life and recovery; both prieft and people, rich and poor, all ranks and forts joined in this litany. A univerſal groan was ecchoed to thofe prayers through our churches and ftreets. We were afraid to afk after that facred health; and yet we were impatient to know how it ftood. It feemed our fins cried louder than our prayers; they were heard, and not the other.

But how feverely foever God intended to vifit us, ſhe was gently handled; ſhe felt no inward depreffion nor finking of nature. She then declared that ſhe felt in her mind the joys of a good confcience, and the powers of religion giving her fupports, which even the laft agonies could not ſhake : her conftant foftnefs to all about her never left her. That was indeed natural to her, but by it, all faw vifibly that nothing could put her mind out of its
natural

natural fituation and ufual methods.   A few hours before fhe breathed her laft, when he who miniftred to her in the beft things, had continued in a long attendance about her, fhe was fo free in her thoughts, that apprehending he might be weary, fhe com- manded him to fit down ; and repeated her orders till he obeyed them.   A thing too mean in itfelf to be mentioned, but that it fhewed the prefence of her mind, as well as the fweetnefs of her temper. Prayer was then her conftant exercife, as oft as fhe was awake ; and fo fenfible was the refrefhment that her mind found in it, that fhe thought it did her more good, and gave even her body more eafe, than any thing that was done her.   Nature funk apace ; fhe refolved to furnifh herfelf with the great viaticum of chriftians, the laft provifions for her journey ; fhe received the blefled facrament with a devotion that inflamed, as well as it melted all thofe who faw it : after that great act of church-commu- nion was over, fhe delivered herfelf up fo entirely to meditation, that fhe feemed fcarce to mind any thing elfe.   She was then upon the wing.   Such was her peace in her latter end, that though the fymptoms fhewed that nature was much oppreffed, yet fhe fcarce felt any uneafinefs from it.   It was only from what fhe perceived was done to her, and from thofe intimations that were given her, that fhe judged her life to be in danger ; but fhe fcarce knew herfelf to be fick by any thing that fhe felt at heart.   Her bearing fo much ficknefs with fo little emotion, was for fome time imputed to that
undifturbed

undisturbed quiet and patience in which she possessed her soul : but when she repeated it so often, that she felt herself well inwardly, then it appeared that there was a particular blessing in so easy a conclusion of a life that had been led through a great variety of accidents, with a constant equality of temper.

The last and hardest step is now to be made; our imaginations, which must still be full of the noblest and augustest ideas of her, may be apt to represent her to our thoughts as still alive, with all those graces of majesty and sweetness that always accompanied her. But, alas ! we are but too sure, that all this is the illusion of fancy. She has left us ; she is gone to those blessed seats above, where even crowns and thrones are but small matters, compared to that brighter glory, which rises far above the splendour of triumphs, processions, and coronations.

The measuring of so great a change, and so vast an advancement in its full latitude, as it is the properest thought to mitigate our sorrows, so it seems to be too lively a one for us' now, and above what we are capable of in our present depression. This may make us conclude with a sudden transport of joy, that she is happy, unspeakably happy, by the change ; and has risen much higher above what she herself was a little while ago, than she was then above the rest of mortals.

But black and genuine horror still returns, and seems to wrap us, and all things about us, with so

thick

thick a mift, that fo bright a thought, as that of her prefent glory cannot break through it. While we are perfuaded of her happinefs, and that fhe has gained infinitely by the change, yet felf-love is fo ftrong, and fenfe makes fo powerful an impreffion, that when we confider what we have loft in lofing her, we fink under our burthren; difpirited, as if our life and joy were gone with her, as if black night and lafting winter had chilled all our blood, and damped all our powers.

It may feem a needlefs feverity to aggravate all this, as if we were not loaded enough already; but that a further black fcene muft be opened, and that we muft be filled with the gloomy profpect of that which we may but too juftly and too reafonably look for. God feems to be making a way for his anger; and to be removing that interpofition which we have reafon to believe did effectually ftop thofe miferies, for which we may well fear that we are more than ripe.

We are not quite abandoned; God does ftill preferve him to us, by whofe means only, confidering our prefent circumftances, we can hope either to be fafe or happy. That duty and refpect which was before divided, does now center all in him. All that we payed her, does now devolve to him, by a title that becomes fo much the jufter, becaufe we have all feen (I wifh we may not feel it) how deep a wound this made on him, whofe mind has appeared hitherto invulnerable, and where firmnefs feemed to be the peculiar character. It is indeed but natural

tural that he who knew her beft, fhould value her moft. The beft tribute that we can offer to the afhes of our bleffed queen, is to double our duty, and our zeal to him, whom fhe loved fo intirely, and in whom her memory is ftill fo frefh, that tho' for our own fakes we muft be concerned to fee it fink fo deep; yet for his fake, we cannot but be pleafed to fee how much his character rifes, by the juft acknowledgments he pays her, and by that deep affliction for her lofs, which has almoft overwhelm-ed a mind, that had kept its ground in the hardeft fhocks of fortune, but loft it here.

If our apprehenfions of his facred life, grow now more tender, and we feel more fenfibly than for-merly, that it is he who makes us fafe at home, as well as great abroad ; if we do now fee, what is that interpofition that is now left, and that keeps off mifery and deftruction from breaking in upon us, as the fea to fwallow us up ; if that life itfelf is fo often expofed, that this creates a new cloud upon our minds, gloomy and black, as if charged with ftorm and thunder ; if all this gives us a me-lancholy profpect, we know that nothing can divert or diffipate it, but our turning from our fins, which lay us fo naked, which have brought one fevere ftroke already upon us, and by which God may be yet further provoked to vifit us again. Another ftroke muft make an end of us.

To conclude,

The

The trueft as well as the ufefuleft way of lamenting this lofs, is, after that we have given fomewhat to nature, and have let forrow have a free courfe, then to recollect our thoughts, and to ftudy to imitate thofe virtues and perfections which we admired in her; and for which her memory muft be ever precious among us: precious, as ointment poured forth, ever favory and fragrant.

Her death has indeed fpread a melting tendernefs, and a flowing forrow over the whole nation, beyond any thing we ever faw; which does in fome meafure bear a proportion to the juft occafion of it: how difmal foever this may look, yet it is fome fatisfaction to fee that juft refpects are paid her memory, and that our mournings are as deep as they are univerfal. They have broke out in the folemneft as well as in the decenteft manner: thofe auguft bodies that reprefent the whole, began them; and from them they have gone round the nation, in genuine and native ftrains, free and not emendicated. But if this fhould have its chief and beft effect, to drive the impreffions of religion, and the terrors of God, deeper into us, then we may hope that this fatal ftroke, as terrible and threatning as it now looks, might produce great and even happy effects: fo different may events be, from the caufes, or at leaft from the occafions of them.

How lowering foever the fky may now feem, a general repentance, and a fincere reformation of manners, would foon give it another face: it would break through thofe clouds that feem now

to be big, and even ready to burſt.   If u... is u
much to be expected, yet if there were b··t · f ·
that did heartily go into good deſigns, even .h(
might procure to us a lengthening out of our trai
quility, and a mitigation of our miſeries, and tha
though they were fixed on us by irreverſible d·
crees.   A number of true mourners might hope
leaſt to ſtop their courſe, till they themſelves ſhou
die in peace ; or they might look for a mi
if they ſhould happen to be involved in a
calamity.

*Mark the perfect, and behold the upright, ,
end is peace.*

F I N I S.